Y0-BQR-512

A SUMMER PLACE

A Novel by

SLOAN WILSON

A Ridge Press Book

Published by Simon and Schuster

New York

A RIDGE PRESS BOOK

PUBLISHED BY SIMON AND SCHUSTER, INC.

ROCKEFELLER CENTER, 630 FIFTH AVENUE

NEW YORK 20, N.Y.

MANUFACTURED IN THE UN[illegible]ES OF AMERICA

For Elise

CONTENTS

Part One

NO TRESPASSING

1

Pine Island, Maine, thrust itself out of the sea like a huge medieval castle. There it stood, the only island in sight, with its Gothic cliffs defying the combers rolling in across the North Atlantic. The question of how it got there teased the mind. By the look of it, there must have been some explosion underground or a collision of massive forces which cast up this one island and left it as a frieze of violence. Although some of the narrow meadows in the interior were good for sheep, and the water in the pond was sweet, the mountains were dangerous. Beautiful in silhouette against the sky, they beckoned picnickers to attempt their paths, but often in a storm there was a roar of loose rock and the trees bowed down before an avalanche. Old John Hunter warned all visitors that this was no place for summer climbers.

The island sloped from east to west. It was about fifteen miles long, and on the south end there was a small harbor used by fishing boats and yachts. On one side of this harbor was the Hulberts' boathouse, and on the other side was a long wharf owned by the Hunter family. On both structures stood unusually large signs which proclaimed NO TRESPASSING. VIOLATORS WILL BE PROSECUTED TO THE FULL EXTENT OF THE LAW. Similar signs were posted at every possible landing place the island afforded.

From June till October a cut-down Gloucester schooner named the *Mary Anne* made daily trips under power from Harvesport, Maine, and, when the weather permitted, weekly trips in winter to bring mail and provisions. Twelve big summerhouses had been built long ago by families who had incorporated the island. Each owned ten acres around his own house, and the rest of the land was held in common. The descendants or successors of these families gathered there during July and August to renew old friendships and enmities. They came from New York, Boston, Chicago—almost every major city in the United States was represented by at least a cousin. Some of the "Islanders," as they liked to call themselves, were wealthy idlers, most were hard-working businessmen, and a few were failures who hung onto the island with the tenacity of the stunted birches that grew from cracks in the cliffs. The houses changed hands frequently, going to those who could afford them, with old residents paying frequent visits as poor friends or relations. Death made the houses change hands, and divorce and business disaster. The real-estate deeds recorded by the County Clerk in Harvesport could tell quite a story.

To strangers, the island was only another "summer place," but to its owners it was more. It was so much more beautiful than the cities where they spent their winters that they liked to think of it as their home. They came from there. Some of them maintained their legal residence there, in spite of the fact that often they could get down only for a two-week vacation. These people made long, painful automobile trips to Maine in November to vote, and they got into all kinds of trouble with automobile registrations and other legal documents that had to be attended to in Maine in winter. Even when most inconvenienced by it, they boasted of the fact that the island had no telephones. They liked to think of themselves as "down-Easters"; they half hoped their children would pick up a Maine accent. They envied Todd Hasper, whom they employed to live the year around on the island taking care of their houses. Some of the "Islanders" were willing to go into careers they disliked to make enough money to keep going there. They loved the place, they said.

Todd Hasper also loved the island, but only in the wintertime, when he usually had it entirely to himself. A morose and solitary man, he raised sheep and goats for his own profit, and he liked them better than his employers. One winter night during the depression of the Thirties, some impoverished fishermen landed and stole some of his lambs. The next week Todd went to the mainland and bought a huge dog named Satan which he methodically trained to attack on sight any human being but himself. When this dog died, Todd Hasper replaced it with another. He had a whole series of them, usually of great Dane or mastiff blood. No matter how gentle these big dogs were when he acquired them, they always turned fierce inside of a few weeks, and he gave them all the same name. During the summertime the current Satan raged at the end of a long chain outside Todd Hasper's cottage, or from a hand leash, but in the wintertime he roamed the island at will. Each winter week the mail-boat put into the bay, the dog came racing out on the wharf with clear intent to kill. When Herb Andrews, the captain of the boat, complained, old Hasper told him to keep the mail—he never read it anyway.

Hasper was infuriated when, as sometimes happened, a house-owner decided to live on the island the year around. Recently divorced women tried that every few years. They set up Franklin stoves and kerosene heaters in the drafty summer cottages, and they stuffed the windows with rags, but they were usually gone before Christmas. Men who had suffered business failures sometimes lasted it out a little longer, but Hasper was usually able to unchain his dog by February at the latest.

Many unkind things could be said about Pine Island and often were said by people who moved away. Big Ken Jorgenson, for instance, used to think that it was simply a haven for the curiously cruel and pretentiously rich. Even when he himself made money, his memories of the island were bitter. For a long time its name alone brought back the summer of 1935 and the picture of a disdainful girl in a bathing suit and an imitation mink coat. At the age of seventeen, Sylvia Raymond had sported that combination when the wind got chilly on the beach. Ken laughed about her when he got older, but the image of her stuck in his mind, along with the sound of her mocking laughter. Ken Jorgenson's memories of the place made his whole youth seem far more bitter than sweet until he finally was able to return.

Bart Hunter loved the island if anyone did, but even he was fond of pointing out that he wasn't the only person there who drank too much, and the incidence of divorce and adultery was unusually high. "We're all fearfully snobbish and tend to be anti almost everything but ourselves," Bart occasionally remarked with an amiable if self-indulgent smile.

The families who owned the island became dangerously ingrown.

Some of them had been coming there for three generations, and Bart's son, young John, for instance, was a fourth-generation Islander. The girls of Pine Island families usually married boys they had met there, and a lot of joking was done about the island being "a marvelous place for romance." Sylvia was once heard to remark somewhat acidly to her husband, Bart Hunter, that the salt sea air and the scent of pines must act as an aphrodisiac, for people who no more than nodded at each other on the mainland often fell into bed together soon after arriving. Bart, who prided himself on his "intuitive knowledge of psychology," said no aphrodisiac was needed to explain the phenomenon. Most of the people on the island had a great deal of leisure, at least while they were there, and the island abounded in hidden places: long lonely beaches, caves, barns, boathouses and cottages temporarily unoccupied. It really was a good place for romance, he said; it had marvelous accommodations.

Barton Hunter was born on Pine Island in 1916, in a Victorian mansion overlooking the bay. His mother, Martha, had planned to go to Boston to have the baby, but she lingered as long as she could on the cool beaches, a pregnant woman dreading the heat of the big city, and the baby came three weeks before he was expected. Barton's father, a fastidious banker, officiated at the birth of his own son, along with Todd Hasper, who was skilled at delivering goats and lambs. The experience was a terrifying one for all concerned, but both mother and baby survived. So Barton was a real native, not just a summer visitor, he used to tell people, and as he grew up he was proud to list as his place of birth: Pine Island, Maine.

Barton came to the island every summer until 1937, when he was expelled from his senior year at Harvard for drastically poor marks and started a search for a job which he would "really like." His family had lost money during the depression, and it seemed unwise to keep the big summer mansion on the island; but no one wanted to sell it, even when old John Hunter, Bart's father, was drowned there and it was discovered that his losses had been greater than anyone had known.

During the Second World War, Bart was happy to leave the investment firm where he had labored for six months and enter the Navy. A cousin of his was heard to remark that the war probably wouldn't last very long, because every job that Bart took ended quickly, but he served as a naval officer with considerable distinction. For four years he regularly sent money home to help pay the taxes on the island. When he did not prosper in business after the war, the part of failure he hated most was the prospect of losing the house, the wooded paths and the beaches where he had played as a boy. As he remarked bitterly to Sylvia, the island was a perverted Garden of Eden from which one was expelled for the sin of poverty.

Bart was almost dangerously disconsolate in those days. Long before the Korean War, he tried to get back into the Navy. It came as a great shock to him when the doctors found, during the course of his physical examination, that he had stomach ulcers and rejected him. Although he was only in his early thirties, a premonition of death overtook him, and he brooded about robbing his children of their heritage, which to him meant Pine Island. The discovery of his sickness rendered him philosophical for a few weeks. He asked himself questions about why he was remaining in a business and city he didn't like, and the upshot of it all was that in the year 1951 he decided to sell his house in Boston, to move permanently to Pine Island, and to convert the old mansion into a summer inn, catering mostly "to friends and the friends of friends." The installation of additional plumbing and other alterations took most of his remaining resources, but to the indignation of Todd Hasper and his dog, Bart and Sylvia and their two children, John and Carla, lasted out two winters. Until Ken Jorgenson came back in August of 1953, it looked to Todd Hasper as though they would be there forever.

2

THROUGHOUT THE SPRING of 1953 the mail was unusually upsetting for Bart Hunter. It almost always brought bills which were difficult to pay, unforeseen debts resulting from income taxes of bygone years or annual insurance premiums which had been forgotten. Because his name was in the Boston Social Register, and because in the old days his family had been on many mailing lists for luxuries, the mailboat brought him a flood of appeals for the blind, for starving children in Greece, for funds to conquer cancer, heart disease, infantile paralysis—everything. People were always trying to sell Bart cruises to the Caribbean, Italian sports cars, horses, yachts, and liquors of unusually high cost. He hated the mail, and after leafing through it to seek letters requesting reservations at the Island Inn, he usually left it unopened on his desk for days.

The mail he received on June 12 was even more upsetting than usual. There was a bill from the Bibliophile Club in Boston which brought to mind the old question of whether he should resign from all his clubs, now that he rarely left the island. There was a letter from a Harvard classmate he hadn't seen in ten years asking that he invest a hundred thousand dollars of "risk capital" in a new company being formed to drill for oil wells. And then there was the letter from Ken Jorgenson, of all people, asking for reservations at the inn.

The Island Inn stood high on a hill at the north end of Pine Island, and with the servants' quarters over the garage used for Bart and Sylvia and the children, it accommodated twenty-three guests, at least in theory. In practice, a dozen people, most of them widows of men who had owned houses on the island, made up the clientele. Bart had begun advertising in *The Saturday Review,* and he scanned the mail eagerly for replies, but he had never dreamed of hearing from Ken Jorgenson.

Leaving the mail in the small room he used as an office, Bart walked out on the wide veranda and began pacing back and forth. The view of the bay and the mountains on the mainland six miles away was spectacular, but Bart rarely noticed it any more. A slender, rather dapper man, he walked with his eyes turned downward. Bart had never learned to mask his emotions, and his face looked precisely as troubled as he was. Mrs. Hamble, who was sitting in the sunlight knitting, took one glance at him and moved inside. "Poor man," she told Mrs. Brackin, "something terrible must have happened to him; some relative must have died."

It's ridiculous to allow myself to get so upset, Bart thought as he paced. A man should pick up his problems one at a time and make brisk decisions. There is no need to feel overwhelmed. This is, after all, a simple situation: an old acquaintance has applied for a reservation, so I shall give him one.

But of course it wasn't that simple, and it was memories and the terrible impact of change which were overwhelming, not the need to make decisions.

Bart remembered Ken Jorgenson well, and even knew of his business ventures, which had been written up in the *Wall Street Journal* and the news magazines to which he still subscribed. It was impossible for Bart to think of Ken as successful. Jorgenson came back to him in memory as a clumsy, rather oafish ox of a scholarship student from Harvard whom few people on Pine Island had liked during the years he had served as a tutor and lifeguard.

It's not as though an old friend were coming to stay here as a guest, Bart thought, walking from one end of the wide veranda to the other, just as he had paced the quarterdeck of the destroyer escort he had commanded during the war. Ken Jorgenson had not been a friend. Bart and his younger brother, Roger, and Sylvia, who was now Bart's wife, and the other young people on the island those summers, all had despised Ken Jorgenson, partly because they had had to study under him and obey him while he was serving as a lifeguard on the beach, and partly because—well, it had to be admitted, Bart thought—because they had all been trying hard to be sophisticated in those years and had succeeded in being pretty dreadful. That is the trouble with the memory of a conscientious man, Bart thought; it plagues him always with the echoes of past sins.

He and Sylvia and the others had ridiculed Ken's flat, Middle Western accent, his loud sports shirts and his green felt hat. They had thought it amusing that he didn't know how to sail, that he was a clumsy dancer and that he was incredibly earnest about continuing his studies, even during the summer. They had made fun of his enormous physical strength, the methodical way in which he had exercised his huge body, doing push-ups on the beach and chinning himself from the limbs of trees. Most of all they had laughed at his serious attitude toward girls, especially Sylvia. Ken had been incapable of light flirtations, small talk or laughter. He had tried to be courtly, always rushing to open doors or to light cigarettes, and standing up even when a maid came into the room. The girls had soon found that all they had to do to make him blush was to stare at him for more than a second. In conversation with Sylvia, especially, Ken had always sweated freely and had occasionally stammered. "The Beast," Sylvia had called him laughingly, and the nickname had stuck, not to be used to his face, of course, but not always beyond his hearing. During the three summers Ken had worked for the Hunter family, he had rarely been asked to the dances, the parties and picnics. "Oh, don't ask the Beast," Bart could remember Sylvia saying, Sylvia at the age of seventeen, her voice dissolving into musical laughter.

We were children, Bart thought now as he paced, and it is a mistake to attribute one's own sensitivity to others. Ken Jorgenson had never seemed to mind the steady rain of insult under which he lived. His face had appeared stolid; he had never attempted to join in repartee. In the mornings he had given Roger his Latin lessons, and in the afternoons he had sat watchfully on the swimming beach, picking up a megaphone occasionally to warn in swimmers who had strayed too far from land. During the evenings he had retired to his room over the garage to read, and in the fall he had taken his pay and left. He couldn't have been too unhappy, for he had worked there three summers in a row.

Still, such a man could hardly be called an old friend. An old enemy perhaps, for though there had never been any real display of resentment, Bart could still remember the dogged, almost desperate way Ken had played tennis with him.

That had been a curious thing. Bart had never been an athlete, not a professional, practically, like Ken. But tennis had been Bart's game, and Ken had hardly ever seen a court until he came to Harvard. Bart had been sixty pounds lighter than Ken in those days and five inches shorter, but he had always been able to beat the big man effortlessly at tennis, at least the first year.

Ken had grinned good-naturedly during these contests, but every month or so he had renewed them, charging around the court like a bull, and occasionally tripping over himself so awkwardly that it was hard not to laugh.

Toward the middle of Ken's second year on the island, he had defeated Bart for the first time at tennis, and his face had betrayed a glimmer of something, not a smirk, for Ken had been careful to be gracious, but a shadow of something that had nothing to do with playing games. The realization that some obscurely important issue was at stake inspired Bart to greater efforts the next time they played, and he could still remember the look in Ken's eyes when the big man had been beaten three straight sets. After that, Bart declined to play with him. As he said to Sylvia, no gentleman should make an issue of winning, and Sylvia agreed.

Ken Jorgenson, the Beast—how the name brought back the atmosphere of those distant summers, and how appalling they were in retrospect! At sixteen, seventeen and eighteen, Bart and Sylvia and the others had been drinking cocktails and smoking incessantly. Ken had seemed ridiculously unsophisticated. He did not disapprove of smoking and drinking on moral grounds, he explained, but he had to keep in training. Somehow Ken Jorgenson had acquired no glamour from being a football player; instead he had made the game appear to be only a dull, practical business for the poor.

"The trouble with you is that you have no sense of humor," Sylvia had said to Ken once on the swimming dock when Ken had soberly reproved Roger for putting water wings on his chest and strutting up and down in full view of a staid and overly buxom old woman.

"I know," Ken replied seriously, "but it's a hard thing to develop." Shortly afterward he began to tell jokes, apparently memorized from some anthology of humor. The trouble had been that he became embarrassed before finishing, and usually delivered the punch line in a monotone. Sylvia had been addicted to puns, and she had come up with one which Bart and the others had thought hilarious: "Beast is Beast and Jest is Jest," she had said, "and never the twain shall meet."

Oh, those had been funny years. And now it was really funny to think that Ken Jorgenson was coming back to the island a rich man. Now Ken would not sleep over the garage. No, Bart and Sylvia were living there with their children; that was the amusing, the really killing part of the whole situation. It was hilarious to anyone with a sense of humor, for Ken Jorgenson and his family would have to be given the two master bedrooms in the big house if he were to have the accommodations he asked for in his letter. He would have to be given the very rooms that had been Bart's and Sylvia's.

I shouldn't mind a reversal like that, Bart thought. I should be a good sport, I should have a sense of humor, and, more than that, I should be philosophical. Democracy in action, it is; this is what I fought the war for. For five minutes Bart continued to pace. There is something unhealthy and sinister in all this, he thought. Why is the Beast coming back?

Good Lord, he thought, I've got to stop thinking of him as that. Why is Ken Jorgenson—Mr. Jorgenson, he may want to be called by an innkeeper—ha! Look at the way he started his letter, "Dear Barton Hunter." What lack of ease is shown there! But why is he coming back?

This isn't the kind of place he'd pick ordinarily, Bart thought. These Middle Western get-rich-quick fellows like fancy hotels with a bar and an orchestra and all that. Why would he be coming here?

To gloat I suppose, Bart thought, and there is something especially hideous about that. The son-of-a-bitch hears I was wiped out, and that I'm running this place as an inn, and he says to himself, By God, I think I'll go and stay there. Maybe old Bart Hunter will carry my bags, and I'll give him a tip.

So he's going to have his triumph, Bart thought; he is coming back in his splendor to visit us in our defeat. He grinned wryly as he remembered two sentences from Ken's letter: "We are chartering a schooner for the month of July and will be cruising up the Maine coast. August we would like to spend with you, and the captain could let us off before taking the boat back."

How nicely it was worked in, the mention of a yacht! And what a dramatic entrance a big schooner would make for the Beast. He could sail right up to the dock where he once had sat watching the children swim, and he could step ashore in white flannels probably, for God's sake, and a blue coat with brass buttons and a yachting cap: that's the way those Middle Westerners usually got themselves up when they went aboard a boat.

The fact is, this is going to be horrible, Bart thought. For an entire month I shall have to endure being triumphed over. He considered writing Ken that the inn was full. That would be fine, except . . .

Barton Hunter did not enjoy thinking of himself as a snob. He was self-conscious about it; he fought snobbery the way he fought drunkenness, disliking both and capitulating to both. In an agony of indecision he went to the kitchen, where Sylvia was leaning over a table helping the cook to bake pies. "Sylvia," he said, "do you remember that fellow named Ken Jorgenson?"

Sylvia turned toward him; she almost wheeled. As Bart had observed, her nerves had been getting pretty jumpy lately. She put her hand up and brushed her hair back from her forehead, leaving a streak of flour on her face. At thirty-five, Sylvia was an unusually handsome woman, with a full, still narrow-waisted figure, and a face which was youthful except when she was tired, as she was most of the time. "Ken Jorgenson!" she said. "Whatever made you think of him?"

"He wants to come here. He wants two rooms for August." Bart's voice was a little querulous.

"That's funny," Sylvia said.

"I thought it might be wise to turn him down," Bart replied, testing her and himself.

"Why?" Sylvia's eyes could turn curiously opaque sometimes, and they were that way now. It was impossible for Bart to tell what she was thinking.

"Sylvia, you're so damn insensitive! Don't you remember him?"

"I do."

"Well, it's kind of ugly, his coming back here, don't you think? Any amateur student of psychology could tell you why a man like that—"

"If I hear that word 'psychology' again, I'll scream," Sylvia said. "I mean that literally, not as a figure of speech."

"All right, but . . ."

Lillian, the Negro cook, came in with a bag of sugar.

"Let's talk this over in our room, Bart," Sylvia said.

He followed her to their room over the garage, a small chamber which had been built for a chauffeur and wife. The walls were covered with a pale green paper now discolored by smoke from the new kerosene space heater which made the place habitable in winter. Because all the good furnishings had been needed for the other rooms, almost everything here was defective: the water pitcher was chipped, the rug had an inkstain on it, and even the chair Bart sat on had a rudely mended arm.

"Now listen," Sylvia said. "We're running an inn. A man wants two rooms, and we have them. It's as simple as that."

"He may give us a hard time . . ."

"So what?" Sylvia retorted. "So what, Bart? We're in business, aren't we? This isn't a hobby any more. We need the money. If it makes it any easier for you, think of it like that."

"Just because we lost our money doesn't mean we have to lose our dignity."

"Dignity!" Sylvia said. "The wharf is rotting, we've got leaks in the roof, and you want to turn down money for dignity. We're fighting for our lives, Bart! You never seem to realize that."

In the hall outside, their son, John Hunter, a handsome, unusually mature boy of fourteen, stood listening. He had been unable to find his tennis shoes, and he was sure his mother would know where they were, but long experience had taught him not to interrupt his parents while they were fighting. Most of what he heard as he waited for the argument to stop made no sense to him, but it was clear that an emergency of some kind existed. John fondled a Boy Scout knife in his pocket, and imagined himself saving his mother from an army of ruffians. With his back against the door, he stood like a sentry braced to meet all comers.

3

WHEN SHE LEFT the bedroom, Sylvia met her son in the hall, and went to his room with him in search of tennis shoes. Patiently she examined the floor and the shelf in the closet; she looked behind the door and finally found the shoes under the bed. "Here," she said with a weary smile. "When are you going to learn to use the eyes in your own head?"

John grinned. "Thanks!" he said, and, taking the shoes, dashed off.

Sylvia had intended to return to the kitchen, but she felt suddenly tired and sank down on her son's bed. Ken Jorgenson—whoever would have thought he'd come back? It will be hard to face him again, but that is ridiculous; there is no need to be ashamed, she thought. Every woman and every man has someone like that in the past, some memory to make the blood rush to the face at midnight when sleep won't come. I am not unusual in that. Think of the women who have had many lovers, a whole parade of men to recall, perhaps with pleasure and not embarrassment. Why now, after all these years, she thought, putting her hands up to her face, why now does the very mention of his name make me begin to blush?

The trouble is, the thing between us was not a love affair; there was something incredibly ugly in the way I acted with him. No, this is not like remembering a love affair; it is like remembering an act of perversion, and that is why I blush.

Yet it was not all my fault, she thought. There are always excuses to be made, explanations, but beyond that . . .

It was in 1934 that Sylvia, at sixteen, first visited the island with her parents, the Raymonds, who wanted to build a summer place there. Danton Raymond, her father, was a business associate of old John Hunter, Bart's father, and the Raymonds stayed at the Hunters' house. Although it was never expressly stated, the purpose of the visit was to enable the other Islanders to look the Raymonds over, and to decide whether to admit them to the corporation of householders. The Raymonds had two strikes against them because they came from Chicago, and, as old John Hunter said, not long before he died, they were "part organ-grinder Italian, part Mick Irish, and God knows what else." The Islanders often formed close business ties with people they did not consider socially acceptable, and it was always more tactful to make believe that one really wanted these people on the island oneself, but that the others—well, that was a matter which no one person could control, because people were admitted to the corporation by unanimous vote only. The Raymonds were on trial on Pine Island that summer and they knew it.

Sylvia, at sixteen, seemed to the Islanders to be an almost indecently beautiful young woman, and nothing more. Old John Hunter, seeing her in a bathing suit, said that no real Yankee ever had such a figure, and his wife, Martha, replied dryly that perhaps the girl should be run in for disturbing the peace. It was not socially acceptable to be that pretty, really. Chorus girls and models and hat-check girls had figures of that sort, but nice girls, the ones nice people knew, were too fat or too thin, or had bad skin or thick ankles, or some defect. Really beautiful girls were the stuff that dreams are made of, movie stars, and such nonsense. A girl like Sylvia appearing in the flesh on Pine Island was startling. There was a lushness about her, a sensuousness inherent in her body, in her innocently downturned eyes, in little mannerisms she had, such as flicking the end of her tongue over her lips; there was that about her which immediately made people interested in knowing whether she was chaste. That summer a lot of people watched Sylvia closely, trying to divine the answer to that question. Old ladies peered at her sharply over their knitting, middle-aged men stared at her musingly, and the mothers of errant boys worried. She *couldn't* be chaste and look like that and walk like that, yet good heavens, the poor child was only sixteen, and there was no real reason to doubt her innocence.

Such beauty was a serious liability. Other girls her age became distant. They did not like to go swimming with Sylvia or play tennis with her or be seen near her at dances. Even the boys shied away, some of them; the timid ones, the modest ones with no high opinion of their own ability as suitors, the humble ugly ones and short ones, these were afraid of Sylvia, for it would be so easy to fall in love with her and to lose her to someone else. Sylvia's appearance exercised a terrible selection on the people who became her friends. She got those with self-confidence, the honestly assured, but also the braggarts, the self-styled Romeos, the self-assertive, and the clowns. Someone was always splashing water on her at the beach, or trying to put sand down the back of her bathing suit, or walking on his hands in front of her. It was all rather confusing to a girl who only two years before, even a year before, had been nothing but a child to whom no one paid much attention.

Still, there were advantages. It was interesting to find that if she stared at almost any of her father's friends for more than a second, they started squirming on their chairs, even the most dignified-looking ones. It was encouraging to discover that the boys who seemed distant and unfriendly became enthusiastic friends if she went out of her way just a little to encourage them. If she just said good morning, for instance, in a cheerful way to a boy, he was almost sure to tag along, trying desperately to develop a conversation.

No one on the island penetrated the disguise of Sylvia's beauty, no one except Ken Jorgenson, who, for a little while at least, had an instinctive understanding of her. She was frightened. The Islanders seemed hostile and superior to her. Her parents did not dress correctly, she was sure; they did not speak properly. Her father talked too much about money. She found she was terrifyingly ignorant of important subjects of conversation on the island, such as Miss Windsor's School in Boston, the Elliot Hall dances and S. S. Pierce's grocery store where, she imagined, only a select few were permitted to buy food. She felt herself to be an outcast, as she had all her life, even in Chicago, where her family had changed houses almost every other year.

Sylvia had been born in a two-family house in a section of Chicago only a little better than the slums, and the first move had taken place when she was two years old. Her childhood came back to her in memory as a series of houses, each a little better than the last, and each with a different set of neighbors and customs with which to become acquainted. By the time she was ten, the houses had large lawns around them, and her mother was employing a teacher of diction for the entire family. There was always a battle to be fought each time a new house was acquired, parties to be given with infinite worry over details of dress, menu and decoration, club memberships to be sought, inner circles to be penetrated.

Sylvia was always "the new girl," for by the time she began to feel at home in any neighborhood or school, her family moved up again. At parties she usually sat quietly with her hands folded in her lap, hoping only to be inconspicuous. When, at fourteen, she was first sent to a private school, she obeyed her mother's instructions not to talk about schools she had attended before. At fourteen she already felt her past to be cause for deep shame, and she blushed when on a drive through the city her father pointed out to her the house where she had been born.

When Sylvia first arrived on Pine Island, she interpreted the coldness of the people she met not as envy of her looks, but as scorn. When she first saw Ken Jorgenson striding along the beach in his swimming trunks, she admired his strength, and she was both astonished and flattered to find that he obviously liked her. On the first day they met, he offered to give her swimming lessons, and very gravely, as he did everything, he held her in the water. Suddenly the youngsters all around them began to giggle, and that afternoon they kidded her about Ken Jorgenson; oh you and Ken, they said, and they laughed, but at first she didn't mind.

The third night she spent on the island Ken Jorgenson took her rowing around the edge of the harbor. She sat in the stern of the boat trailing one hand in the water, watching his powerful shoulders outlined against the sky, and feeling an unaccustomed sense of peace. It was as though she had fought a battle alone since childhood, and had suddenly, without words, found herself to have acquired a mysteriously loyal and powerful ally. When they returned to the wharf, Ken kissed her as he helped her out of the boat, a shy and gentle kiss upon her lips, and they were both confused when without explanation she broke into tears. He held her tightly against him until the sobs stopped, and then with clumsy gallantry escorted her to the house without trying to kiss her again.

No one saw that kiss, but it was soon assumed by almost everyone on Pine Island that she was having an affair with Ken. One reason was, of course, that they looked as though they belonged together. They both had that irritating superiority of physique—a match between them was good casting. Ken, who was blond and big and "charming until he talked," old John Hunter said, appeared at first glance to answer the question in the minds of many, of what kind of a man would eventually get a girl who looked like that. There was a sort of inevitability about it. Beyond that, of course, there was the way he looked at her, his lack of ease in her presence, and perhaps, a little, the way she looked at him. It was a dull summer on the island, with many people giving up their boats for economy, and it was fun to have something to gossip about, to have a scandal, perhaps. Some of the girls found it comforting to write Sylvia off as competition, and some of the men felt it almost a relief to believe that Sylvia was not available, even if they had the courage to try. Within a month it was being widely said that this new tutor, Ken Jorgenson, was sleeping with the Raymond girl, and the atmosphere, whenever they met at an island get-together, became charged with excitement; the tempo of conversation audibly changed, and old ladies scowled with delight.

The rumors soon reached Sylvia's parents, who were alarmed both for their daughter and for themselves. The way to get accepted on Pine Island was not to have one's daughter start sleeping with the hired help.

Sylvia's father, Danton Raymond, asked her to his room, and it would not be fair to say that he warned her against Ken Jorgenson on the simple grounds that she could do better. Danton Raymond would have been shocked at the thought of advising his daughter to marry for money or for social position, and Sylvia would have rebelled indignantly if he had. Danton started that conversation by saying, "Sylvia, you are no longer a child now, and I know I can't organize your life. You can do what you want, and in the end I won't be able to stop you, but I'm your father, and I would like to be able to discuss matters such as Ken Jorgenson with you. Do you mind if I do?"

"No," she said, feeling immensely guilty, as she had when he had lectured her long ago about being rude to her mother.

"I think Ken Jorgenson is a very fine young man," Danton continued. "It would be a mistake, however, for you to take any young man too seriously at your age. Your sense of values will change as you get older. Good looks may not always be so important to you. Even football may not always seem so exciting."

"It's not football . . ." Sylvia started to say, but her father interrupted her. "As you grow older, matters of taste, even convention, may seem more important to you. Allowing a young man to monopolize your attentions and to make a public display of affection may seem fine and brave to you now, but later you may realize that the old-fashioned virtues are not without charm."

"I haven't made a public display of affection!"

"You are a very beautiful young woman," Danton said. "It's time you learned that there is always some foundation to gossip. I'm sure this will sound hopelessly old-fashioned to you, but a lady should be above suspicion."

Sylvia blushed.

"I know you haven't done anything wrong," Danton continued hastily. "The thing is, it's not enough for just me to know that. Don't underestimate the importance of a reputation."

"I haven't done anything!" she protested. "I don't even *like* Ken so terribly much. Can I help it if he keeps following me around?"

"I think that all young ladies eventually learn how to handle that sort of situation."

Sylvia said nothing.

"Your mother and I have high hopes for you, dear," her father went on. "One reason we've worked so hard is that we want to achieve a better life for you. You're getting old enough to think seriously now about your future."

"I guess I'll go to college," Sylvia said.

"If you wish. I'm also hoping we can arrange a coming-out party for you. But beyond that, I want you to realize that when a woman chooses a husband, she gets more than a man: she marries a whole way of life. Some ways of life would be a great deal more fun for you and more meaningful than others. My point is that when you find yourself thinking seriously of a young man, you should look beyond the man himself, and see what he stands for. Love should be more than just an animal attraction."

"Yes," Sylvia said.

"You're a good girl," her father concluded. "You've just got to learn to use your head."

It wasn't that talk alone which influenced Sylvia. There was the gradually deepening realization that almost everyone on the island treated Ken with clear, if amiable, condescension. He was unfashionable, and at sixteen, Sylvia felt that a peculiarly embarrassing sin. The Hunters, on the other hand, were the height of fashion on Pine Island. Sylvia's mother tried to learn how to arrange flowers the way Martha Hunter did, and almost imperceptibly began to acquire a few of her mannerisms of speech. "Why don't you get Bart Hunter to teach you tennis, dear?" she often said to Sylvia. "He plays so beautifully."

After the talk with her father, Sylvia did not argue with Ken or fight with him, but she began to feel that in some obscure way he had cheated her, that he had misrepresented himself to her, that she had been betrayed into making a fool of herself. Her father advised her to let the swimming lessons "taper off" rather than terminate abruptly, but her body was so rigid that Ken kept asking her in bewilderment what the trouble was. "Nothing!" she said. "I guess I'm just scared of the water."

The other young people on the island, Sylvia saw, made fun of Ken a good deal, and she soon found in ridicule a way to disprove the gossipers, and at the same time to achieve a reputation as a wit. The insults she fired at Ken were relatively mild at first. She was a good mimic and imitated his Midwestern accent, but when he only smiled good-naturedly at that, she repeated a few funny jokes about Swedes and dumb football players, and other little things which weren't so bad by themselves, but which in sum made his good-natured smile turn into a hurt look. In spite of herself she had strong impulses to hold tightly to those shoulders, but these feelings, she told herself, were the sort of "animal attraction" which had to be disciplined. He was a beast, she thought, and first turned that into a joke one day when he was doing push-ups on the diving board. "Observe the Beast at play," she said to Bart, and was rewarded by an appreciative laugh.

The nickname, "the Beast," seemed to so many of the Islanders to be apt for Ken that it stuck. It really was an inspired instrument of ridicule, because he could never admit he had heard it without creating a scene. Of course they never used that nickname to his face. It was a game to use it just within his hearing, when one could pretend one didn't know he was there. Once when Hasper's dog was heard barking, Sylvia said, "Did you say something, Ken?" and it got so she could produce a laugh simply by mentioning a leash or a chain in Ken's presence.

But even that didn't turn out to be enough; sadism, like dope, is never satisfactory for long in mild doses, and neither is exhibitionism, Sylvia thought with self-disgust now so many years later. Getting up from her son's bed restlessly, she paced the narrow room, finally sitting down in a chair in front of the window. This was not the room in which Ken Jorgenson had slept; no, he had occupied the one farther down the hall, but the view from all the windows was the same: they looked across a narrow courtyard to the back of the old mansion. Staring over there now, Sylvia could see the window of the room where she had stayed when she visited the Hunters that summer long ago.

Late one August afternoon Sylvia, at sixteen, went to the window of that room and, glancing across the courtyard, saw Ken at his window, looking up at her. The way he was sitting, with his elbows on the window sill, it seemed apparent that he had been gazing up at her for some time. It gave her a funny feeling to know that he was watching her, that he perhaps watched her often. Impatiently she pulled the window shade, and she wondered if there had been times when she had forgotten to do that.

An idea came to her then, more daring than any she had had before, that she could accuse Ken of being a Peeping Tom, and cause him to lose his job in disgrace. Naturally she wouldn't do such a thing, but the discovery that the power was in her hands was startling. Of course, she couldn't accuse him of peeping from his window as he had, because that was her fault for not pulling the shade, but she could accuse him of peeping in other circumstances. She could, as a matter of fact, accuse him of almost anything, and she would be believed. A simple accusation would set all the rumors at rest for good and all. It was quite an interesting thing to think about.

That summer Sylvia got a new black bathing suit which set off her figure well. She strolled down to the beach in the morning and, finding it was chilly, let Bart run up and get her fur coat. When the sun had warmed the air, she threw the coat back, and slipped the straps of her bathing suit off her shoulders to get an even tan. Ken, who was sitting on his lifeguard stand under a big umbrella, glanced down at her, looked away quickly, and buried his face in a book.

"What are you reading, Ken?" Sylvia called, making her voice friendly. That was one of the things that worked best with Ken, like alternating fast and slow balls in tennis; a combination of friendliness and insult was more deadly than insult alone.

Ken climbed down from his lifeguard stand and walked toward her. "*The Decline and Fall,*" he said. For some reason, Bart, who was only a little older than Sylvia, thought this was uproariously funny, and he laughed. Several young people who had been sunning themselves on the beach gathered around, sensing that some bearbaiting was about to begin.

"Tell me about it," Sylvia said. "I always wanted to read it."

Standing before her as though he were giving a lecture, the Beast began to talk, describing "marvelous prose rhythms," "a genius for government," "a study in decay." "How interesting," Sylvia said gravely at two-minute intervals, encouraging him to go on, and "Really?" Ken conducted a monologue for ten minutes, getting excited about his subject, gesticulating with enthusiasm. He looked almost like a preacher standing there waving his arms. Bart, lithe and dapper with a towel over his slender shoulders, and all the rest of them had to struggle to keep straight faces. "I'm awfully glad you're telling me this," Sylvia said finally, and Bart couldn't stand it any longer; he let out a suppressed snort, and that set all the others off. Ken looked up, his big face full of confusion, unable to understand for a moment why everyone was laughing. "Were you pulling my leg?" he asked Sylvia. For some reason this seemed awfully funny to everyone, and the laughter increased.

"You can be sure I'd never pull your leg," Sylvia said, a really screaming remark, the way she said it, making it sound mildly bawdy.

"I ought to throw you off the end of the dock," Ken said, his face flushing with anger.

"Go ahead," she said.

He stood over her, a mountain of a man, and he put his right hand on her shoulder, preparatory to picking her up, but it became immediately obvious that if he did so, her bathing suit would come down around her waist. He froze.

"Go ahead," she said again, folding her hands behind her head, a gesture which made everyone roar with laughter; it seemed unbearably sophisticated and modern, the whole thing. Ken leaned toward her and she had a quick stab of fear that he actually was going to pick her up and carry her squirming, half naked in his arms, to the edge of the dock, an action which would make her appear ridiculous, but which also would be quite likely to get him fired, she knew, thinking quickly; a tutor twenty years old could not do that to a young girl, no he couldn't. He put his left hand on her waist, and he seemed about to pick her up. Everyone's laughter stopped. A sudden silence shivered in the air. But then, abruptly, Ken turned and walked determinedly away, with his fists clenched at his sides, and the laughter started again.

The teasing of the Beast continued in many secret ways. Once the whole group of young people went for a moonlight sail in Harry Hulbert's big sloop, the *Gull's Wing,* and Ken was invited for once, because the boat's big, gaff-rigged mainsail was hard to hoist and get in. It was fun to sit drinking beer and singing while the sloop skimmed over the moonlit bay with Ken at the wheel. He said he liked to steer and he had learned to sail pretty well for a Midwesterner. Sylvia asked Bart to go forward and they sat silhouetted against the white curve of the jib. Feeling Ken's eyes upon her, Sylvia allowed Bart to kiss her, and she put her head on Bart's shoulder, making their silhouetted figures merge. Everybody said later that Ken had looked furious; it had been really funny to see.

Adolescent sexuality on Pine Island, Sylvia thought now with the horrified candor of added years. Some anthropologist should study it, the way they study Samoa and New Guinea and places like that. On Pine Island the young teen-agers talked openly about sex; it was very modern and sophisticated to be frank about everything, but it wasn't fashionable for girls "to go all the way," oh no; only waitresses and shopgirls did that. It was all right to have lighthearted necking parties on the beach at night. Sometimes, incredible to remember, the laughing young people changed partners at a given signal. "Switch" was a good game; in the early Thirties all anyone had to do was say it to get a laugh.

The laughter was important, the banter and the jokes were necessary, because it was not fashionable "to get serious." "Getting serious" was a creepy thing to do. That was one trouble with Ken Jorgenson—he "got serious" about Sylvia, oh God, how serious he got.

Now, almost twenty years later, Sylvia could still clearly remember the hungry expression in Ken's eyes, the earnestness with which he gave her love poems he had written, some of them in Latin, which she couldn't read at all, and which he wouldn't translate for her. He said she'd have to learn the language herself; it might be an added incentive for her studies, because it was a wonderful language in which to write love poems. He told her once in a soft voice that he wished they lived in some other land, where sixteen-year-old girls could get married and not waste their youth away. He was on the point of proposing, it seemed, but then he stopped and his eyes looked haunted when she laughed.

We were children, Sylvia thought now as she pressed her hands to her face. We were the foolish children of foolish parents, and we cannot be blamed too much. Oh, the Islanders were very sophisticated about their children—they allowed them to sip cocktails sometimes when they were as young as fourteen, and a few of them laughed when the youngsters' speech got thick. The drinking was part of what happened; it helped determine the end.

Restlessly, half unwillingly, Sylvia now got up and sat in the chair before the window in her son's room. Directly across from her, high up on the old mansion, was the yellow square of the draperies at the window which had been hers so many years ago, new draperies now, but they had always been yellow in that room. It had been a curious sensation for a young girl to live there, knowing that a man like Ken Jorgenson often sat staring up at her from his room over the garage. Now, as she watched, the wind swayed the draperies at that window, and a figure was half visible behind them. It would be old Mrs. Hamble, no doubt, who occupied that room now, but Sylvia had the eerie feeling that the curtains would open, and that she was about to see herself, aged sixteen, staring at her older self across the courtyard.

But the draperies did not open, and a few minutes later Mrs. Hamble pulled the shade; perhaps she felt that eyes were upon her. Sylvia got up restlessly and stretched out again on her son's bed. She covered her face with both hands.

Her second summer on the island, when she was seventeen, she came home from a dance late one night, a dance to which Ken had not been invited. It was a hot July night with little wind. She was slightly drunk; that had to be taken into account. Bart had had a silver flask full of warm Martinis saved from a cocktail party. He had kept passing it to her. It had been difficult to refuse and even more difficult to gauge how much she had drunk. Her position on the island was difficult that year, because her parents had just been turned down by the organization of householders. She was visiting the Hunters as Bart's guest, in spite of the fact that her family had been weighed and found wanting. Anyway, she had got a little drunk that night. Her head had started to swim, and the kisses and embraces from Bart in the back seat of a Chris-Craft on the way home with the other couples laughing all around them had seemed suddenly nauseous to her. She had been glad to get out of the crowded boat and to be alone in her room. Locking her door, she put on the lights and opened her window. Across the courtyard the light in Ken's window flashed out. Sylvia pulled back the draperies and, standing before the open window, breathed in the cool air and the fragrance of the garden. While unfastening the hooks at the side of her blue evening gown, it occurred to her that perhaps Ken might be watching, but on the other hand, he probably was in bed. Slowly she undressed and, feeling a new kind of exaltation, let the night air blow over her body, evaporating the small beads of sweat on her skin, making her so cold that she suddenly shivered. She began to tremble, and pulling the shade down, she went to bed. Lying there in the dark, she felt conscious of having done a monstrous thing, and she took comfort from the thought that she really had been drinking a great deal; she had taken several swallows from the flask, four or five at least, and a girl who has been drinking can easily be forgiven for forgetting such small niceties as pulling a window shade before getting undressed.

Still, the memory made Sylvia blush, because it had to be admitted that she was forgetful more than once. It became a teasing game, an intensification of a game that had been going on for a long while. Some nights she pulled the shade down and some nights she did not, and in the mornings when she saw Ken at the beach, he looked at her with those dumb, hungry eyes, and he would sometimes blush and turn away, and he would sometimes go running off the end of the dock, diving into the water with a tremendous splash and flailing his way out to the float, hauling his big body through the water, kicking up a storm of spray, surging through the sea as though pursued by sharks. She was always demure and circumspect with him. When he asked her to go sailing with him, she said no, sounding mildly shocked, as though he had made an indecent proposal. She held herself away from him when they danced, and was coldly aloof on the beach.

The climax came a year later on the twelfth of August during another visit Sylvia was paying the Hunters. When she stepped off the schooner, the *Mary Anne,* at the small wharf in front of the old mansion, Ken, as well as Bart, was there to meet her. She threw her arms around Bart and gave him a welcoming kiss of unusual warmth. Turning to Ken, she held her hand out and said, "Oh, hello! It's nice to see you again."

"Hello," Ken said, and he seemed as ill at ease as the first time they had met.

There was a dance that night at the Hunters' house, and Japanese lanterns were strung all around the wide veranda. The guests came in cruisers and motorboats from other parts of the island and from the mainland. At ten-thirty in the evening everyone gathered at the wharf and Bart fired some skyrockets he had saved from the Fourth of July. He said it was much better to shoot them on August twelfth. There must be all kinds of things which had happened on August twelfth that never got celebrated, and he was righting a great wrong.

"Like what?" Roger, his younger brother, asked solemnly, weaving a little from side to side. That was the first night Roger ever got drunk; he had always been pretty good before.

Ignoring him, Bart turned to Sylvia and said, "Let's get engaged. We've got the skyrockets to celebrate, so why not?"

"Now don't get serious," Sylvia said.

"Who's serious?" Bart replied. "I just want to get engaged. You don't want to waste skyrockets, do you?"

"I'm yours," Sylvia said, and the assembled guests laughed.

Bart touched her ceremoniously on the forehead with a skyrocket and said, "I dub thee mine." Then, putting two skyrockets in the wooden trough which had been built as a launching platform, he solemnly said, "Stand back! This is going to be a very symbolic ceremony. Two skyrockets are going up together, representing two souls beginning their journey into eternity together. This is a great tradition, a famous nuptial rite practiced by the wild Hunter tribe of Pine Island, ever since they invented gunpowder in the year ten, antedating the Chinese discovery by many centuries."

"Hear, hear," Roger said in his high voice. He was only sixteen that year, and fairly fat. Looking like a little old man, he stood and clapped his hands. "Hear, hear," the others chanted, while Bart lit a sparkler with which to ignite the rockets.

Out of the crowd came Ken. "You're not really going to try to fire those rockets together, are you?" he asked.

"Sure," Bart said. "Stand back, slave!"

"It's dangerous," Ken said. "The chute isn't made for . . ."

"Are you questioning the judgment of the tribal prince?" Bart asked, and standing very erect at the end of the wharf holding a blazing sparkler aloft, he did look oddly noble and savage.

"They'll go wild!" Ken said, stepping forward, but he was too late. Bart stooped and touched off the two rockets. A fountain of sparks spurted. One rocket soared into the sky, but the other jumped the chute and turned toward the crowd, a wailing banshee trailing fire, twisting and turning erratically, exploding finally with a crash against a window high up in the attic of the house. Speechless, the crowd stood looking up, and there was the pungent smell of gunpowder, the sound of falling glass. Smoke floated from the window. Ken was the first to speak. "We better get water up there," he said. "It's started a fire."

Fifteen of the young men raced into the kitchen and carried pans full of water up the four flights of stairs to the attic, where a small fire had been started, all right. It was soon extinguished, and they all trooped back to the kitchen, laughing together. The only damage was a broken window and a lot of water slopped on the attic floor and in the kitchen, where Roger had slipped with a whole dishpan full, so the episode could hardly be called a tragedy. In fact, it was good to have some excitement for a change. Old John Hunter, who was both sick and a little drunk, said it was nothing to worry about. "Strike up the band!" he said. "Strike up the band!" He kept repeating that until someone turned the electric phonograph up a little louder. That was the first year the Hunters didn't have an orchestra come over from the mainland.

For an hour the excitement over the rockets killed the party. When the water on the kitchen floor had been wiped up, people divided into small groups talking seriously, but then Bart brought out a whole case of bourbon and some salt fish he had bought in Harvesport, which produced a fierce thirst. By midnight things were really rolling. Bart's father, who was sixty-two years old, staggered out on the floor in spite of his bad heart and tried to do a tap dance before he was hustled off to bed by his wife. A half hour later he appeared at the foot of the stairs dressed in his pajamas and a bathrobe, clamoring for a drink. "I'm not a party pooper," he said.

Sylvia was dancing with Bart when Ken put a heavy hand on his shoulder. She was surprised, because he rarely cut in on her; he usually went to his room to read when the dancing started. "Go 'way, Beast," Bart said. "I am dancing with my fancy, I mean my fiancée, and . . ."

He never finished the sentence, because Ken pushed him away with one swipe of his arm, and Sylvia felt herself crushed against Ken's massive chest. If Bart had been sober, he might have resented it. He was far smaller than Ken, but no one had ever accused him of lacking physical courage. As things were, he shrugged in a debonair way, and walked to the table where the liquor was.

Ken danced without talking, and was even clumsier than he

usually was. Sylvia realized gradually and with great astonishment that he was drunk; she had never seen him touch liquor before.

"Breaking training?" she asked mockingly, and was sorry, because the reply was a bear's hug that almost broke her ribs.

It must have been about three in the morning that everyone decided to go swimming.

"But I didn't bring a bathing suit!" a girl from the mainland cried.

Laughter followed. "Your bathing suit is the night," Bart said, and bowed in what he felt was just tribute to his own poetic eloquence.

Old John Hunter in his bathrobe pulled himself up to a sitting position on the couch where he had been dozing. "Drunken swimming very dangerous," he said, holding out his hand with the forefinger extended, and looking very much like the poster with the caption, "Uncle Sam Wants You."

"We're not really drunk, Dad," Bart said.

"Take Mr. Jorgenson," old John Hunter said. "You'll need a lifeguard. Knew a girl who drowned once like this."

"All right," Bart said. "Ken, you come along."

Ken thought they made a sad procession in the moonlight, the girls in their pastel summer evening gowns and the men in their white dinner coats, as they headed for the beach. Some of them weaved a little, and many of them bent their faces downward. They looked oddly like people in deep grief, and for Ken, whom the liquor was depressing, there was the sudden sensation of walking in a funeral march. With incongruous giggling, the girls gathered behind a clump of pines to take off their clothes, while the men disrobed brazenly on the beach. Quickly the men rushed into the water, and swam in circles waiting for the women.

The girls came running in a group from behind the pines, their bodies white and lovely in the moonlight. They were visible only for a few seconds before they plunged into the water. Ken swam slowly toward them, looking for Sylvia. He found her twenty yards apart from the others, apparently swimming straight out to sea. Her face and shoulders were white in the moonlight. He kissed her, and they sank, coming to the surface in an explosion of spray, gasping for breath. "Don't!" she said. "Do you want to drown me?"

"Yes," he said.

"You son-of-a-bitch!" she retorted, and started swimming as fast as she could toward the shore. He swam easily beside her, shouldering her to the south, so that when she reached the beach, it was a good hundred yards from the others. As their feet touched bottom, he grabbed her and carried her across the beach toward the grove of pines. "Let me go!" she said fiercely between clenched teeth. "Put me down!"

"Scream if you want," he said.

She hit him in the face with her clenched fists; she made his nose bleed, and battered his eyes before he succeeded in pinning her arms behind her, but she didn't scream. Their battle was silent and deadly. He put her down on the pine needles, and when her struggles turned into the motions of love, the world seemed his. Afterward there was a moment of peace during which they lay on their backs, with her head on his shoulder. The tops of the pine trees looked black against the sky. He turned to caress her and was bewildered when she started to struggle away from him again. Imprisoning her with one huge arm, he kissed her and said, "I want to marry you."

"You bastard!" she replied with venom.

He rolled over and pressed her shoulders down with both hands. "Why not? We love each other."

She called him everything she could think of then to hurt him. He was a vile Swede, a boor, an idiot, a pauper, she said, and she concluded with the simple statement that she wanted to marry a gentleman, not a beast. In reply, he took her again, finding that she did not give in this time, that she fought him to the end. When he was through he held her cradled in his arms, struggling to a sitting position and rocking her back and forth in a strange combination of passion and grief. Her mouth was clenched so tightly shut that he could not kiss her. The wind in the pine trees rustled. Seemingly far away, there was the sound of laughter and shouts. Suddenly, above the other voices, was the question in Roger's high, panic-stricken soprano: "Where are Sylvia and Ken?"

In reply there was a babble, broken by Bart's clear tenor voice drunkenly singing, "Who is Sylvia? What is she?"

Laughter followed. Suddenly Ken released her. "You can go back," he said.

She stood up, quick to jump away from him, but he lay there, stretched on his back, like a naked corpse in the moonlight. She looked down at him.

"Go ahead," he said. "Call the pack."

Whirling, she ran, plunging into the water, swimming fast to rejoin the others. There was still a chance, she thought, that her absence could be joked away.

The next morning Ken appeared on the beach in his bathing trunks and a garish sports shirt, because her fingernails had raked his back. He did not blush when he saw her; he just turned away. That night he told old John Hunter that his mother was ill, and he would have to return to Nebraska right away. To Sylvia he said no goodbyes.

For a ridiculously long while, Sylvia feared that she was pregnant, but that did not happen. After all, she concluded, nothing had occurred which she could not forget. Convinced that she was doing the right thing, she married Bart not long afterward. Soon the Raymonds were offered admittance to the Pine Island Corporation, but her father's business was falling off by that time and they had to decline.

I wonder what Ken Jorgenson will look like now, Sylvia thought as she lay on her son's bed seventeen years later. I think I have been imagining him returning exactly as he was, the young athlete with brooding eyes, striding along the beach. He probably will be fat and will smoke cigars. It would be absurd for me to apologize now, she thought. It would be ridiculous for me to point out the obvious fact that in a thousand ways I've been proved wrong. He probably will be kind; he usually was. There is no reason for me to be afraid to see him again.

4

THAT SUMMER Ken Jorgenson, at the age of twenty-two, returned to Boston after quitting Pine Island and got a job with a construction firm until it was time to resume his studies. In former years he had worked hard and had spent his few spare hours dreaming foolishly of marrying Sylvia, but there was not that any more. Everything seemed dreary. Talk of war in Europe was increasing. The whole world seemed to be gradually disintegrating. In the back of his mind was the fear that Sylvia would find she was pregnant, or was it a hope? Probably she wouldn't come to him even if she was—she would prefer an abortion to marrying a beast, he thought.

Ken labored hard as a carpenter's helper for a month, helping to build a warehouse. It was dull work. He was glad when college started, but the long evenings of Indian summer in the dormitory also palled. Chemistry, his major subject, was the only thing that made any sense, a rational analysis of the physical world, the neat symbols on the printed page, the experiments that could be controlled. Whenever Ken saw a sex crime in the newspapers, he had a certain sympathy for the offender. Us rapists should form a union, he thought, and laughed at himself, but there it was; he had committed rape, hadn't he?

During football practice that fall, the coach had to warn Ken that, after all, the purpose of the game was not to kill. He became a much better player than he ever had been, and was given considerable publicity in the Boston *Herald*, which nominated him for All-American. Invitations to cocktail parties poured in, and at last he was put on the list of people asked to the debutante parties. He went to a few, but the girls had small appeal for him. In comparison to Sylvia even the few really pretty ones looked to him like shadows.

Sylvia, he decided after much reflection, was a form of mental illness for him. After all, she was not really more beautiful than any one of thousands of women. She wasn't stupid, but she had a lazy, uncultivated mind. She was a snob without being an aristocrat. A petty bourgeoise, he enjoyed calling her in his thoughts, a sloppy little strainer, trying to marry her way up. She had no soul, and he was well quit of her. Certainly he was clever enough to recognize an illusion when he saw it, and to steer clear.

Still, he could not get her out of his mind. Occasionally he caught sight of other women on the street who, from a distance, looked like her, and once he ran for a full block to make sure it was not she. When the telephone rang, he imagined it might be she, and he always jumped to answer it. Folly, he knew, perhaps insanity—he certainly was old enough to understand when a thing was hopeless, but still he thumbed through his mail each morning feverishly, imagining there might be a letter from her saying she was pregnant and asking him to marry her.

Another woman, he decided, was necessary to expunge her from his mind. He disliked the idea of setting out for deliberate conquest, but it was foolish to stay obsessed by a girl beyond his reach. Debating this, he spent most of his time moodily pacing his room.

One night in early December his telephone rang, and he leaped to answer it as he always did. "Is this Ken Jorgenson?" an elaborately seductive woman's voice asked.

"Yes."

"I've heard so much about you, and I think it would be fun if we could meet," the woman said. "I live at 29 Easterton Avenue. Would you care to come up for a cocktail?"

"What's your name?"

"Catherine Gray," the woman said.

Ken had heard of her. She was a nymphomaniac who used the Harvard yearbooks as Sears, Roebuck catalogues, telephoning the young men whose pictures she liked, and paying special attention to the members of the football team. As a matter of fact, she had called him before, and he had politely refused. But now, why not? Some of his friends had told him she wasn't bad. "I feel like a cocktail right now," he said. "Wait for me."

She turned out to be an overly plump divorcée with greedy eyes, and with a photograph of her mother and father hung over her bed. It was this picture which bothered Ken, as much as anything: the picture of a kindly old man sitting beside his sweet-faced wife, her hand locked in his. The experience was small pleasure, and he hurriedly left, hoping he could forget the name, "Catherine Gray," which was of course false, but still indelibly fixed in his mind.

Ken tried a variety of brothels next. The thought of them had always disgusted him, but most of his friends talked of visiting them, and why not? A man was a fool to allow the body of a foolish girl to obsess him. Perhaps it was time to learn that the net value of a well-made body without a mind and soul was in the neighborhood of twenty dollars. A girl fully as symmetrical as Sylvia could be had for that, and one looking as Sylvia would in a few years could be had for much less.

The brothels were curious places, some of them like clubs for the unhappy, the possessed. The girls laughed too high and too loud. In their eyes was not so much the look of tragedy as of mania. In one establishment which he frequented for a few months, two girls tried to commit suicide, one by leaping from a window and the other by swallowing hot coals from a fireplace. She ate them greedily, the madam told Ken in awe. She crawled into the fireplace on her hands and knees and gobbled them up, burning her legs and her fingers and her lips and tongue and throat horribly, but surviving to be placed in a mental hospital.

The customers were not much better. In the kitchen of one small Negro establishment, Ken saw an honors student from the law school bare his arm and smile while, for a fee, a naked brown girl burned her professional name into his skin with a series of lighted cigarettes. The cigarettes kept going out, and the girl repeatedly asked the madam for a light. "Don't go," the honors student begged Ken, and during the whole operation there was a look of serenity on his face. When it was over the madam bandaged the man's arm, but underneath the gauze there was the whore's name, burned in rough letters: "Cindy."

After that, Ken lost his taste for brothels. A friend took him to a fireman's ball in Salem, where he met a seventeen-year-old Polish girl who responded avidly when he kissed her, but suddenly Ken realized that she was in love with him, and he felt no love for her at all. Victimizing her seemed even more obscene than the brothels, so Ken left her without fully seducing her, and hardened his heart when she cried.

At about this time he read the autobiography of Benjamin Franklin, who recommended that a sensible young man find an older woman, who would be grateful for his attentions without either suffering or causing trouble. The difficulty was, he couldn't find any. In search of one, he started haunting night clubs and bars, buying one bottle of beer in each place, to keep the bill down. It was important to save money, because his marks were suffering. There was some danger of losing his academic scholarships, and in graduate school football would not pay the bills.

On a snowy evening in early March he went to a place called the Hi-Ho Club and at the end of the bar saw a dark-haired girl with ivory skin and a figure almost like Sylvia's. She appeared to be about twenty-five. Usually, Ken had found, women that good-looking were waiting for somebody, but this one returned his glance, and when he offered to buy her a drink, she accepted. For an hour they danced to the music of a jukebox, jammed amongst a group of sailors and their girls. Speaking in a slight Italian accent, she told him that her name was Rosa Gilatano, and that she had just become separated from her husband. Her cheek felt wonderful against his, and her hips were responsive. A little after midnight, he asked if he could take her home, and she said that she had her own car, but she would be delighted if he would care to drop in for a nightcap. He said he'd like that, and they danced one more number, her body feeling so good that he decided he was in love again.

When they left the Hi-Ho Club they were quite drunk, and were surprised to find that it had been snowing hard all evening. Already the drifts were more than three feet deep. Not many people were on the sidewalks, and the street lights cast golden circles in the snow. Walking by her side down an alley, Ken had a rare moment of complete elation. Morality or no morality, he thought, I have established contact with something; I am alive for the first time. The snowflakes settling on her black hair looked fragile and beautiful. In the shadow of a garage he caught her by the arm and started by kissing the snowflakes.

Her old Ford stood in the middle of a deserted parking lot, with the snow banked around it. There was no watchman or attendant and the only light was in the window of a warehouse across the street. It was an ominous, eerie place, and he placed his arm around her as they approached the car. Just as he put his hand on the cold handle of the door, it was violently pushed open in his face, and before he knew what was happening, a large man jumped out and knocked him down in the snow. He lay there dazed, gradually becoming conscious that the man and the girl were arguing shrilly in Italian over him. "Enrico!" the girl kept saying. "Enrico, Enrico!" Then the man raised his fist and delivered a crushing blow to the girl, who went down. Ken struggled to his feet, and the man rushed at him, with something shiny in his upraised hand—a wrench, Ken saw, a large crescent wrench. Ken ducked with the skill of a practiced athlete, and brought his left arm across in a vicious hook, but the man wasn't there—he was dancing back with the wrench held high again. They faced each other, crouched forward like boxers, Ken a little bigger than the stranger, but unarmed. Suddenly the man was at him in a rush. Ken put his arm up, but the wrench numbed it, and grazed his head. Before he knew what was happening, he was down again, with the man kicking him. Ken rolled, spinning in the snow away from him, springing to his feet, already crouched; and this time, he butted his head under the wrench into the man's hard chest, driving him back with the disciplined fury of a man who had been drilled to do that as a bread-earning football player for years. The man fell on his back, immediately pulling himself to a sitting position with the wrench upraised, and Ken, jumping high in the air, landed on his stomach with both knees. The man dropped the wrench and lay limp.

Ken hurried to the girl, and helped her up. She was crying. Her nose and lips were bleeding, and he handed her a handkerchief. While she used it, she saw a welt on his forehead, and with a whimper of alarm, insisted on feeling his head and face with her extraordinarily delicate fingers, as though she were blind. Forgetting the throbbing pain in his head, he kissed her, tasting the blood on her lips, and she said, "Let's hurry home."

In spite of their wounds, Rosa Gilatano gave Ken the first good night he had ever had in his life, and the last one he was to have for many years. In the morning he awoke, still elated, and looking out the window of her tenement, he saw that the snow had piled six feet deep. It had been a real blizzard. That seemed only mildly interesting until he remembered that he had left a man unconscious and perhaps mortally injured in the snow many hours before. With a sense of inevitability, it occurred to Ken that he was turning out to be not only a rapist but a killer.

He awoke Rosa, and in terror they drove back to the parking lot. The drifts had piled waist high.

"Don't go near," she said. "Someone will see."

They sat huddled in her car, staring at the undulating banks of snow, under which there could be anything. Ken's eyes sought the spot where he thought he had left the man, and jumping from the car suddenly, he rushed toward it, plowing through the snow, expecting at any minute to have his feet strike a corpse, but there was nothing. In panic, he blundered in erratic circles, but still there was nothing. Half frozen, he returned to the car.

"Did you . . . ?" she asked in agony.

"No."

She leaned forward, with her hands to her face, and cried. "Enrico!" she said.

He went back to his room and sat there thinking. Obviously, there were only three possibilities: the man could have recovered consciousness and walked away; he could still be lying hidden under the snow in some part of the parking lot where Ken had not looked; or his body might have been reported to the police and picked up earlier. If the man were dead, the police would undoubtedly go to his wife, who would have to point to Ken. It was self-defense, Ken thought, with the sweat coming to his brow; I should go to the police now and report it. Putting on his coat, he walked to the police station, but paused outside it. If the man weren't dead, it would be ridiculous to cause a scandal, to get himself involved in a mess which might cause his expulsion from college. Imagining that Sylvia would take grim satisfaction in his dilemma, he clenched his fists, turned and walked away from the police station, keeping his dark secret to himself. For a guy only twenty-two, he thought bitterly, he was building up quite a record for himself.

It took two weeks for the snow to melt, and until the parking lot was bare, Ken could not be sure a body would not be found. He read the newspapers and listened to news broadcasts with dread. It's not worth it, he concluded. Even that elation, that moment of feeling he was alive for the first time, that he had established some mysterious contact with the life-giving force of the world, even this was not worth becoming a criminal, which was where this road apparently led. The moment he had stooped to kiss the snow crystals on the dark hair of the pretty girl, the things he had imagined might be possible with Sylvia, the dreams, illusions of love—these things had to be forgotten. With sudden insight Ken understood for the first time the pinched, wintery look of most of the older people he knew. His dead father, bent by long lonely labor, his mother haunted and querulous; this is what they all had faced, one way or another, the realization that for them at least there was no real love, and there would never be.

All right, Ken thought, I'm tough, I shall endure, and by God, I'll make something of myself. Passing a derelict blundering along the sidewalk with red-rimmed eyes, he had a sudden lust for respectability. I shall consort with no more whores and maniacs, he thought. There shall be no more cheap bars, no fights in the snow. I am a respectable man, by God, I'm not a derelict. I shall be chaste, I shall be celibate.

As it turned out, this was more than a passing fancy. Except for one drunken night during which he celebrated reading about Sylvia and Barton's wedding and seeing her picture in the Boston *Transcript*, which represented her as tall and virginal, Ken's only solace was work. His professors eyed him with interest, and after he finished his graduate work, they tried to persuade him to remain at the university as a chemistry instructor, but he said no. He didn't want the life of a college teacher, he didn't know just what he wanted. Driven by winds he didn't even try to analyze, he got a job as a research chemist with the biggest corporation he could. When he was sent to Buffalo, he felt the city to be immaterial. The important thing, the only important thing, was his work, and that could be done in any laboratory.

Still, life in a furnished room got lonely. When an elderly colleague at the laboratory, Bruce Carter, asked him home for dinner one night, Ken was glad to accept.

The Carters lived in an immaculately kept small house in a rather run-down suburb of Buffalo. Their daughter, Helen, was a thin girl who never had had many friends, male or female, and who was then finishing her course at the Buffalo State Teachers College. Except for her eyes, she was not beautiful, but she appeared to be decent and her figure, though slight, was well-proportioned. She was not the sort of girl who would start undressing in front of open windows, Ken thought bitterly. She was no whore, no maniac, she came from a background not unlike his own. Lower middle-class, dull, respectable, but something to hang on to, something that didn't blow up in one's face. The very fact that she appeared devoid of passion was almost an attraction to Ken at the time; she seemed comfortable and safe.

He took to visiting the Carters often. On weekends Bruce, a tired pear-shaped man, polished his elderly Ford and trimmed his tiny lawn, making it neat as a putting green. His wife spent almost all her waking hours cleaning the house. From the first, Ken felt he knew everything the Carters thought, simply because they were so much like people he had known in Nebraska. They disliked modern furniture, modern houses—in fact, anything modern. Old Margaret liked cloth dogs, Teddy bears, all sorts of soft children's toys which cluttered her room. She was vaguely apprehensive whenever she entered an expensive store, hotel or restaurant, because she felt she didn't look right, and someone might ask her to go. She had, Ken was sure, never left a child untended, never kissed a man other than her husband and never cooked a meal with dirty hands.

Her daughter, Helen, at twenty-two, was almost an exact duplicate of her mother, but there was an appealing quality of struggle about her, as though she were trying to be more. The professors at the State Teachers College had introduced her to the fine arts, and she spent a great deal of time at the Albright Art Museum, solemnly trying to copy great paintings. When Ken danced with her, she held herself stiffly and awkwardly in his arms. But once when he visited her house unannounced, he heard the music of a radio on the small concrete terrace old Bruce had built in the back yard, and going there, was astonished to find her dancing by herself with surprising grace. She was so preoccupied that she did not see or hear him, and fearing that he would embarrass her, he walked back to the front door and called to her. The music immediately stopped. "Hi, Ken!" she replied. "I'm back here." When he arrived on the terrace, she was sitting in a deck chair knitting, with her usually sallow face strangely aglow.

That evening he proposed to her, and with a quick intake of breath, she said, "Yes, if Daddy and Mother approve." Her kiss was the kiss of a decent girl, he thought, one which bespoke virtue and restraint.

Old Margaret inquired about his income and extracted a promise that he would always remain in Buffalo before touching him on the cheek with her dry lips and wishing him happiness. That evening she called up all her friends to tell them "the great news," making a special point of the fact that her prospective son-in-law had been graduated from Harvard.

They were married in the neighborhood Methodist church a month later, and flew to New York for their honeymoon, arriving at their hotel at seven in the evening. When Ken closed the door of their room behind them, he took Helen in his arms, but she was so painfully frightened that he was swept with pity for her, and found himself explaining seriously that a marriage does not have to be consummated right away, and that sex really isn't a bit important, anyway. She seemed immensely relieved, and after pulling all the shades in the room, and putting the lights out, contrived to change into her night clothes without a moment of nudity.

During the first three days of their honeymoon Helen was as modest and chaste as a nun. On the third night Ken lay sleeplessly at the very edge of their double bed. Memories of Sylvia which he thought he had forgotten obsessed him. At three in the morning he got up, and, lifting the shade, stood at the window, looking twelve stories down at the streets of New York. To his astonishment, he had a sudden impulse to jump. It would be so easy to release the catch on the sash, to raise the window silently, and to slip out, head first, and go hurtling down through the cool, lavender night air, finding surcease on the pavement below. Shocked at his own thoughts, he turned toward the bed, where Helen's head was dimly visible on the white pillow. On a small table beside her was a water carafe. Noticing it, Ken had an even more horrifying vision: that of picking up the carafe and hitting her over the head with it, beating her to death. The image of himself standing beside her corpse with the carafe still upraised was startlingly clear in his mind. He could even see himself putting the carafe down and raising the telephone receiver to his lips, saying to the operator, "Call the police. I've just killed my wife." Impatiently he shook his head to clear it of these thoughts, and climbed back into the bed, being careful to lie without touching her. Sleep finally came.

When he awoke in the morning, Helen was already dressed, sitting in an armchair reading a Gideon Bible. She smiled at him nervously as he climbed out of bed in his rumpled pajamas. He meant to embrace her reassuringly, almost paternally, but her shoulders felt so good in his arms that he found himself entreating her, carrying her to the bed, kissing her, stopping only when he realized she was crying. Abruptly he stopped, trying to dam the rush of anger within him, saying desperately, "I'm not angry at you, Helen, it's not you I'm angry at, it's fate, I guess, God, I don't know—it's not your fault!"

Abruptly the tables were turned, and it was she who was comforting him, apologizing, earnestly begging him to take her, which he did, without pleasure to either of them. Afterward she cried a lot more, and neither of them could eat breakfast. That day they went to two double features and a Broadway play. Following a large dinner that night, he had such an acute attack of indigestion that the hotel doctor had to be called, and the next day he lay weakly in bed while she read magazine stories aloud to him.

A week later they moved into a small house he had bought in the town of Kenmore, a suburb of Buffalo, and Helen decorated it according to the best advice of the magazines on homes and gardens, which she read incessantly. As the months slipped by, he learned to control the almost constant irritation he felt at her. Visions of suicide and violence occasionally plagued him, but he learned to live with them, confident of his own self-control. In his work he found comfort. Because evenings and weekends at home dragged with painful slowness, he began spending almost all his time at the laboratory, gradually discovering that new, hitherto unimaginable degrees of concentration were becoming possible for him. His mind learned to store all the details surrounding a research problem in chemistry, and to feed upon them to the exclusion of all else for weeks, emerging suddenly, sometimes in the dead of night, with a startlingly complete answer. During these periods of deep preoccupation Ken was hardly aware that Helen existed, even when he was sitting across the breakfast table from her. He was surprised and sympathetic when she complained that she was lonely, and for a while he forced himself to return home early each evening to play cards with her. But his thoughts remained so concentrated on his work that conversation was almost impossible, and once, after asking him twice whether he wanted a glass of beer without getting an answer, she threw her cards down on the table and fled to her room in tears.

Gradually Helen began to spend more and more time at her parents' house. In old Margaret, her mother, she found a loyal confidante. At first she tried to defend Ken when her mother accused him of being a bad husband, but it wasn't long before she found herself agreeing with her, and the two women spent most of their days cataloguing his sins. He did not dress properly; he did not keep the lawn cut; he cared nothing for their automobile, for the household budget; he seemed to be "going to pieces," Margaret said darkly. Even when Helen announced she was pregnant, he seemed only mildly interested.

Throughout her pregnancy, Helen was so stricken with nausea that it seemed more practical for her to pack up and move in with her parents, for it was clearly impossible for her to remain in her own house alone so much of the time. Toward the end of her term, Ken became conscience-stricken and waited upon her with almost ludicrous solicitude, bringing her flowers or baskets of fruit almost every evening when he came home from work. But by that time the hostility between them had become so deeply ingrained that their conversation was stilted, and after a meager supper at the Carters', he was grateful to return to his laboratory or to his own empty house.

In 1940 when Molly was born, Ken insisted that Helen move back with him. To everyone's astonishment, he showed great interest in the baby, often coming home from his laboratory in time to play with her for an hour before her bedtime, even when it was necessary for him to drive back to work immediately afterward. It was at this time that the administrators of the laboratory began to appreciate his talents, and in quick succession he received a series of advancements which put him far ahead of his father-in-law and enabled him to employ a nursemaid to help Helen. The criticisms which old Margaret leveled at him became sharper than ever. He cared about nothing but money, she said, and sacrificed his poor wife to his own unruly ambitions. When the war came they criticized him first for trying to enlist and then for accepting his status as an essential worker without complaint.

Even before Molly could walk, Ken began spending his weekends with her, taking her in her perambulator to the zoo. At first Helen accompanied them on these expeditions, but as she said, the walking hurt her feet, and now that Margaret was growing older, she needed Helen's help at home whenever possible. As Molly grew, the range of Ken's weekend expeditions with her lengthened. By the time she was seven they had visited every museum in Buffalo, been to Niagara Falls countless times, seen the Corning Glass Works and Toronto.

The hostility between Ken and Helen did not increase—it reached a kind of plateau which never varied. Helen enjoyed the results of Ken's success at the laboratory. When Molly was eight, he got a big promotion, and they bought a larger house in a prettier neighborhood. Helen asked for and got a car of her own, and she had hopes of being asked to join the Garret Club, which she often saw mentioned in the society section of the Buffalo *Evening News*. She never went to the Albright Art Museum any more, but she became so active in the local chapter of the Daughters of the American Revolution that she had hardly more time to spare than Ken did.

It never occurred to Helen that her marriage would not continue almost exactly as it was until death concluded it. As she told her mother, she had forgiven Ken for his weaknesses, and that was that. She had no knowledge of the torments Ken went through with a young French Canadian woman who served as a technician in his laboratory, a girl whose fine, slender hands trembled when she worked beside him, and whose dark eyes showed that she understood him completely, though they had hardly exchanged a sentence which did not have to do with their work. Lillian Bouchard, her name was, and she was engaged to a young doctor serving his internship in a local hospital. In spite of himself, Ken found himself obsessed by a fantasy of asking her to stay late with him at the laboratory some night, of turning toward her and taking her into his arms, and then going, hand in hand, down through the dimly lit halls to his car, and a nearby motel. I cannot ruin a young girl's life, he told himself sternly. I cannot disrupt her engagement unless I am willing to give her more than I can without divorcing Helen and giving up Molly. That was a thought he could not face, and he tried his best to put aside his fantasies concerning Lillian Bouchard, almost succeeding until one warm night in May, when Molly was nine years old, he left his laboratory and found Lillian Bouchard waiting in his car for him, and the whole fantasy abruptly became a reality.

But not a very good reality, a long, tawdry affair which had the curious effect of making him dream more intensely of Sylvia than he had in years. The half-nights he stole with Lillian Bouchard under the pretense of working late at the laboratory distressed him more than they delighted him. He could not accept her matter-of-fact assurance that their excursions would affect neither his marriage nor her engagement. There was something so deeply wrong in the whole arrangement that she began to appear ugly to him, and he was deeply relieved when she told him casually one night that they would have to break off, because she was soon to be married.

After that Ken gave himself with more abandonment than ever to his job. In 1951 he and an associate named Bernie Anderson began work on a plastic tissue in their laboratory which was unlike anything anyone had ever seen before. It looked like paper, but it stretched, and when two pieces were pressed together they stuck. It took color easily, and a battery of tests showed it was durable, and resistant to both fire and water, although not actually proof against them. It also had the virtue of being cheap. Ken thought that all kinds of uses could be found for it, and when he passed the samples and formulas on to the head of his department, he expected a large bonus at least, and probably a substantial salary boost which would enable him to take Helen and Molly off somewhere for a long vacation.

But that didn't happen. There was a delay of months, and finally the word trickled down through the layers of executives and administrators that the firm was not going to manufacture the product. It had been examined and judged a poor gamble.

Ordinarily, Ken would have accepted this decision stoically. He did not regard himself as an entrepreneur or a businessman of any sort. A research chemist's job was to invent and to develop, and to leave the decision of what to manufacture, promote and market up to the big brass.

Bernie Anderson, however, did not feel that way. Bernie Anderson had worked hard on the plastic tissue, and he too had expected a bonus and a raise. He was furious when he heard about the executive decision, and he said one thing positively and angrily: "They're wrong."

"So what can we do about it?" Ken asked.

"We can start our own company and manufacture the stuff ourselves."

To Ken, this was the fabric of fantasy. He had never imagined himself doing such a thing, but Bernie Anderson kept talking, and he kept bringing in other people, promoters and engineers and people who knew men who had risk capital to invest. "Do you have faith in the stuff?" Bernie kept saying. "Will it do the things your report says?"

"Yes," Ken said, "but the big guys know what to market. They're experts, for God's sake!"

"They're human, aren't they?" Bernie retorted. "Can't they make a mistake?"

So Bernie kept talking, and he talked fantasy into reality, but first he talked it into a sort of nightmare. Ken found himself quitting his job, giving up the pension plan and the stock bonuses and a salary of eighteen thousand dollars a year; Bernie Anderson talked all the security away. Both Helen and her mother were aghast. Ken found himself borrowing on his life insurance and taking a second mortgage on his house, selling his wife's car and taking out a personal loan at the bank. Helen's mother said openly that Ken was having "some sort of breakdown"—he had always seemed odd to her. But even that wasn't the hardest part of it. He found himself doubting everything and everyone, including Bernie Anderson. Bernie was a Jew who had changed his name, and this seemed suddenly sinister to Ken, who had never been anti-Semitic before. A man named Jacobson who put fifty thousand dollars into the venture was also a Jew, and a phrase he had read somewhere, "I have fallen into the hands of Jews," came back to Ken, and suddenly he was terrified, knowing this was absurd but still feeling it. Before the thing was over, he began to doubt his own sanity as much as his family did. What would make a man quit a good job and incur great debt voluntarily? Bernie Anderson talked constantly of "the enormous possibilities" of the project, and Ken found himself dreaming for the first time in his life of trips abroad, a huge house with a swimming pool, and more. Wasn't that the classic symptom: delusions of grandeur?

During those months Ken lost forty pounds, and was thin for the first time in his life. Old friends stopped dropping in to see them, and friendly shop people became less friendly. Ken began to doubt his whole view of the world, and to become a cynic.

But Bernie Anderson kept talking, and gradually a new concept of the issues involved came to Ken Jorgenson. Success, or the attempt to get it, was not a matter of cleverness, as he always had thought. It was only in small part a matter of intelligence. It was mostly faith. He had to keep faith, he told himself in his despair. He had to keep faith with Bernie Anderson, who had changed his name, all right, but who was a tall man of enormous energy and integrity and hope. He had to keep faith with his research. He had to quit doubting that the tests meant what they said. And most of all, he had to keep faith with himself, to stop fearing that he was going insane. No, he was not a madman, he was a courageous person intent on seizing a great opportunity; yes, he was.

When Ken reached the conclusion that his faith was being tested and not his mind, he still was scared, but he worked harder. He began to help Bernie Anderson draw together the corporation they were forming. He began to try more as a salesman when he was called in by bankers to explain the product. Somewhat to his own astonishment, he found he could talk hard and long with enormous effect, his detailed knowledge and his air of diffidence combining to produce an atmosphere of earnestness, sincerity and confidence which gave others faith. Within a year the money was raised, over a half million dollars, a terrifying sum even to think about, and a large building was leased in which to start manufacturing.

For more than a year Ken worked day and night, often getting only three or four hours' sleep. He helped to set up the machinery, and to sell—that was the important thing, not the manufacturing, but getting orders, the money, the cash on the barrelhead before the payments on their many loans had to be met. Ken wrote a long booklet on the uses of the new tissue which a promotion man named "Marfab," a name which Ken once would have ridiculed, but which he now accepted eagerly on the premise that the promotion man knew what would sell. Selling was the only thing which counted that year.

Ken found that Marfab would make an excellent material for wrapping packages; no string or tape had to be used at all; department-store officials showed interest. There were moments of elation, such as the time when an automobile salesman accepted the idea of wrapping a whole car in it, and when a construction man agreed with Ken's suggestion that the stuff could be used as insulation when building houses. "Marvelous Marfab," the advertisements called it, marvelous, marvelous, marvelous, it could do anything. One night Ken Jorgenson, a research chemist, not a promoter, sat down to work up a list of things that could be done with it. Orange trees could be covered with it to protect them from the frost. The army could use it when transporting machinery across rivers. Marfab could do anything. While groping for ideas, Ken's mind turned grotesque. Undertakers could use it as shrouds for the dead. It could take the place of condoms; there could be condoms of many colors. Marfab. In a frenzy he drove his imagination, and out of it all came a booklet of a hundred practical ideas, or ideas which at least sounded practical, a booklet which at any rate helped to attract a force of good salesmen.

There were moments of panic. The ownership of the formulas he had developed while working for a large corporation came under close legal scrutiny, even though that corporation had declared them impractical, and even though Ken varied them, changing them to make them a different legal property. There were threats of lawsuits, of attachments, the clear possibility of bankruptcy, debt, disgrace, a bad reputation, the man who tried to pull a fast one and failed. On one dark night even Bernie Anderson lost his nerve, and overcome by exhaustion, put his head on his arms and cried. "Faith," Ken said to him, "we've got to have faith, faith in each other, faith in ourselves, faith, faith in God, I guess, and have a drink, Bernie. We'll come through this yet."

In the end, faith was what did it, faith and courage and hard work. The memory of a girl with a fake mink coat over her bathing suit who, Ken imagined, would laugh if she heard he had failed, and who would be astonished if he became a success—this had only a little to do with it.

The development of the Marfab Corporation was not a gradual thing. From beginning to end, it only took two years. For a month bankruptcy seemed certain. Ken went to bed with fear, brushed his teeth with it and ate it on his bread. He looked around his house, realizing that the walls were transient, seeing that soon they could all be taken away by the bank. When he passed tenements he said to himself, Someday I shall be living there. The gaiety of his daughter, Molly, seemed ironic to him. She doesn't know, he thought, she doesn't know, and he shouted at her when she asked to buy a hat for two dollars, "No, you've got to learn the value of money, damn it, no, you cannot buy a lot of foolish things." His nerves were shot after eighteen months of pressure. He started to drink too much in order to get to sleep. He quarreled with Helen, he told her she was extravagant, that she put too much butter on the vegetables, that she was a bad manager, and she had to learn to be poor, damn it, poor, because that was what it was almost certain that they were going to be. He had nightmares in which he heard a girl's derisive laughter.

But then the lawsuit was called off by the big company, and an offer was made, not a large one, but enough to enable them to repay their loans and make a small profit, an offer to buy them out, and to make them paid administrators with a salary three times what they had had before. "We've made it!" Ken said exuberantly.

"Not yet," Bernie said grimly. "We've got to hold on!"

"Why? Let's pick up our winnings!"

"No," Bernie said. "They wouldn't make such an offer if they didn't know they were licked. If we hang on, we can make it big."

So they hung on and the buffeting continued, warnings of each offer being the last one, threats of running them out of business, putting them on the street without a dime. Oh, the executives of the large corporations, the big men with the soft voices and money in the bank, they knew how to play hard ball with petty beginners like Ken Jorgenson and Bernie Anderson. Who the hell had ever heard of them?

Ken got mad, finally. He and Bernie made a good team, for when one was down, the other was up, and they talked fast together and they held on while the offers mounted. A big firm in New York got interested, and one in Chicago, and three in Buffalo, and then the bidding really got hot.

"Let's hold out and run it ourselves," Ken said. "The hell with 'em."

But the lawyers started talking. There were sober explanations of complex deals involving capital gains, deferred payments, all kinds of ways to reduce taxes. The lawyers kept talking with the well-groomed men carrying briefcases who arrived in rented Cadillacs from the airport, and finally the deal was made. It was concluded so quickly that it made Ken's head swim; he picked up a pen and signed his name and found himself in possession of more than a million dollars. Ken Jorgenson was in Wonderland, and the well-remembered sound of a girl's laughter in his ears almost stopped.

That afternoon Ken drove his old Chevrolet home slowly, and pulled up in front of his small suburban house which had seemed so expensive when he bought it for fifteen thousand dollars only a few years ago, and again he had the sensation of everything being ephemeral. Inevitably, the house would be sold now; it was not a rich man's home. Old Paul Crandon who used to call, "Come on over for a dipper," meaning a drink, on hot summer evenings when they were working in their gardens; and Mary Harper, next door, the prettiest girl on the block, who volunteered to take Molly any time Ken and Helen wanted to go out—these people would disappear, they would fade into Ken's past as surely as though they had died. Getting out of his car, Ken knew a moment of dizziness, of disorientation which blurred his triumph. He walked into the house, and Helen came out of the kitchen wearing a soiled apron, a thin woman whom he saw objectively for the first time in years, her sad eyes, the poor weak chin, the nice black hair. Suddenly he remembered stories about people who get suddenly rich; they get divorced. They go out and buy themselves new wives, and even Helen seemed transient, a leaf that could be easily blown away in this strange new wind. He swept her into his arms then and hugged her so tightly that she gave a little cry of pain, and he kissed her more passionately than he had in years. "Did everything go all right?" she asked.

"Yes," he said. "Signed, sealed and delivered!"

"Do we actually have the money?"

"The checks are being sent to the bank."

She shook her head, a gesture of sudden confusion, and she said, as though naming a duty, "I guess we ought to celebrate."

"Yes," he said, and an idea came to him then. As a tangible act of celebration they would buy a new car.

When Molly, a slender, serious child worrying about her arithmetic, came home from her junior high school, Ken said to her, "How would you like to go out with us and buy a convertible?"

"Now?" Molly asked, sounding surprised.

"Yes, now!"

"I promised I'd go over and see Kay Harper."

"This is a big day," Helen said. "Call Kay and tell her you'll see her later."

"All right," Molly replied, and made the telephone call, her clear voice explaining, saying, "Yes, Kay, yes; I'll see you tomorrow or the day after . . ."

So they went and they bought the car, a new blue-and-white Oldsmobile. Helen wanted to buy a Cadillac, but Ken said nuts, he wasn't going to play a part. They drove it home and the neighbors all came out and admired it; they were most polite, even effusive, only old Paul Crandon didn't say, "Come on over and have a dipper," and there was a tired look in his eyes. Margaret and her husband, old Bruce, acted as though they had suffered a personal defeat when they saw the car.

The next afternoon the Buffalo *Evening News* carried a big story on "The Marvelous Sale of Marfab," and the telephone started ringing, and the doorbell. Old friends showed up whom Ken hadn't seen in years; bright young men came to sell life insurance, stocks, automobiles, real estate—all the goods of the world.

I shall not let success go to my head, Ken thought, I shall move slowly and cautiously. When Helen wanted to go out and look at new houses, he said, "No! For at least a month, we stay here."

"Why?"

"I don't even know what city I want to live in," he said. "We don't have to stay in Buffalo any more. After all, it isn't Athens, it isn't Paris in the spring!"

"No . . ." she said, sounding puzzled—Helen, a Buffalo girl, who had never thought of living anywhere else. "Where do you want to live?"

"It depends partly on what I want to do," Ken said. "I might want to start another business, or just loaf, or do research. Anything."

"What do you really want?"

"I don't know!" he said, his voice suddenly sharp. "I don't know yet!"

"All right," she said soberly, her face worried. "Let me know when you make up your mind."

"I'm not making the decision just for myself," he said, replying to her implied accusation. "I've got to figure out what is best for all of us. What do you want to do?"

"First of all, I'd like to take a vacation," Helen said. "At least a year . . ."

"Where?"

"This is kind of silly," Helen said, her cheeks growing pink. "My cousin Faye always used to talk about cruising the Maine coast in a yacht. Her roommate's grandfather had one once, and it always seemed to me the most glamorous thing in the world, and I used to dream that some day . . ."

"Do you want to buy a yacht?" Ken asked in astonishment.

"No, but couldn't we rent one?"

"I guess so," Ken said. And then the memory came to him, the old, sore memory of those three summers on Pine Island, the laughter, and with the memory an idea.

A ridiculous idea, to be sure. Why go back to a place where one has experienced nothing but pain and humiliation? Why open up the memories of a poor, stumbling scholarship student from Nebraska who got way over his head? Why try to recapture the days of what, after all, could only be described as a ludicrous adolescent love affair, a sordid chapter from some book of psychiatric case histories, one's personal fling at juvenile delinquency? Why try to go back to the scene of a sick youth?

No, it wasn't that bad, he thought. Oh sure, I made a fool of myself, I was an ass, an idiot compounded, only that and nothing more. But even so, why should the idea of going back to Pine Island in such new circumstances be so attractive, why should the temptation be there, like the temptation to keep wiggling a sore tooth?

Regardless of the reasons, there was no doubt about the result; Ken wanted to go back to Pine Island, to buy a house there perhaps, but at least to pay the place a visit. I just want to see what it is really like, he told himself. I want to check my memories. I want to see how I exaggerated. The time is beyond recall now, thank God, but the place and perhaps the people . . .

The people. He remembered Bart Hunter as a slender young man, cocky, elegant and dapper, the sort of man who could turn almost any action into a graceful gesture. As though quoting the wisdom of the ages, Bart Hunter had said a gentleman is a man who never insults anyone unintentionally; Ken had always remembered that. It had applied to everyone on Pine Island in those years. Those gentle folk had never insulted anyone unintentionally.

If the definition held for gentlemen, Ken had thought, it certainly must apply to ladies. Ladies are women who never insult anyone unintentionally, and that certainly was true of Sylvia, the girl with the fake mink coat, a person he never thought about, the image he had expunged from his mind, almost. Sylvia had never insulted him unintentionally, he could be sure of that.

What nonsense, Ken thought; the affairs of one's youth are meaningless and best forgotten. A middle-aged man, a great success, a man supposedly of some intelligence, should certainly not waste time with that. A married man with a wife who, regardless of her weaknesses, had suffered with him on the way up, who took his ill temper, tolerated his nerves, no, a man with a wife and daughter should not be dreaming of a girl who never insulted him unintentionally, a girl in a shining black satin bathing suit, the wheat-colored hair, the brown shoulders, no, it was absurd to remember that.

Good heavens, he thought, she's almost forty now, thirty-five at least. She probably is fat with large sagging breasts. She had the kind of figure which is magnificent at sixteen or seventeen, but which ages badly, I'm quite sure. And anyway, we are both married, and the state of Sylvia's breasts is hardly a matter for my concern.

Still, it would be fun to go back, in all innocence. It would be interesting to see how the friends of one's youth, even the tormentors, had turned out. The purpose of making money is to earn the freedom to do what one wants to do, isn't it? What else? And if one wants to take a leisurely journey through one's past, to revisit the site of old agonies, even, well why not? It would undoubtedly turn out to be therapeutic; it would be wise to replace his memories of Sylvia with the image of a stolid, workaday woman approaching forty, the mother of a great many children perhaps, with the harsh face of reality, not a stereotyped golden girl fuzzed by the aches of memory.

For his wife's sake Ken wrote a yacht broker and arranged to charter a schooner for the month of July; and for his own sake he wrote a real-estate broker in Harvesport to inquire into rentals on Pine Island. The reply informed him that the island was still owned by a corporation of families, and that they still ran it like a club, screening applicants for admission carefully. If he really wanted to go there, the broker suggested, the best thing was to begin by staying for a few weeks at the Island Inn, which had been opened by Mr. Barton Hunter two years ago.

This astonished Ken. It was impossible for him to think of Bart as an innkeeper and Sylvia as an innkeeper's wife. He wrote requesting accommodations, and waited impatiently for the reply.

On the morning he heard from Bart, Ken came down to breakfast late. Helen had left the house to take Molly to her new private school, but his mail was piled neatly by his plate. While the new maid poured him his coffee, Ken leafed through the stack of envelopes, which contained more letters than he used to get in a month. The one from Barton was immediately identifiable, because it was written on the same cream-colored stationery which the Hunters had always used—in fact, the paper tore easily when he opened the envelope, and crackled like dry leaves. Bart wrote:

DEAR KEN:

We have the accommodations you request, and are pleased at the prospect of having you back on Pine Island again for August this year. The rates, American plan, would be eleven hundred dollars for three people for the month. If that is satisfactory, please let me know, and I'll be glad to make the reservations.

Sincerely,
BART

Ken was musing over this letter when the doorbell rang. The maid admitted Nancy Brankist, a portly woman who for some months now had been Ken's secretary. Nancy gave her coat, a poor worn tweed, to the maid, and came into the dining room. Ken stood up, a habit which had been so deeply ingrained in him by his schoolteacher mother that he had never been able to give it up, even when people made fun of him; one stood up when a lady entered the room. Nancy smiled.

"Good morning, Mr. Jorgenson," she said, and sat down at the end of the table.

"Want some coffee?" Ken asked, sitting down again.

"No, thanks," Nancy said, sitting as erect as though she were in an office. From her handbag she took a pad and a pencil. "Want me to open that mail?"

Ken handed her the pile, keeping the letter from Barton. An idea was beginning to develop in his mind. Excusing himself, he went to the telephone and called Bernie Anderson, the one person with whom he felt any identity in these strange days. A new maid answered: "Mr. Anderson's residence."

"Hello," Bernie's voice said, suddenly cutting in on an extension.

"Good morning," Ken said. "Want to go yachting?"

"What?" Bernie said, and yawned sleepily, the sound of the yawn coming clearly over the telephone.

"Helen wants me to charter a boat and cruise the Maine coast, and after that I'm going to rent a place on an island. Want to bring Rachel and the kids and come along?"

Bernie laughed. "Boy, you're really going!" he said.

"I mean it. Want to come?"

"I'd like to," Bernie said seriously, "but Rachel always wanted to see Paris. We're off next week."

"Oh," Ken said, feeling disappointed. "Well . . ."

"I'll see you before we go," Bernie said. "We've got to get going on plans for the fall."

"Good," Ken said. "See you, Bernie . . ." He hung up and returned to the dining room. Nancy extinguished her cigarette.

"This is a letter to Barton Hunter, Pine Island, Maine," Ken said. "Dear Bart, My family and I are glad to hear you have the accommodations for us, and the financial arrangement you suggest will be fine . . ."

5

On the first of August 1953 the big schooner, the *Fairy Queen*, bowled along at eight knots, with her lee rail awash, bound for Pine Island. Below decks, Helen Jorgenson pressed her lips tightly together in exasperation as she tried to iron Molly's best dress on the table in the main cabin. The flatirons grew cold rapidly and had to be reheated in the galley by the Negro cook. The cabin was hot, both from the midsummer sun beating down on the decks, and from the roaring fire the cook had had to build in his stove. Helen found it was difficult to avoid letting the sweat from her brow drip on the delicate fabric of the dress. While the schooner rolled and pitched, she braced herself with one hand and ironed with the other. She felt ill, and suddenly burned her finger painfully on the iron. "Oh!" she cried in anger, for Helen never swore. "Oh! Oh! *Oh!*" Yachting, she decided, was not all it was cracked up to be.

In fact, it was rotten. Molly had been hopelessly seasick from the beginning. Helen worried about shipwreck, about people falling overboard, and most of all, she worried about flags. While under charter to the Jorgensons, the *Fairy Queen* flew only the national ensign, for Ken had no personal owner's pennant, and belonged to no yacht club. The lack of an association with a yacht club meant that the big schooner could not moor at the clubs in any of the ports she visited, and as a result she had been doomed throughout this cruise to tie up alongside oily commercial wharfs, or to lie in lonely anchorages away from the other yachts. Helen hated this; it made her feel like an outcast.

The whole etiquette of yachting confused Helen, and she was a woman who wanted to be "correct" above all else. Ken point-blank refused to wear anything but a sports shirt and slacks, and Helen doubted that that was right. The stout professional captain, Mr. White, who said he had worked for the Vanderbilts, looked contemptuous, even when Helen talked to him about her cousin Faye, who had done quite a lot of yachting long ago.

The worst aspect of the cruise was the sense of homelessness Helen felt. The home port of the *Fairy Queen,* written in gold leaf on her transom, was Boston, and the people they met in the anchorages assumed they came from there. No, Buffalo, Helen always said at the first opportunity, and sometimes they asked, "Where in Buffalo?"

Helen couldn't say, because before leaving, Ken had sold the house. There was no point in keeping it, he said, because even if they went back to Buffalo, they'd want a bigger place. The furniture was in storage, and all Helen had for a home was this pitching, rolling, sickening boat. Some nights she lay in her tiny stateroom and cried, and now, when she burned her finger on the iron, tears mixed with the sweat on her face.

On deck Ken sat comfortably in the cockpit enjoying the sun. "There it be!" the captain said, pointing over the bow, and sure enough, the pinnacle of Pine Island was just beginning to show over the horizon. How well Ken remembered it, this Gothic mass of land, with the cliffs like walls. He had seen it last in 1936, sitting on the stern of the *Mary Anne,* a dejected young man carrying a small zipper bag. He had had a dream that someday he would return as a rich man with the world at his feet. He would arrive with an enormous mink coat for Sylvia, real mink, but even then he had known it was a silly dream, and he had tried to put it out of his mind.

"Ken!" Helen called now, sticking her head up the hatch. "Come change your clothes!"

"Plenty of time," he replied in his deep voice. "The island just came in sight."

Helen sighed. "Please," she said. "I have your things all laid out."

"All right, dear," Ken said, and went to his stateroom. Lying on his bunk was a new white linen suit which Helen had bought for him. Ken stared at it a moment and put it back in his closet. From a drawer he took a clean green sports shirt, exactly the sort of thing he often wore in Buffalo, and a pair of freshly pressed slacks. Thus dressed, he walked into the main saloon of the schooner.

Helen was on her knees, pulling and adjusting Molly's dress. The child stood erect, still pale from seasickness. At thirteen, Molly was thin, with a heart-shaped face of great sweetness and glossy black hair cut in a Dutch bob. When Ken came in, Helen glanced over her shoulder at him and in a strained voice said, "Ken! You aren't going ashore like that!"

"Why not?"

"You look terrible! Why didn't you put on the clothes I laid out?"

"This is the way I like to dress."

"Not for this place!"

"Now, Helen," Ken replied. "I think we've passed the point where we have to pretend to be anything we're not."

"You're so stubborn!" Helen retorted, and with her mouth full of pins, plucked and pulled at Molly's dress. "Hold still!" she said to the child. "Don't wiggle so much!"

"You look nice, baby," Ken said.

Molly smiled at him gratefully. "You do too," she replied.

6

"LOOK OUT THERE!" Todd Hasper said, and his great dog strained at the chain leash. Young John Hunter looked. Rounding the end of the island only a thousand yards away was the big schooner, the *Fairy Queen*, her white jibs reaching over the blue sea, her bow raising a storm of spray, her fore and mainsails straining upward.

"Whose is she?" he gasped.

"Never saw her before," Hasper said. Satan began to bark.

John had never before seen at close range any large vessel under sail in a stiff breeze. Oh God, she was beautiful! He ran along the shore, just able to keep up with her, his eyes so riveted upon her that he stumbled on a root and fell headlong, bruising his knee to the bone; but he picked himself up without an outcry, and kept running to avoid losing sight of her. The sky that day was an intense blue, like a stained-glass window.

Off the entrance to the harbor the schooner luffed suddenly into the wind, so close that John could hear the violent slatting of her sails as they were lowered. Under power the vessel crept into the bay and there was a splash as she let go her anchor.

By that time John was on the end of the wharf, watching breathlessly. A gleaming motor launch was dropped from davits on the schooner's starboard side, and a boarding ladder with polished brass stanchions was lowered. Several people descended.

First there was a sailor in faded blue dungarees and a shirt of the same material, then a young girl in a white dress, followed by a thin woman in navy blue. Last of all came a tall man wearing a green sports shirt. The sailor held the launch alongside the boarding ladder while these people seated themselves. When they started toward shore, John whirled and ran pell-mell to tell his mother of the arrival of such wondrous guests.

Bart had already seen the yacht. "Sylvia," he said to his wife, "I think they're here."

Todd Hasper chained his dog to a tree and was dispatched in an ancient Ford to carry the Jorgensons and their baggage up the hill from the harbor. John rode with him, but Bart and Sylvia waited on the big veranda. Sylvia sat with her eyes closed, seeming to be asleep, while Bart paced. When the Ford stopped at the bottom of the steps, Sylvia stood up suddenly and Bart went to her side. Ken was the first one out of the car. His shirt flashed brilliantly in the sun, and Bart glanced at Sylvia, but Sylvia did not look back. Ken, seeming to be a bigger man than could be believed, stared up at her, the broad face so well remembered, the heavy shoulders, the incongruously diffident smile. He came up the steps toward her, his eyes upon her face, and he said, "Hello, Sylvia. Hello, Bart."

"Hello!" Bart said in his thin dry voice. "We're glad to see you again."

"Yes," Sylvia said.

Ken turned and helped Helen and Molly up the stairs. "I want you to meet my wife and daughter," he said, and made the introductions. Helen started to offer her hand, but unsure that it was correct for a lady to do that first, she pulled it back. Molly, who was now standing beside her, looked at her feet. There was a short embarrassed silence during which John, who had been helping to unload the baggage, ran up the steps and stood by his mother.

"John," Sylvia said, "this is Mr. and Mrs. Jorgenson, and their daughter, Molly."

Looking up, Molly smiled, her fragile face suffused with great warmth. "I'm glad to meet you," she said. John gave a short bow of acknowledgment, a mannerism he had picked up from his father, and which even at fourteen he performed with the older man's touch of elegance and grace, but his smile was boyish. "That's a keen boat you've got," he said.

"Come, and I'll show you your rooms," Barton said, and they walked through the big living room of the old mansion. Behind them came Todd Hasper and John, carrying suitcases.

The living room looked almost exactly as Ken remembered it, although the old oak paneling had been painted white, and a stag's head which had been over the dining-room door had been taken down. In a corner cupboard a French clock with its innards clearly visible under a glass dome and an ivory chess set remained as they had been almost twenty years ago, when they had seemed to Ken to be the epitome of elegance and wealth. Three old ladies, one of whom Ken recognized vaguely, peered sharply at him over their knitting. The carpet on the wide curved stairway was worn, but the big airy bedrooms to which Bart led the way had been newly papered, and each had a modern bath. John and Todd Hasper put the suitcases in the middle of the floor, and Ken reached into his pocket. For a moment Bart thought he was going to tip John, but he gave a dollar to Hasper only, and, turning to the boy, said, "Thanks for doing my work for me. If you'd like to see that boat, I think the captain would be glad to show you over her before he sails."

"Thanks!" John said, and dashed for the wharf.

"If there's anything you need, just give me a call," Bart said, struggling as he always did to be courteous without being obsequious.

"They're beautiful rooms!" Helen said. "What a lovely view!" Her voice was sugary and false.

Sylvia smiled mechanically. "Dinner's served from six to eight. Would you care to join us at our table tonight?" Everything she said that day sounded awkward and stilted.

"That would be nice," Ken replied in his deep tones.

Sylvia avoided his eyes. "We usually start at seven-thirty," she said, "but the children often eat at six. Molly, would you care to join John and my daughter, Carla? You'll meet Carla later—she's swimming with friends."

"Thank you very much," Molly said. Hers was the only voice that sounded entirely natural.

Early that evening the children ate at a table by themselves. Carla, a stout eight-year-old, started by spilling her milk, and John glared at her, feeling the family honor had been ruined. "There, there," Molly said, and helped the waitress to clean it up. Throughout the meal, however, Molly ate little. She sat with her head bowed over her plate, as though saying a sort of perpetual grace, and she didn't seem very interested in John's enthusiastic talk about the *Fairy Queen*.

"Does she sail fast?" John asked her.

Only then did Molly smile. "Yes," she replied. "It was terrible. Have you ever tried to live at sea?"

Helen and Ken rested in their room all afternoon. When Sylvia sat down to dinner with them and Bart that night, she glanced at Ken's tanned face, and she thought, The trouble is we are strangers and we are not, we know too much about each other, and too little. In her flat Buffalo accent, Helen carried on a rather nervous conversation with Bart, answering the questions he gallantly fed her. What ports had they visited on their cruise? Which one had they liked best? Helen talked fast, punctuating her sentences with apologetic little laughs. When there was nothing more to say about the cruise, she began telling Bart about the Buffalo PTA.

She's doing better than I am, Sylvia thought in sudden panic. This is ridiculous, but I can't think of anything whatever to say, and I can't just sit here throughout the meal without uttering a word.

"You have beautiful children," Ken said to her, and she looked at him, thinking how wonderful that a voice can be both so deep and so soft. She had almost forgotten that.

"Your Molly is a real charmer," she replied, thinking, Yes, that's true; she has your face in miniature, turned feminine, but the same symmetry, the same straight nose, and lucky for her she got her father's chin.

"What school do you send them to?" Ken asked, the deep voice sounding a little stilted now as he fought the silence.

"There's no school on the island," Sylvia replied. "I have to teach them myself."

"You live here the year around?" Ken sounded shocked.

"Yes," Sylvia answered, and felt obligated to add, "It's really quite lovely with the snow." The phrase kept repeating itself in her ear. Her mind raced, and she was breathing too fast.

Lovely with the snow, she thought, oh it's lovely with the snow, all right. I wish you could know what it's really like. Someday I would like to tell you. When he said, "Tell me about it," she was startled. "Oh, there's really not much to tell," she replied.

"I remember the winters out in Nebraska," Ken said, the word "remember" sounding suddenly startling. "They were fun sometimes."

"Tell me about Nebraska."

His face was thoughtful, and it was absurd to think there was the same old hunger in his eyes; he was just a man who always had a brooding look about him, as though his thoughts dwelt always in some sad and distant place.

"I left Nebraska when I was so young I hardly remember," he said, and there it was again, the word "remember"—a beautiful word really, the way he said it in his soft, deep voice; "remember"—a word that should not hang like that, resonant in the air between them, "remember."

"I've read Willa Cather," Sylvia said, and was suddenly chattering about books, her voice racing along, seeming entirely detached from herself; she could even sit back and listen to it and make silent comments on it, as though her words were coming out of a machine. Oh, let's talk about books, she thought, and yes there is a power in the West as Willa Cather describes it, even a warmth in winter, quite lovely with the snow, and it's better to chatter like this than to sit silently. She blundered along, feeling that she was headed for disaster. "In the winter," she said, "we have plenty of time to read. I was never much of a reader before. As a girl I was so stupid . . ."

Her mind went blank. "As a girl I wasn't much of a student . . ."

she continued, and then she heard herself say, "I'm sorry! Excuse me!" and saw she had turned over a glass of water.

Somehow the meal came to an end, and they walked to the living room. Old Mrs. Hamble excused herself from her bridge table and approached them, with a smile on her sunken-cheeked face. "Aren't you Mr. Jorgenson?" she asked.

"Yes," Ken said, "I . . ."

"Oh, you wouldn't remember me, but I remember you!" Mrs. Hamble said. "Dear, dear, yes. How nice to see you back!"

There were introductions all around the room then, and Sylvia had a problem; she didn't want to keep following Ken around. She didn't want to keep up that tortuous conversation, yet when she walked away, she was drawn back, so that she kept getting up and sitting down. The absurdity of this frightened her, and at nine she told Bart she had a headache and went to bed.

Lying in the dark, in her room above the garage, the word "remember" seemed to repeat itself, merging with the phrase, "warmth in winter, lovely with the snow," and to her horror, she couldn't stop remembering, not just Ken and all that had happened with him, but the winters, the terrible two winters over the garage alone with the children, and with Bart.

"Tell me about it," Ken had said.

In the beginning it had seemed like a fine, brave idea to winter on the island. All their friends remarked upon the decision being so courageous and all that. They were going to read Thoreau together, Bart said. They were going to sit before a roaring fire while it was snowing outside and read all the books of their youth over again. They were going to get "reacquainted with the outdoors." They were going to go fishing through the ice, and have just a marvelous time alone on the island together.

But it didn't work out that way at all. Sylvia never told anyone about those two winters alone on the island; the memory lay within her too horrible to admit. Even the word "winter" was one which Bart and she never mentioned to each other. They talked about "next year" or "next summer," but even the word "fall" was best not used any more.

The trouble started that first fall, when the families from the other cottages on the island prepared to leave and, reasonably enough, brought cartons of food from their iceboxes which, they said, would have to be thrown away if the Hunters didn't take them. There were quarter pounds of butter, and milk, partially eaten roasts, and canned goods which would freeze if left on the shelves, quite a store, altogether, when the leavings of eleven families and many guests were counted. Bart accepted this provender not happily, but as he said, it was a shame to let good food go to waste, and they were not yet low enough to have to refuse gifts from old friends out of pride. The trouble started when Todd Hasper, coming into the kitchen to deliver wood, saw the pile of groceries on the table. "I used to get that stuff," he said.

"Take it!" Bart immediately replied. "We just didn't want it to go to waste."

"I guess you people need it more than I do," Todd said, breaking a record of twenty years of sullen courtesy to the Hunter family, and he stamped morosely out of the house. That night Bart delivered the groceries to Todd's cabin, leaving them in a box in front of the locked door when no one answered, and on that small issue, apparently, the two men stopped talking to each other for the rest of the winter.

From late September through May, Todd Hasper was the only person on the island other than the four Hunters. Throughout the fall Sylvia saw him walking his dog or working around the cottages with a ladder, putting shutters on windows and taking down awnings. He never glanced at her or Bart, never raised his hand in greeting, and they felt like intruders on their own land.

Fall, Sylvia thought now as she lay in bed. My God, in another month it will be fall again!

Shortly after Labor Day, the rowboats and canoes and sailboats always were hauled out and stored in boathouses with the paint peeling from their bottoms. The leaves fell from the big maples, oaks and elms, leaving the old mansion on the hill naked and forlorn, its crumbling paint dreadfully exposed.

Huddled in an overcoat, Bart sat for hours on the veranda watching the yachts owned by people he knew heading back for Boston or New York or Florida. "There go the Johnsons," he'd say. "There go the Depews."

During the evenings Bart lay in their tiny bedroom with the windows stuffed with newspapers and the air smelling of kerosene and whisky. He did not read Thoreau. No, he read the *Wall Street Journal.* Every evening he read it, making notes of the investments he would make if he had any money to invest. One night he got even more drunk than usual because he said that he had just made a theoretical profit of a million dollars.

The atmosphere in the cramped garage apartment became so tense that the children erupted from it and played outdoors regardless of the weather. "At least they have each other," Bart used to say, but what little real love had existed between the children withered that winter. Carla and John fought each other with a cold, deadly bitterness which Bart called "a perfectly normal sibling rivalry," but which Sylvia thought was a tragedy. "All we've got is each other!" she used to say. "We've got to learn to get along together!" The children listened solemnly, but at the first opportunity Carla, at six and seven, would openly strike her brother, kick or even bite him, and John, who was six years older, would go pale, and stalk out of the house with his fists doubled up in his pockets.

Occasionally the children played together in the snow. Just before their first Christmas on the island John built his little sister a snowman. He became interested in the job himself after he got started, and ended by making it an enormous, surprisingly well-sculptured rendition of Santa Claus. Standing at the window of her room, Sylvia watched the children working together in the snow, putting the final touches on their creation, and for a little while she thought they might be solving their differences; but then, before Sylvia's horrified eyes, poor little Carla lost her temper and attacked the snow Santa Claus in a fury, butting it with her chucky little body and flailing at it with both arms, and John, turning abruptly, ran off like a wild thing into the icy woods which surrounded the house like a glass forest.

In the fall, before it grew too cold to use the piano in the big, unheated living room of the inn, Sylvia gave John music lessons, and she was both touched and horrified to find that in dead of winter he often let himself into that frigid place, left his wool mittens on top of the piano, and played until his hands were blue. He taught himself to play remarkably well, but the image of him huddled over the keyboard in an overcoat and filling that great deserted house with music seemed to Sylvia to be small cause for parental pride.

During the mornings Sylvia laid the school materials sent by the State on the kitchen table. "No!" she said countless times. "No, Johnny! No, Carla! That's not right! Oh dear! Remember, you've got to keep up with the children on the mainland!" She became so nervous and so irritable that she shrieked at the children, and occasionally they all put their heads down on the kitchen table and cried together.

Todd Hasper's dog appeared to bark more when winter came, or perhaps the sound just carried more clearly through the leafless trees. His growling and whining seemed never to cease, and sometimes at night he rattled his long chain and bayed at the moon in a way that made the children tremble. That first winter on the island instilled a lasting fear of dogs in both children, and the following summer Carla screamed in panic when a small fox terrier owned by a guest at the inn came toward her unleashed.

Remembering this now, Sylvia twisted and turned in bed. Yes, summer was almost gone. Within a month it would be fall again, and fall brought terrors of its own, because the only thing worse than winter on the island was waiting for it, knowing it all lay ahead, like a horror movie which one must sit through time and time again, knowing each terror that is coming, but having to see it again, sitting frozen in a dark theater with no exit.

Not that everything was precisely the same. Bart drank much more the second winter, although he was rarely sober between November and April of either year. He apologized for it a lot. "I know I'm impossible to live with," Bart often said.

Poor Bart. One of his troubles was that he knew everything, or almost everything, that was happening. He played the parts of both participant and spectator simultaneously, and when he lost a game, when he kept losing, he seemed amused.

Only occasionally did Sylvia allow herself to fight with Bart. Once when she became convinced that John should be sent to the mainland at any cost, she asked Bart to see if a small trust fund his mother had left for her grandson's college expenses could be used for boarding school instead. Bart refused to consider it. John was bright enough to get into college under almost any conditions, he said, and the money should be waiting for him, as had been planned.

"You're deluding yourself!" Sylvia shouted. "No child can get into college by himself, and I'm a terrible teacher!"

"Then I'll teach him," Bart said, but that course of instruction petered out within a month. Sylvia finally became so enraged that she slapped Bart's face, and she was appalled when he cried.

Ken would not be like that, Sylvia thought. The two men were almost as different as they could be, not only in character but in aspiration. Both men were sensitive, for instance, but Bart not only suffered from a thin skin, he valued it. He thought that being sensitive was synonymous with being intelligent or beautiful. He was always talking about people with such sensitive faces, and such sensitive hands and such sensitive heads.

But Ken Jorgenson did not look sensitive. His hands were like hams; and although his face was well-shaped, it was the face of an aging semi-professional football player, or of a fighter who has been good at keeping his gloves up, but no one can ward off the blows every time.

Ken Jorgenson was sensitive but he was also tough, and that was one of Bart's favorite words of condemnation, "tough." "She has a rather tough face," he often said of professional beauties, and Sylvia had often agreed with his scorn; but now she thought it was wonderful to be tough, to endure, to win once in a while.

It's not just that, Sylvia thought; Bart has perverted a legitimate respect for sensitivity into a love of weakness, almost. He takes everything and twists it around. When, for instance, he said Mrs. Pitten was "a very cheerful woman" he meant she was a fool. At first he had said, "She's one of those terribly cheerful women," but Bart kept refining all his phrases, as did the other families on the island. They worked out their own language, almost, and if anyone on Pine Island said a person was cheerful, that person was being insulted, whether he knew it or not.

Yes, Sylvia thought bitterly, this is a great place. The weak are eulogized for being sensitive and the strong are criticized for being tough. Gloom is highly fashionable and cheer is regarded only as a symptom of a vacant mind. The clever Islanders, the wonderful sophisticated people who find it so funny to understate or to put everything in reverse! "A nice little animal," is what Bart called Hasper's dog. Industry was frowned upon and indolence revered. Only fools sweated, Bart often said; this constant preoccupation with work is an American neurosis. Truly mature men like Bart were glad to escape the hubbub of the city and just sit on an island winter and summer, enjoying the beautiful view from the veranda, which in winter especially was a real killer, the frozen bay stretching away to meet the icy hills, the whole landscape indistinguishable from the North Pole.

Bart and the other Islanders also made a virtue out of incompetence. He couldn't fix automobiles or dripping faucets or broken chairs and he was proud of it. "I'm afraid I am just one of God's helpless people," he often remarked.

Ah, Sylvia thought, what fun lies in self-condemnation and in the denial of all they stood for! Money was said not to be important, while hardly a husband on the island wasn't bleeding and dying either for it or for the lack of it. The men of Pine Island said that at heart they wanted to be painters or writers or musicians; they were all a bunch of frustrated artists to hear them talk. But they became advertising men and salesmen and brokers who explained seriously to their sons that money isn't important, not worthy of a second thought.

Sylvia's reflections were interrupted by the door opening. Bart came in, sighed and took off his coat. "Are you awake, dear?" he asked in a stage whisper.

"Yes, Bart."

"How do you like our new guests?"

"All right. What do you think of them?"

Barton slipped out of his trousers, managing to do even that gracefully. "Of course, the woman's impossible," he said. "But I suppose she's about what you'd have to expect."

Sylvia said nothing.

"That little girl of theirs is pretty," Bart continued.

"What do you think of Ken?"

"Well," Bart said, "he seems cheerful, even more cheerful than he used to be, don't you think?"

7

IN THE MORNING Sylvia awoke to find it raining hard outside, a driving August rain, almost like a tropical storm. She hated rain, because she feared the roof of the inn would develop more leaks. Last month one had developed in a bathroom on the third floor, fortunately enough, just over the tub. Bart had been content simply to pull the stopper and let the leak drip. God takes care of his own poor helpless people in mysterious ways, he had said, making quite a joke of his solution. But the dread had been there, the fear that the whole roof would soon have to be repaired at enormous cost; that the inn, the one asset they had left, was rotten at the core, and might even come tumbling down around their heads. Sylvia had wanted to have a contractor examine the roof, but Bart was so sure that something terrible would be found that he refused to do it. Let it go, he had said, let it go; if there is something drastic the matter with it, what good will it do us to know? If a contractor examines it and finds the frames are rotten, he might talk about it, and it wouldn't be good for business. He might report it to the building inspector in Harvesport, and the inn might even be condemned.

For a while Sylvia had argued with him, but his worry became so acute that "roof" became one of the many words that never could be mentioned between them, like the names of the partners of the investment firm which had not appreciated Bart. Oh, there was a whole list of words which agitated him, and could not be used without causing distress. So they had both tried to forget the roof, but of course that was impossible, because if one leak had developed, might not there soon be others in places which could not be joked away?

As she lay in bed the steady drum of the rain on the garage roof seemed ominous to Sylvia. Bart stirred drowsily and opened his eyes. He sat up, looked out the window, and lay down again. Obviously he was thinking the same thing. He closed his eyes, and twisted restlessly as he tried to go back to sleep.

"Bart," she said gently. "It's eight o'clock."

"Hell with it," he said.

She got up and dressed. This apparently was going to be one of the days which Bart spent in bed—he had such days, a dozen or so a year. Looking into their rooms, she saw that the children were still asleep. With the sky so gray, they might sleep another couple of hours, she thought, and there was no use awakening them. Sylvia welcomed opportunities for a little privacy; they came seldom enough.

She went to the room used as Bart's office because it was the only place she could be alone, and she was inside it before she remembered that it had been where Ken Jorgenson had slept in the old days. The plaster was badly cracked, as it must have been even then. Sylvia stood at the window, looking through the rain-splattered panes at the gardens, now unkempt, because gardeners were almost impossible to get on the island any more, even if one could afford them. The hydrangeas were in full blossom and waved their leaves wildly in the storm. The formal garden, in which triangles and circles of snapdragons had grown, was now grassed over. The rose garden was a tangle of underbrush with a narrow swath cut through it by a power lawn mower, and with a patch of reasonably good lawn around the old fountain in the center. Snowberries, lilacs, and other flowering trees had gone untrimmed so long that they pressed their branches together, like a forlorn army closing ranks before attack.

Down by the bay she could see the roofs of small houses which had been built by some of the children of the corporation members. The children of the association of householders were admitted automatically, which posed a problem, because many of them were poor and never made money. On their parents' property they built cheap cottages which offended the eye, but one could not expel the children, even those who were now fifty years old. In spite of the bylaws established by the corporation of householders, Pine Island was changing, growing shabby, not what it used to be at all.

Well, if Ken wanted revenge he got it, Sylvia thought. If he stood there on the beach seventeen years ago and placed a curse upon us, the curse worked. I wonder what he thought when he sailed into the harbor aboard his yacht and saw those shacks along the beach, the untended gardens, and found Bart with his hands already trembling a little when he lifts a glass. I would like to know, was he glad or sorry?

What did he think of me, Sylvia thought; he must have been curious to see what kind of woman I became.

The woman I became, she thought, and with sudden, horrified objectivity saw herself, her own personal history of the past years, as though for the first time.

After marrying Bart she had thrown herself energetically into playing the role of the perfect wife, and she had succeeded, or at least that's what everyone had said. Such a handsome couple, old ladies had exclaimed, and dear Sylvia is as smart as she is pretty, a brilliant organizer, really, and a person with great social sense. Oh, she had been a great organizer, all right. She had been a leader of the Junior League, and had started a crusade with the League of Women Voters to help clean Boston up. She had organized a book-review club devoted only to the most serious reading. She had been voted chairman of the arrangements committee at the country club, and had served as a patron of many dances. Even when Bart could no longer afford servants, and she had all the cooking and house cleaning to do for her husband and two children, she had been chairman of a half-dozen committees. She was an absolute wonder, everybody had said; there never had been anyone with so much energy and so much charm.

Soon after her marriage, she had become afflicted with asthma, and had spent many sleepless nights with her breath rasping as though she had just run a long race. There had been allergy tests and special bedding to be bought. A specialist had seriously told her that her house should be vacuum cleaned twice every day, that she should wear no cotton and no wool, and that she should avoid a list of foods which contained almost every dish she liked. All this she had tried to do, but the asthma had continued. Slowly the fear had mounted in her that her breath might start coming short during one of the speeches she had to give at the book-report club or before the League of Women Voters, that she would be left gasping in public, unable even to apologize to her audience. Acute stage fright had overtaken her, and she had been so nervous before standing up to chair a meeting that she had occasionally feared she would faint. Still, she had persisted in accepting new "community responsibilities," and the telephone had rung in their house from early morning until eleven o'clock at night. "I love to keep busy," she had said. "A woman just stagnates, sitting around the house all day long."

The asthma had not been her only trouble. She was, Bart had remarked bitterly, the most aching person he had ever met. Before her monthly periods, she had suffered severe stomach cramps. Her breasts often were sore; she had occasional attacks of bursitis in her left shoulder and recurrent "sick headaches." On waking in the morning, she often suffered from a sore throat. The joints of her fingers pained her so that she had been examined to see if she had arthritis. Her eyes often ached, and she was surprised when an oculist told her she needed no glasses.

During the years she had lived in Boston, courage had come to seem to her to be the only meaningful word in life. In spite of her aches, and in spite of her "full schedule of community activities," she had been a model mother, everyone said. Immediately upon becoming pregnant for the first time, she acquired many volumes of books on child care. She nursed her children until her breasts became abscessed; she saved special hours in her day to kiss and fondle the babies. She read aloud to them when her head throbbed so she could hardly remain erect in the chair; she had taken school clothes from the dryer and pressed them at two in the morning.

And she had been a good wife too, even Bart had admitted. Hardly ever had she refused her attentions to him, even when she was most exhausted. When he complained that she did not seem to appreciate the pleasures of the bed with much intensity, she had tried hard to drive herself into some simulation of what he considered passion. The possibility that she was frigid had terrified her. Often she had caught herself remembering a long-ago night on the beach with Ken Jorgenson as dim proof that she was not, and once she had bewildered Bart by asking him to take her forcibly, begging him not to mind if she appeared to struggle against him, saying there was something abnormal in her perhaps, but that she needed the sensation of trying to resist. She had cried when that strange pantomime had produced nothing in her but frustration and weariness.

Added to her other troubles had been a growing conviction that in spite of her most determined efforts, she was turning out to be a ruinous mother. Her despondency had showed, no matter how hard she tried to conceal it. "Mother, are you all right?" Johnny as a small boy often had asked her. "Why do you look so sad?"

"I'm not sad," she had replied, forcing herself to smile. "I'm perfectly fine!" Often she had become so preoccupied with her worries that the children had difficulty in penetrating her consciousness at all. Once Carla had screamed at her, "Mother, Mother! *Why don't you answer me?*"

"I didn't hear you, dear," Sylvia had replied.

"You never hear!" Carla had retorted, her face red with rage. "*You never do!*"

Oh, she had been a great mother, with her habit of brooding about herself, and the indefinable apprehensions raging within her, until the children began imagining disaster on all sides. Carla had gone through a stage of fearing the house was going to burn down, and at the age of six, John had often come to her in the middle of the night to ask her to put her hand upon his chest to see if his heart was beating all right. "Yes, darling," Sylvia had said. "There's nothing the matter with your heart!"

"Are you sure?"

"Of course."

"Is it beating the way it should?"

"Of course it is!"

"Exactly?"

"*Yes.*"

"Thank you," John would say. "I'm sorry to bother you . . ."

"It's *all right.*"

While Johnny ran back to his bed, Sylvia had lain with her own heart beating too rapidly, thinking that something must be terribly wrong with the whole household to produce children that fearful. A house without love, a house without hope—what kind of children could such a place be expected to produce? When the children fought together, as they often did, Sylvia occasionally startled them by hugging them and covering them with kisses, as though to prove with her intensity that there was enough affection to go around.

Although Sylvia had not liked to admit it, she had been happier when Bart had been away during the war. She had worked hard at the Red Cross and had helped to organize a USO center. When Bart returned, however, the tension in the household had redoubled. Sylvia's asthma had grown worse, and she had been seized by a sudden fear that she would burst into tears on the street, while answering the telephone, or while serving as chairman of one of her committee meetings. Once, when asked to stand and deliver a report, this fear had grown so acute that she pleaded sudden illness, and had gone home in confusion, attended by two solicitous friends.

That night Bart had advised her to see a psychologist. In fear that she would be found mad, she had gone to a small office on Commonwealth Avenue in Boston, and in a sudden torrent of words had told a small, bald, bespectacled man about her whole relationship with Ken Jorgenson, about the teasing, about undressing in front of the window, about the rape which was not a rape really, she had stammered out, no, not really, I always thought it was, but lately I've realized that it was not. His comments, delivered in a mild, dry, matter-of-fact voice had astonished her. "You must not forget," he had said, "that such actions are not entirely unnatural, they are not wholly bad in motivation." In most primitive societies, he had said, there are rituals provided with dances during which young women can flaunt their beauty before young men with the full approval of their elders.

"There is nothing unhealthy about that," he had said. "The difficulty always comes when these natural impulses collide with countercurrents within yourself and with society."

Oh, the psychologist had made everything as clear as day to her; she had seen him several times, paying ten dollars for each visit, money which she had hoped to spend for a summer camp for John, and the only trouble had been that the asthma had continued, and the fear of crying, the sensation that there was no joy in life, and the growing conviction that she was ruining her children.

"What do I do?" she had asked the psychologist.

For the immediate future a little rest would help, he had said; long walks in the country and some activity with her hands, such as weaving, would be more beneficial than committee meetings. In the long run, a complete psychoanalysis might help, he had said, and had recommended a doctor who was twice as expensive.

She had dutifully followed directions and had started the analysis, but when Bart's financial affairs had gone from bad to worse, she had stopped it. Courage, she had finally decided, had to be her answer; not lying on a couch and talking at a cost of a hundred dollars a week, but courage, only that and nothing else.

The difficulty had been that taking care of her house and children, weaving and long walks in the country had not been enough to cure her restlessness. After having made the decision to give up her clubs and her "community activities," she had grown so nervous that she could hardly remain seated for more than five minutes. Part of the trouble, she had decided, was Boston, a city which had seemed to her to personify false standards. The clubs which she had so eagerly joined had begun to appear to be the epitome of hypocrisy. Her old friends had seemed to act like marionettes pulled by complex strings of convention, never by their own emotions. Long before Bart's business problems became acute, she had talked to him of pulling up stakes and moving to California, perhaps, or back to Chicago, where she still had distant relatives. When Bart suggested that they convert the old mansion on the island to a summer inn and live there the year around, she had agreed with enthusiasm. Indeed, she had egged him on, and had turned what had begun as a tentative proposal of his, little more than a dream, into reality. It would be so wonderful for the children she had said.

The decision to move permanently to the island had been hers as much as his: this she remembered now with grim self-criticism. It was not all his fault, she thought; those horrible winters were of my own making. Oh, she had had bright dreams of abandoning all convention, of walking naked on the beaches in the sunlight alone, of losing herself in some new, mystical union with nature. She had bought books on how to become self-supporting on one acre of land; she would abandon the phony and get back to essentials. They would weave their own clothes with wool from their own sheep, and make brandy from their own apples. They would grow potatoes and learn how to smoke fish, and the children would learn how to relax.

Of course, she had not taken into account the almost constant weariness which plagued her, the lack of privacy caused by Todd Hasper's ubiquitous presence on the island, and the depressive atmosphere which surrounded Bart after his business failure. But during that first fall on the island, in the false reassurance of Indian summer, she had achieved a few days of exaltation. Once she had gone to the end of the island alone, and slipping off her clothes, had lain on a warm granite rock, with the surf curling around her, and she had felt herself washed of years of falseness. Looking down at her body, still full-hipped and narrow-waisted, but with the skin on her belly striated by childbirth, and with her breasts beginning to sag a little, she had not felt old; she had had the curious sensation of ripening, of being far more beautiful than when she had stood tightly corseted before the ladies' meetings with white gloves to her elbows, and more desirable for any man than when she had lain smugly on the beach in a black bathing suit and a fake mink coat. If Bart had not been drunk that night when she returned home, it might have been possible to achieve a new beginning.

But, of course, he had been drunk, and the first snow had come a few days later, and the memory of that short period of exaltation had seemed like a dream. Grimly she had returned to her creed of courage. Meals had had to be cooked and clothes to be washed and bills to be paid, for Bart soon became upset at the very sight of a checkbook. There had been the children to teach and to comfort, with determination if not with joy. How efficient she was, Bart had said; how remarkable that she remained so young. An automaton held up by courage, living by rote: that was the kind of woman she had become.

But not entirely, she thought now in the quiet of Ken's old room. I'm lucky: I have a point of pride, unlike poor Bart. In spite of everything I've still got my vanity, I've aged no more than Ken, I'm no old lady yet, no bridge player, no longer a PTA–garden-club expert. By God, I'm still a woman, and that's more than his wife can say.

I shouldn't admit this even to myself, she thought, but I'm glad he married an ugly woman. I shall not fool myself: in this I delight. I should be kind to her; I should feel sorry for her; I should try to help her out here on the island, her with her poor fluttery hands, and her nervous giggle, poor soul; but I'm still glad that she's ugly, I'm still bitchy and honest enough to feel that.

But all of this had little to do with Sylvia's practical question of how to spend the day at hand. The rain was a problem for more reasons than the leaky roof. The guests at the inn would be confined to the living room and the glass porches. Instead of dispersing to the beaches and the gardens, and instead of taking walks, they would be gathered in the living room playing bridge and gossiping. Any uneasiness that she displayed with Ken would be much more closely scrutinized than it would be in sunny weather. Mrs. Hamble, the dean of all gossips, had said she remembered Ken, but she hadn't said how much she remembered. Probably it would turn out to be a lot. If Sylvia knew anything about Pine Island, the story of the tutor returning as a rich guest paying the son of his old employer to sleep in the master bedrooms of the old mansion, oh, Pine Island would make a lot of that. And if Mrs. Hamble's memory were good enough to rake up the old rumors, the gossip of almost twenty years ago, why then the summer might not end up so dull after all.

Maybe Bart was right when he instinctively felt we should turn Ken down, Sylvia thought. I did not think this through. I did not imagine that I could be robbed of my poise by any man; I did not know that he would look so nearly as he did, or that age can in so many ways improve as well as destroy.

Sylvia's eye was caught then by a figure moving in the rose garden. At that distance it was difficult to see who it was, but she knew. There were only two men who would put on a coat at eight-thirty in the morning to go striding around Pine Island in the rain, and this one didn't have a dog. She watched him circle the inn. When he came to the courtyard which separated the garage from the old mansion, she stepped to one side of the window, behind the curtain. He stood there on the concrete driveway below staring up at his old room, with the rain splattering on the pavement around him and dripping off the brim of his felt hat into his face. For perhaps twenty seconds he stood there, then turned brusquely and stared up at the back of the inn, where the yellow draperies closed off the window of her old room. With both hands in his pockets, he turned impatiently and, with his feet splashing heedlessly in the puddles, headed down the path toward the beach where he had sat guarding children long ago.

8

THE THING TO DO is to keep busy, Sylvia thought as she put on her raincoat to dash across the courtyard to the inn. I shall count the sheets today, and take an inventory of the canned goods, and pay the bills. Letting herself through the kitchen door, she sat with Lillian, the Negro cook, at the old marble-topped table and drank coffee. After two cups she felt better and went to the living room, where the bridge games were already in progress. Helen Jorgenson had been included in one, and sat biting her lower lip as she studied her cards. In a corner Ken sat reading a large volume aloud to Molly, his voice little above a whisper. The child sat with a chair drawn tightly against his; she was leaning forward, and their faces were only about two feet apart. When Sylvia entered the room, everyone glanced up and perhaps Sylvia imagined that there was hostility in Molly's look, something more than simple annoyance at being interrupted.

"Good morning," Ken said in his deep voice. His hair was still wet, she saw, and the cuffs of his trousers were muddy.

"Good morning."

"Sylvia dear," Mrs. Hamble said, "this isn't a good way for me to start the day, but I must tell you there's a leak in the roof."

"Where, Mrs. Hamble?"

"In my bathroom."

"Where in the bathroom?"

"It's odd," Mrs. Hamble said, "but it's right over one of the conveniences. It is causing no damage, but I thought you ought to know."

"That's funny; we have another one like that," Sylvia said. There seemed to be something eerie about such incidents, almost as though Bart were right about the Lord taking care of his own helpless people in curious ways.

"I do hope you'll call someone to fix it," Mrs. Hamble said. "I must admit it causes some difficulty."

Helen Jorgenson laughed, a high nervous twitter, and a few of the others joined in.

"I'll see about it," Sylvia replied, and put her hand up to her forehead, stroking it back across her hair, the way she always did when she was confused. It was very hard, as well as expensive, to get repairmen to come from the mainland.

"Would you like me to look at it?" Ken asked, his deep voice filling the room.

"Do you know about roofs?" Sylvia asked in surprise.

"A little."

"I'd be grateful," Sylvia said.

First they inspected the two leaks, one over the toilet in Mrs. Hamble's bathroom, and one over the bathtub on the third floor. With a flashlight Sylvia showed Ken up the narrow attic stairs, and he poked around the eaves for ten minutes. Then he opened a trap door and emerged onto the wet tiles, crawling over the roof on his stomach, examining every inch. When he came down, he was dripping wet and grinning.

"Nothing to worry about," he said. "They ran ventilator pipes into your new bathrooms, and the flashing was poorly put on."

"Will it cost much to fix?"

"If you've got tools, I can do it."

"Oh, you don't want to take the time!"

"I like to keep busy."

She screwed up her courage and said, "Is the roof itself all right?"

"My God, it's slate. It will last a thousand years."

"Thanks," Sylvia said. "I can't tell you how worried we were about it!"

"Do you have the tools?"

"You're sure you want to bother with it?"

He grinned again. "I get restless," he said. "I was never born to be a gentleman of leisure."

Looking resentful, Todd Hasper lent Ken his tool chest. As soon as the rain stopped, Ken clambered to the roof again and sat there working with a blazing blowtorch and a soldering iron. To Sylvia's astonishment, he next began to plane a porch door that long had jammed, and to replace some torn screens.

Sometimes Sylvia sat and watched him work, although she too

tried to keep as busy as possible that week. Ken talked lightly about the month he had been a carpenter's helper while a student at college. There was of course no mention of that other job he had had, the one on Pine Island he had quit. He just said he had been a carpenter's helper for a few weeks toward the end of one summer, when he happened to need some money, and that's how he learned to handle tools. Watching him with his big hands moving quickly on the door he was planing, Sylvia felt less tension than when they sat talking at the dinner table, for usually he kept his eyes on his work. It was his eyes that robbed her of her poise, the deep-set, brooding eyes, the smoldering tormented look which hadn't changed in so many years.

To get away from those eyes and from Mrs. Hamble's bright, inquiring stare, Sylvia began taking long walks by herself for the first time in many years, knowing it was all right for her to stay out of sight so long as Ken remained at the inn, within full sight of the gossips. Often starting immediately after breakfast, she hiked clear to the south end of the island, where the granite hills frayed out in a tangle of surf, boulders and sand. Once she met John and Molly on the beach, walking with their thin backs bent into the wind, looking oddly like an elderly couple. The gulls wheeled about their shoulders, and the crash of the surf drowned out her words when she called to them. Smiling, Sylvia let them go.

Tiring of the beach, she climbed mountains, where she had never been before. A narrow trail led along the brink of the cliffs up one hump, which was about three hundred feet high, and into a ravine, on the steep rocky sides of which cedars and white birch grew, clinging to crevices in the rock, stunted but enduring. A trail of fallen hickories and pines marked the path of a small avalanche during the past rainstorm. Goaded by an urge for discovery, Sylvia picked her way carefully to the depths of the ravine, where gray stones at the bottom of a dry brook turned white in the August sun.

It was almost dark when Sylvia returned to the inn. Ken met her on the veranda, and she could tell from the look in his eyes that he knew she was avoiding him and that he was hurt; she also recognized that perhaps this was what she had been trying to do. There was still the echo of the instinct to hurt him. Stepping directly in front of her, he said, "Sylvia, could I talk to you for a minute?"

Her head jerked up. "What about?" she asked.

"It's kind of important, to me anyway. Let's go out in the garden."

She looked around the porch, but it was dinnertime, and no one was in sight, not even Mrs. Hamble. "All right," she said, and followed him as he led the way across the lawn toward the old fountain. Fireflies throbbed in the dusk, and she remembered how at some party long ago everyone had pursued them with Mason jars to see how much light a large collection of them would make. She could remember the young boys in their white flannel trousers and blue blazers dashing among the lilac bushes, and the girls in their swirling pastel dresses, but she couldn't recall whether Ken had been there, or whether he had been alone in his room. "Do you remember when . . ." she began, and stopped, wishing she hadn't spoken.

"What?" he asked.

"We used to chase fireflies here."

"I remember," he said. "Bart bet me a dollar he could catch enough to read by."

"Who won?"

"I did."

In the silence that followed, the tree frogs croaked, and the katydids rasped their wings. Far away in the woods, a whippoorwill called shrilly. As they entered the rose garden, the trailing branches of one of the bushes reached out and snagged her dress. He helped her disengage it, and they continued to walk without talking. In the center of the lawn was a small circular pool with a marble Cupid who once had spouted water from his pursed lips, but now the statue looked simply as though it were kissing air, and the water beneath it lay stagnant and mottled with green scum. Although a cool wind blew from the sea, Ken began to sweat, and his sports shirt was soon plastered to his chest. Delicacy had never been his strong point, she remembered without contempt. "You said you wanted to talk to me about something," Sylvia started to say, but did not. With his silence and his lack of ease he had already started to say it. Sylvia looked up and in the last rays of the sun was shocked to see that the leaves on the big maple tree by the north corner of the house were already beginning to turn a pale yellow. Fall was coming, all right. She shivered. Far away, down near the beach, she could hear the children shouting, and then there was no sound but the wind in the leaves.

The silence became increasingly oppressive. "I was wondering," Ken blurted out suddenly, his deep voice sounding unnatural, "if we could come back next year and spend the whole summer."

"Why do you want to?" She made it sound like a simple inquiry, without overtones.

He wheeled and looked down at her. "Why do you stay?" he asked.

"Because I'm married to it." Her voice was flat.

"The winters must be hard," he said. "I wish I could help."

"Of course they're hard!" she said with a catch in her voice, and in a sudden burst of words, she started to tell him about it. The memories of the last two winters, which had been bottled up, too horrible to admit, even to herself, came out in a rush of confidence. She told of the oppressive loneliness. She told how her children had grown pinched and thin, how her daughter, Carla, had got bronchitis with a temperature of 104, and how it had taken two days to get a doctor. She told of her fear that Todd Hasper, the morose superintendent, was really insane, that he had started muttering to himself when going about his work, that he never spoke to her now without rage in his eyes, apparently because his winter solitude had been violated, and that he had begun to tell dark stories to the children, stories which she at first had thought they had dreamed, but which they attributed to Todd Hasper when they came running to her in terror late at night.

"What kind of stories?" Ken asked.

Sylvia brushed her face with her hand. "He told them about his brother who hung himself with a piece of wire," she said. "I found out that really happened—they didn't dream it. He told them about it last winter, over and over again."

"You ought to get rid of him," Ken said.

"There has to be somebody here—and oh, he's been here for so many years. It's not easy to get someone to work on the island." Sylvia went on then, her last reserve collapsing, and told about Bart's drinking, his cycles of accusation and apology, his gloom, his violent temper when aroused, about the time when deep in his cups he had accused her of being a whore at heart, a phrase he had repeated over and over, a whore at heart, a whore at heart, and Johnny at the age of twelve had heard it and had attacked his father, a small boy with his little fists doubled up and flailing. Bart had shoved him up against the wall, banged him down on the floor, and then had stood over him crying, and had ended by throwing himself down and embracing him there on the floor, the two of them lying together and sobbing.

Sylvia paused in confusion, silently crying, with both hands covering her face. "I deserved it," she said. "They didn't."

"You ought to get out of here," Ken said, his deep voice sounding to her almost like thunder.

"How?"

"Something could be arranged."

"What?" Her voice was tragic.

"Go back to Boston in the winter. Or Florida."

"We can't afford it!"

"Can't he get a job?"

"He won't try."

"You could."

"With the children?"

"Yes."

"Like what?" Her strength was coming back now, and she sounded bitter.

"Lots of Maine people run hotels in Florida in the winter."

"You want me to buy one with our savings? A big hotel in Miami?" Her tone was ironic.

"No. A small motel maybe."

"For God's sake," she said. "Don't you understand that we're broke?"

"I have money. I'll lend it to you."

There was a brief silence.

"You could take Bart too," he added heavily. "I'll pay him a salary."

"No," she said, her voice barely audible.

"Your pride still comes first."

Her breath came rushing out then between clenched teeth, and there were her hissed, agonized words, *"Oh Jesus!"* She crouched with her hands clenched tight to her belly, as though she had been stabbed. Suddenly he was towering over her. She felt herself crushed to him, and she flung both arms around his neck as though he were saving her from going over a waterfall. Without kissing her he said in her ear in a strange choked voice, almost a sob, a cry of despair, the one word: "Love?"

"Yes!" she replied, and then there was the sound of laughter, high and clear, and children's voices coming closer. In panic they sprang apart, just as John and Molly and Carla burst into the garden, carrying flashlights. Ken melted into the underbrush. Without seeing him, the children ran to the pool and knelt before it, shining the lights

into its dark waters. "This is the place!" Carla said exuberantly. "There always used to be lots of them here!"

"Did you ever catch any?" Molly asked.

"No," John said. "We weren't supposed to. But some of them were enormous."

"Hello, kids," Sylvia said. "What are you looking for?"

They both glanced up, startled. "Goldfish!" they said almost in unison.

"I'm afraid they all died last winter," Sylvia replied. "We forgot to take them in, and the pool froze solid."

"The poor things!" Molly said, her alert face suddenly clouded with grief, her mind possessed by the image of a clear cake of ice containing a neat pattern of goldfish.

"There's something down there!" John said, stabbing the water with the beam of his light. "I just saw it move." Suddenly he darted his hand into the murky water and came up with a frog, its bulging eyes glowing brightly. He held it in front of him and shone his light on it. Molly bent over it, her face full of wonder. "Don't squeeze him!" she said.

Sylvia admired the frog, then turned and walked haltingly up the path. Ken silently rejoined her on the other side of the lilac bushes. He kissed her and she clung to him hard before breaking away. "Ken, Ken!" she whispered, "I don't want to wreck everybody."

"No."

"They'll be wondering where we are, even now. Meet me here at three in the morning. It's the only time on this whole damn island we can be sure of not being missed."

"All right," he said, and was suddenly gone, the shadows of the lilacs swallowing him as though he had never existed.

9

THAT NIGHT Sylvia lay sleepless beside her husband, and tried to think rationally.

There are only five possibilities, she thought; the whole situation is perfectly clear-cut. Remaining a faithful wife, I can cut this thing off with Ken before it starts, and put the winters through on the island somehow, but I cannot do that and nothing could be worse than things are for the children.

Or I can take Ken's money and give him nothing but interest of four per cent, but there's a kind of immorality about that too. My pride would not allow it, and anyway, it's not the way it would work out. The money would keep us tangled together. We are not the sort of people to manage a small platonic affair.

Or we could each get a divorce, and then we could marry, she thought. It was this possibility that her mind hovered longest over. But of course it wouldn't work. Bart's pride would be hurt, and Bart with hurt pride was like a small wounded lion. Perhaps he would insist on keeping the children, and that would be impossible.

Or she and Ken could have an affair, as civilized as possible, and as discreet as possible, but only an affair, with false names signed in hotel registers, probably, excuses to be given, lying explanations of absence and constant subterfuge. I never thought of myself as a particularly decent person, Sylvia thought. But an affair is not what I want now, I am too old for that, it's not what I want at all! It is too ugly.

Or we could do what most people would probably do, she thought; we could drift along, making no real decisions, being both unchaste and unfulfilled. We can have an affair without planning it, the quick clinch in the night. We can have the gossip, the recriminations. We do not have to choose our mess—it is easier to drift into it.

No, she thought. That I won't do, and Ken is too much of a man for that. If I'm going to have an affair, it's going to be a good one, deliberately planned to last a lifetime and to hurt other people as little as possible. I do not want to go blundering around in the night.

But divorce and remarriage—her mind kept returning to that. It ought to be possible, she thought, for four civilized adults to sit down and work out an intelligent solution to a problem. She imagined herself and Bart and Ken and Helen sitting ceremoniously around a bridge table, and she imagined herself prattling in a high bridge-table voice, "The problem is that when I was young I was a fool, and now I am no longer, and I would like to marry a man I've always loved. Does anyone mind?"

"Why, of course not!" she imagined Bart replying. "It's perfectly all right."

"I pass," Helen would say, but of course the whole thing was a travesty. What could she really say to Bart, how could she put it in a letter, the truth with no holds barred?

"Dear Bart," she imagined herself writing, burlesquing the classic note to be pinned to a pillow, "The truth is I never loved you, I was confused. I loved what I thought you stood for, or something. I was addled by my parents and I don't know what, but now, you see, we have to face the truth, and the truth is, dear Bart, that you are becoming an alcoholic and a little insane. I hope you don't mind my saying this, but we have to be frank, you know. So I would like to leave you and I would like to take the children and I want to be kind if I can, although I realize that this note is not exactly tactful, but don't be hurt."

In the bed beside her Bart stirred restlessly in his sleep. Dim moonlight from the window illuminated his face, fine-boned and angular, and she thought, Poor Bart, God help him. God help us all, I do not like to do this.

Divorce, she thought stonily. I don't even know whether Ken wants one. He would lose his daughter, and it's perfectly obvious that they love each other, those two; I've never seen a man's face light up so at the sight of his child. They're always sitting together and talking together. That is a beautiful thing that I would be smashing. And it's strange, that young girl looks at me with those great alarmed eyes as though she knew her enemy on sight.

Sylvia turned over in bed with her heart pounding, and there was a moment of panic when she thought, What has happened, what are we doing, how did we get into this situation? Why can't we all just relax, she thought, and take care of our children, and . . .

Because I'm in love, she thought, and though it sounds stupid and sentimental, it's true and I'm glad. Only the dead at heart find virtue easy, the dead at heart or those few fortunate ones who marry for love and do not change.

Easy virtue, she thought, what a strange phrase, meaning, of course, no virtue. I suppose a clergyman would tell me that virtue was never meant to be easy, that I should grit my teeth and spend the winters on the island with Bart and hold him up with my strength.

I could do it, she thought with a curious sense of self-revelation.

I actually could; but even if the children could survive such a thing, even without considering them, that kind of virtue, the gritted teeth, no, no, no, that kind of virtue is a sin.

I am beginning to understand, Sylvia thought. I am beginning to understand a lot of things, oh, I'm becoming a great expert on morality. And I am about to shrivel and die, or to have an affair, or to make a man lose his daughter. Is it possible to have an affair that is not shoddy?

Perhaps the truth is this, she thought, imagining that on the skin of her wrist she could almost feel the hands of her watch crawling toward the hour of three, perhaps the truth is that there is no way out of this business, because there is no absolution, because I have finally arrived in hell. My sins were committed. I have been worrying about the future, but the sins lie in the past, and I committed them in a thousand ways, and now I pay, and Bart pays. Step right up this way, ladies and gentlemen, this is the place to pay.

This is a new installment plan, a payment every month, the debt growing not smaller but larger, for the rest of my life, Sylvia thought. The price was set, and now we pay, both the guilty and the innocent; we come to the cashier.

And that's the unfair part, Sylvia thought. I can see why I have to pay and why Bart does, and maybe even Ken, but what did poor little Molly do, and Carla and Johnny?

The sins of the fathers, she thought, oh this is a very just plan, the torture of the innocent. The system is more immoral than anyone in it.

God help us, she thought. This is the morning to pray, as well as pay, and I wonder if a small prayer composed in complete confusion will be acceptable. *Dear God, I do not understand.*

At two-thirty Sylvia got up silently and dressed without putting the lights on. Bart did not stir, and the rhythm of his heavy breathing was unbroken. She stole down the hall and stairway to the courtyard. The lawn was gray with dew. A soft night wind was blowing, and there was a fragrance in the air from the sea and the gardens that was easy to understand, and a golden sickle moon, and the distant sound of the breakers surging against the cliffs. She ran to the lilac trees, and Ken's kiss was easy to understand, yes, and the feeling of sudden joy. This is a triumph against great odds, she wanted to say, perhaps a small victory prefacing great defeat, but I don't care. Right now, for a little while at least, I understand and I am grateful.

Ken broke away from the kiss, tearing his lips from hers brusquely, still holding her with both arms around her waist, but averting his face, and his voice was tormented when he said, *"We've got to talk."*

"No," she said.

"We've got to plan."

"All right," she said, and took her arms from around his neck. "Do you want to get divorced, or do we just have an affair?"

"I don't know," he said, and in the dim light from the sickle moon, his face looked pale. "What do you want?"

"A divorce if I could have my children."

"Same here."

"Would Helen give you Molly?"

"No."

"I don't want to influence you," Sylvia said. "I'm perfectly willing to have the affair."

"I just have to think."

"Not now."

"Look!" he said, "We're too old to make a mess. Right now, if Bart woke up . . ."

"He won't. He drinks himself to sleep. Will Helen wake?"

"No," he said. "She takes sleeping pills."

"Then we have till dawn," she said. "Two or three hours."

He kissed her again. "I'm afraid I'm too old for the pleasures of dew-covered grass," he said. "There must be a better place."

"The Hulberts' boathouse," she said. Turning, she led the way to a path which cut through the woods and around the edge of the bay to the opposite side of the harbor. The boathouse was a large structure of weathered gray shingles which had stood empty for many summers. In the bottom portion of it were two slips for motorboats surrounded on three sides by a narrow pier. It was pitch dark when they entered. Cobwebs brushed Ken's face and there was a flutter of bats' wings. Under the dock the sea murmured restlessly. "Take my hand," she said, and walked to a narrow stairway. Halfway up he pulled her to him and kissed her. "Wait," she said, and twisted away. His eyes were becoming used to the darkness, and the head of the stairs appeared as a gray rectangle above him, in which her silhouette was framed. He followed her and found himself on a wide-planked floor with the eaves sloping down so steeply on both sides of him that he could stand only in the middle. Through dusty windowpanes there streamed the pale light from the sickle moon and the stars. An old dory sail and kapok life preservers hung from nails. Sylvia walked quickly to a corner and took from a hook a weathered sailbag which was half as big as herself. Letting it fall to the floor, she opened it and drew out a seemingly endless torrent of white canvas which fell in loose folds to the floor and made the loft seem much lighter. "This used to belong to the old *Gull's Wing*," she began. "Remember . . ."

His kiss interrupted her. They sank down on the sail, finding that it was surprisingly soft. The clean smell of hemp and tar was everywhere. After the kiss she knelt beside him and with one hand began to unfasten the buttons of her blouse. In the dim light she did not look young. Her face, downturned, appeared almost gaunt. Her eyes seemed to have grown larger, and her shoulders thin. Misinterpreting his glance, she said with a catch in her voice, "I'm not pretty any more. I'm sorry for that."

He caught her hand and pulled her down to him. "I love you too much to speak," he said.

Part Two

SOMEDAY YOU'LL UNDERSTAND

10

They woke themselves up often after that for secret meetings in the dampness of dawn, and as Ken said wryly, people really have to be in love to do that. Speaking in whispers, they tried to make plans, and they grew tired of whispering. They wanted to talk and laugh and shout, but even in the boathouse they felt they had always to whisper. They had to steal away from there one at a time, they had to keep glancing around to make sure they were alone on the path, even at five in the morning. They had to conduct themselves like thieves.

"It's all so absurd!" Sylvia said bitterly one morning. "Even if Bart let me take the children without a terrible battle in court, things wouldn't be easy. It sounds crazy, but I'd worry about him. I've taken care of him so long! How can I just leave him here on the island, all alone with Hasper? He'll drink himself to death. He won't eat, and . . ."

"We have to make choices," Ken said.

"I wish we were both sons-of-bitches! I wish you didn't give a damn for Molly, and that I hated Bart!"

"You don't wish that."

"I know! But what do we do?"

"I'll arrange some way for both you and Bart to go South. That will solve your immediate problems. The others we'll just have to work out as we go along."

Sylvia bit her lip. In her heart there was a rising sense of disaster too intense to be told.

On the third of September 1953 the Jorgensons left Pine Island. John Hunter looked so lonely when he came up the hill after waving goodbye to Molly that Sylvia wanted to cry for him as well as for herself. Ken had promised her that he'd find some way of getting them off the island before winter came, but she doubted that he could work out any really happy solution to a dilemma such as theirs.

As though in reaction to the whispering he had had to do with Sylvia, Ken found himself having to stifle an almost constant temptation to shout at Helen. They argued about whether to go to Buffalo before spending the winter in Florida. When Ken reluctantly agreed to a two-week visit in Buffalo, they argued about whether to stay at her family's house or in a hotel.

"They'd be terribly hurt if we stayed at a hotel!" Helen said in a shocked voice. "Ken, what's the matter with you? Has all this success gone to your head?"

"No," he replied miserably. "I just don't like sofa beds."

"Not grand enough for you?"

"Not long enough, damn it!" Ken shouted. "My feet stick over the edge."

For two weeks they stayed with the Carters, and from the time they arrived, Ken found himself getting more and more annoyed at them. I suppose I'm being unreasonable and cruel, he thought; my nerves are simply overwrought. But everything he saw fitted into a pattern which appalled him, and he couldn't understand why he had been blind to it so long.

First of all, there was the house itself, and the fetish of the perfect lawn. Old Bruce Carter spent hours fertilizing and watering it. He weeded it on his hands and knees, and chased children and dogs off it with indignant shouts.

He spent far more time with the lawn than with books or newspapers. While on his knees weeding, he looked as though he were worshiping the lawn, and maybe he is, Ken thought, for all I know.

Then there was the car, a blue Pontiac a year old, which the old man rubbed with a rag every night, and washed every weekend. He's in love with it, Ken thought. He's not polishing it, he's caressing it; there is something about his preoccupation with that car and the lawn which is obscene.

Seeing Margaret Carter, his mother-in-law, again, upset Ken, because she was so much like Helen, an intensification of her daughter, really. The characteristics which she made obvious explained too much about Helen, he reflected. It was like parading the poor woman naked through the streets.

Just as old Bruce spent so much time rubbing the car, Margaret was almost constantly polishing silverware or applying liquid wax to her floors or furniture. The sound of the vacuum cleaner in the house was incessant. The washing machine and dryer in the kitchen were always churning, and when any of her towels or sheets didn't come out of them blindingly white, Margaret immediately put them back in the machines again, with the result that linen never lasted long for her.

The shelves in the single bathroom at the Carters' house were full of deodorizers of many kinds, sprays, salves and powders, mouthwashes and toothpastes guaranteed to prevent bad breath. Margaret often went around spraying every room, or hanging up bottles with wicks to reduce smells, of which both she and her daughter lived in terror. Margaret washed her hands so often they became chapped. Dishes and glasses which had stood on the shelves for only a few days since they had been used had to be washed again before the table was set. Any member of the family who got the slightest scratch had to have it elaborately sterilized and bandaged, for it was a dirty world, Margaret Carter felt, against which her guard could never be dropped for a minute. Cleanliness was next to godliness, as she so often said, and as far as Ken could see, she had drawn the conclusion that if it was almost divine to be clean, it must be actually Olympian to be sterile. She gave the impression of wanting to boil herself thoroughly, like a surgical instrument.

Cleanliness and sterility—she had connected them in her mind, all right, and had deduced that fertility must therefore be dirt—or at least, that's the way she acted, Ken thought. Dogs had never been allowed in the house because they might hurt the rugs, but Margaret liked cats. She had three, and all had been desexed, even though one was a blooded Persian of high quality which the veterinarian had told Margaret should be bred. Since childhood Margaret had thought that any animal had to be spayed or castrated before being allowed into the house, and she had told the veterinarian to proceed with the operation, because, as she said, she only wanted the cat for a pet.

Even the decorations Margaret had bought, the plaster-of-Paris statuettes on the living-room mantelpiece and the people depicted in paintings on the walls, had been desexed, Ken noticed. The movies she saw had to omit all reference to any but sentimental love, or Margaret wrote critical letters to the newspapers. Lovers in television plays had to be cute, sad or funny—if they got passionate, Margaret turned off the set. Even words such as "passion" or "sex" had been chopped from Margaret's vocabulary, and had been replaced by such words as "nastiness" and "dirt." Margaret's favorite reading matter was detective stories, the cruder the better, but she complained that the writers of modern mystery novels put in too much filth, by which she meant sex, and not enough action, by which she meant blood and death.

Bruce and Margaret slept in separate rooms in the Carter house, which was one reason why there was no room for Ken. Margaret's room was decorated with pink flounces; even the lamp shades had them. At the south end of it was a table for her collection of figurines: small dogs and kittens and bears, most of them with faces twisted into human expressions, the animal lips distorted into sugary grins, the slanting, oval eyes enlarged and made round to represent innocence, apparently. They were the cutest things, Margaret often said, and when she spied a new one in a ten-cent store she swooped down on it, saying, "How *darling!* You sweet thing! How would you like to come home and live with me?"

She was constantly fussing over Molly. That was what worried Ken most: the thought of what would happen to his daughter if Helen moved in with the Carters after a divorce. On her fourteenth birthday Molly received from Margaret armfuls of little-girl clothes which would have been suitable for a child of ten. The old lady wanted Molly to wear bows in her hair; she objected violently when Molly put on a touch of pink lipstick; she derided Molly's blushingly confessed desire to own a brassière. When Molly asked Helen in a matter-of-fact way to buy her some sanitary pads, Margaret looked appalled and said, "Don't tell me, child, that you already have the curse! How terrible that you should have to begin so young!"

Soon after he arrived in Buffalo, Ken saw his financial advisers and had a conference with Bernie Anderson, who had just returned from Paris full of enthusiasm for starting a "New Development

Corporation" to repeat their success with Marfab on a broader scale, beginning with three new processes he had been studying in Europe. Several tax questions had been settled advantageously and both Bernie and Ken found their financial situation was even better than they had thought. Subsidiary rights connected with Marfab had been sold profitably, and what with annual payments from the company which had bought Marfab, stock dividends, and retainers for serving as an occasional consultant, Ken's income was close to a hundred thousand dollars a year. He made plans to join Bernie in forming a new company, although he said that until some of his personal problems were solved, he'd prefer to play a fairly passive role. Bernie didn't ask what the personal problems were; he'd known Helen a long time. They made plans to get together, perhaps in Paris, in midwinter for another conference.

When Helen learned that Ken's success was continuing, rather than disappearing overnight, as she had more than half expected, she said, "I've been wondering. We've been so fortunate, do you suppose we could do something for Mother and Dad?"

"What?"

"I'd like to buy them a new house," Helen said. "I mean, I know that's a lot, but if we really are so rich . . ."

"Sure," Ken said, but he felt sardonic; buying the Carters a house might be a good way to begin to reduce the bitterness of an impending divorce, and it salved his conscience a little.

The trouble was that the house-hunting expeditions, in which Ken was expected to join, increased the clarity of the pattern he had observed. Margaret Carter talked freely with the real-estate agents about wanting to avoid any neighborhood with Jews; and when she placed her old house on the market, she said proudly that she wouldn't think of selling it to Jews, no matter what they offered. She was, she said, going to remain loyal to her old friends and neighbors; it was terrible the way some people just sold to anyone when they moved away, they had no loyalty at all.

"You wouldn't be getting a new house if it weren't for a Jew," Ken felt impelled to say. "My partner is one, and the idea of starting our own corporation was his."

"Oh, I know they're awfully sharp in business," Margaret replied.

"It wasn't that at all. But anyway, would you refuse to sell Bernie your old house?"

"I don't doubt that he's a fine person, but you know, you get one in, and it's like a crack in the dike," Margaret replied. "It wouldn't be fair to the neighbors."

"Now, don't argue with Mother," Helen said.

But it wasn't only the Jews that Margaret Carter wanted to avoid, Ken discovered as the house-hunting expedition progressed. She didn't want a Catholic neighborhood, and "of course," she said, one had to be especially careful to steer clear of the Polish section and the Italian section—those people were making so much money nowadays, their houses didn't look any different from anyone else's, and one could get fooled. Some of the old parts of the city were being "infiltrated by Negroes," the real-estate agent said, and "of course" they had to be avoided at all costs. Neighborhoods near schools were eschewed, for there would be too many children running around, too much noise.

"Now let's see," Ken said to Helen one night, ticking off the taboos on his fingers, "we are seeking a neighborhood where there are no Jews, no Polish people, no Italians, no Negroes, no children, no Catholics. Do I have the list right?"

"Don't be mean," Helen said.

"I'm just trying to get this straight. You know, out in Nebraska when I was a kid, us Swedes weren't held in too high repute. Do they mind Swedes here?"

"Of course not! What's getting into you, Ken? You've never been so mean!"

Although Ken stopped talking about it, the compiling of the list of Margaret's dislikes became an obsession with him. When she refused to patronize a Chinese laundry, he learned that she was against the Chinese and, it seemed, all Orientals. The Russians she hated with patriotic zeal. The English she thought snobbish, the French immoral, the Germans brutal, and all South Americans lazy. Category by category, she closed humanity out.

At first Ken thought the Carters simply wanted to move into as expensive and genteel a neighborhood as possible, but that proved incorrect. They rejected a rich neighborhood because they said the residents were "too snooty," so Ken added the rich to his list. Other neighborhoods were rejected because they were too poor. Ken finally concluded that Margaret and Helen were simply anti-people, or anti-life, and fantastic though it sounded, every bit of evidence seemed to lead to this conclusion. Added to the desexing of everything, which seemed a logical part of it, was an anti-food prejudice.

Although no one who saw Margaret and Helen cleaning the house all day long could accuse them of being lazy, their chief interest in shopping for groceries was to buy things which could be quickly prepared. The kitchen was full of minute mixes and instant powders of all kinds, and a huge deep freeze chest was devoted entirely to products which could be stuck into boiling water or put on a griddle and served within five minutes. There was a great rush wherever food was concerned in the Carter household. No dish had sauces, nor any of the savor that slow cooking produced. Meat often was served with ice crystals at its center. After considerable reflection, Ken decided that the lust for cleanliness helped to produce this phenomenon. The Carters hated cooking because it messed up the kitchen, and they got it over with as speedily as possible, so they could fall to rubbing the counters and the dishes again. And of course, food gave life, and was therefore disgusting.

Ken's theory of the anti-people people was borne out by Bruce's political tastes, which favored preventive war, capital punishment, and clapping strikers in prison, and by Margaret's literary taste for blood. The converse of Jorgenson's theory, as Ken termed it, was obviously that people who don't like people or life become pro-death.

These thoughts made Ken no happier when he reflected that a divorce would undoubtedly hand Molly to Margaret Carter, for Helen just adored her mother, as she said, and couldn't bear to live alone. He tried to tell himself he was too bitter, that he should be compassionate toward Helen and Margaret, that he should regard them as poor lost souls, the product of their own undoubtedly horrible parents. He also tried to tell himself that he had to take more responsibility for Helen, that if he had really cared enough, he might have succeeded better in weaning her from her mother, that he had abandoned her too readily. These thoughts did not help. Regardless of the reasons, Helen and Margaret had ended up as they were, and he did not want Molly to be subject to them.

The house the Carters finally selected was in a neighborhood much like the one they were leaving: a poor suburban street, where one large California ranch house had been built on a double lot. It was by far the biggest and most expensive building on the block. In fact, it looked so out of place that it had been difficult to sell, and the contractor had reduced his price from sixty to forty thousand dollars. After thorough investigation, old Bruce found that there were few Catholics and Jews nearby. At least the postman, a small dark man of indeterminate ancestry, said that, and he ought to know. The postmen are a great help when you're buying a house, Bruce said; for five dollars they'll tell you almost anything. The names the city directory listed in that block were not Polish or Italian, and no Negroes could be seen walking about. No school was within a mile, and fortunately, Margaret said, there was no land in the neighborhood where one could be built. It was easy to see from the threadbare lawns of the neighbors that they wouldn't be snooty. The house, in fact, made the neighbors look poor and rendered them miserable. It was, Margaret exclaimed, "exactly right!"

At dawn on the morning after the "exactly right" house had been discovered, Molly stole out of her cot in her mother's room in the Carters' old house, and down the stairs to the living room, where her father was sleeping. In her nightdress and kimono, she perched on the foot of his sofa bed. He opened his eyes and smiled when he saw her.

"I didn't mean to wake you up," she said.

"I was already awake. Want to come under the covers?"

"Yes."

"Did you have a nightmare?" he asked when she was lying beside him.

"No. I just wanted to be with you."

He hugged her and she hugged him back, as she had so often when she crawled into bed with him after a bad dream. Since babyhood Molly had had a marvelous capacity for warmth, Ken thought. At the age of seven she had put her arms around his neck, her small face full of adoration, and had asked him to marry her. Now she snuggled against him, completely unself-conscious about being a woman, but full of small sighs of contentment, and wiggles that were as unabashedly sensual as they were virginal. He brushed her hair with his lips. "Glad to be back in Buffalo?" he asked.

"Not very."

"Why not?"

She wrinkled her nose. "Too flat," she said. "I like the mountains and the sea."

"So do I."

"Are we going back to the island next year?"

"I hope so."

"It was a funny summer," she said.

"Did you have a good time?"

"I didn't like the boat."

"And the island?"

"I liked that," she said, but her big eyes looked troubled. "Daddy, can we talk? Like we used to, I mean. Serious."

"Sure."

"Well, Johnny Hunter kissed me, and I kissed him back. Do you think I should have?"

"Do you like him?"

"Sort of."

"Then I think it was all right for you to kiss him back. I wouldn't let that kind of thing go too far, though. It's a little early yet."

"He didn't try to do anything bad. It was just that last day, before we went down to the boat to go. He asked me to go for a walk with him, and he said he thought I was a keen girl, and he kept saying that, and then all of a sudden he kissed me—here." Molly touched a delicate forefinger to her lips.

Ken smiled at her.

"Then he apologized, and he seemed, I don't know, so kind of *desperate;* so I kissed him back."

"I'm glad you did," Ken said.

"And then he asked if we could write letters this winter. They get mail once a week on the island, except when the ice gets too bad, he says. He asked me if I would write, and I said I would."

"That'll be fun."

"Do you think Mother will mind?"

"I don't see why she should."

Molly sighed and stretched. "Gee, I love you, Daddy," she said. "I better go upstairs now, or Granny will *murder* me."

"Why?"

"I'm supposed to make my bed before leaving the room—it's always been her rule, as though it were written down in the *Bible* or something, and Granny gets *very upset* if people don't obey—anyway, that's what Mother said."

"Sounds terrible," Ken replied, giving her a glance of mock ferociousness. "You better obey."

Molly grinned and jumped from the bed. As she disappeared up the stairs, her laughter, kept muted to avoid waking people up, was low and throaty.

Ken lay looking out of the window of the living room at the flat suburban landscape. If I leave Molly with those two, he thought, what chance will she have? They'd spay her. They'd spay her, just the way they spay the cats, and by the time she was twenty, she'd be just like them. Ken doubled up his fist and brought it down hard in the palm of his hand. The people who concentrate their love on automobiles and lawns, he thought bitterly—at least they have easier problems than this!

The next day Ken got a bad cold which turned into bronchitis. He lay in the sofa bed with his legs awkwardly curled, and morosely coughed. Winter came early, even for Buffalo, that year, and in mid-September there was a brief flurry of snow. Ken wondered whether it was snowing on Pine Island, and how Sylvia was. He could picture her standing nervously, while Bart went through the mail, waiting for the letter Ken had promised to write.

The bronchitis lingered, and Margaret didn't like the sofa bed lying open in the daytime. It looked terrible, she said, yet no woman or girl could give up her room to sleep in the living room because there were no shades on the windows, and *anyone* might look in. Old Bruce offered his bedroom as a sick chamber, but to reach it, one had to go through Margaret's room, and Ken declined. Molly put a pillow on an armchair in such a way that he could stick his feet out straight.

"Maybe you could go to the hospital," Margaret said hopefully. "With a cough like that . . ."

"I'm not going to the hospital!" Ken thundered.

"But Mother and I have to start packing to get ready to move into the new house," Helen said. "We're going to be awfully busy . . ."

"You go ahead," Molly said. "I'll take care of Daddy."

For two days Molly kept a precise chart of Ken's temperature, which varied from normal to a hundred and one and back again, and gave him his medicines on the very minute the doctor had prescribed. She brought him books from the library, astonishing him by selecting volumes which really interested him.

"How did you know I'd like this?" he asked her, holding up a new novel, a newspaper review of which he had recently torn out and placed in his wallet.

Molly looked pleased. "I just guessed," she said.

On the third day of her ministrations Molly herself came down with a sore throat, and was confined to her cot upstairs. Margaret and

Helen, who were busily wrapping each of seemingly numberless teacups in paper and packing them in barrels of excelsior, looked harried. "I don't know what we are going to do!" Margaret said. "It isn't *sanitary* to have *two* sick people here. Really, Ken, it's silly not to go to the hospital."

"I can get up now," Ken said. "I'll take my turn as nurse."

Ken was sitting on the foot of Molly's cot reading to her later that morning when Helen came in. "You've got a letter, Molly," she said, and handed her a square cream-colored envelope.

Molly took it and gravely opened it. Helen stood watching her.

"Come on, Helen," Ken said. "I'll bring in some more barrels for you now if you want."

On the stairway Helen said, "That was a letter from John Hunter that Molly got."

"Oh?"

"Do you think she should be getting letters from boys at her age?"

"Why not?"

"Mother doesn't think it's right."

"Sometimes," Ken said, "I would like to crumple your mother up into a small ball and pack her in one of her teacups."

"Ken! Keep your voice down! This is a small house!"

At that moment Margaret came out of the kitchen, looking tired, with pieces of excelsior stuck in her gray hair. Her lips were pursed tightly. Ken went to the cellar, where the barrels for the china had been stored, and brought one up. As he approached the dining room with it, he heard Margaret say, "I'd talk to her anyway, dear. You can't take chances with things like that."

"Talk to who?" Ken thundered, and dropped the barrel with a bang.

Margaret put her hand up to her hair.

"Mother was talking to me, dear," Helen said.

"Were you talking about Molly's letter?"

"It was a private conversation," Helen said.

"Private or not, I'm telling you here and now not to mention it to the child!"

Helen put on her virtuous look, which meant that she tilted her chin up and half closed her eyes. "Ken, don't be rude to Mother!" she said.

"I'm not being rude! I'm just setting a rule concerning the upbringing of my daughter!"

"She's my daughter too," Helen said.

"Of course. And please make decisions about her with your husband!"

Margaret bent over and took a teacup from the table where they were stacked. "I'm just thinking of the child's own good," she said.

"I'm sorry, Mother," Ken replied, "but that's up to us."

"Boys and girls that age get into trouble all the time," Margaret continued. "Just read the paper."

"That has nothing to do with this!"

"Well, I didn't mean to butt in. Bruce always left the upbringing of my daughter to me."

"Families do things differently," Ken said, regaining his patience. "Now, if you don't mind I'm going to take a glass of milk up to Molly, and then I'm going to take a nap."

With the milk in hand, he started to walk through the living room, and it was then he got his idea. In her room he found Molly reading a book. The letter was not in sight, and he was careful not to mention it. She smiled at him, but also said nothing about her mail.

"Honey, do you feel well enough for a plane ride?" he asked.

"Sure! Where we going?"

"I thought it might be a good idea to go down to Florida and bake these colds out. Just you and I."

Her eyes widened with wonder. "That would be *marvelous*."

"I haven't talked it over with your mother yet, but we'll see." He went downstairs, and going through the living room, decided that the proper stage setting for the conversation he was planning would help. Briskly he unfolded the sofa bed. After taking his pants off, he hung them quite artistically, he thought, from a doorknob. His shirt he left over the back of a reproduction of a Chippendale chair, and he put his shoes and socks on a window sill where some of Margaret's best teacups had reposed to be admired by passers-by. Stretching out in his underclothes, he pulled a blanket up to his waist, and surveyed the disarray with pleasure. "Helen," he called. "Could I talk to you a minute?"

"Can't you come in here?" Helen asked.

Wrapping a blanket around him like a toga, but leaving large portions of hairy leg exposed, Ken went to the dining room, where he appeared like an apparition, Margaret told her friends afterward; really, it was hard to say what that man *did* look like.

"This cold seems to have jumped up in me again," he said, hawking elaborately. Picking up a cup, he added, "Is it all right to spit in this?"

"No!" both women said in horror.

"Where do you want me to spit?"

"I'll get you some Kleenex and a paper bag," Helen said. "Are you really sick?"

"Feel pretty weak. I'll be in the living room lying down."

When Helen returned with the paper bag and the Kleenex, he was rolled up in the blanket on the sofa bed with his big, naked feet sticking out grotesquely. She gave him her burden, and he spat explosively.

"I may have to stay in bed here some time," he began. "A couple of weeks."

"I'm sorry you're not feeling well," Helen said, and her eyes traveled around the disordered room.

"Maybe I ought to go to Florida," Ken continued. "Molly's cold seems worse too—it would do us both good to bake out in the sun."

"I can't leave now! Mother needs me to help with the moving!"

"I know she does," Ken said sympathetically. "Why don't you stay here and get her straightened out? You can join Molly and me later."

"Well . . ."

"This is no place for us to be sick."

"No. But who'll take care of you?"

"We'll take care of each other, and the sun will cure us in no time."

Helen's eyes came to rest on the shoes on the window sill. "If you're sure you're well enough, that would be fine."

"We'll leave tonight," Ken said.

When they took off from the airport six hours later, Molly, who had never before flown, held tight to his hand. The engines thundered and vibrated as the heavy plane strained upward. Beneath them the multicolored lights of Buffalo stretched like a sea of jewels, beautiful in the distance. "This is fun," Molly said.

11

It was a blustery October afternoon in 1953 when the schooner *Mary Anne* put into the harbor at Pine Island to deliver the mail. On the end of the rickety wharf in front of the Island Inn, John Hunter, a strong, dark-haired boy waited. Dressed in frayed skiing pants which Sylvia had made for him out of a pair she had had as a girl, and a heavy Navy raincoat Bart had had in the war, John stood bracing himself against the wind as the old vessel battered her way up the bay. When Herb Andrews, her captain, brought her alongside the wharf, John leaned far out over the water and accepted the limp mailbag Claude, Herb's brother, held out to him. "Hi there, Johnny!" Herb called. "What happened to Hasper?"

"I told him I'd get the mail."

"You must have a girl! Or are you expecting something from the catalogue?"

John grinned. "The catalogue!" he called, and as the schooner spun on her heel and headed out to sea, he ran with the mailbag up the hill.

Snow already covered the island, and the trees gnashed their bare branches together in the wind. John went to the small room over the garage which served as his father's office. Bart was sitting there reading, a pale man now dressed in a worn lieutenant-commander's uniform. He had taken to wearing his old uniforms during the winter and fall because, as he said, there was no one on the island to give a damn, and it was a shame to let warm clothing go to waste. The ribbons over his left breast showed he had served in the North Atlantic, the European theater, and the South Pacific. He had three battle stars and the Navy Cross. The two and a half gold stripes on his sleeves were worn to the color of silver, and as was usually true, he was a little drunk. Starting promptly at noon, Bart began to drink from a bottle of California port he kept in the icebox. At five the cocktail hour started, and he drank Martinis until seven. The highballs began at eight-thirty and lasted until one in the morning, when Bart was able to go to sleep. He wasn't a truly vicious alcoholic, as he analyzed himself aloud to Sylvia quite often. Only rarely was he stumbling, or thick-speeched or abusive. Usually he spaced his drinks pretty well, and was able to maintain an edge of saintly beatitude. Now there was a serene smile on his face when his son arrived with the mail. "Right on time, eh, Johnny?" he said, and from a hook on the wall took a key, which, after considerable fumbling, he inserted in the padlock at the neck of the mailbag. Lifting the bag higher than necessary, he spilled the mail on the floor.

There were a week's copies of the *Wall Street Journal* and three appeals from charities for Bart, as well as a dozen bills, which he put aside for Sylvia to handle. There was an envelope addressed to Todd Hasper in the almost illegible, spidery scrawl of his ninety-year-old mother, who lived in Harvesport, and who wrote him once a week, winter and summer, despite the fact she never got an answer. There was an advertisement from a shop called "My Lady's Hat" for Sylvia, and in the midst of all this were two light-blue envelopes from Palm River, Florida, one addressed to John in a large, still-childish scrawl, and the other expertly typed to Bart.

Bart handed John his letter without comment, and the boy took it to his room. Bart was glad to be alone—for many months now, he had been developing a sense of annoyance when anyone was in the room with him. He opened his letter from Ken with curiosity.

DEAR BART,

While down here in Palm River, Florida, for a vacation, I ran into a good investment opportunity: a small motel on the beach. These establishments are apparently very profitable and offer certain tax advantages to the investor, but the problem is to find responsible couples to operate them. The thought occurred to me that you and Sylvia might be interested in entering into the venture with me as partners. I'll put up the money if you'll supply the administrative ability and professional skills necessary for running such a place. The usual arrangement is for the manager and his wife to be supplied an apartment and a suitable salary or percentage of profits. Helen and I have acquired a house nearby which I hope to get down to for vacations, but for the most part, the entire responsibility would be yours. I enclose a photograph of the establishment, and I can't tell you how grateful I would be if this appealed to you. I'm sure that we could reach agreement on details if you cared to come down and talk it over. While in New York a few weeks ago, I ordered a car which is supposed to arrive from Italy soon, and I would count it as another great favor if you drove it down with your family. Otherwise I shall have to have it shipped, and that takes ages.

Perhaps this is presumptuous of me, but I thought it worth a try.

Sincerely,

KEN

Bart read this with a thin smile on his lips. Holding the letter in his hand, he went to the bedroom, where Sylvia was making a dress on an old-fashioned foot-treadle sewing machine. She looked up sharply when he came in, and brushed her hair back from her forehead. "What have you got there?" she asked.

He put it on the pink cotton material before her and said nothing.

She read it slowly, her face grave. Then she handed it back to him. "What do you think of it?" she asked.

Bart smiled. "Sylvia, there is an old joke with the tag line, 'I may be crazy, but I'm not stupid.' I think that applies to me."

Her face showed no sign of emotion, except that her eyes seemed to widen a little. "No one said you were crazy, Bart."

"I know about you and Ken," he said quietly.

She bowed her head.

"You've had another admirer for a long time," Bart continued, his voice dry and ironic. "He knows more about you than you think."

"Who?"

"Our old friend."

"What old friend? Don't play cat and mouse with me, Bart!"

"Todd Hasper. Apparently you and Ken had difficulty sleeping last summer, and Hasper walks at night too."

There was a brief silence. "What a rotten way for you to find out," she said finally.

"Oh, I don't know. It kind of brought Todd and me together."

"Stop it, Bart! Don't try to make this funny!"

His face was pale, and the mocking smile went. "I wouldn't for anything," he said. "It seems that Todd has been a sort of distant admirer of yours, ever since you were a girl."

She jerked her head up. "What do you mean?"

"Todd isn't the most coherent man, but he said something about undressing in front of windows, and all sorts of rot. Evidently he's made a lifetime study of you. He wasn't a Peeping Tom, really, to hear him tell it. Just a scientist, a bird watcher, perhaps. And he used to have a certain admiration for you."

Sylvia closed her eyes. "I have no defense," she said.

"That surprises me."

"Except one."
"Ah."
"I've grown up, Bart. I've changed."
"You're suggesting that we forget the past?"
"No. That we face the present."
"How?"
"I'm in love with Ken."
"Very touching," he said.
"I can't live here on the island with you and the children."
"You want a divorce?"
"Yes. And I don't want to hurt you."
He was standing very erect, an officer at attention, almost. "I appreciate your concern," he said.
"You know the truth about me, and I don't deny it. Don't deny the truth about yourself."
"And that is?"
"You ought to get off this island, Bart! It's no good here in the winter, for you or for any of us."
"But you are leaving and you want to take the children?"
"Yes."
"I could make it dirty in the courts. I'm the aggrieved party, the innocent one." Bart twisted his lips into a parody of a smile.
"I know."
"I think Todd would like to appear as a witness. He's been brooding about this for a long time, and it seems to do him good to talk about it."
Sylvia put her hand over her eyes. "That would be fine for the children," she said.
"You're the guilty one."
"If it comes to that, I could prove you're an alcoholic," she said in the low tones of despair. "Anyway, you don't really want to keep the children here on the island yourself."
"It would prove a point."
"Yes. It would prove a point, but you're not that bad."
"No," he said. "Thank you for recognizing that."
"Why don't you come to Florida with us?" she said miserably. "I don't want to leave you here alone."
"Really," he said, assuming an air of detached amusement. "I've lost money, dear, but I'm not ready to be kept by Ken Jorgenson's mistress. Or will it be his wife?"

"I don't know."

"I imagine you'll have a fight with that woman, Helen. She's not as reasonable as I."

"Perhaps."

"I may be crazy, but I'm still perceptive, dear. She's got a weapon. Your old Beast won't like losing his daughter."

"No."

"I don't think he'll ever marry you."

"Perhaps not."

"What I'm trying to say is," Bart said, slumping suddenly, as though someone had barked "*At ease!*" "I'm willing to let bygones be bygones if you care not to reply to this letter."

"No."

"I was afraid of that," Bart said, his face looking tortured. "Most women don't want to be forgiven."

"It has nothing to do with that."

"I'll give you Carla," he said, his voice flat. "I can't take care of her."

"And Johnny?"

"I would like to keep my son." The tone was final, and not without dignity.

"There's not even a school for him!"

"He's old enough for boarding school. I'll let your friend pay for that."

"How about his summers? You're not a fit father, Bart! Any court would recognize that!"

"And what kind of a mother are you? Would they want him brought up by Jorgenson's mistress?"

Sylvia closed her eyes again.

"I'll make you a deal," Bart said. "Take Carla, leave me Johnny, and I'll spread no dirty linen in court."

Sylvia shook her head silently. "I can't leave you Johnny."

"Why not?"

"You'd kill him. Remember . . ."

"Yes. I was drunk. But I'll tell you this. I'll send him to boarding school and summer camp. He'll be here hardly ever."

"Then why do you want him?"

"He'll still be my son."

"Pride," she said.

"If you wish to call it that. But in all truth, Sylvia, he's better away from both of us. Boarding school is best."

"That's true," Sylvia said hopelessly. "Oh, God, I guess that's true."

"For Carla there's no choice—she's too young," Bart continued soberly. "So you can take her. But John is mine, and I want him to stay mine."

"Can he visit me?"

"What is gone is best forgotten."

"I don't believe that."

"I do. You're going to do this my way."

"Let me see him sometimes! It's ridiculous to forbid that!"

"No," he said. "You'd try to get him back. I don't want you even to speak to him about this without my being there. We'll break the news to him together."

Putting her head on her arms, she began to sob. He stood looking down at her, and once he started to touch her gently on the back, but instead he did an abrupt about-face, his face drawn hard, and strode from the room.

12

"Dear John," Molly wrote. "I am in Florida. We have a funny house colored green. The swimming is great, but the surf is much bigger than on the island. They have hurricanes sometimes, but none yet. Mother has been in Buffalo, but she's coming tomorrow. I can't wait to see her face when I show her the Toad Fish I caught in the river. Daddy pickled it for me in a bottle of alcohol and it's *so ugly!*"

There were four pages of observations of this kind, and the letter was signed, "Sincerely, Molly."

"Johnny's getting love letters!" Carla said.

John blushed. "It's nothing like that," he replied indignantly. That night he wrote Molly the latest news about a seal that had been seen off the island.

It was on a cold day that Barton Hunter, wearing a uniform Sylvia had pressed for him, came into John's room over the garage on Pine

Island at four-thirty in the afternoon. He found his son lying on the bed reading *Tarzan and the Moon Maiden.*

"John, could you come into our room, please?" Bart said in his perfectly enunciated tenor voice. "Your mother and I have something important to discuss with you."

"Sure, Dad," John said. He put the Tarzan book under his pillow, where Carla would not be apt to find it, and followed his father down the hall. In the corner of his parents' room he found Sylvia sitting in a small armchair. She was wearing a pale-blue dress she had recently made. As John entered, she took a cigarette from a case in her purse and put it in her mouth. When she struck a match it made a surprisingly sharp rasping sound. "We have something important to talk over with you, Son," she said, and her eyes seemed to be pleading.

"What?" he asked.

Bart sat down on the nearest of the twin beds, both of which were covered with white lace spreads he had inherited from his mother. "It's not very good news, Son," he said.

"What is it?" John asked. His mother's perfume pervaded the room, lilac, and the scent of talcum powder. On Sylvia's mirrored dressing table was a glass vase containing three red maple leaves.

"Your mother and I are going to get a divorce," Barton said.

Sylvia struck another match and relit her cigarette. Except for the scraping sound, there was complete silence.

"A divorce," Barton repeated, thinking from John's reticence that the boy did not understand.

"Why?" John asked. He stood erect near the door and his voice was steady.

For a moment a stricken look flickered on Barton's face, but then his voice acquired a curious tone of falseness. "People marry because they fall in love," he said. "Sometimes they stop loving each other, and then it is better for them to get unmarried. That is called a divorce."

"You'll understand when you are older," Sylvia said, her voice sounding strained.

"Yes," Barton said. Outside the window Hasper's dog started to bark.

"When?" John asked.

"When you get older," Barton repeated.

"No. When are you going to get the divorce?"

"Your mother is leaving this afternoon."

"This won't affect you much, John dear," Sylvia said. "You'll be going to boarding school soon. We've made arrangements with a very good one."

John said nothing.

"Your mother is going to take Carla with her," Barton said. "I am hoping that you will stay with me when you're not at school or camp."

John made a sound then, a sudden exhalation of breath, and turned toward his mother. She gave a forced smile. "Someone has to stay and keep your father company," she said.

"You're taking Carla?"

"Yes."

The sudden dizzying thought that his mother had simply chosen the child she liked best swept over John, leaving him speechless.

"You mustn't take it hard," Bart said nervously. "You and I will get on just fine together."

"And you can visit me someday," Sylvia added.

"No," John said, the word barely audible.

"What, dear?"

"Never!" John said, his throat so tight he could barely get the word out.

"Johnny!" Sylvia said, getting up from her chair. "Don't be like that, please!" She put her arm around him, her bosom soft against his cheek. The scent of her perfume was overwhelming. Against his will he clung to her a moment, but then he pulled away. "There's no reason to be sad," she said. "When you're older, we'll see a lot of each other."

John made no sound, but he was crying, and he made a convulsive effort to stop, inhaling sharply, almost as though to suck the tears back.

"We'll have a good time together, you and I," Barton ventured timidly.

John stood mutely looking from one of his parents to the other. Then he whirled and ran down the hall to his room. He heard his mother scream, but kept running and locked his door.

In time his tears stopped. There was no moisture in his eyes, and even his mouth and throat were dry. The sweet smell of his mother's perfume seemed to follow him into his room and to permeate everything there, like the smell of funeral flowers.

Suddenly he heard his mother's footsteps and there was a knock on his door. He said nothing. "Johnny," she said, "let me in."

Clenching his fists, he lay in silence.

"Please!" Sylvia said.

A door slammed violently and there was the sound of Bart's footsteps. "God damn it, leave him alone!"

Outside the window the sound of the surf pounding the cliffs was low and ominous. John turned on his back and lay staring at the ceiling. He was careful to make no sound. Let her think I'm dead, he thought. Let her think I'm dead. In the white plaster there was a long crack with many branches, like the map of a river, a river that would be fun to explore. Tarzan and the moon maiden might explore a river like that in a dugout canoe, and John might go with them, shooting the rapids with the black heads of the crocodiles bobbing in the white water, and wildcats screeching ashore.

"Hold on, John!" Tarzan would say.

"Let's go!" the moon maiden would shout, sounding and looking like Molly. "We're off to the mountains of the moon!"

Later John was awakened by the sound of an automobile door slamming, and there was the grinding of gears as the old Ford started. John was aware that his mother was leaving for the wharf, and the boat. There was the thought that this might not be true, that there would be another knock on his door, and she would be there in her blue dress, with the smell of perfume, but that did not happen. He thought of pursuing her, of running wildly after the car, but his pride stopped him. He lay rigid in bed and finally slept.

Later he awakened with a start. The room was pitch black, and someone was pounding on his door. There was a moment of ringing silence, and then his father said, "John! Let me in!"

John lay motionless, breathing hard, but did not answer.

"Please!" his father said.

Still John did not answer.

"John!" Barton said with pleading in his voice. "Are you all right?"

"Yes," John said.

"I want to talk to you, Son. Let me in!"

"No."

"Why not?" There was desperation, not comfort, in Barton's voice.

"Because I want to be by myself," John said in a monotone.

"All right!" his father said with anger, and there was the sound of his footsteps going down the stairs.

John remained motionless in his bed in the darkness. The wind was rising outside, sighing through the naked branches of the trees, and the surf pounded.

At three in the morning there was another knock on John's door, followed by a guttural noise, almost an animal sound, the nature of which made John sit bolt upright in bed, trembling. Silence, and then the noise came again, half sob, half whisper, a wounded sound. John jumped to open the door, and his father, still in uniform, half fell into the room, catching himself on the bed, turning and smiling slowly in the dim light from the hall. Barton was crying. The smell of his whisky and sickness filled the room. John's breath stopped. He said nothing.

"You and I," Barton gasped, holding himself erect with sudden dignity.

"Yes."

"We're self . . ."

There was a pause during which Barton appeared to be meditating deeply. "We're self . . ." he repeated, "we're self-sufficient."

"Yes," John said.

His father turned and stretched out on his back on the bed. "Don't need a woman," he said.

"No," John replied.

"No more arguments," Barton continued. "No fights. No more being a goddamn cuckold. Do you know what that is?" Barton put his fingers up to his head like a devil's horns.

"No," John said.

"You shouldn't know. Not at your age."

John said nothing.

His father sighed. "Things happen to people, Johnny," he said. "Even nice people. Someday you'll find out."

John did not answer.

"Do you hear me?"

"Yes."

"Sylvia used to be a nice woman. I lost the money—all the goddamn money. Winner takes all, losers weepers."

"I guess so," John said.

"You can't keep a woman like that without money. Poverty is against her nature. She goes to the highest bidder."

No reply came from John.

"Always plenty of takers for a woman like that," Barton said. "Odd man out."

"Out," John repeated without knowing what he was saying.

"Shirt sleeves to shirt sleeves in three generations," Bart said. "That's me. You're lucky. You can start all over again."

"Yes."

"Start up the ladder, boy. From the bottom up, not the top down. No, sir. Do you understand?"

"Yes," John repeated.

"Good. But that's not the point. The main point is . . ."

Barton struggled to sit up on the bed. "The point is," he said again, "the point is that you and I don't have to worry. No worries. That's absolutely final." Swinging his legs over the side of the bed, he tried to stand up, but sank back again. "Give me a hand, will you, Son?" he asked.

John gave him a hand. He gripped his father's arm and found it shockingly thin and weak. Barton struggled to his feet, slack-boned, leaning on his son's shoulder, and said, "Thanks, Son. Mustn't think I'm a drunk, understand. Unusual circumstances tonight. Very unusual circumstances. Just give me a steer down the hall, and I'll be all right."

Teetering down the hall with his father leaning upon him, John was astonished at his own strength. Always before he had imagined his father to be big, but now he found he could almost carry him like a baby. Upon reaching his room, Barton staggered toward his bed and, without undressing, collapsed. His face lying on the white lace counterpane was gray with the bones showing clearly through it, almost in the outline of a skull. His cheeks were still wet with tears. John covered him with a blanket, then put out the light and returned quietly to his own room.

An hour later he heard his father get up and stumble to the office down the hall where he kept his liquor, but John didn't try to help him.

Just before dawn John awoke, shivering violently. The room was very cold, and there was no sound but the steady sighing of the wind, the distant surf, and the whimper of Hasper's dog. He went to Bart's room and saw his father lying motionless and uncovered, with both arms flung back, and his mouth open. A quart bottle of whisky lay beside him, leaving the sheet stained where it had spilled. Stricken with the fear that his father was dead, John stood stock-still, listening, hoping desperately to catch the sound of his breath, but there was nothing that could be heard above the sound of the wind and the dog. "Dad!" he said, flinging himself in panic upon Bart. "Dad! Wake up!"

Bart remained inert, but he groaned, and grateful for even that sign of life, John gave up trying to arouse him. After covering his father with a quilt, he stood at the foot of his mother's empty bed, shivering. Of course, he thought, the heater must have gone out, that is why it is so cold. Finding some matches on the bedside table, he tried to light the stove again, but the wick wouldn't catch. Discovering that the tank was empty, John went outside, pushing the door open against the wind, and got a five-gallon tin of kerosene from the bottom section of the garage. When he came back to his father's room, he found Bart lying with his position unchanged. John stared hard at his chest, and was relieved to see that he was breathing. After getting the stove going, he went back to his room and fell asleep.

It was almost noon when John awoke, but the light in the room was dim, and sleet was rattling against the windowpanes. Running to his father's room, he saw that Bart had turned over in the night, and was now lying on his stomach with his face in the pillow, so that there was no way to tell if he was alive.

"Dad!" he called. "Dad! It's time to wake up!"

Bart didn't stir. John seized his shoulders and turned him over. Bart opened his eyes, and his head lolled back weakly. "Let alone," he said thickly, and groped for the bottle. Finding it was empty, he produced a full one from beneath the covers.

John went to the kitchen, where he cooked himself toast and bacon, and drank a glass of milk. He cleaned up after himself carefully before returning to his room, where he lay on his bed all day reading his Tarzan books. Every hour or so he checked on his father, but Bart had apparently fallen into a coma.

Shortly after six o'clock John heard his father groan. Running to his room, he saw that Bart had vomited, and that his eyelids were fluttering oddly. In panic John rushed outside to get Todd Hasper. It was bitter cold, and he clutched the collar of his coat around his neck as he ran.

The sleet had left a brittle crust over the snow, which cracked like glass as John ran over it. Smoke was coming from the chimney of

Hasper's cottage, he was glad to see—he had had a dread that on this day of nightmares even Hasper would be dead or missing. When he pounded on the door there was no answer. He opened it, and suddenly the dog was upon him, knocking him to the ground. Todd Hasper, dressed only in long woolen underwear, appeared simultaneously and dragged the dog back. John stood up, trembling, with his collar and coat badly ripped. "Dad's sick," he said.

"Ha!" Hasper retorted. "You hurt?" He chained the dog to a ring in the wall at the far side of the room.

"No, but hurry!"

"He'll still be there," Hasper said, drawing on his trousers. "He ain't going no place."

On the way to the garage Hasper refused to run, and they trudged slowly over the splitting ice crust. The odor in Bart's room was sickening. Hasper leaned over Bart and turned him on his back. Bart opened his eyes, which looked yellow, and made an effort to smile. "Sick," he said, his voice barely audible.

"We'll get the Coast Guard and send him to the hospital," Hasper said to John in matter-of-fact tones. "You can stay with me."

"No," Bart whispered. "Johnny."

John bent over, with his face only a few inches from his father's. "Go to your mother, address and money in my office."

"I want to help you!"

"Hospital. Go to Mother. Come back later, when I'm better."

With Hasper, John drove in the old Ford to the south end of the island. Balancing themselves carefully on the icy ground, they carried two five-gallon cans of kerosene to a finger of rock extending into the bay nearest the mainland. They wet down a space about fifty feet square with the kerosene, and standing back, Todd casually lit a ball of paper with a match and tossed it into the center of the area. There was a flash, and for about five minutes the flames burned brightly. When they went out, Todd stared into the darkness toward the mainland where only a few dim lights could be seen. Without comment, he went back to the car and got more kerosene. They had to repeat the performance twice before a signal light blinked on Harvesport Point. "They see us," Hasper said, and they returned to the garage.

Three hours later a Coast Guard picket boat arrived, and two cheerful young bluejackets, their faces full of concern, put Bart on a stretcher and loaded him aboard. John accompanied his father to the doors of the hospital. Bart was able to smile when he left and to say, "Don't worry about me—Navy will take care."

From Harvesport John telephoned his mother, reaching her soon after she arrived at the Seaside Motel in Palm River. In rigidly calm, almost formal tones, he told her what had happened. "Oh, Johnny!" she said. "I'll come get you!"

"I can come alone!"

"Are you sure?"

"Of course," he said, and his high boy's voice was curiously stern.

"Johnny, are you all right?" she asked hoarsely, and he was filled with the sudden horror that he was going to cry there over the telephone, that he was going to sound as though he were crawling, coming on his belly to his mother who had abandoned him, and he said, "Yes, I'm all right! I'm just coming to you to get money!"

When John got off the plane at Palm River twelve hours later, Sylvia ran to embrace him, but he stood stiffly as a soldier at attention, and he did not kiss her back. "Oh Johnny!" she said, stroking his cheek with her hand. "Don't be like that!"

A muscle under the skin of his cheek flickered. "I'm glad to see you, Mother," he said, his voice tightly controlled. "I'm sorry that I have to bother you like this."

Wearily she turned, and gripping his hand tightly, led him to her car, a new Ford Ken had had waiting at the motel for her. When they got in it, she put both hands around John's neck and tried to pull his face down on her shoulder, but he reared back violently with his eyes blazing and said, "No!"

"You don't have to hate me," she said in a soft voice. "That doesn't do any good."

"I want to go to boarding school," he said, his fists clenched.

"You can if you want. But there's a good school here I'd like you to attend for a while first."

"Have it your way!" he said, and bending over, averted his face because the tears were beginning to come. He crouched there in the car covering his face with his hands, but when she tried to comfort him he turned on her in agony and said, "Leave me alone! All I want is to be left alone!"

A stout woman leading a child by the hand peered into the car curiously as she passed. Sylvia started the engine and drove slowly to the Seaside Motel, a small barrackslike building of white stucco on the beach. She parked by the manager's apartment and went in. Carrying his suitcase, John followed her. Carla was helping a colored maid to fold newly ironed sheets. When she saw John she ran toward him with her chubby arms out, but he turned away from her, too, this girl whom his mother had preferred to him. "Nice to see you, Carla," he said, his voice bitter. "How have you been?"

"All right," she said, letting her arms fall to her sides. "What's the matter, Johnny? Are you mad at me?"

"No!" he said. "Nothing's the matter! Nothing, nothing, nothing!" Tears were starting to come again. Leaving his suitcase in the middle of the room, he bolted out the door.

The dry sand near the dunes was soft, and the wind sent it up like puffs of smoke from his feet. Possessed, he ran as fast as he could, zigzagging in crazy pursuit of sea gulls, waving his arms wildly in vain attempts to catch them and perhaps rend them as they wheeled past his shoulders. Exhausted, he finally sank down on a log and sat there with his breath rasping out in hot gasps. The wind from the sea was strong, and the breakers curled in endless rows flashing in the sun. He rested for ten minutes and then for the first time stood up and looked around. The Seaside Motel stood alone on the dunes beyond the city boundaries of Palm River. To the south of it, several houses had recently been built a thousand yards up the beach, and beyond them an almost unbroken row of cottages began. In the other direction, the beach and dunes were deserted, all the way to the inlet, which was now barely visible in a blaze of reflected sun. John put his hand to his eyes and it was then he saw a girl walking down the beach toward him, barefoot at the very edge of the sea, a slender girl in blue dungarees rolled up to the knees and a fresh white shirt that fluttered in the wind. She was leaning forward with her eyes cast down, and she was walking slowly, looking forlorn against the background of the pounding surf. Although they did not recognize each other, there was a feeling inherent in the wind on that barren beach which drew them together as though they had met on a desert, and she changed her direction toward him as he started walking to her. When John got about a hundred feet from her, he realized she was Molly, and he stopped, suddenly confused.

"Hello, Molly," he said.

She was hurt because he did not seem more glad to see her, and the memory of the letters they had exchanged suddenly embarrassed her; perhaps he thought she had been trying to write him love letters, or something. "Hello," she said in guarded tones. "I heard you were coming."

"Where do you live?" he asked.

She gestured down the beach toward one of the houses which had just been built, but she kept her eyes cast downward. The wind was whipping her long dark hair, and she brushed it back impatiently. Her face was tan, and so were her arms, her long, coltish legs, and her feet. Suddenly she bent over, darted a hand into the sand, and picked up a dark brown object, shiny as a chestnut, but flatter and larger.

"What's that?" John asked.

"A sea heart," she said, turning it over in her hand. "I am collecting them."

"May I see it?"

She handed it to him and he inspected it with interest. It was as smooth as though it had been varnished, and was indeed shaped roughly like a heart.

"Do they grow in the sea?" he asked.

"No," she said seriously. "Daddy says they grow in Africa or South America or some place and float over." The wind blew a strand of dark hair across her lips, and she brushed it away.

He returned the sea heart to her and she polished it on the rolled-up sleeve of her shirt. "I collect all kinds of things on the beach," she said, her voice sounding almost academic. "Coquina shells make good necklaces—they come in every shade of every color. There are even striped ones. Look!"

She darted her hand into the sand again, and came up with a pale-pink shell shaped like a fan. "I don't know what this one is yet, but I can look it up in a book."

"It's a nice one," John said. "I'd like to learn about shells."

"There are more than shells to find," she said. "There are sea beans, some brown, some gray. There are things that fall overboard from ships. Daddy heard of somebody once who found a bottle with a message in it."

"It would be fun to find a bottle with a message," John said enthusiastically.

"But you have to watch out," Molly continued. "My mother says you have to be terribly careful on the beach."

"Why?"

"There are jellyfish and Portuguese men of war which sting. They look like little blue balloons, but they have poison in them, and long tentacles which float out all around them, and if you touch one in the water, you might drown."

"I'll stay away from them," John said.

"Then of course there's the sun," she continued, speaking faster, but still looking down. "People die from sunburn sometimes. And there's the undertow—several people are drowned on this beach every year. There are sharks and barracuda in the water, and don't go near the coral reef, because the Moray eels live there."

"What are they?" John asked in astonishment.

"Big eels with teeth," she said. "Their bite is poisonous or something. And there are sting rays with poisonous tails."

"I won't go near the reef," John said.

Suddenly Molly glanced up at him and he found himself looking directly into her startlingly light blue eyes. "They always try to scare people about the beach," she said. "Daddy says that whenever anybody new comes, the old ones try to scare him. We don't know why."

"I'm not scared," John said.

Molly smiled. "I've got to get home now," she said, and before he could reply she stepped quickly past him and started running along the very edge of the sea toward her house, with the surf reaching up and erasing her footprints behind her, so that she appeared to be skimming six inches above the earth, leaving no trace of her passage. In front of her the sandpipers scattered, and gulls wheeled around her head. John watched her out of sight. Then he glanced down and saw that she had dropped the sea heart at his feet.

13

HELEN JORGENSON, looking thinner than usual in a severe white linen dress with a low-cut back which exposed too much of her spine, clearly outlined beneath her tanned skin, walked into the drugstore in the shopping center near her house, and giving the clerk a twenty-dollar bill, asked to have it broken into quarters and dimes.

"All of it?" he asked.

"Yes," she said. "I have to make a long-distance phone call."

Going to a telephone booth, she inserted a dime from her purse, and dialed the operator. "I want to place a long-distance call to Buffalo, New York," she said, and gave the number.

It took ten minutes to get the call through, and the telephone booth was hot with the door shut. Finally she heard a buzzing, and her mother's voice said, "Hello?"

"Mother!" Helen said.

"Helen, dear, is everything all right?"

"It's about Ken. You know, Mother, you were right. He is having an affair with her. You were absolutely right!"

"I knew that from the beginning," Margaret snapped. "As soon as you told me he was having her down there, I knew it."

"Well, it's absolutely *fantastic,*" Helen said. "I couldn't believe it at first. I mean, last summer there was a lot of talk, but you know, he's never been the type."

"Does he know that you know it?"

"Not yet."

"How did you find out?"

"Well, it was *strange!* Last Sunday he told me he was going fishing. He's been doing that a lot lately, and I thought it was queer, because you know in Buffalo he never did it—he never thought of going fishing. Well, he went off with his pole and his bait and all that, the way he always does down here, and Minnie Apton saw them."

"Who's Minnie Apton?"

"You know, she's that nice woman I wrote you about, the president of the Garden Club."

"Would she act as a witness?"

"Gosh, I don't know. I never thought of that. Anyway, she and Jack—that's her husband—and their children wanted to go swimming, some place away from the crowds. There's an awfully trashy element coming in down here now, you know—sometimes it's just *disgusting* on the beach. Well, anyway, Minnie and Jack decided to go way north, about a mile from here, where they could have some privacy, and she saw Ken. He was with *her*. They were *behind the dunes,* mind you, not on the beach."

"What were they doing?"

"Oh, they were just talking."

"Oh." Margaret's disappointment was clear.

"But you know what that means. When he came home, I asked him how the fishing was, and he said he didn't have much luck. I mean, if he *weren't* having an affair with her, why would he lie to me?"

"*Of course* he's having an affair with her! But to get a divorce, you've got to catch them doing more than talking."

"He'd give me a divorce, Mother, if I asked him. I told you that."

"Now don't start that again. Your father has talked to a lawyer, and we have to be *very careful.* If it ever appeared that it was *you* who wanted the divorce, we wouldn't get half as much, not a third."

"But he never has been bad about money. All right, operator, I don't care—I've got plenty of change here."

"What's that, dear?" Margaret asked.

"The operator said the three minutes are up. Now, Mother, I think I should just tell him. I don't think he'd even deny it, and then it would be just the same for the lawyers as if we caught them."

"But you can't be *sure!*" Margaret said in exasperation. "I'm telling you, dear, the lawyer said men act differently in circumstances like these than at any other time. He *might* deny it, and if you told him you knew, you would be giving him warning, and they'd be *much harder* to catch. They might even break off altogether for a long time."

"I suppose that's true," Helen said.

"Does he still want to—you know—with you?"

"No!" Helen said. "He hasn't for ages."

"Well, don't refuse him. The lawyer says you have to be willing to be his wife, to avoid a nasty countersuit."

"Mother! You didn't talk about *that!*" Helen sounded aghast.

"Why, dear, that's what lawyers are for. They're like doctors."

"I'd be so embarrassed if I met him!"

"You have nothing to be embarrassed about. You are the one who is innocent."

"I know. But even talking about it!"

"Lawyers hear that sort of thing often. And he said that in Florida that might be grounds for divorce. I mean Ken might be able to get one from you, for refusing for a long time, if it all came out in the courts, and you might not be able to get *anything* from him. It could be very dirty. And if Molly said she wanted to stay with him, I mean a girl that age, why they even might let her!"

There was a brief but pregnant silence.

"I can see we have to be careful," Helen said.

"But you mustn't refuse him any more! I know it sounds terrible, but it's *important!*"

"Mother!"

"Well, there's no way around it. It's the law. If you're a man's wife . . ."

"Mother! We don't have to talk about it, anyway. He never asks me any more."

"You could try . . ."

"Mother!"

"Well, a great deal is at stake here, dear. If you could prove that you'd been *willing* . . . But, of course, if we could *catch* them and had a *witness,* none of that would have to come up. He could bring countersuit, but the lawyer says he wouldn't have a chance. We've got to *catch* them."

"How?"

"Now listen, dear. Your father and I have been talking. How would you like us to come down and help you out?"

"But Daddy's job!"

"He's almost ready to retire anyway, and he has a month's vacation due. We'd be willing if you want us."

"Of course, I'd love it!" Helen said.

"We could help you. This can be a nasty business: hiring detectives and all that. You need our help."

"Yes," Helen said. "Mother, you're a wonder!"

"We'll start driving down Saturday," Margaret said. "By the way, how's Molly?"

"She's still seeing that boy all the time. That's another *fantastic* part of this. Ken seems to think I'm *wicked* when I try to warn her, or keep her home."

"It's fantastic, all right," Margaret replied. "But if we play our cards right, we won't have to worry. See you Wednesday, about noon. Will he *mind* our coming?"

"Oh, I can handle him," Helen said.

They said goodbye with great affection, and Margaret hung up. It took quite a long while to feed the machine enough quarters and dimes.

14

Palm River, Florida, was a paradise for bicycle riders. A bankrupt real-estate development called Garden Heights, which had been started in 1927, stretched through the palmetto jungles, the concrete roads crumbling and split by weeds, but still passable. There were almost eight miles of roads crisscrossing each other in the wilderness with lamp posts and fire hydrants regularly spaced, but few houses, no traffic and no people. The reason was that the Garden Heights Development Corporation had gone broke in 1929, and had traveled through so many bankruptcy courts, inheritance squabbles, attachments, and other legal entanglements that it was cheaper for later-day real-estate speculators to clear the almost limitless palmetto scrub land with bulldozers and start afresh than to bring to realization the tarnished dreams of their predecessors. These old roads usually began at a fancy gate with an arch of rusting iron proudly proclaiming Hillside Avenue or Oceanview Terrace and they ran through acres of pine and palmetto waste across the flat Florida landscape, where the buzzards perched solemnly in the few tall trees and the quail whistled in the underbrush. Rattlesnakes and an occasional coral snake sunned themselves on the warm concrete, and mourning doves cooed from the crossbars of rotting telephone posts. Down these empty roads with tall, bright-blossomed weeds growing in the cracks, Molly and John at the ages of fourteen and fifteen sped on bicycles as though they were the only two people left in the world.

Some of the lamp posts had had ornate shades of milk glass, but most of these had been broken by boys with slingshots, and presented only jagged edges to the sky. In a clearing choked with high grass they came upon an old mansion built as a sample and abandoned by its owners. Too isolated, too big and too dilapidated to be reconditioned, it had been rotting for years. Feeling that eyes were upon them, they pried open a broken window, crawled in and wandered through the dusty rooms. In a bureau drawer John found an old golf ball with the white cover brittle and cracked, and they marveled at the tightly wound rubber inside, an elastic a thousand miles long, they guessed, if it could only be stretched out without being broken. On a window sill near an old-fashioned mahogany table Molly spied a lizard, a perfect alligator in miniature, only sleek and striped with green and brown, crouched to gobble flies caught in spiderwebs. In the cellar they found a tattered pool table and attempted a game, with the brightly colored balls leaving tracks on the dusty, disintegrating felt.

Tiring of this, they fished from the bridges which crossed the inland water route to Miami, in which Palm River formed a link. Negroes in faded blue shirts fished for their dinner beside them. Occasionally there was a loud blare from an air horn, three blasts in succession, and the bridges opened to allow a stately yacht from Detroit or Chicago, New York or Boston to pass. The children and the Negroes on the bridge usually waved at the people on the yachts, and the yachtsmen often waved back.

Some of the yachts tied up at the Palm River Municipal Docks, where Molly and John often went. Aboard one shiny houseboat lived a beautiful woman with her hair dyed lavender and a lavender wolfhound to match. She walked her dog along a path beside the river every evening, sometimes accompanied by a fat old man with a yachting cap and a cigar. Molly and John met them several times and accepted them as a matter of course.

Oh, there were all kinds of things to be seen at the Municipal Docks. There was a man living with his wife and two children aboard a dwarfed four-masted schooner he had built himself in Ohio and had trucked to the nearest water, in hopes of sailing around the world. He started every month on his magnificent voyage but invariably ran aground or broke down before leaving the inland waterway, and had to put back for repairs.

There was an old man with a grand piano built into his tiny motor cruiser, taking up the whole cabin, with a bunk on top of it, and storage lockers under it, but just the piano in the cabin, and no room for anything around it. This man lived on top of his piano and under it, and he anchored out in the river alone playing Beethoven sonatas late at night. He said he lived on a dollar a day sent to him by his daughter, and the fish he could catch, and that he had enough cash left over to send his grandchildren Christmas presents every year. He liked to talk to Molly and John and told them to be sure to learn to play a musical instrument, there was nothing more important in life. John delighted him by playing his piano well.

On the beach in downtown Palm River were great hotels with floor shows brought in from New York and kidney-shaped swimming pools lying jade in the sun, but John and Molly rarely saw those. They rode their bicycles in the depression-haunted jungles, and they explored the river in an old Barnegat Bay sneakbox that Ken bought to teach his daughter how to sail, because he said he thought that was a skill all children should acquire young. The *Oyster* was the boat's name, and they thought her prettier even than the big schooner, the *Fairy Queen,* aboard which John had first seen Molly. At first Ken and Sylvia were very careful about allowing the children to use the boat. They were permitted to sail only in the narrow part of the river, within sight of the boathouse, and a servant from Molly's household was posted to keep an eye on them. When they demonstrated their competence, however, the watch was relaxed, and they were allowed to go around the bend, where the river offered more room for sailing. There was, as Ken pointed out to Helen, little danger for, outside the dredged channel, Palm River was shallow, and if they capsized, all they would have to do was to hang onto the boat until she drifted to a place where they could crawl through the mud and get ashore. Even this freedom, however, did not satisfy them. There was always another bend in the river which they wanted to see around; the curiosity of explorers got into them. They had never seen a chart and were only dimly aware that such things existed. The river was as new to them as though it had never been sailed before, and as far as they were concerned, anything could exist beyond the place where they could see.

It is conceivable that the trouble might never have happened if Ken had not bought the boat, or if he had not, above the violent objections of his wife and her parents, been adamant in giving the children permission to go on an all-day exploration and picnic. Old Bruce Carter, who spent most of his days in Florida silently rubbing his car in the driveway of Ken's house, was convinced that the river was a place of great danger, full of alligators, sharks and God knew what else, including sewage and germs of all kinds, and as he told Ken, he washed his hands of the situation. Margaret, his wife, said that she might be old-fashioned, and she didn't want to be a prying mother-in-law, but in her day, fourteen-year-old girls weren't allowed to spend the day with boys in boats without chaperones. "They're old enough," she said several times. "You've got to remember that they're old enough to get in all kinds of trouble." Helen echoed her parents' sentiments. As far as she could see, Ken was subjecting Molly to a variety of perils that defied the imagination, but he was so stubborn, he had always had that mulelike streak in him, and he wouldn't pay a bit of attention to a word they said. So late in December the permission was given, and the day was set to take advantage of the New Year holiday from school.

The trouble might have been less if Ken had not had to go to Paris. That was coincidence, of course—a circumstance that could have happened at any time, but that happened then. Bernie Anderson's plans for a new development corporation were proceeding faster than he had anticipated. He had met businessmen in Paris who were willing to invest money in it as a sideline; the deal was going to be a spare-time project for everyone concerned except a small staff which was to be hired, and Bernie himself. Some of the prospective investors wanted to take advantage of the long New Year weekend to bring together a lot of busy people from New York who might be interested, and Bernie wanted Ken to fly to Paris for the meeting. There didn't seem to be any reason why he should not go, so Ken agreed. Before he left, he told Molly to be careful on the voyage, and to remember all the details so she could tell him when he got back.

The Saturday for which the children's expedition had been planned dawned clear and, for Florida, quite cold. A "norther" was blowing, but in the narrow part of the river near the boathouse its weight was not fully felt. At eight in the morning Molly and John stowed their picnic boxes under the deck, hoisted the sail, and went flying down the channel dead before the wind, with the boat rolling and tossing her boom up in perfect expression of their exhilaration. Within an hour they reached the bend around which they had never seen. As the familiar landmarks dropped astern, they observed that the river ahead of them became narrower and more crooked. The water was interlaced with small marsh islands, and swampy areas where white herons fished in the tall green grass and alligators lay looking dead in the sun. A flock of red-winged blackbirds scattered like a handful of stones before the boat. Although the wind blew harder as the day wore on, the surface of the river lay black in the confinement of the marsh, and as they rushed along, their wake stretched out astern like a path of suds. At ten in the morning they came upon a drawbridge, and exercising the right of all craft, however small, they bravely blew three blasts on a mouth horn and forced an old man to labor mightily on a huge crank to open it. He stood staring mournfully down at them as they swept majestically through, and squirted a brown stream of tobacco juice into their wake.

They had planned to turn back at noon, but at eleven-thirty they sailed into a broad estuary, across which land could be only dimly seen. "I think there are big islands over there," John said.

"We ought to start home," Molly replied.

"I'd just like to sail out enough to make sure what's on the other side."

"All right," she said.

On they went with the seas becoming larger as they drew away from the shore. The old sneakbox rolled wildly, and it took an alert eye and both hands on the tiller to prevent her from jibing. When they were about a quarter of the way across the bay, the islands ahead seemed to materialize into a headland, but it was hard to be sure. Plunging down an especially high wave, the sneakbox dug her blunt bow under, and shoveled a bucketful of water into the cockpit.

"I think we ought to go back," Molly said nervously. Her shirt was wet with spray, and she looked cold.

"Just a minute," John said. "I can almost see . . ."

They passed a channel post and noticed that a strong tide was running with the wind. It's going to be tough to beat back against this, he thought, but was stubborn and held on. Ahead of them stretched more channel posts, between some of which were sand islets cast up by the dredge which had deepened the channel, low and without vegetation. On they rushed until they could see clearly that a big point of land cut across the estuary ahead of them.

"I wonder what's on the other side of that," John said.

"I don't know," she replied, glancing worriedly at the sky. "It's getting cloudy, and I think we ought to start home."

Reluctantly he agreed. They came about, and immediately found that running before it, they had underestimated the force of the gale. On the wind, the old sneakbox lay pounding heavily. John started the sheet and left the mainsail almost empty. Spray drenched them, and in spite of all they could do, enough water slopped into the cockpit to keep Molly busy with a bucket. She glanced over her shoulder at him, and he saw that her face was pinched with fear.

"We'll be all right," he said, but as they sailed by a channel marker, he noticed that the tide was sweeping them sideways, and that they were making little progress. For perhaps an hour they tacked back and forth near the same channel marker, while the sun grew lower in the sky and the clouds grew darker. The water became roiled with mud, and in the worst puffs of wind, the surface of the waves took on a curiously tawny color. The luffing sail made an ominous thundering noise. At about four in the afternoon a gust flattened them, and they capsized, suddenly finding themselves clinging to the overturned boat with the water up to their necks. The old sneakbox floated like a low-lying raft.

"Now what do we do?" Molly asked breathlessly. With the sail in the water it seemed strangely quiet. The waves slopped against the hull, and the water was warmer than the air.

"We hang on," John said grimly. "We mustn't try to swim to shore."

"We couldn't," she said, staring around wildly. The shore looked very far away, barely visible.

"With this wind and tide we'll drift fast," he said. "Are you tired?"

"I can hang on."

"Look at that channel marker," he said. "You can see we're moving by it."

He crawled closer to her and put his arm around her thin shoulders to help her hang on.

"When it gets dark, they'll come looking for us," he said.

For about an hour they clung there, their bodies warm in the water, but their arms and shoulders chilled in the wind. "Are there alligators here?" she asked.

"They don't bite people. Only crocodiles do, and they're different."

"Sharks?"

"They don't come up rivers like this."

Finally they saw that they were drifting down on one of the sand spits cast up by the dredge. Suddenly his feet touched soft mud, barely thicker than the water.

"Maybe we can pull the boat up here and bail it out," he said.

"Let's swim in and rest first."

"No, wait till we drift in. It's still farther than it looks, and we couldn't walk in this stuff."

"Will there be alligators?" she asked.

"They don't bite people," he said.

Quietly they waited until the boat came to rest in the soft gray mud. Half swimming and half crawling, they made their way to the sand spit, pulling themselves out on their stomachs as though they themselves were alligators. The place smelled of seaweed and sewage. Above the waterline the sand was firm, and they stood up, shivering in the wind, but delighted to be on their feet. The sand spit was about thirty feet wide, a hundred feet long, and only about two feet above the water in the center. The gray sand was covered with broken white shells.

"I'm freezing," Molly said.

"We could haul the boat up to break the wind, and maybe we could make a tent from the sail."

Caught on the bottom and flooded with water, the boat would not budge, and John realized that it would be impossible to move her even if he could get footing in the mud. Quickly they removed the sails and spars and contrived a rough tent in the very center of the island. Splashing back and forth from the boat, even their heads became covered with mud, but they found their water bottle and a can of corned beef hash.

"I wish we could build a fire," she said.

"Me too." But of course everything was wet, matches included. Huddled in the shelter of their improvised tent, they ate and drank. By that time the sun was setting, and it was very cold. Molly's teeth were chattering. Only the surface of the sand was warm.

"Maybe if we dug a hollow it would be better," John said.

Immediately they set to work, scooping up the broken shells with their hands. Beneath the surface, the sand still retained the warmth of the sun. John cut his hand on a sharp shell, and sucked the blood.

"Let's get the paddle and dig with that," Molly said.

Emerging from the tent, they saw that the tide was receding, leaving the boat stuck in the mud. The paddle was nowhere in sight, but a loose floor board had drifted in, and they dug with that. In a few minutes they made a long hollow like a shallow grave. Wrapping themselves in the jib, which had partly dried, they lay down together and covered themselves with warm sand. The delivery from the cold was delicious.

"I'm sorry I turned the boat over," he said. "It was my fault."

"It's all right," she said, snuggling her thin, mud-soaked body against him drowsily. "They'll be along to pick us up soon."

"Still cold?" he asked.

"No."

In the last glimmer of daylight a variety of long-legged birds could be seen stalking the mud flats around them. The tide continued to go out, expanding their island to the very edge of the channel. John hadn't realized the tide went out so far. I wonder how high it will get when it comes in, he thought. The idea struck him that perhaps their tiny island would be awash at high tide; perhaps it had been only half tide when they arrived. But no, he thought; the sand would not be so warm if it had not been lying all day in the sun. Maybe, he thought. Why doesn't anything grow on this place? How deep could the water get here at high tide?

We could cling to the boat again, he thought. Help will be here before long. They'll miss us and go searching. Glancing down, he saw that Molly had gone to sleep, with her cheek resting peacefully against his shoulder.

On the distant shore that night the lights of cars could be seen bobbing along a road. Far down the river the red and green lights of a bridge glimmered. There was no sound but the lapping of the waves and the occasional screech of a bird. With Molly against him in their gravelike place, it was warm. He put his head down and went to sleep.

At about midnight the Coast Guard found them there. They were so exhausted that they did not awake when the searchlight swept by their tent. The first thing they knew, a sailor in rubber boots shook them and said, "Get up! Are you all right? Good God, you kids sure need a bath!"

Sylvia, Helen and Margaret were aboard the Coast Guard picket boat. Sylvia smiled with relief when she saw them, but Helen and Margaret were furious. Margaret grabbed Molly's shoulder the moment the sailor set her down on the deck and said, "What do you mean, staying out so late? What have you been doing?"

"We capsized," Molly said.

"You don't have to tell me why he took her out here," Margaret said, glaring at Sylvia. "Like mother, like son."

"Stop it," Sylvia said, aghast. "Don't talk like that to the children!"

Molly and John stared at each other dully, too exhausted to think, but not to record what they heard to be dimly remembered later.

The next day Molly did not show up in front of her house at her usual time. Instead, old Bruce appeared. His skin had not tanned even during hours of polishing his car in the Florida sun, and he had a nervous habit of scratching himself on the seat of the pants. "Come here," he said to John, in an attempt to sound friendly.

"What do you want?" John asked, immediately suspicious.

"I want to talk to you."

Diffidently John went to him. "About yesterday," Bruce said.

"What about it?"

"You can tell me," Bruce said. "We men can talk about things like that." He grimaced.

"About what?"

"What did you do, you two out on the island? You're old enough."

John said nothing.

"Her mother has to know," Bruce said.

John ran, and Bruce started after him, but the lithe boy outdistanced him with no difficulty. John returned to the motel, and with sobs bottled in his throat, burst in the front door of his mother's apartment surprising a colored woman on her knees scrubbing the tiles. "What's the matter, honey?" she asked.

"Nothing!" John said. Rushing to his room, he threw himself on his bed and sobbed as though to mourn the end of all innocence.

15

THE NEXT DAY Molly showed up on the beach in front of her house at dusk. She looked almost as she always did that year, a slender girl, quick to smile and quick to frown, but now her fists were clenched, and on her face was the deathlike look of shock.

"Hello," she said to John when he ran to meet her.

"Are you all right?" he asked.

"Yes," she said and sat down on the sand. He sank down beside her, and the ocean looked black beyond the white line of the crashing breakers which still gleamed in the last rays of the sun. "She won't let me see you any more," Molly said.

"Why not?"

Molly shrugged, a quick emphatic gesture that was to become characteristic, but she said nothing.

"I'll see you anyway," he said.

Molly was staring down with her face turned from him. "Mother says that my father and your . . ."

"What?"

"Mother," she said. "A doctor . . . I can't . . ."

There was a moment of silence during which they sat stricken by the terrible helplessness of childhood. A kind of shudder went through Molly's body. At length, without saying anything, she shrugged again. Darkness fell and a dim half moon appeared, veiled behind streaks of dark clouds. It was about a half hour afterward that they heard, faint in the wind, the voice of someone calling.

"What's that?" he asked.

"Her," she said. They sat still while the word in the wind grew louder, clearly resolving itself into *"Molly,"* Helen's voice full of anxiety and anger. John glanced at Molly and in the dim light from the moon saw she was smiling. "I've got to go," she said. "Tell her you haven't seen me." Before John could answer, Molly was on her feet, running down the beach away from the voice and her home. John got up to follow her, but she seemed to dissolve into the night, and after a few minutes he stopped and turned around. Way down the beach he saw a flashlight bobbing, and the voice borne on the wind was clear. "Molly, Molly!" Helen was calling. John walked toward Helen slowly, his arms limp at his sides, his body bent forward, stalking, unconsciously stalking, not running, for the first time in his life.

"Molly, Molly!" Helen kept calling.

When John was about fifty feet from her, she saw him outlined against the sky, a tall fifteen-year-old boy, broad-shouldered, thick of chest, and already muscular of arm, a shadow in the night.

"Who's that?" Helen called.

He said nothing.

"Molly, is that you?"

John walked toward her quietly, his feet making no noise on the sand. Helen shone the flashlight in his face. "Ah," she said, "it's you! I should have known!"

"Now you, Mrs. Jorgenson!" he said, his boy's voice suddenly shrill in the night, high but commanding, a trumpet note.

"What?" A gasp of astonishment.

"Don't you hurt her!" he said. "Don't you hurt her! If you hurt her, I'll kill you!"

"You're mad," she said, turning and running. "A crazy boy from a crazy family!"

He stood, his arms still slack at his sides, looking after her, watching the flashlight go bobbing erratically down the beach. Then he turned and walked back to the motel.

"Sit down for supper, Johnny," Sylvia said when he got there. "You're late."

He sat down in the corner of the dining room of the small apartment and took a spoonful of heavy bean soup. He had half finished it when the young Negro who served as an attendant at the motel came and said something to Sylvia in a low voice. "Tell her I'll call her back," Sylvia said.

"But she said it was urgent, ma'am."

"All right." Sylvia left the table.

A moment later she came back, looking distraught, moving the fingers of both hands convulsively. "Son, come to my room," she said.

John followed his mother across the small living room. As they climbed the stairs to her bedroom, he ran his hand along the railing, trying to think only of the way the cool wrought iron felt against his fingers. They went to her bedroom, and Sylvia shut the door. "Son," she said, "Mrs. Jorgenson said you threatened her on the beach. Is it true?"

"I told her not to hurt Molly."

"Where is Molly?"

"I don't know."

"Mrs. Jorgenson says she's missing. Son, this is very serious. Mrs. Jorgenson has called the police."

The police station in Palm River was a small stucco building, pale yellow in color, with different lavatories for the white and the colored people, but one jail cell for both. It smelled of a drunk who had been sick there the night before, disinfectant, whisky and stale cigar smoke. In a back room there was a desk, an unmade cot and a calendar with a picture of a naked girl coyly holding a small spaniel against her abnormally inflated breasts. "Lucky Dog," the caption said.

"Now look," said the chief of police, a mild-appearing little man dressed like a hardware clerk. "This is a serious situation. A girl is missing. She has been absent from her home for more than five hours. And a boy threatened a grown woman on the beach at night. We have to put two and two together."

"You want to watch it, chief," a lean lawyer with a brown vest said in a low voice at his ear. "You're dealing with minors, and prominent families at that."

"I ain't said nothing except the facts," the chief said.

John stood erect with his back against the wall. Beside him Sylvia sat on the cot, her head in her hands. Helen stood in the center of the room. "There was murder in his eyes," she said. Margaret and Bruce, sitting at the side of the room, nodded as though they had been there.

"Now let's play this thing over again," the chief said in very reasonable tones. "Mrs. Jorgenson, did you do anything to upset the girl recently?"

"Not a thing," she said. "I just had the doctor give her a physical examination to see if anything happened out on that island. I had to make sure. You can see that."

"And the doctor's report?"

"She was all right," Helen said. Margaret and Bruce nodded again.

"But she seemed upset?"

"Yes, she seemed very upset. She's always been a difficult child."

"And you confined her to her room?"

"Yes."

"But she wasn't there when you went to bring her her lunch."

"No."

"You thought she was hiding in the house to be spiteful, but couldn't find her, and finally went looking on the beach."

"That is correct," Helen said in her flat Buffalo accent.

"And you met the boy and he threatened to kill you."

"He did," Helen said.

"And you don't deny this, do you?" the chief asked, spinning to face John as he had seen detectives in television dramas do.

"No." John's voice was low. He knew better than to try to explain things to adults.

"When did you last see the girl?"

"Yesterday," John said. "Last night, when we got back from the boat."

"I think you're lying," the chief said. "I think you met her on the beach, and I think you . . ."

"Take it easy, Bob," the lawyer whispered.

The chief sat back in his chair and lit a cigar. "Nothing to do but wait, I guess," he said. "We'll search the beach and dunes. We'll drag the river. We've already notified the highway patrol. We usually don't act so fast, but I don't like the look of this case."

"Let the boy go home," the lawyer said. "Suggest that he stay in his room."

"Will you keep the boy in his room?" the chief asked Sylvia.

"My son is innocent!" Sylvia replied. She didn't lift her head.

"Will you be responsible for him?"

"Of course!"

That night John stood at the window of his room staring out at the beach and the dunes, where lanterns were circling, tracing out the search. His mother tried to comfort him, but he said he didn't want to talk to her; he was all right, he maintained stiffly as he had since he arrived in Florida, and needed no help. The surf pounded and the palm trees rustled in the wind. The clouds made a kind of island reaching up for the moon, and three stars could be seen from the window. By four in the morning, most of the clouds had changed from gray to white, and it really wasn't a bad sort of night.

The next day Molly was found wandering in a daze along the highway three miles north of town. For a week she was in the hospital recovering from exhaustion, and then she was confined to her bed.

When Ken got home and learned what had happened, he struck Helen for the first time in his life. Helen screamed, and Margaret and Bruce came running. In the heat of anger Margaret said they knew about Sylvia, and Helen shrieked that she wanted a divorce. She could have it any time, Ken said, but he wanted Molly. A fine father he'd make, Margaret replied. Aside from the question of his morality, hadn't his judgment about the boat trip been proved wrong? They'd all been against it from the beginning, but Ken had got his way, and now look what had happened.

"We have you cold," Margaret said, lying, but sometimes, as she told Helen, a lie is effective. "We have witnesses."

The argument lasted all night, and most of the next day, and the Carters had many hurried telephone conversations with lawyers. The upshot of it all was a suit for divorce. It was agreed that during the proceedings it would be best to send Molly to boarding school.

Ken spent a lot of time talking to his daughter, but she was withdrawn and wouldn't speak to him at all. After Helen got through telling her about Sylvia, she wouldn't even look at him.

Briarwood Manor in Virginia, a school which Miss Summerfield, its headmistress, said was the best in the United States, was selected. The Carters escorted Molly to the train and seemed enraged to find

Ken there with a large, elaborately wrapped box under his arm. John also came to see Molly off. It was a strained group which assembled around her. Ken gave her the box and told her to open it after the train started.

"Thanks," Molly said meekly, and allowed herself to be hugged.

John had nothing to give her—only a look of naked, despairing love that made the Carters say it was lucky she was leaving. Molly shook hands with him and said she hoped she'd see him again, but there was an almost deathlike passivity in her voice. She didn't look as though she cared much about seeing anybody again. Before the porter called "All aboard" she turned from her family and insisted on going alone to the compartment Ken had reserved for her. She sat there with the large box on her lap, staring out the window. It was an hour before she unwrapped her gift and found it to be a glossy mink coat, real mink. Bending double, she buried her face in the soft fur, and it was only then that she cried.

16

THERE WAS SO MUCH TALK about the divorce that Sylvia decided it would be better to send John off to boarding school too as soon as possible, but it took several days to make the arrangements with Colchester Academy, which had been decided upon. Meanwhile, she told him, he didn't have to go to the local school—he could have a real vacation. Most of it he spent wandering around the Municipal Docks.

"Now I want to tell you, sonny," Captain Shay said. "You sit here long enough, and you can see almost anything come down the Inland Waterway."

John, who looked as lonely as he was, sat with his feet swinging off the edge of the wharf. Captain Shay sat at the wheel of the big auxiliary yawl he was paid to command for an owner too busy to use the boat. The captain had plenty of time on his hands, and loved to tell stories.

"The things I've seen!" he said. "Just this last trip, in Norfolk, a homemade cruiser, just a motorboat, really, came alongside with two retired firemen aboard her. Bound for Florida and never sailed before. They asked if they could follow me down, and I said there was no law against it.

"Well, these firemen—I never did learn their names—had grown about a hundred bushels of potatoes in their back yards before they left home, and had stored them all aboard, and they had filled five-gallon oil cans with corn whisky they made themselves.

"That's all they had: potatoes and whisky, and the fish they could catch. Their pension money went for gas and oil. Well, you never saw a happier pair—in their seventies at least. They followed me along down the canals, drinking that corn whisky and throwing those five-gallon tins overboard. By the end of the day they weren't steering a very straight course, but all they had to do was stay in my wake. One of them had a banjo, and they'd sing and drink and eat those potatoes. Hell! You never saw a happier pair! They got to Miami without ever running aground, and I don't think they were sober a mile of the journey."

John laughed. "They sound nice," he said.

"Lots of nice people," Captain Shay said. "A good many of the amateurs follow me down every fall, because they know I'm a pro at the game. Sometimes I feel I'm driving the engine of a long train. If I ever ran aground, a good many people would be stuck." He lit his pipe.

"I'd be proud to be followed," John said.

"Hell! It's my profession and their play. I'll tell you a funny one, though. A fellow came aboard in Atlantic City once and asked to follow me down, and I couldn't figure it. He had a motor cruiser almost fifty feet long, looked like one of the old rumrunners. Fast. And he was a guy, you could tell, who knew the water. A little man sixty years old, who looked to have been to sea all his life. Why did he want to follow me at eight knots, I thought, why the hell?"

"Why?" John asked.

Captain Shay spat over the gleaming mahogany rail of the yacht. "I didn't find out for a few days," he said. "The guy followed me along, and anchored a few hundred yards from me every night.

Then one night we were anchored in the Dismal Swamp with a full moon overhead and I heard it."

"Heard what?" John asked.

"Ever heard a madwoman laugh?"

"No!"

"It ain't pretty. It went on half the night, and I had a good mind to up anchor and get out of there, but I didn't. The next morning he rowed over and told me."

"Told you what?"

"His wife. She was nuts, and he didn't want to put her away. Wherever they lived ashore, the neighbors started to object. So this guy was a commander in the Navy, and he retired and bought a boat and kept her there, on the move most of the time. But he liked the company of another vessel. Sailed in convoy, so to speak. That's what he told me once."

"Did you ever see her?" John asked.

"Sure. Little old woman sat on the fantail knitting most of the time, looked like anybody. Only sometimes, usually at night, she started to laugh. You've never heard a sound like that."

"I guess not," John said.

"You sit here long enough and you can see almost anything come down the Inland Waterway," Captain Shay concluded.

17

It was obvious that the divorces would take many months to negotiate because there was agreement on so few issues. Barton came out of the Naval Hospital shaken, but he was still determined to maintain legal custody of his son. Sylvia told Ken she wouldn't be able to sleep on any night she knew John was on the island alone with Bart and Hasper.

"Hell," Ken said, "I think the court would rather give a child to an adulteress than an alcoholic, if it comes to that, and your position will be much better when we can get married."

But of course they couldn't get married until the divorce took place, and Sylvia had to be judged as a woman who had left her husband to become another man's mistress. And Bart was careful to get a long technical report on his condition from the Navy doctors. On paper, he had an excellent record, marred only by one episode of acute alcoholism which had as a contributing factor the strains a man undergoes when he is abandoned by his wife. He was on the wagon now and as long as he didn't drink he had a pretty good case, the lawyers said. His position was, of course, much improved by the fact that the boy apparently did not want to stay with his mother, and displayed a fierce loyalty toward his father.

Ken was in a hopelessly weak position when negotiating with Helen. She had all the top cards in her hand, her lawyer said with satisfaction. There was no way to dispute her custody of Molly, but she was going a little far, her lawyer admitted, in trying to deny Ken the privilege of having his daughter visit him for at least a few weeks a year.

It was lucky, everyone acknowledged, that Molly was at boarding school. The newspapers got hold of the story, and there was nothing pretty about it. Bart was described as a "Socialite War Hero"; Ken appeared in the tabloids as the "Marfab Man," and the editors ran old photographs of Sylvia which had reposed in their files since her days as a "community leader." One difficulty was that Helen could not be convinced that it was wrong for her to talk to newspaper reporters. She loved sympathy, and publicity brought her that in quantity. She had nothing to hide, she said, and if the papers wanted the truth, why let them have it, and Margaret agreed. It gave them both a sense of importance to have the reporters and photographers visit their new house in Buffalo. They were nice young men, really, and were never impolite. The world might as well know what a beast Ken Jorgenson was, Margaret said bitterly to one nice young man and a New York tabloid carried a lighthearted wrap-up story on the whole thing, with several pictures of Sylvia, a take-out on the Marvelous Sale of Marfab, and even a resumé of Ken's football record.

When Sylvia took John to her room to explain that she was going to marry Ken as soon as the divorce became final, John said he hoped she'd be very happy. "This is a hard thing for a boy," Sylvia said. "Someday you'll understand."

"I understand now," John said without raising his voice; and although his muscles were tense, he did not pull away when she kissed him. He just stood there.

The day before they took John to the airport in Palm River, where he was to start his journey to Colchester Academy, Sylvia arranged for Ken to take him fishing. While the divorce was being negotiated, it was, the lawyer had said, desirable for Sylvia and Ken to stay apart, so she did not go, but she told Ken it might be easier on the boy if the two of them got to know each other better. Ken agreed, and chartered a fishing cruiser to take them offshore, where the bluefish were running. John said he didn't want to go, but Sylvia begged him. "Look," she told him, "Ken Jorgenson is a good man, and someday you've got to learn that. We have to face realities in life, and there's no point in building up a lot of horrors in your mind. He's a good man who loves both of us, and you're going to hurt his feelings terribly if you refuse to go."

"I'll go if you want," John replied quietly. "It's just that I don't really like fishing." He was beginning to acquire the preternaturally wise look of the children of the divorced; he was developing a poise she could not break through, a courtesy of the sort his father could show strangers when he wished. John always stood when she entered the room now, coming to attention, almost, the way Bart did; and with that same touch of elegance which his father had even when he was quite drunk, John now was lighting her cigarettes for her and opening doors for her, until she wanted to cry.

The day of fishing was not a success. John said, "Thank you, sir," when Ken handed him a rod, and "No thank you, sir," when Ken offered to show him how to bait a hook for bluefish. With a touch of arrogance he added, "Sir, I've been fishing all my life."

With sad eyes Ken watched John move around the boat, admiring the easy grace, the flair for doing small things well which he had always admired in Bart as a young man, even when Bart was beating him at tennis. He liked the easy way the boy handled the fishing equipment, never getting anything snarled, and the quiet assurance with which he braced himself against the roll as the cruiser lunged through the inlet and the going got rough. After they had fished with a good deal of success for a few hours, the captain of the boat asked John to take the helm while he went below to get lunch. The boy stood balanced on his toes, turning the wheel hardly at all, knowing instinctively, apparently, how to meet the boat's yawing before it started.

"You're quite a sailor, aren't you?" Ken said admiringly.

"Thank you, sir," John replied. "My father taught me, sir. He was the captain of a ship in the war. Did you know that, sir?"

"Yes," Ken said gravely. "He was a fine Naval officer. That is something of which you ought to be proud."

"Were you in the war, sir?" John's voice was polite.

"No, I wasn't," Ken replied, and felt obliged to add, "They seemed to think us research men should stay home."

"Yes, sir," John said.

At the end of the day Ken put his big hand on the boy's shoulder and said, "Johnny, could we talk for a few minutes?"

"Certainly, sir."

They sat alone on the flying bridge, while the boat plowed placidly up the Inland Waterway returning home. Ken's voice was deep and soft. "I just want you to know that we'll all come through this time of trouble," he said. "Your father and your mother and I are all decent people, and we'll solve our difficulties. We all want to help you in any way we can."

"Thank you, sir."

"Someday next year maybe we can all get together on Pine Island, or down here. You and Molly and your mother and I. I hope you can spend some of your vacations with us."

"Maybe, sir."

Ken wanted to grab the boy and say, Don't be like that; don't think that you have to stand alone; come here and put your head down and cry if you want to, or hit me, or shout, but get it out, damn it; say it and let's have it over with; you've got to get it out before you can learn it's not as bad as you think. But that hadn't worked with Molly, and he knew it wouldn't work with John.

That night Sylvia disregarded for the first time the advice of her lawyers, who told her she shouldn't even telephone Ken until the divorce was final. From the hotel to which she had moved she called him to ask how the day had gone.

"I couldn't reach him," Ken said sadly. "It will take time."

Sylvia sighed. "Yes," she said, and after a brief pause she added, "I love you, Ken. I love you for trying."

"I love you. Don't worry about the kids. They're going to be all right."

"I hope so!"

"We just need time," Ken said.

Part Three

DO YOU EVER GET LONELY?

18

Colchester Academy, which stood in an isolated section of the countryside about fifty miles from Hartford, Connecticut, was, as such things are counted, a good school. It catered not only to the children of the divorced, the widowed and the sick, but to those with intellectual or social ambitions unattainable at home. It was an old school, started in 1803, and many famous men had gone there. Barton Hunter himself was an alumnus of Colchester Academy, and it was his influence which enabled John to enter midterm, in March of 1954.

The morning John arrived, Mr. Nealy, one of the teachers, met him at the station. Mr. Nealy was a mournful-appearing man of middle age and size who had wanted to be a professor of the classics at Harvard, but he had failed to get his doctor's degree, and for twenty-one years had been an instructor at Colchester Academy. He had foolishly bought a secondhand car in which to escape to Hartford for weekends, and the payments on it were more than his slender budget could maintain. His wife had told him that morning that the ache in her shoulder was persisting and that she might have to go to the hospital. Mr. Nealy was preoccupied when he met John, and there wasn't much warmth in his handshake. The two of them rode silently to the office of Mr. Caulfield, the headmaster, who explained to John that he would have to work hard to make good at Colchester Academy.

"I'll try, sir," John said.

Mr. Nealy then took John to his dormitory and introduced him to his roommate, a thin boy named Bill Norris, who was also fifteen years old, and who had a slight stutter. "I'm-a, I'm-a, it's good to meet you," Bill said, smiling pleasantly. "I didn't like rooming alone."

"Could you tell me where the post office is?" John asked after shaking hands.

Before unpacking his bag, John crossed the muddy quadrangle of the school without even glancing at the handsome brick buildings which distinguished alumni had given to Colchester Academy because it had done so much for them. Following Bill's directions, he entered a small room beside the dining hall which was used as a post office. There was a strange smell, a compound of paste, ink and cheap perfume used by the janitor's wife, who served as postmistress. No one was in sight. John knocked softly on a sliding panel beneath a sign reading STAMPS, and a female voice said, "Yes?"

"My name is John Hunter. Is there any mail for me?"

"No," the voice said without any hesitation. "You new?"

"Yes, ma'am."

"Wait a minute and I'll give you a box." There was a pause before a withered hand with a large artificial diamond ring placed a small slip of paper at the window. "Box 135," the voice said. "There's your combination."

John read the figures: 18-25-02. Going to his box, he twirled the dials and opened it once or twice, just for practice.

Going back to his room, he sat down at his desk and wrote a letter. "Dear Molly," he said. "I'm at a place called Colchester Academy. My roommate's name is Bill Norris, and he seems like a nice guy. I flew here from Palm River, and some of the people on the plane were sick, but I wasn't. I like flying, don't you?"

It was hard to know what to put in letters. John nibbled the end of his pen, and after staring around his room, decided to describe that for her. "The walls are green," he said, "and from the window there's quite a nice view." He put an airmail stamp on this communication and walked across the quadrangle to put it in the post-office slot.

Molly's answer came four days later. "Dear Johnny," she wrote. "Your school sounds like mine; my walls are *exactly* the same color. I think that's marvelous, don't you? I hope the food you get is better than ours, though. Frankly, I couldn't *exist* here if we weren't allowed to go to the drugstore to eat."

This was the beginning of a steady interchange of letters. Neither John nor Molly ever mentioned their parents. They talked about food and movies they had seen and books they were reading. The meaning of the letters lay in their existence, not in what they said.

Quite often during that first period at school, John heard from his mother. Sylvia wrote short, cheerful letters about the fishing in Florida, and about the shells she was beginning to collect on the beach. "It looks as though Ken and I will be able to get married next summer," she said in one letter, mentioning it casually, along with plans for a trip abroad. John didn't answer that letter. Every month he sent his mother a dutiful postcard, but that was all.

Bart wrote irregularly, often enclosing small checks. His letters were rarely more than three or four sentences long. "Dear Son," he said once, "Hope you're well; we're all well here." Bart always used the word "we" when he wrote from Pine Island, even when he was living in the big house alone. His letters were always signed, "Hastily yours," as though he lived an incredibly busy life.

As the weeks wore on, Ken, Sylvia and Bart seemed to fade from John's life; he didn't think about them much any more. Molly was more real, especially when she sent him a copy of a school photograph she had had taken. It showed a serious-faced young girl sitting very erect on a straight-backed chair with her hands folded on her lap. "Don't I look like a *gump?*" Molly wrote in her letter, and John replied, "I like your picture very much." He wanted to add that he thought she looked beautiful, but of course he couldn't say that; he blushed at the very thought of writing such a thing in a letter. A few days later he sent her a picture of himself, feeling embarrassed because he thought it seemed so much better than he really was, yet grateful to the photographer for making it look as though he weren't beginning to get spots on his face.

At night when the lights were out, John and Bill Norris talked for hours. Bill's father had recently died from shrapnel wounds suffered in the war; he had been bedridden for many years. Bill had a theory, almost a conviction, that another war was coming soon, and that he too would be killed by it. "They'll be using hydrogen bombs and we're all going to get it," he said casually. "We're just the right age."

"I guess so," John said without alarm, simply trying to be agreeable. It was a matter on which he had no opinion.

Bill Norris had a harder time at school than John did, and sometimes he cried at night. There was something about him which made the larger boys pick on him. They were forever jostling him in hallways, flicking him with towels in the shower baths, and making him the butt of jokes. He detested athletics, which amounted to heresy at Colchester Academy, for the great rivalry with Hampshire Academy thirty miles away demanded the earnest efforts of all the boys, even the little ones who could only carry buckets of water. Because he spent most of his unsupervised study hours lying on his bed staring at the ceiling, Bill also had trouble with his studies. Goaded to exasperation, Mr. Nealy sometimes picked up the edge of the big table around which the class sat and let it slam to the floor. "You've got to study, Bill!" he said. "What do you think you're here for?"

"I don'ta, don'ta, don't know, Mr. Nealy," Bill replied.

In his bottom bureau drawer under his sweaters, Bill kept, among other things, an album of pictures his father had taken during the Second World War, which he had found in the attic of his mother's house in New Rochelle, and had stolen. It contained cracked and yellowed snapshots of groups of young men in soiled uniforms, big guns in the mud with their barrels tilted skyward, crashed airplanes, and one terrifying picture of a tangled pile of the dead, showing one corpse in the foreground with his mouth open and a hand outstretched. "My father saw that," Bill said proudly. "He was there."

"My father was the captain of a ship," John replied with equal pride.

Bill also had hidden under his clothes in the bottom bureau drawer a forbidden object, his father's old service pistol, his most treasured possession.

"No firearms shall be kept in the rooms," the school's rules said, but the pistol had been given to Bill by his own father shortly before he died; it was his inheritance, and he smuggled it in. For hours he sat polishing it, and at night quite often John saw him steal from his covers, get the pistol, and take it to bed with him, as younger boys might take a Teddy bear.

"You can see," Bill said many times, pointing to a headline in the paper. "They're getting close to it."

Bill Norris had a second album of pictures hidden away which John stumbled on by mistake while attempting to borrow a pair of socks, a collection of photographs of nude women. They were not pornographic photographs, such as a boy from Florida named Dick Woller surreptitiously invited friends into his room to see; Bill's were routine art shots, some of them quite beautiful. John always remembered one of them, a photograph of a young woman leaning against a Grecian pillar on the steps of a ruined building, with dark braids falling down on each side of her full, perfectly formed breasts. Bill came into the room while John was poring over this collection and furiously grabbed it from him, both boys blushing piteously. "You shouldn't have taken that!" Bill said, almost in tears.

Bill Norris' Latin went from bad to worse during the few months John knew him, and John himself had so much trouble making up for his lack of instruction in Latin and algebra on Pine Island that at Mr. Caulfield's suggestion, he dropped back a year. Mr. Nealy's temper kept getting shorter. He threw pieces of chalk and blackboard erasers at Bill and John, and in supposedly mock fury picked up a chair once and threatened to let them have it. John had a capacity for hard, driving work, and before long he had his studies under control, but Bill Norris kept lagging farther and farther behind, like a wounded ship falling out of convoy. Because he lived with him, John shared his agonies, and of all he learned at Colchester Academy, the story of the short, sad education of Bill Norris stuck in his mind longest.

Colchester Academy Builds Men, as its brochure proclaimed. Mr. Caulfield, the headmaster, and Mr. Nealy had themselves been built there, but they weren't sure that Bill Norris was "good material." The curriculum they prescribed for him included a dead and a foreign language, mathematics and English. The boys' personal lives were not considered to be the school's business, and some kinds of ignorance were thought to be beyond its province. Many of the students, including Bill Norris, believed that masturbation would drive them insane, that their backbones would turn to liquid, and that hair would grow on the palms of their hands. Horror beyond the imagination of an adult dwelt in their minds.

Bill Norris was caught in a toilet booth. Dick Woller spied on him through a crack in the door, and called a dozen others. They quietly brought in chairs and stood on them, looking over the wall of the booth, and in unison called, "Hey Bill! What are you doing?"

He bolted, panic-stricken, holding up his pants, and ran to his room, bursting in upon John, who was trying to translate Caesar. "What's the matter?" John said.

Bill's eyes were crazed. From the hall the boys followed him. "Go ahead, Bill," they said. "Don't mind us!"

"Well, now, we'll hear a recitation from Bill Norris," Mr. Nealy said the next day in Latin class. "You, I suppose, Bill, have again got your lesson letter-perfect today?"

Laughter. As in the Congressional Record, laughter had to be noted often in any true report of the doings at Colchester Academy. Bill looked up, his face pale, and said, "I'm-a, I'm-a, I'm afraid I haven't done my lesson today, Mr. Nealy."

"How strange!" Mr. Nealy retorted with relish. "You mean my star student has come to class unprepared?"

"I'm-a, I'm afraid so, Mr. Nealy," Bill said.

"Try to translate the first line anyway. Page ninety-two, in case you don't know."

Laughter. Mr. Nealy was a great comedian.

"Caesar," Bill stammered, "Caesar was merciful to the Gauls."

"Very good," Mr. Nealy said. "After two years of my expert tutelage you can now translate six simple words of Latin almost right. I guess this is as much of a triumph as we can expect today. Time's up—class dismissed!"

A few weeks later the boys played another prank on Bill Norris. They cut letters from a newspaper to make a headline reading "Bill Norris Found Dead in Bed"—this, in the atmosphere of Colchester Academy, being an obviously obscene reference. Bill saw it on the bulletin board and blushed, but hurried on to class, anxious to escape the knot of boys waiting to see his reaction. It was John Hunter who took the sign down.

"You leave that up!" Dick Woller said. He was a broad-faced, red-haired, freckled boy a year older than John and bigger.

John walked toward him slowly, holding the pasted-up newspaper clipping in his hand. "Did you make this?" he asked quietly.

"Who wants to know?"

Quickly, without premeditation, John hit him, a full man's blow in the mouth. The boy staggered back with blood welling from his lips, and John was all over him, pounding his fists into his face and belly. It took three boys and a master to haul him off.

"I hear you started it," Mr. Caulfield said to John that night.

"Yes, sir."

"Why?"

John said nothing because the subject was unspeakable. A wall lay between the generations through which one could not talk or see or hear.

"Do you have anything to say for yourself?"

"No."

"Twelve demerits for fighting," Mr. Caulfield said. "Remember, if you get twenty demerits, you'll be expelled."

"Yes, sir," John said.

John went to the music building and sat for three hours playing the piano that afternoon.

There were a few good teachers. One of them, Albert Newfield, tried to tutor Bill Norris every night to help him catch up in his Latin, but Bill did not prove very co-operative. "To tell the truth, Mr. Newfield, I don't see much point to Latin," he said.

"It's mental exercise. Learning it will help you to do any kind of intellectual work well."

"Will it?"

"Of course."

"I don't think I'm really much of an intellectual," Bill said. "I mean, I don't really have many ambitions that way." With Mr. Newfield, Bill didn't stutter so much.

"What are your ambitions, Bill?"

"I don't know," Bill replied. "I guess I just don't have any. I think there's going to be a war, and I guess that will take care of that."

"But you need an education to fight in a war, even if one does come."

"Do you?"

"Of course. You want to be an officer, don't you?"

"No," Bill Norris said.

In late April there was a dance at Colchester Academy, and John asked Molly, but her school would not allow her to come without her parents' permission and her mother said no. Only about a third of the boys got girls for the dance. On the great night a line of Japanese lanterns was hung from the administration building to the gymnasium, where the orchestra was playing love songs at one end of the basketball court. The lucky boys in white dinner coats walked with the girls to the gymnasium after supper. It was twilight, and the paper lanterns glowed against the sky. The girls wore evening gowns, and John, leaning out of his dormitory window to watch, found it almost impossible to believe that they could be so beautiful, and still walk with the boys from Colchester Academy. Even Dick Woller had a girl, a stout young lady before whom he was painfully shy, but whom he later claimed to have seduced. Dick Woller always carried a condom in his wallet and boastfully showed it to his friends.

"Foolish not to carry one," he said in his slow Florida drawl. "After all, they don't weigh much." Dick Woller caused John always to hate a Southern accent.

During those lonely months John's face and body, plagued by the difficulties of adolescence, grew more splotchy, and he felt himself to be unclean. Looking at himself in the mirror, he was certain he was growing up to be ugly, hideous beyond redemption, and it did not seem in the least surprising to him in retrospect that his mother had chosen his sister to take with her. How could any woman love a face like his? It was nice that he and Molly just exchanged letters, he thought.

As the brochure also said, Colchester Academy fits its program to the individual child. Early one Sunday morning a group of the individual children led by Dick Woller stole into the room where Bill Norris was sleeping and ripped the covers from his bed. "Just want to make sure you're behaving yourself, boy!" Dick Woller said.

But the joke didn't work out quite the way Dick Woller expected. Bill Norris in his rumpled pajamas awoke with a start, sat up, his eyes wild, and in his hand was a gun. The evil black pistol emerging suddenly from beneath the white pillow was such an astonishing sight that the boys stood gaping, crowding back against the wall. There was a click as Bill cocked the gun. His hand did not tremble. "You bastards leave me alone," he said, "or I'll kill you, every one."

The boys fled, but the story, or at least part of it, soon got to Mr. Caulfield, the headmaster, who was shocked to learn that a Colchester Academy boy would do such a terrible thing, that he should have a gun he hadn't registered with Mr. Nealy, who was in charge of the rifle range. Bad stuff. Not in the tradition of Colchester Academy. Not at all. Mr. Caulfield called all the boys who had seen the incident to the administration building. They stood in a semicircle around his desk.

"Was the gun loaded?" Mr. Caulfield asked.

"No," Bill Norris replied. "I didn't put the bullet in it."

"But you have a bullet?"

"Yes. One."

"Where did you get it?"

"I found it in my father's collar box."

"This is very serious," Mr. Caulfield said.

"He never loads the gun, sir," John Hunter said, trying to be helpful.

"It's always the unloaded guns which kill people," Mr. Caulfield said. "To think that a Colchester Academy boy kept a gun in his room is bad enough. To think that he threatened other boys with it is intolerable. I will of course have to confiscate the gun."

"No," Bill Norris replied.

"Bring it to me immediately," Mr. Caulfield thundered. John and the other boys who had been called as witnesses glanced apprehensively at each other. "You will have to leave this school immediately if you do not conform to the rules," Mr. Caulfield said to Bill Norris.

"All right," Bill replied in a low voice.

"That's better," Mr. Caulfield replied, sounding relieved. "Just tell us where you've hidden it, and I'll ask one of the masters to pick it up."

"I'll get it myself," Bill said and walked out of the room, looking as he always did, a little pale, but not visibly upset.

Mr. Caulfield picked up the telephone. "Mr. Nealy," he said. There was a pause. "He just left here to get it for me," Mr. Caulfield said. "I think you better stay with him."

Putting the receiver down, Mr. Caulfield turned in his swivel chair and faced the witnesses. "How did this incident start?" he asked.

"We were just teasing him a little," Dick Woller said.

"How were you teasing him?"

"Just fooling around," Dick Woller replied. "We pulled the covers off his bed."

"You shouldn't have done that," Mr. Caulfield said, "but of course it's no excuse for him to . . ."

"But you don't understand," John said.

"Don't understand?" One of Mr. Caulfield's eyebrows went up. He was quite proud of being able to make one go up that way, while the other stayed still.

"No, you don't understand," John repeated.

At that moment there was a scream from outside. John looked out the window and saw Mr. Nealy running in the quadrangle, his mouth agape. He arrived, gasping for breath, in Mr. Caulfield's office and said, "He's gone! He's gone!"

Mr. Nealy wasn't very coherent, but finally he was able to explain what had happened. His car had been parked in front of his apartment in the dormitory; he had left it there because his wife had planned to drive to the hospital to continue special treatments for her shoulder. Bill Norris had stolen it. Coming out of the dormitory beside Mr. Nealy with the gun in his hand, Bill had threatened to shoot himself if anyone tried to stop him. He had got into the car, had started it, still holding the gun in one hand, and a half dozen boys, besides Mr. Nealy, had been afraid to stop him because of the look on his face, Mr. Nealy said; a terrible look. Suddenly Bill had raced the engine, and with a screech of tires had careened right across the lawn to the school's driveway, disappearing in the direction of the state highway.

"Sit down, Mr. Nealy," Mr. Caulfield said. "You boys run along and leave us alone now."

But Mr. Nealy couldn't wait. "He was going to shoot himself," he said, and put his face on his knees and wept.

"You boys run along and come back here in half an hour," Mr. Caulfield said, and picked up the telephone.

John and the others walked outside. All the masters in the school appeared almost by magic, like the crew of a ship in time of disaster. The superintendent of grounds immediately began to erase the tire marks on the lawn. An elderly football coach walked around the quadrangle saying, "Let's get up a game, boys! We'll set up two teams chosen by lot, and I'll put up a trip to New York for the winners!"

"Tonight we should have a special movie," a mousy English teacher said. "I'll arrange it."

"Where are you going?" a French instructor asked John.

"I thought I'd take a walk."

"Why don't you come up to the room with me and have a glass of sherry? I think you're old enough."

It was an order, not an invitation. John followed him dutifully, and sat on a couch sipping the cheap sweet wine.

Mr. Caulfield didn't like to call the police when the boys ran away from school. It wasn't good to give the youngsters even a juvenile record, and it was bad publicity for the school. Usually a quiet telephone call to the home did the trick, or the homes if the son of a broken marriage was the offender, as was so often the case. Some judicious waiting usually produced the boy within twenty-four hours, but this case seemed to Mr. Caulfield to be different. The image of a fifteen-year-old boy careening along the highway with a gun on the seat beside him was appalling. As soon as he got Mr. Nealy to the infirmary, where he was given a sedative, Mr. Caulfield called the state police.

A trooper caught sight of Bill Norris in Mr. Nealy's car about twenty miles outside of Hartford. He was driving toward New York at a normal speed, but when the trooper tried to wave him down, he stepped on the gas. The chase lasted almost an hour, because the trooper was a fifty-year-old man with four children and he didn't want to risk his life unnecessarily chasing some crazy hopped-up kid with a gun. Some of these juvenile delinquents are worse than the hardened criminals, the trooper reflected darkly as he held his speedometer at eighty, and tried to get headquarters on the radio to have a road block set up ahead. I don't know what the world is coming to, he thought; for Christ's sake, a fifteen-year-old kid with a gun, and from a rich family too, coming from a school like that. If he points his goddamn gun at me, I'll shoot his eyes out, the trooper thought, and unbuckled his holster. "Yes," he said, when he finally got contact on his radio. "I've got him—just keeping him in sight. Get the boys in Draytown on the job, will you? The way he's going, he'll roar through there in about ten minutes, so for Christ's sake get the people off the street."

Bill saw the road block way ahead; they had put it on a straight stretch of road so he would have plenty of room in which to stop. Two state police cars were parked there with their red lights blinking and their sirens going full blast, and beside the road three men stood with drawn guns. I might kill somebody if I sailed into those police cars, Bill thought, and picked a telegraph pole instead. The car snapped it and ripped a swath two hundred yards long through the earth before it stopped, and by that time it was so crumpled and enveloped in flame that it was hard to tell whether it was right side up or upside down. The policemen came running and stood in a semicircle around it calling for fire extinguishers. It wasn't necessary for Bill to wait for a hydrogen bomb: the flames in the automobile were quite hot enough.

A special meeting was called in the study hall with all boys who knew Bill present.

"A very sad thing has happened today," Mr. Caulfield said. "Bill Norris was killed in an accident."

He paused. "Now it would be very unfair to repeat much about this," he continued. "Unfair to Bill Norris, and to his mother."

None of the boys said anything. "Poor Bill was probably having trouble at home, and felt he had to get there quickly," Mr. Caulfield said.

Still no one said anything.

"It is a tragic accident," Mr. Caulfield said. "A fine boy is dead, and we must all respect his memory."

"Yes suh," Dick Woller said. His lip trembled.

"I appreciate the maturity with which you're all acting," Mr. Caulfield said more briskly. "Classes will of course be held as usual, but anyone who wishes may join the football game out at the gym, and there will be a special movie tonight."

He hesitated, and for a moment he looked confused. "Boys," he said, "things like this happen sometimes in life, and no one can be blamed. We have to trust in God, I guess. Run along now, and try not to dwell on it too much." He sank wearily into his chair.

The boys filed silently out and joined the others in the quadrangle.

"Where did it happen?" a thin boy asked.

"Outside Draytown," someone said.

A crowd of boys gathered around. "Mr. Nealy sure took it hard," a fat one said. "He's gone to the hospital. An ambulance came in the back way and got him."

"I thought he was dead," a tall thin boy said.

"Bill is. I'm talking about Mr. Nealy."

"Ted Whitely heard on the radio that the car was completely demolished," a solemn child about thirteen years old with the puffed-out cheeks and mild blue eyes of a cherub said. "It burned him up."

John turned away, nauseated. He walked across the muddy quadrangle into the woods, and leaning against the cold bark of an oak, vomited. Then he started to walk slowly through the woods, aimlessly, his tracks circling widely and crossing, twisting back again, forming a pattern of agony and confusion in the mud.

Exhausted, he finally returned to the school. A police car was parked by Mr. Caulfield's office, and a master was shooing the boys away from that part of the quadrangle. John headed for the dining hall and sat there without eating.

Later that afternoon he went to his room. Bill's bed, with a new counterpane, was neatly made up, and looked shockingly empty. The silence in the room seemed to hum. John turned to the drawer where Bill kept his collections of photographs, and found it too was empty. John wondered what Mr. Caulfield would think of the collection of faded snapshots of the war, and of the nudes, of the girl with the dark braids leaning against the pillar of the ruin, of her wondrously rich, symmetrical body. Mr. Caulfield would have these things burned, probably. Everything, even Bill's clothes were gone, and the room was lonely as a tomb.

Three days afterward Mr. Caulfield told John that Bill Norris' mother would like to talk to him. "You realize, of course, that we're in a rather difficult situation," Mr. Caulfield said. "Bill's death was an accident, as you know, but the boy was disturbed—there's no doubt about that. Yet we can't say that. Mrs. Norris is herself a highly strung person, and we can't do anything that would hurt her."

"I'll try not to," John said.

Mrs. Norris sat in the living room of Mr. Caulfield's home, a handsome brick house at the north end of the campus, where a formal tea was held for the students once a month to give the students a little home atmosphere. She was a thin woman who looked shockingly like her son done up for a costume ball, with long hair and a black dress. She leaned forward on the reproduction of a Hitchcock chair, with her hands clasped tightly in her lap. "So you're Bill's roommate," she said. "He wrote so happily about you."

"I liked Bill very much," John said.

"I don't want to make things difficult for you," Mrs. Norris continued. "I know this is a hard thing for a young boy. It must be almost as hard on you as it is on me."

Mr. Caulfield, sitting in a gold upholstered easy chair, cleared his throat. John stood in the center of the floor. He was too nervous to sit down.

"Still," Mrs. Norris said, "there are some things I do hope you'll tell me, which I'm sure you'll understand I have to know."

"Yes," John said.

"Do you know where Bill was going when he left here, and why he stole a car?"

John stared at his feet.

"I think he did it on a dare," Mr. Caulfield said. "He was always such a venturesome boy. Some of the others may have dared him to take the car, and of course he didn't really know how to drive . . ."

"That's what I think," John heard himself saying. "It must have been a dare."

Mrs. Norris sighed. "It's strange," she said. "He always seemed to me to be such a timid child . . ."

"I think we ought to have a glass of sherry," Mr. Caulfield said gravely.

Colchester Academy used sherry the way the British Navy uses rum. John never liked it much, but that day he sat sipping it, trying to think of nice things to say about Bill to his mother. "He was liked by everyone," he heard himself saying. "He was one of the most popular boys in school."

Fifteen minutes later Mr. Caulfield accompanied John to the door and squeezed his elbow approvingly while saying goodbye. John felt obscurely venal, but what truth could he have told Bill's mother? How could he have explained the things that had happened, and who, after all, knew why?

19

THE NEGOTIATIONS for the divorce dragged on, and Sylvia and Ken did not realize their hopes of getting married quickly. Sylvia remained in Florida throughout that summer of 1954, walking on the beach with Carla, seeking shells. Ken made many trips to New York, where Bernie Anderson had moved to start their new business. Helen would not let him see Molly, at least until everything was settled, because it upset the poor child too much, she said. Ken wrote Molly once a week, and often sent her little gifts: a pair of white angora mittens which were certainly out of season, but which somehow reminded him of her; a necklace of cultured pearls, and a light gray, rather adult hat with a cocky little feather which he saw in a store window and thought would look nice on her. In return he got short notes which in rather stilted phrases expressed gratitude for the gifts and nothing else.

The year 1954 was hard for everyone concerned. John refused to go to summer camp and stayed with his father on Pine Island. Barton wrote Helen, inviting her and Molly to pay them a visit, but he got a polite refusal. Molly hadn't been awfully well lately, Helen wrote, and they were going to keep her home.

There were no young people his age on the island that year, and for the first week of his summer vacation John wandered by himself over every inch of the place, exploring the highest mountains, the deep ravines and the most deserted sections of the beach. During the evenings he sat in a dim corner of the inn playing the old piano, teaching himself new songs, but the piano was badly out of tune and it would cost a great deal to have a man come from the mainland to fix it. At the end of a week, John told his father it was stupid to waste time, and he wanted to work.

"At what?" Bart asked.

The wharf was badly rotted, John pointed out, and the gardens needed a great deal of attention. "I could trim bushes if Todd would show me how," he said. "The wharf is a much bigger job."

Hasper had had arthritis badly that winter, and his hands were gnarled as the limbs of old trees. Glowering silently, he gave John a lesson in pruning, and John got to work. His ambition was to put the whole garden in shape, which was impossible for even a grown man to do in one summer, but he worked feverishly, often arising at dawn and continuing until dark. Although he was not yet sixteen, the muscles of his back and shoulders were beginning to develop like those of a professional athlete.

Bart fell off the wagon frequently that year. He had trouble getting women from Harvesport to stay as housekeepers at the inn, but only a dozen old ladies requested reservations, and there wasn't much which Lillian, the cook, couldn't handle by herself. On warm summer evenings Bart often stood talking to John while the boy was working. They made an odd sight together. John, wearing only a pair of soiled khaki trousers, wielded the big pruning shears without comment during most of the conversations, while Bart, dressed in a white linen suit, followed him from bush to bush, glass in hand.

What Bart talked about most of the time was the war, and the part he had played in it; he had a compulsion to make his son understand this; it seemed extremely important that he know, and Bart talked about it almost incessantly, repeating himself over and over again not only through drunken forgetfulness, but because he was nagged by the feeling that John didn't fully understand. By the end of summer the story was so deeply ingrained in John's mind that it was almost as much a part of the boy's personal experience as his father's.

The story began when Bart joined the Naval Reserve at college in the belief that it might increase his skills as a yachtsman. "Naval Science," as it was called at Harvard, was his only good subject, and when the war broke out, he was able to get an ensign's commission in spite of the fact that he had never graduated. In January of 1942, he was called to active duty and stationed aboard an old four-stack destroyer which was escorting ships to England.

As soon as the ship left Boston Harbor, Bart was, to his great astonishment, hopelessly seasick. All his life he had sailed boats, but the destroyer racing at twenty knots through the winter seas was something entirely different. The convoy she was escorting had to zigzag, and the destroyer had to patrol around the basic zigzag pattern. She was changing course constantly, first rolling forty-five degrees, then pitching her bow under green water up to the five-inch gun. The men aboard her were shaken like dried peas in a rattle.

But although he was sick, Bart never missed a watch. Often he stood on the wing of the bridge with a bucket hooked over his left arm. He lost twenty pounds and got so weak he had to hang onto a stanchion with both arms, sometimes, just to keep upright, but he braved it out, and after a month the seasickness diminished. Within two months he was allowed to stand a deck watch by himself.

The most junior officer was usually given the graveyard watch, as it was called, lasting from midnight to four in the morning. In March of 1942, on only the third night that he had stood his own watch, a heavy gale was blowing. The convoy consisted of a dozen naval tankers taking gasoline to bases in Britain. Heavy-laden, they were smothered in foam by the Arctic combers, and the convoy speed had to be reduced to four knots. There were no moon and stars that night, and Bart's ship had not yet been given radar. Depending on eyesight and echo sounding devices alone, Bart's destroyer and three others tried to keep close to the unlighted vessels without running into them. It was bitter cold, with the spray freezing on deck and on the portholes of the pilothouse. On the port wing of the bridge Bart huddled against the wind, staring with binoculars into the rush of blackness.

It was eighteen minutes after two in the morning when a star shell suddenly burst over the convoy, turning the raging sea white. A wolf pack of five black submarines, almost invisible in the night, came charging arrogantly in on the surface with their deck guns stabbing the fat-bellied tankers. It hadn't been necessary for the submarines to send up another star shell, for in the few seconds that the first one hung blazing in the sky, a gas tanker exploded, sending a column of fire a thousand feet in the air.

Bart rang up general quarters, and before his commanding officer came on deck, changed course to race in the direction of one blurred shape, which he dimly saw through his binoculars. The submarines seemed to be all around them, lying low in the water just beyond the circle of fire made by the tanker, which burned fast. The convoy broke formation and scattered in many directions. The big tankers lumbered along like panicked cows in the night, while the lean destroyers knifed in and out of their ranks, but in the blackness it was almost impossible to tell friend from foe. The shadowy shape toward which Bart had altered course was still indistinct when the captain got to the bridge; it was low in the water, almost awash, and while they stared at it through their binoculars, there was a flash of a gun on the forward deck.

"Open fire," Bart's captain said, and it was fortunate that the destroyer had a green crew; fortunate that the seas were so rough that accuracy was impossible; fortunate that most of the first barrage missed, for when one shell hit that indistinct shape it blossomed in fire and became not a submarine but a tanker.

The gun crews aboard the destroyer realized this even before the order to cease fire came from the bridge; it became apparent instantaneously to everyone on deck, and a deathly, sickened silence reigned aboard the ship. Astern of them another tanker, hit by a submarine, exploded, spilling yellow fire over the sea. Oh, there was oil on troubled waters that night, Bart said. The gasoline blazed for many miles around when eight of those tankers went down together, and there was oil on troubled waters indeed.

Bart's destroyer wheeled, and at full speed charged right through the blazing sea. It was possible to see now, oh it was possible to see quite clearly, Bart told his son. Exposed in the glare of the destruction they had created, the five submarines lay naked in the night, long, black and obscene, with the seas breaking almost over their deck guns. At point-blank range the three destroyers opened up with everything they had, the bull-throated five-inchers, the sharp-cracking three-inchers, the chattering machine guns of many different calibers—all these exploded in crescendos of fury, and they sank three of those submarines before they had a chance to submerge. Afterward the destroyers prowled the burning seas, searching for the other two. One of the submerged submarines doubled back and lay under the burning oil spilling from a tanker, for that is where Bart's destroyer followed its echo. The ping of the echo-ranging gear came through the machines on the bridge of the destroyer quite clearly, and the man with the headphones on Bart's ship chanted in a deep Southern accent, "Bearing zero two one, range two thousand yards and closing rapidly; bearing zero two five, range fifteen hundred yards; bearing zero three zero, range one thousand yards; bearing zero three five, range . . ."

Bart stood on the wing of the bridge while all around the waters blazed. There was a series of short sharp barks as the K-guns of the destroyer tossed the heavy depth charges out on both sides. More depth charges rolled over her stern, and suddenly the burning sea exploded. Geysers of fire shot into the night; the ocean boiled as the deep-set charges went off, and in the midst of all this more oil from the wounded submarine floated to the surface and ignited.

That is what happened, or that, at least, is what Bart told his son on the warm summer evenings in their garden, and John listened understandingly, it seemed, or at least half-understandingly, although most of the time the only sound from him while his father talked was the steady *clip, clip, clip* of the pruning shears.

The other destroyers went looking for the surviving tankers, which had scattered over the horizon, and Bart's ship returned to the one tanker that was left burning, the one she herself had hit. Smoke was still pouring from her pilothouse and bridge, while on her rolling deck her crew scrambled back and forth, seeming to be dragged by the serpentine hoses rather than dragging them. The destroyer blinked her signal light at her, and from the bow of the tanker the tiny pinprick of a flashlight answered. The lights talked for ten minutes, after which it was clear that it seemed possible to bring the fire under control, although there was still great danger, because the ship was loaded with gasoline and might explode at any minute. All the officers were dead except the engineering officer, for the shell had hit the bridge. The crew was exhausted from fighting the fire.

Bart was standing beside his commanding officer when the signalman gave this information. "Sir," Bart said, "let me take a boat over."

"Too risky," the captain replied; that's what he really said; the captain thought it much too risky, Bart told his son.

But Bart insisted, and a boat with fifteen volunteers was swung over the side of the destroyer. Bart, who had always been good at sailing small boats, stood at the helm.

Lowering a boat at sea is a precarious business, John learned from his father. The ship rolls the boat into the water at one moment, and before the blocks and tackle can be disengaged, lifts it fifty feet into the air the next. Oh, it is a fine art to lower a boat in a raging sea, and a finer art to pull away from the ship before being hurled against her topsides and smashed.

But that night Bart did it perfectly; his timing was exact, and suddenly the boat was free of its murderous mother ship. With the men straining at the oars, the boat sank into a great valley between two mountains of water, while the destroyer shot up to the peaks overhead, and then the boat shot up and the destroyer slid into the valley. But by that time they were a hundred yards apart, with the men grunting at the oars to make the distance grow, and the destroyer's engines whining in reverse, as she tried to wrench herself away.

They pulled into the darkness and great skill was needed to keep the boat from capsizing. Ahead of them a small bloom of fire still glowed rose red in the middle of the heavy smoke pouring from the tanker's bridge. Coming alongside the ship was just as precarious as leaving the destroyer; it was the same operation in reverse, but again Bart judged it right, and the tanker's men, almost collapsing in exhaustion, cheered.

Bart began to help fight the fire aboard the tanker. Trying to forget the great pool of gasoline under the hot decks beneath his feet, he led a crew of men with hoses to the very base of the flames. The engineering officer, a huge man with a bulging paunch hanging out over his belt, led another group, and within an hour they got the fire out. After examining the damage, they decided they could limp into port unaided, steering from the stern with a jury rig.

The destroyer left them; far to the north the remnants of the convoy needed her help. An escort vessel could not be spared for one wounded tanker, not in the winter of 1942. As the destroyer sped into the darkness, her captain, who had never been friendly with Bart before, signaled with a small red blinker light which could be seen for only a very short distance, a message which Bart never forgot: "Well done, and good luck."

"Well done, and good luck"; that's what the skipper of the destroyer said, Bart told his son beneath the lilac trees; "well done, and good luck." And Bart kept repeating it.

Alone on the raging seas, in command of a ship for the first time in his life, Bart headed for Iceland, the nearest port. The ship had been strained, they soon found, and somewhere gasoline was leaking into the bilges. The smell of gasoline was everywhere. Mr. Redding, the fat engineering officer, found that the pump room was flooded with gasoline, and donning an oxygen mask, he descended into it. Standing in gasoline to his waist, he covered his wrench with a rag so it would not make a spark. At the hatch above, Bart and the other men wore rubber boots so the nails in their heels would make no spark, for a spark was all that was needed to blow them up. Listening to this on a warm summer evening, John almost smelled the gasoline fumes, and he jumped when a firefly throbbed a few feet from his nose.

But the spark was avoided, and Bart brought the ship to port. As a reward he got the Navy Cross, a thirty-day leave, during which he was drunk most of the time, and later, the command of one of the first destroyer escorts built.

"It was supposed to be an honor to get command of a ship so young," Bart usually concluded, and then he sometimes would start to tell the story all over again, while his son steadily pruned the snowberries and the lilacs and hydrangeas, the big shears going *clip, clip, clip*. "Sure I understand, Dad," was all John ever said, and it was impossible to tell from his youthful face whether he really did.

Oh, that was a great summer for stories. Not only did Bart tell them incessantly, but Todd Hasper, lurking with his dog behind the bushes, began to strike up conversations with John, coming to squat down beside him morosely, saying once that this was the first time he had ever seen a Hunter work, saying another time that he wouldn't expect such a boy from such a mother, and finally telling all the stories he knew, bringing them out gradually, giving John first a small glimmer of what he meant, and then confirming it, until in a rage one day late in August John turned on him with the pruning shears upraised and told him he didn't want to hear any more, even if it was the truth.

That night John wrote Molly the first emotional letter he had ever written to anyone. He didn't mention his mother, for she had become a subject which he now thought unspeakable, but he did describe more of his own problems than he ever had before.

"Dear Molly," he said. "This is a lonely place. To tell you the truth, I've had a lousy summer. I guess it's pretty awful to feel sorry for myself, but I hate school too, and I don't like the idea of going back. Do you ever get lonely or is this just something funny about me? I don't know what's the matter, but it's been a real lousy summer, and I just had to tell somebody.

"I wish you were here and we could go sailing together. The next time I promise I won't capsize you. A fellow down at the other end of the island has a catamaran, and sometimes he lets me use it.

"Well, that's all for now. I've been working in the garden all day, and I'm pretty tired. The garden is beginning to look nice, though. Someday I hope you can see it."

He reread this before adding, "Sincerely, John." It seemed to him to be a pretty silly letter, but he felt Molly would understand, and he mailed it.

20

MOLLY WAS SITTING in an armchair near the front door of the Carters' new house in Buffalo when the postman brought John's letter. She usually managed to be there for the arrival of the mail, because she hated the expression on her mother's and grandmother's faces when either of them handed her a letter from John. The postman, the small, dark-complexioned man whom old Bruce had asked about the neighborhood, smiled at her and gave her John's letter first, as he almost always did. Molly hurried with it to her room. Her face was serious as she read it. When she was through, she put it with a packet of John's letters in a cigar box with a rubber band around it, which she kept carefully hidden under some spare blankets on the top shelf in her closet. Taking some new stationery Helen had given her with her own name on it, she lay on her stomach on her bed, and using a collection of poetry as a desk, she wrote, "Dear John, It's lonely here too, and I certainly know how you feel."

There was the duty to write something else then, a thing which embarrassed her, but it had to be explained. "You can see by this paper," she wrote, "that my name has been changed from 'Jorgenson' to 'Carter.' I don't like this very much, but Mother and Granny seem to think it's *very important*. Mother's changing her name back to 'Carter' too. I guess 'Jorgenson' wasn't a good name, as Mother says, but it's a funny feeling to change it like that. Anyway, I guess you better address your letters to 'Molly Carter' after this, because the mailman has been told about it and everything."

Molly paused. That was the part she had dreaded most to write, and now that it was on paper she felt better. Rereading it, she added, "This whole divorce business is pretty silly, if you ask me. Mother says we can't go to Pine Island again *ever,* so I guess I won't be able to go sailing with you, although I'd love to see a catamaran. My dictionary has a good picture of one, and it looks as though it would be fun to sail. I'd also like to see your garden. Is it the one where we looked for goldfish? I'm getting quite interested in some tropical fish I keep in an aquarium I have here in my room. I have two neon tetras, two black mollies, two angel fish, and some guppies. Mother says they're *disgusting,* but I love to watch them swim around. I put a light over the aquarium, and the neon tetras especially shine beautifully."

Molly added a few more sentences about the fish, and finished with, "Sincerely, Molly." Putting an airmail stamp on it, she hid the letter under her sweater and walked down to the mailbox at the corner.

Margaret, who at seventy was still unusually spry, was on a stepladder washing windows. She watched Molly go, knowing exactly what had happened. The child always answered that boy's letters immediately, and whenever she went out for a walk soon after the arrival of the mailman, it meant that she'd got another one. Still carrying her polishing cloth, Margaret got down and walked to her granddaughter's room. She didn't hurry, for it always took Molly fifteen minutes to get to the mailbox and back. Going to the closet, Margaret took down the cigar box and with practiced hands slipped off the rubber band. Standing by the window, she took her glasses from her apron pocket, and put them on. Then she read John's latest letter through twice.

When she had first started reading John's letters, as soon as Molly had returned from boarding school in the spring, Margaret had been surprised at their innocence. Maybe they had a code, she thought, and were saying things which weren't apparent. Helen had agreed with her that it was wise to let the letters continue as long as they were carefully watched. Soon, Margaret thought, the children would betray themselves, if they were trying to put something over, which after all, would not be surprising. Things like that happen every day,

Margaret knew. You don't reach the age of seventy for nothing, she often told herself.

Now she read this letter from John a third time. The talk about loneliness was dangerous, she thought; that's the way men always began. They started by saying how lonely they were, as though all they wanted was companionship, oh sure.

The talk about sailing also deserved close scrutiny, Margaret felt. Remembering the last sail John and Molly had taken together, and the way it had ended up, she felt that the reference to boats and the sentence, "Next time I promise I won't capsize you," were vaguely leering. Margaret replaced the letter in the packet carefully and put the box back on the closet shelf under the blanket. It was time to stop this foolish correspondence, she was sure.

For the last year Margaret had been worried about Molly. Already she was beginning to develop a rather startling figure. Surely it was unnatural for that to begin so young, Margaret thought; she felt there was something almost obscene about it. Both she and Helen had always had "dainty" figures, by which Margaret meant flat-chested, and no member of the family had ever looked like Molly.

It was the Swedish blood that did it, Margaret told Helen; for although Molly had, luckily enough, inherited dear Helen's dark hair, she was a Swede at heart, Margaret was sure, and everybody knew how the Swedes are. They walk around naked on the beaches even today, Margaret had heard, and in a magazine article she had read that they have trial marriages, and legalized abortion, which certainly was sensible enough when it was necessary, but making a law about it obviously would encourage all kinds of things. If anybody doubted that the Swedes were immoral, all they had to do was to follow the careers of the movie stars who came from Sweden, which Margaret did with malignant avidity.

Although it had been a struggle, it was lucky that Helen had succeeded in convincing Molly to change her name, Margaret thought. Not only would it be inhuman to force a girl to explain why her name was different from her mother's every time she was introduced, but it would be wrong to pin the name of an evil man like Jorgenson on an innocent girl, whether a former wife or a daughter. Helen had made a mistake in marrying Jorgenson, but there is such a thing as forgiveness, and there was no point in commemorating a sin with a name. Beyond that, a Swedish name like that for a young girl would be an open invitation to seduction, Margaret thought. "Jorgenson" indeed—how vulgar it sounded!

In spite of her good marks at school and a medal she had been given for writing poetry, Molly was really stupid, Margaret thought; she was so slow to realize the practical advantages of a fine name like "Carter" over "Jorgenson." The girl had insisted on "maintaining her identity," a ridiculous phrase, for heaven's sake, something she had picked up in one of the books she was constantly reading. It had been necessary to explain to her in some detail what an evil man Ken really was before she became convinced. All the gossip which Margaret and Helen had heard about Ken and Sylvia had had to be repeated, with all the elaborations they could devise.

After reading this latest letter from that woman's son, for heaven's sake—really, you'd think that Hunter family would be content with seducing one generation—Margaret went to the dining room, where Helen was polishing silver. Quickly they agreed that the time had come for the correspondence to stop.

When Molly came home from the mailbox she found her mother and grandmother sitting in the living room. "Dear, have you been getting more letters from John Hunter?" Margaret began directly.

"Yes," Molly said, looking startled.

"Well, your mother and I have been awfully worried about it."

"Why?"

"Well, you know, he's a nice boy, dear, but we can't forget the kind of woman his mother is, and his father, you know—the drinking and all that. Your mother says that everybody was talking about it at the island that summer. He drinks like a fish, they say, like an absolute fish."

"What's that got to do with John?"

"There is such a thing as bad blood, dear," Helen said sadly. "I know it's difficult to face, but it's a scientific fact."

"John isn't bad!"

"No, dear, it hasn't shown up yet, perhaps, but it will. And anyway, it isn't good form for a girl your age to be engaging in steady correspondence with a boy. It isn't correct."

"I don't care."

"Not now, but it's already hurting you, dear," Helen said. "You haven't made any friends here this summer. Peggy Talbert next door said her Anne has been quite hurt."

"I don't like Anne Talbert."

"Why not?"

"She belongs to fan clubs."

"What's the matter with that, dear? It's innocent fun."

"It's goony," Molly said.

"That's beside the point. What I'm trying to make you understand is, these letters must stop. You may write him once more and tell him that."

"I won't," Molly said.

"Don't be rude, child," Margaret interjected. "You must honor your mother."

"You don't have to tell him if you don't want to," Helen said, "but you must stop answering his letters. That might be more correct."

"No," Molly said.

"Are you defying us, dear?" Helen asked, her eyes narrowing.

"There's nothing wrong in writing letters!"

"There doesn't seem to be anything wrong in his letters," Margaret said, "but if you examine this last one closely between the lines . . ." Margaret stopped, not greatly embarrassed at having made the slip, but annoyed.

Molly's eyes blazed. "Have you been reading my letters?"

"It's our duty, dear," Helen said. "A young girl . . ."

Molly turned, ran to her room and locked the door. Blushing furiously, she took down the box of letters and read every one, trying to make sure there was nothing her mother and grandmother shouldn't have seen. No, it was only her imagination that they were love letters, but still Molly blushed. Carefully she tore the letters up in minute pieces and walked to the bathroom, where she flushed them down the toilet. Never again would she keep letters, she thought.

For about an hour Molly lay on her bed, staring at the new plaster ceiling. Then she took out her letter paper, and placed it on her volume of poetry.

"Dear John," she wrote. "Mother thinks that we shouldn't write each other, so until I go back to school you better address me care of general delivery at the post office, and I'll go downtown to get my mail. Otherwise there will be a stupid fuss every time a letter comes."

She wanted to stop there, but the slender black fountain pen in her hand and the white paper beckoned. A rush of thoughts came to her head, and her hand seemed to be detached from herself as it wrote, "I hate my mother and I hate my father and I hate my grandparents. I hate them all, every last one of them, and I hate your mother too. They're all rotten people, and I wish they'd die. You write me if you want to, and I'll write you."

She signed it, "Sincerely, Molly," and knowing that she'd tear it up if she reread it, she shoved it immediately into an envelope. Her hands shook as she addressed it. Walking through the living room, she said to Margaret, "I've written him. No more letters will come."

"Good, dear," Margaret said. "I knew you'd see reason."

Molly ran down the street to the mailbox, and she clanged the metal door covering the slot defiantly after she had dropped the letter in.

21

KEN AND HELEN'S DIVORCE soon went through the Florida courts, but it was December 1954 before Sylvia and Bart's divorce became final. Both Sylvia and Ken won the right to have their children visit them a month a year, but it was a hollow victory, for John never even answered Sylvia's letters any more, and Molly had stopped answering Ken now too. The day he got a letter from Helen's lawyer saying briefly that Molly was changing her name, Ken got drunk for one of the few times in his life, and Sylvia cried. They both agreed to keep writing their children, even if they never got replies, and they did so regularly once a week, but the letters were difficult to compose. They had not seen their children for so long now, that it was like writing strangers. Children grow so fast, Sylvia said sadly. She didn't know what books to send John for his birthday, and Ken had to quit sending Molly clothes because he knew her size had changed, and anyway a Fifth Avenue shop where he and Sylvia had picked out some dresses for Molly returned his check, because they said the dresses had been sent back, and the person to whom they had been shipped declined to have alterations made or to accept replacements.

Well, Sylvia said grimly, we shouldn't expect this sort of thing to be easy; it can never be. She was becoming more and more moralistic, obsessed with the conviction that sins have to be paid for in full. *He* is a just God and an angry God, precisely as the Bible says, and there was proof of that enough for anyone with the wits to look around.

But the Bible says there is forgiveness if there is repentance, Ken said angrily, and God knows we've repented enough. No, Sylvia said bitterly; perhaps it's an Old Testament world, not New Testament, and there is only damnation. In that case, the only choice, Ken said, is to be not penitent but defiant, and what was getting into them anyway to have all this solemn talk? "We've got our wedding coming up," he said. "Let us forget the divorces, and if we have to, let us forget our children. We have a life of our own to lead, and a man and woman would have to be extremely foolish to deny themselves happiness after going through so much hell to get it."

"No, Ken," she said wearily, "we can't be that rational. Not you and I. Neither of us can be really happy if we know our children are miserable. It's funny, in a way. When the children were born their happiness was in our hands, and for one reason or another, we haven't done a very good job. Now I can't help feeling that the tables have been turned, and in a strange way, our happiness is in their hands. There's not going to be much for you and me, unless some day we are convinced that the children are all right."

"But that will take time!" he replied. "Meanwhile, we have to do the best we can!"

So a wedding was planned. Sylvia said flatly that she wanted to be married in a church. She had never been religious before in her life, but now was the time. Her father had been an ardent atheist and her mother Catholic, so it seemed logical to her to become a Protestant. A Congregationalist minister agreed to marry them, and said that after a series of talks with her, he would accept her as a member of the church. Rather uneasily, Ken agreed to become a Congregationalist too. His father, whom he hardly remembered, had become a stern Swedenborgian, almost a fanatic, shortly before he died, when Ken was only twelve years old, and religion had terrified him ever since.

The question of whom to ask to the wedding was a troublesome one. Sylvia did not like the idea of just having an official witness there; she wanted to be surrounded by friends and relatives. But her parents were dead, and all their old friends were split into factions over the two divorces, and it was hard to know where anyone stood. Since she and Ken had been living together, a lot of people they knew had dropped out of sight.

She wanted more than anything to have John attend the wedding; she wanted him there so much that she telephoned him at Colchester Academy the moment the date was set. "Ken and I are getting married," she said, her voice tight. "We want you to come."

"I have examinations," he said, without inquiring about the date. Apparently, every contact she had with him worsened matters, because shortly after that she got a brief note from him saying that he had got a music scholarship and wouldn't need any financial help from her any more. The checks she sent him after that were not cashed.

Molly also declined to come to the wedding, but Ken had assumed that Helen wouldn't let her accept. The only person who seemed happy was Carla, who acted as though a big sister were getting married to an old beau long beloved by the family. She asked if she could be a bridesmaid, and delightedly tried on dress after dress.

Ken arranged for his seventy-five-year-old mother, who still lived in Nebraska, to come. Old Mrs. Jorgenson agreed to accept plane fare when he told her it would really mean a great deal to him to have her at the church. Bernie Anderson and his wife said they'd arrive "with bells on," and sent a case of champagne with which to celebrate.

While the preparations were being made Sylvia found herself making comparisons with her first wedding, and the more she remembered about it, the more horrified she became at herself. Her father's business had not been going well, but on her mother's insistence he had borrowed a great deal of money to make the wedding "a proper affair."

Oh, it had been proper all right. The invitations had been engraved on the most expensive paper, and the gowns for all the bridesmaids had come from Paris. Sylvia had worn "white for purity," and Bart had ridiculed her. It had been very sophisticated to assume that no bride was pure, but there had been more to it than that, Sylvia realized: Bart had known perfectly well from the beginning that she didn't love him. He had got hopelessly drunk the day before the wedding, and had asked her if she was in love with someone else, if she had ever loved anyone else, and she had said no, thinking that was the truth, almost. Bewildered by her coldness toward him, Bart had boasted of his virility. At one time or another, he had slept with every one of the bridesmaids she had picked, he had said, standing before her on the day before the ceremony, so drunk he could hardly stand up. They were all Pine Island girls, and the Hunters always exercised the *droit du seigneur,* he had claimed, and Sylvia had realized that in a sense he was right; he probably had slept with most of her bridesmaids, or come close to it. The old rules about not "getting serious" and not "going all the way" had applied only to teen-agers, and the parties on the island had been getting wilder lately.

The knowledge of this had made her first wedding a parody; it had been necessary to be very sophisticated, to smile as she leaned on the arm of her poor tired father. The smile had been hard to maintain as she followed her procession of pretty bridesmaids down the aisle to stand beside Bart at the altar. It had been difficult to look amused when he dropped the ring, obviously because he was drunk, not nervous.

In the middle of the night before her second wedding Sylvia covered her face with her hands when she remembered this. Suddenly all Bart's troubles seemed her fault—she had caused his drunkenness, and the misery of the children; she had put Ken through a special kind of hell; and she had been evil from start to finish, she thought. Smothering her face in her pillow, Sylvia started to cry.

But the second wedding on January 31 was much different. Her only bridesmaid was Carla, a chubby young girl in a new white dress; and instead of leaning on the arm of her debt-worried father, she now had the strong arm of Bernie Anderson, who had gone out and licked the world, but who looked a little like her father—yes, there was the same sad kindness in his eyes. And instead of Bart standing stiffly at attention while he swayed by the altar like a tin soldier too loosely attached to its base, there was Ken, big and relaxed, with a quiet smile upon his face.

Except for Bernie's wife, Rachel, and Ken's mother, no one was sitting in the church, and the rows of empty pews seemed to extend back to infinity through the shadows; the darkened ceiling seemed to arch up to the sky itself. Behind the altar there were fourteen candles and a golden cross. On one stained-glass window was a poorly rendered picture of a shepherd and a lamb, and on another was Christ on a cross, his face tortured and compassionate. All this appeared beautiful to Sylvia. There was no music, and she felt none was needed.

An old minister with a tired face stood on a raised platform near the altar, towering above Ken and Sylvia. Ken's mother started to weep, emitting tiny snuffling sounds, like a small animal hurt. Rachel Anderson put a reassuring hand on the old lady's shoulder.

"Dearly beloved," the minister said, reading from a small red prayer book, "We are gathered here in the sight of God, and in the face of this company, to join together this Man and this Woman in Holy Matrimony; which is an honourable estate, instituted of God . . ."

The ceremony didn't last very long. The minister's voice was mellifluous but subdued; outside the church a fire engine whined in the distance. Ken glanced at Sylvia. She was pale. When she said, "I do," her voice was clear but faint, contrasting strongly with Ken's basso profundo "I do," which echoed through the church like an organ note.

"Let us pray," the minister said.

After the wedding Sylvia, Ken and Carla went to live in France, where Ken had work to do with Bernie Anderson. A year or two abroad would do them both good, he said, and the children might have grown up enough to feel differently by the time they got back. Sylvia felt bad because she had no source of news concerning John; he might be terribly sick and she might not hear about it in time to get there, and she was sure he would want her if he fell ill. She had nightmares of his dying and calling for her. Before sailing she had premonitions of disaster so acute that she telephoned Colchester Academy to see if he was all right. The absence of news about his daughter bothered Ken too, and acting on a sudden inspiration, he wrote Mr. Caulfield, and Miss Summerfield, the headmistress of Briarwood Manor, asking to subscribe to the school newspapers, the yearbooks, the literary magazines—in short, any publication in which the children's names or pictures might appear. Soon after they got to their apartment in Paris, a stack of these materials arrived, and more came every month. From the *Colchester Academy Arrow* they learned, to their surprise, that John, who was then in his second year at the school, had become a member of the boxing team, the pianist and singer for the school band ("Say, Bing and Frank, move over!" a campus gossip columnist wrote), and that he was on the dean's list, with top marks. Molly wasn't mentioned much in her school newspaper, but a copy of the *Briarwood Literary Review* which arrived in March 1955, after Ken and Sylvia had been in France three months, carried a small poem by Molly Carter. It read, Ken found to his astonishment, as follows:

NO

BY MOLLY CARTER

Sometimes I do not want the world to know
That I exist.
I want to see but not be seen
Like gulls in mist.
I envy arctic things upon the snow,
White bear, the fox.
In jungles I would like to be pure green
And gray on rocks.
I know some people want to be admired
Or to be kissed,
But I find too much heartache is required.
Do not insist.

"Isn't that an awfully good piece of verse for a girl her age to write?" Ken asked Sylvia.

"Don't forget that she's almost sixteen now," Sylvia said. "Weren't you writing love poems in Latin when you were only a little older?"

"Yes," Ken said bewilderedly, "but they weren't that good, and anyway, I never wrote a poem called 'No.' All mine said 'Yes.'"

Sylvia laughed. "Molly's a girl," she said.

22

MOLLY WROTE A LOT of verse that year. It was easier for her to say things she felt deeply in that impersonal way than in letters. At boarding school she was a solitary child and all sorts of things were happening which disturbed her.

In the first place, there was the matter of popularity. Everyone kept saying how important it was to be popular, especially at the dances the school held once a month in conjunction with Teaberry Academy, a boys' boarding school in a nearby Virginia town. To Molly these dances were terrifying occasions. It wasn't that she was a wallflower, far from it. There was always a procession of boys waiting to cut in on her. It was easy to make friends, but the difficulty was in keeping them, in overcoming her shyness. When dancing, Molly held herself stiffly erect in the boy's arms, and although she learned to make small talk, her voice sounded mechanical. When, as sometimes happened, a boy tried to squeeze her too tight, or allowed his hand to move around to the side of her breast, she had all she could do to keep herself from breaking away in panic. Almost always the boys kept telling her how pretty she was, how beautiful, how absolutely terrific, and she was never sure how to reply. At first she thought modesty demanded denials, and she said, "Oh no, I'm not," or, "Oh, go on," but that sounded silly. "Thank you," she ended up by saying, "thank you very much," and she didn't realize how cold she made that sound.

Although there were always plenty of new boys to dance with her, they didn't come back many times, and this hurt Molly. There was one earnest boy with glasses who was able to quote A. E. Housman's poems, which she had been studying, and she liked to talk to him; but he was one of the ones whose hands kept straying toward her breast when they danced, and conversation with him soon became impossible. Even when they sat out dances together he seemed to be under great emotional stress, and it wasn't long before he began avoiding her, the way most of the others did. Once at a dance she heard one boy say to another, "Sure, she's a knockout, but all ice."

Girls didn't like Molly, either. They thought her stuck-up, because of both her looks and her grades, which usually were the best at the school. She rarely laughed and never joined in dormitory bull sessions about "boys and stuff like that." Her paleness, the delicate bone structure of her face, her habit of holding herself so erect, and her almost constant silence made her appear to her classmates to be aristocratic and aloof. As Ken saw in her school yearbook, her nickname was "the Countess," and as he guessed, it wasn't meant to be kind.

So Molly stayed by herself, studying, reading far more than her courses required, and pouring out letters to John. When she began writing poetry she sent him a few restrained verses, and his letters of appreciation were enthusiastic. Gradually she began mailing him everything she wrote. The only trouble was it embarrassed her to think of some of the poems which dealt, however mildly, with love. When John wrote her that he would like to hitchhike to Virginia to see her, and that he was sure a meeting could be arranged without her mother finding out, she became terrified. She was sure she would blush piteously when she saw him, and would stammer. Furthermore, there was no reason to believe that he would like her after the first meeting any more than the other boys did. He might go away disappointed, and then their correspondence, the greatest pleasure in her life, indeed, the only one, would stop. Still another danger was that she herself might be disillusioned by John, now that they had both grown older. As things were, she imagined him as tall, handsome and kind, perfect in every respect, and she suspected he might turn out to be something else. She wrote him that the school had very strict rules against male callers; it was practically a nunnery, she said, and there would be all kinds of trouble if he came. A little later she sent him the poem entitled "*No,*" which was published in her school literary magazine.

John was hurt and puzzled by her refusal to see him, but a little relieved, for though his complexion had cleared up during the past year, it still wasn't perfect, and perhaps it would be better after all for Molly not to see him right away. He liked the poem. It sounded almost like a song, he thought, and when he reread it, the beginnings of a melody seemed to be stirring deep down in him, teasing him to try to write it down.

John's interest in music was increasing. He practiced on the piano two hours a day, and played in the school band at all the dances. One small advantage of this was that he didn't have to dance. In spite of his acute sense of rhythm and the inherent elegance of movement which he shared with his father, John, even at sixteen, found that he got so confused when he danced that his feet tangled. The girls' perfume bothered him; the very idea of their being so close to him threw him into a panic; their soft dresses and the feeling of his hand on a girl's shoulder or back, this was all too much to be borne calmly. Dancing inspired a rush of thoughts and emotions which were so overpowering it rendered him as thick-tongued and stumble-footed as though he were drunk.

But at the piano John was a different person. There he was no longer earthbound; he could glide and fly and soar. He could make love to a girl on the piano, very delicately with the little high notes, and passionately with the pounding basses, and often when he put his head back and sang, the dancers stopped and gathered around to listen. His clear tenor voice was so charged with emotion that it made the tired words of old Tin Pan Alley songs flash into life. His singing appeared effortless, as though all he had to do was just sit there and let the music pour out.

Playing at the dances John often forgot his audience entirely. When he looked up after finishing a song and saw the semicircle of faces around him, he sometimes blushed, as though he had been caught naked. The girls from Miss Arden's Academy in Hartford were always teasing John, trying to get him to dance. They said they bet he was a marvelous dancer, but none ever found out, because John was too embarrassed to try.

For months John had been trying to compose a song. He had sat up half the night in his dormitory after the lights were supposed to be out, holding a flashlight under a blanket, staring at the neatly lined music paper and painstakingly writing down notes. The results were so bad that he had given up, but Molly's poem, "*No,*" teased him to try again.

For two weeks he worked on his song in every spare moment, and when it was finished it was a long way from great, he was quite aware, but it wasn't a bad little tune. The only trouble was that Molly's words didn't seem to go very well with it—it bothered him to sing or to write as though he were Molly; he wanted to sing about her. Hoping she wouldn't mind, he changed the words a little. He wasn't as good at writing verse as she was, and for a person who still signed his letters to her "Sincerely yours," the words were pretty embarrassing for him to set down; but in a song he hoped such talk was permissible. This is what he wrote:

NO

LYRICS BASED ON POEM BY MOLLY CARTER

MUSIC BY JOHN HUNTER

My Molly doesn't want the world to know
Her charms exist.
She wants to see but not be seen
Like gulls in mist.
She envies arctic things upon the snow,
White bear, the fox;

She envies jungle birds whose hue is green
Or gray on rocks.
My Molly doesn't want to be admired
Or to be kissed.
Of me I fear she'll soon get sick and tired
For I insist.

John blushed painfully when he reread it, and he became enraged when Dick Woller caught him singing it at the piano. For weeks he polished the music, putting off the decision of whether to send it to her, but finally, in March of 1955, he mailed it.

Molly was both embarrassed and pleased to find he had set her verse to music. Early one Sunday morning she crept into the common room at her school when no one was there, and sat down at the piano. She couldn't play well, and it took her an hour to pick out the tune with two fingers. After she had caught the melody she ran through it ten or twelve times. Played with two fingers, it had its limitations, but she thought it sounded pretty good.

23

THAT SPRING Helen decided to satisfy a lifelong ambition and buy a Cadillac. There was no reason why she shouldn't, her mother said. After all, she hadn't yet done a thing to celebrate her freedom from Ken, and if anyone had earned a Cadillac, God knew she had.

Old Bruce was commissioned to buy the car. He had always prided himself on being able to purchase anything cheaper than anyone else could, especially automobiles, and he began touring every Cadillac garage in the Buffalo area. He and his wife and daughter read all the brochures available, and spent their evenings discussing the relative merits of Fleetwoods, Eldorados and the other models. Helen had a clear idea of what she wanted: the biggest and most impressive limousine made, but she felt she couldn't say that. When Bruce drove smaller models up to the house to demonstrate, she said, "Don't we need more room, Dad? I mean, some day we might take a long trip."

Finally Bruce found the exactly right car, an immense black limousine which had been used by an undertaker to carry mourners in funeral processions. The undertaker himself had recently died, and the car was only a year old, a much better buy, Bruce said, than a new one, and after all, it had hardly ever been driven at more than twenty miles an hour.

Helen and Margaret were ecstatic. Sitting on the soft gray upholstery of its back seat, they felt like duchesses. The car also had a marvelous device, a telephone connecting the rear seat with a small speaker over the driver's head. Margaret, who had always been a zealous back-seat driver, found it a joy to sit comfortably back with the telephone at her lips, a great improvement over the old days, when she had had to lean forward and raise her voice when she wanted to berate her husband. Bruce enjoyed the telephone too. The second day they owned the car, he took it back to the garage "for a checkup" and had a switch installed beneath the little speaker. It gave him a wonderful feeling to let Margaret talk for a few minutes and then, with a touch of a finger, to shut her off. When he didn't answer her through the mouthpiece attached to the dashboard in front of him, she spoke loudly enough to be heard without the telephone, but Margaret had long been used to one-way conversations with her husband, and if he just nodded his head a little from time to time, the secret switch protected him from most of her comments.

They all loved the car, and decided that as soon as Molly's summer vacation began, they would take a trip across the country to see the Grand Canyon and to visit several distant relatives in Wisconsin who might be expected to be properly flabbergasted by their mode of travel. In June they drove to Briarwood to pick up Molly at her school, and immediately set off for the West. Molly spent most of the summer sitting beside her grandfather in the front seat, or standing with dutiful awe before national monuments. Sometimes they covered as much as six hundred miles a day, and as old Bruce often said, it would have been a terrible trip in any car but a Cadillac.

John started that summer as an unpaid counselor at Camp Mantawana in Maine. Bart's drinking habits had not improved, and his conscience bothered him less when his son was not around. Camp Mantawana was run by Mr. Newfield, the teacher at Colchester Academy who had befriended Bill Norris. Some of the boys at the camp were the sons of parents in large cities who worked hard to help their children to escape the heat, but others had, in effect, no parents. Almost a third of the youngsters at Mantawana simply shuttled from summer camp to boarding school and back again, seeing one divorced parent or another only for an occasional weekend, or for Christmas. Through long experience, Mr. Newfield and Dora, his sweet-faced wife, recognized these lonely youngsters at a glance, and treated them with special kindness. When a boy was discovered crying at night, Mr. Newfield often took him into his own cottage, and Dora would quickly slip on her bathrobe to prepare hot chocolate. It was surprising what Dora could do with a cup of hot chocolate and her soft, understanding eyes.

In search of the rare talents he needed, Mr. Newfield picked his counselors carefully, and kept a sharp eye on them. Before the end of July he promoted John to Senior Counselor, with a small salary, and asked him to help with some of the more difficult cases. There was, for instance, the son of a famous actress, a boy named Teddy, who at ten was painfully fat, and who wet his bed so consistently that he had to have rubber sheets. If the others had found out about the rubber sheets, Teddy would have been unmercifully ridiculed, so it fell to John to change the sheets secretly, slipping them quickly into a canvas bag. To facilitate this operation, John moved Teddy's cot into a corner suitably screened from the others by a large chest of drawers.

One of Teddy's difficulties was that no one wanted him for a partner when the boys were divided into mutually protective pairs for swimming. Feeling hurt, Teddy refused to swim at all, and on even the hottest days, remained sweating on the shore. It was John's job to try to sound convincing when he invited Teddy to go swimming with him on the pretext that he himself didn't want to go swimming alone.

John was so successful with Teddy that, before long, the boy was following him around like a large, mournful puppy. Mr. Newfield congratulated John and put him unofficially in charge of a whole group of misfits, including a boy who was prematurely tall and bent at the age of fourteen, a frantic little bully who got into fights almost every day, a stutterer, and a child suffering from a mild form of kleptomania. Finding that exhaustion appeared to be at least a temporary help to everyone's problems, John often took his charges on long hikes over mountain trails and country roads. They made up an oddly bedraggled little army as they trudged along in their green uniforms, with their canteens wagging at their belts and their knapsacks bobbing on their backs. They liked to sing, John found, and there was curious pathos in their cracking voices as they piped, "Over hill, over dale, we will hit the dusty trail . . ."

Late in August Teddy's mother arrived in a red sports car to visit her son and to introduce a new father, his third. A striking blonde who looked almost as good as her photographs, she seemed markedly ill at ease as she strolled with Teddy under the tall pine trees which ringed the camp. Apparently Teddy told her about John, for before she left, her husband, a small man who was beginning to get bald, took John aside. "We're very grateful for what you've done for the boy," he said nervously, and slipped a hundred-dollar bill into John's hand. Then he got in his sports car with his wife, adjusted a plaid cap on his bald spot, and they drove off with the engine roaring. That night it was necessary to give Teddy several cups of hot chocolate.

"You show unusual sensitivity in dealing with troubled children," Mr. Newfield said to John gravely a week later. "Have you ever thought of going into teaching?"

"I haven't really made up my mind what I want to do," John replied to avoid hurting Mr. Newfield's feelings, but he knew he didn't want to be a teacher. The loneliness of his charges increased his own until sometimes he grew so restless that he couldn't stand still. The desire to escape the oppressive atmosphere of the camp got so bad one night that John bolted from his cot to take a stroll in the woods. His walk soon turned into a run, until he was zigzagging through the trees like a wild thing in full flight, with the branches whipping his face, and his breath coming hot. Finally he tired himself out and walked back in the moonlight to take a shower and try to sleep.

John couldn't write Molly often that summer because her address was constantly changing. The communications he received from her were briefer than usual, because Molly had to share motel rooms with her mother, and had scant privacy in which to write. Often she sent postcards which she had hastily scrawled in lavatories. Wherever her family stayed more than a night, Molly insisted upon being allowed to take a walk alone, and sitting in some secluded spot with a pad, she wrote John descriptions of the sights she had seen. One long letter was devoted almost entirely to Bruce's switch on the telephone, which Molly had observed without betraying the secret. She wrote a long rollicking account of her attempts to keep a straight face while Margaret droned criticisms of Bruce's driving into the mouthpiece, and the old man sat at the wheel with a happy smile. From time to time he reached up and turned the speaker on for a few moments just to have the pleasure of flicking it off. Other than this, the tone of Molly's letters was somber. "I try to think about the old settlers who crossed this country in oxcarts, and how brave they were," she wrote once. "I wish I could be like them."

On the first of September Helen returned with her family to Buffalo, and John was able to resume his half of the correspondence. His first missive was as close to a love letter as he had ever come. "Dear Molly," he wrote, "I can't stand this business of not seeing you much longer. I'll be through here at camp next Monday, and Dad would never know the difference if I took a few days off before going back to the island and to school. Couldn't I come up to Buffalo to see you? I have a little money now and would like to make the trip. If we had to, we could meet some place away from your home. I hope more than anything that we can arrange something like that. It's been more than a *year* now! Please try to think of some place we can meet, and I'll be there any time you say."

He signed it, "Sincerely, John," and addressed it "General Delivery, Buffalo, N.Y.," as she had asked him to do.

When Molly read this letter she was not surprised. In spite of her fears, she had been hoping that he would ask to see her again, and on the long drive across the continent, she had enjoyed thinking about what she would do if he did. Locking herself in her room, she took out her paper and without hesitation wrote, "Dear Johnny, I certainly would like to see you, if you really don't mind making such a long trip." She paused and tried to think of a good place to meet. Delaware Park would be nice, but what would happen if it rained? She had a vision of standing there in a pouring rain waiting for him, and that wouldn't be good at all. A movie house? It would be awkward to wait in the lobby with people walking by, any one of whom she might know. Suddenly she had an idea. Outside a small Catholic church which she had often passed on her way to the post office was a sign giving the schedule of Sunday services with the notice, "Always open to the public for meditation and for prayer." Molly, who had been told by her mother and grandparents that Catholicism was wrong, had once been driven by curiosity to go there. Surprised to find that the interior did not look entirely unlike that of the Methodist church her mother attended, she had sat there for a half hour in the dim light, enjoying the unaccustomed fragrance of incense lingering in the air, and the flicker of candles. Now the idea occurred to her that this church would be a good place to meet John. It appealed to her esthetically, and had the further advantage, she thought wryly, of being the least likely place to run into any of her mother's friends.

"St. Mark's Church on Cottonwood Avenue is open all the time," she wrote John. "I'll meet you in the right-hand pew nearest the door as soon as you arrive. Just let me know the day and time."

By return mail John replied that he could get there by the following Tuesday, and that his train reached Buffalo early in the morning. "I'll have breakfast at the station," he said, "and if it's all right, I'll meet you at the church at nine o'clock."

Molly told Helen and Margaret that the Halseys, whose daughter, Susan, also went to Briarwood Manor, had asked her to join them for a day's drive to Canada. The Halseys had a huge old mansion on Delaware Avenue, and Margaret had been hoping that Molly would get an invitation from them. "That's the advantage of a place like Briarwood," Margaret told Helen. "By going there, she'll meet the best people here." Neither Margaret nor Helen made any objection when Molly said the Halseys were sending a taxi for her at a quarter of nine in the morning. The hour and the use of a taxi seemed a little peculiar, but who were they to question what people like the Halseys did?

Molly awoke at seven that Tuesday and was glad she had chosen the church as a meeting place, for although it was not yet raining, it was cold and gray. She put on a blue dress which she had chosen carefully the night before, and sat brushing her hair for a half hour. She wasn't at all hungry, but she forced herself to drink a glass of milk. Twenty minutes before the taxi which she had called arrived, she was waiting at the window with her raincoat on her lap. When Helen and Margaret come downstairs with Bruce for breakfast, they noticed that Molly looked a little nervous, but who wouldn't be, with the prospect of a day with the Halseys ahead? "You look *very nice, dear,*" Helen said. "You never will have to worry about your appearance in *any* company."

"Thank you, Mother," Molly replied.

When the taxi finally drew up in front of the house, Molly threw on her coat and dashed to it, only to find before getting in that she had forgotten her handbag. After returning for that, she entered the cab and sat back with relief. There was no fear that her mother would check with the Halseys, because Helen didn't know them, and would be too ill at ease to call them in any but the most dire emergency. Molly sighed, and took from her handbag a lipstick. Staring into a small mirror, she applied it with the utmost concentration.

It was only ten minutes to nine when she got to the church, and she was dismayed to find that a funeral was in progress. A hearse was drawn up nearby, and a knot of men in formal clothes stood near the door. Molly paid the taxi-driver, turned and hesitated. Then she saw a young man dressed in a tan trench coat without a hat come across the sidewalk toward her, and recognized him as John—the angular features, the way he walked, yes, it was John, who looked frighteningly sophisticated to her now, and older. He hurried up and stood two feet away from her with his arms held tensely at his sides, and all he said was, "Molly."

"Hello," she replied.

A tired-appearing man in a swallow-tailed coat and striped trousers came toward them with a grave look and said, "Are you members of the family?"

"No," John said. "I'm sorry." He touched Molly's arm, and they started walking down the street together. "I didn't know there would be a funeral there," Molly said to him, her own voice sounding unaccountably strange to her.

"I don't mind funerals," he replied. That sounded peculiar, and he added, "I mean when they're somebody else's." That sounded worse. "I mean they don't upset me when somebody I don't know is being buried," he concluded lamely.

"I feel that way too," she replied.

They walked for another minute before they realized they had not the slightest idea where they were going. It was too cold for the park, and at that hour in the morning, it would be hard to find a movie open. "Would you like a Coke?" he asked suddenly.

"Sure," she said. "There's a drugstore just down the block."

They sat across the table from each other in a booth and she took off her coat. He did not say he thought she was beautiful, and his eyes seemed to avoid her. They sipped Coca Cola from large glasses, and suddenly she heard herself chattering about the Grand Canyon, and Old Faithful, and the bears which came right up to the car and ate sandwiches out of her hand.

After an hour and two Coca Colas they felt self-conscious about remaining in the drugstore so long, and moved on to another one. In all, they visited four such establishments that morning and as an admittance fee purchased more Coca Cola than they could drink. At noon he took her to a good restaurant. It seemed important to him to order a festive meal. Somewhere he had read the phrase, "pheasant under glass," and trying to sound matter-of-fact, he asked the waiter if it were available. Finding it was not, he ordered huge steaks which neither of them felt like eating. Sitting across the table from each other, they suffered a curious reversal of roles. John, who had always been voluble, found it almost impossible to talk, and when he tried, he often got desperately mixed up, twisting even the simplest statements into nonsense. In spite of the photographs they had exchanged, it was difficult for him to believe she looked the way she did. What seemed to him to be her astonishing maturity and her intense beauty brought him small delight. Instead, these qualities caused his heart to sink, for they made her seem distant to him and unattainable. He imagined her being besieged by platoons of men who looked like movie stars. Already he had a clear picture in his mind of Molly in a formal wedding gown standing at a church door beside some enormous paragon of a man. Girls usually get married much younger than men do, and she would never wait for him, he was convinced. Yes, she would be lost to him, and it would be wise to start getting used to that idea now. And what does one do when one is sitting across the table from a girl like that? One cannot stare at her, and one cannot look at one's plate, and one cannot keep glancing nervously around the room.

Molly, who at school and home was habitually reticent, responded by talking constantly. The thought of a moment of silence terrified her. After she had told John about her trip, she found herself prattling about the Buffalo weather, which was caused by warm air from the Middle Western plain meeting cold air from the Great Lakes and Canada, creating a cloud belt, she said seriously, or at least, that's what somebody had told her, and there had to be *some* explanation for the scarcity of bright days, didn't he think? When the meal arrived, she heard herself say, "That certainly looks marvelous, doesn't it? I'm glad you like rare steaks too. I wonder where they get steaks like this? They're Black Angus, I guess. In Texas they have mostly

Longhorns, or at least they used to. I think cattle are an interesting subject, don't you? I'd like to learn more about them."

Yes, he said, he would like to learn more about cattle, and he was grateful when she plunged on, saying she would like to live on a farm some day, but cities are nice too.

After luncheon they continued to walk the streets. A cold drizzle began and they turned into the first movie theater they came to. The first half of the double feature was about a collie dog which was smarter than all the people, and the second film was about a debonair detective who never showed the slightest fear, even when in a dark house full of murderers. They observed this without comment. When they came out of the theater it was only three-thirty and it was raining quite hard, so they decided to go to another double feature. It was dark and still raining when they emerged from that. Standing under the marquee, they looked at the lights reflected on the black streets. A taxi drew up in front of them. "Cab?" the driver asked.

"I guess so," John replied. "I can leave you at your home, Molly, before going to the station."

On the way to her house the silence was such that even Molly couldn't break it. Everything she thought of saying sounded absurd, and she ached to have the visit end on a proper note. Remembering the way she had prattled, she blushed in the darkness.

"Molly," he blurted out as the cab approached her house, "can I see you again?"

"School starts next week," she said, having worked all this out in her mind during the day. "I change trains in New York. Sometimes I have a couple of hours . . ."

So it was arranged. The cab stopped before her house, and just before she got out, he squeezed her hand. "Thank you!" he said, knowing that didn't sound right, but repeating it anyway. "Thank you very much!"

Her reply, which also sounded wrong, was, "I'm sorry!" meaning I'm sorry the day didn't go better, I'm sorry I talked so much, I'm sorry I can't ask you to my house. "I'm sorry you had to come so far," she added, jumped quickly from the cab, and fled.

They saw each other three times during the next few months, once when she was on her way to school later in September, and both before and after her Christmas vacation. The meetings continued to be strained, for they never had enough time together to recover fully from the strangeness of meeting after long absence. They had luncheon in the Pennsylvania Station. They inspected the giant Christmas tree and the skating at Rockefeller Plaza; they listened to a choir sing hymns in Grand Central Terminal, and they sat in the waiting room talking earnestly there till it was time for her train to go. Nothing was said between them which either of them remembered. The important things could not be talked about. They never mentioned their parents, nor long-range plans about the future. A casual onlooker might have thought them a brother and sister.

Although the meetings were curiously frustrating to experience, and although they were difficult and expensive for John to arrange, they were a great pleasure to remember and to anticipate. If it weren't for Susan Halsey, they doubtless would have continued.

Susan, a scrawny girl with a pinched, lonely face, developed an attachment for Molly, and wanted to travel with her on the way to and from school. It proved impossible to keep from her the fact that Molly was meeting John between trains in New York. Susan was touchingly eager to co-operate when she found out about it. Molly seemed to her to be a figure of romance, and she liked to think about her having a passionate love affair. The whole situation seemed wonderful to her, much too wonderful to keep from her friends. She told only her best friends, of course, or girls she hoped would become friends, for Susan had been unpopular, but as she always said before repeating the story, she never told it to anyone who could not really and truly keep a secret. Before long the news that Molly Carter regularly met a *very handsome* boy between trains in New York was common gossip throughout the school. Some of the older girls added elaborations about night clubs and hotels. At sixteen Molly had a figure which seemed to make a platonic love affair implausible, and her reticence among the other girls struck many as secretiveness. Still waters run deep, a tall senior a year older than Molly observed, and confided to Molly that she herself hadn't been a virgin for three years.

It wasn't long before the story of Molly's great romance reached the ears of Miss Summerfield, the headmistress. Usually she let such gossip die a natural death, but this rumor kept mounting until she felt she had to do something about it. Although Miss Summerfield had in one of her more earthy moments observed to a colleague that running a girls' boarding school was worse than trying to run herd on an entire pack of bitches in heat, she displayed small humor to the girls and their parents. Gravely she told Molly that although she was perfectly willing to believe in her innocence, it was not good form for a young lady to meet a young man alone in New York, and that she would have to take the matter up with her mother if it didn't stop. "And I'll know, dear, if it doesn't stop," Miss Summerfield concluded. "You'll find that in actual life, secrets are very difficult to keep."

Perhaps not in actual life, Molly observed to herself, but certainly she had no hope of keeping secrets at Briarwood Manor. Most of the student body went through the New York stations before and after vacations, and speculation about Molly's trysts had reached such a point that she felt herself to have no more privacy than a Golden Plover surrounded by bird watchers. All this embarrassed Molly greatly, and the letter she wrote to John about it was awkward. Certainly she couldn't repeat to him the nature of the rumors which had been circulating, and it was hard to explain what her mother's reaction would be if Miss Summerfield notified her. Molly didn't know what her mother and grandmother would do in such an eventuality, but she was sure it would be ghastly. She shrank almost physically from the prospect of discussing John with Helen and Margaret. Such a conversation would be punishment enough. Furthermore, she was quite sure that if her mother heard she had been seeing John, new steps would be taken to make it harder to see or even hear from him again.

In March of 1956, Molly wrote John that they couldn't meet in New York before or after their Easter vacation, and her explanation didn't sound convincing to him. The gossip of silly girls and the fear of the reprisals of old women wouldn't dissuade Molly if she really wanted to see me, he thought, and the fear came rushing up in him that she was tiring of him, that her excuses would continue now whenever he wanted to see her, that the kind-as-possible letdown he had so long expected was beginning. At seventeen, John felt he knew a great deal about the psychology of women, oh, he was realistic about it, and didn't fool himself at all. The boys at Colchester Academy talked a great deal about this subject, and it was widely known that a woman will do anything for a man she loves, and any display of caution is proof of a lack of passion. John imagined many reasons why Molly didn't want him to come to New York to see her any more. His love for her had betrayed him, he was sure—he probably had been so *obvious*, it had undoubtedly shown in his eyes and in the tone of his voice, and Dick Woller might be at least partly right when he said that no woman really respects a man who loves her, that most women want a man to be casual, a little rough or even cruel. John had been too awkward and stumble-tongued, he felt, and the last time he had seen Molly, he had been having a little trouble with his complexion again, and that probably had disgusted her. Dick Woller said that girls were contemptuous of men who didn't make passes at them, and maybe Molly thought he was too timid. But then again he had held her hand awfully tight in the movies the last time, and maybe she thought he was getting too fresh. Worst of all, she probably had met another man, someone at college, probably, with a car of his own, who could run up to Virginia and bring her to football weekends and dances, who wouldn't expect her to sit around in waiting rooms of railroad stations with him, or to endure one double feature after another. Soon she would probably marry someone like that, John thought in despair, someone who wasn't afraid to try to kiss her. Women really are just animals, Dick Woller had said; and although that scarcely seemed plausible with respect to Molly, maybe Dick was at least a little right. What really affects a woman is not kindness nor steadiness nor intelligence nor even a man's looks, Dick Woller had observed, it's just a matter of sex appeal, and some guys have it and some guys don't. Muscles aren't at all sexy to a woman—it's just a certain something, Dick Woller had concluded, and he had smirked.

John wasn't at all sure what that certain something was, but he was quite sure he didn't have it. At any rate, he felt Molly couldn't think of him as he thought of her, or she wouldn't have cut off the meetings. Probably he had bored her, and she had just been trying to be nice. In despair he sat down and wrote her a note held short by pride saying he had received her letter about not meeting in New York, and that he understood.

In the stern resolve not to press himself upon Molly, John did not suggest any more meetings. When summer came, he went back to Mr. Newfield's camp in Maine as a Senior Counselor. Often she wrote him from Buffalo, but she did not ask him to visit her there, and he had no way of knowing that she was afraid he no longer wanted to come.

24

Ken and Sylvia returned from Europe in October of 1956. Ken wrote Molly a letter which was different from his weekly bulletins to her about books and plays he had enjoyed. He wrote:

Dear Molly,

Sylvia and I have bought a small house in Redding, Connecticut, and I would like you to visit us there, or in Florida. I can easily understand how these divorces have been hard on you children, and a certain amount of bitterness is inevitable, but I frankly think that two years of this foolishness about your refusing to answer my letters is about enough. Judging from your verse in your school's literary review, which I've subscribed to, and from all I know about you, you're a remarkably mature and sensitive young lady. After all, you're almost seventeen years old now. You're growing up, and do you propose to avoid your father for the rest of his life? What would you think of a character in a book who did that? Wouldn't she appear cruel and a little smug to you, not just righteous? Sometimes it helps to think of yourself in the third person, to pretend you're a character in a story. Now, I ask you, do you think a real heroine would be so hurt by her father divorcing her mother that she would refuse to see him ever? *A child, yes, but an adult, no, and you're becoming an adult.*

Sylvia is writing about the same thing as this to John, who's being just as difficult as you, and I propose that the four of us get together during your Christmas or spring vacation, or any other time you choose. I am suggesting two weeks of lying in the sun and getting back to normal. We've all had enough hating lately, and it's time to relax. How about it, baby? Are you your old man's daughter or not?

All my love,

Dad

The letter moved Molly. When John wrote to ask with elaborate casualness whether she were going to Florida for Christmas, she said she would. The plans were all made when Margaret Carter had her accident.

On November second the postman delivered a package to the Carter house from a shop in Buffalo that framed pictures. It contained a framed scroll Molly had received from her school as a poetry prize. If Molly had known her mother would have it framed, she would never have sent it to her. As it was, Molly had hesitated, but any printed honor meant so much to Helen and Margaret that it would have been cruel to refuse, and anyway, they had made fun of her locking herself in her room to write poetry for so long that there were aspects of vindictiveness and practical self-defense in mailing them her pay, the fancy, illuminated scroll. Maybe it would cause them to let her alone.

When she unwrapped the frame scroll, old Margaret stood looking around the house, wondering where she should hang it. The living room seemed best. Anne, the girl next door, was having trouble with her studies at the local high school, and Peggy Talbert, her snooty mother, would die when she saw it. Ordinarily Margaret would have waited until Bruce came home, for he did all small chores like hanging pictures, but he was at the wrestling matches. Since his retirement, he did little but attend prize fights and wrestling matches; it was almost impossible to keep him in the house. Helen was at a meeting of the Daughters of the American Revolution, and Peggy Talbert was there too. Margaret suspected that Helen would ask Peggy in for a cup of tea when she drove her home; Peggy had been only too glad to accept the invitation to ride in Helen's Cadillac, and why not, Margaret thought; that old Plymouth of the Talberts' was nothing in which to ride to a meeting of the Daughters of the American Revolution. Anyway, Helen would probably ask Peggy in for tea when they got home, and Margaret wanted that scroll Molly had won to be on the living-room wall when they arrived. It would make a good conversation piece.

In the new house Ken had bought her there was a molding around the top of each wall from which to hang pictures. Margaret got the stepladder from the utility room and balancing herself precariously, climbed up there to hang Molly's scroll. As she put her fingers on the top of the molding, she made a horrifying discovery: the thin strip of wood, which was about three inches from the ceiling, was covered with dust and dirt. The thought that the four walls of each of the twelve rooms in the house had such moldings, all of them concealing filth, was dizzying to Margaret. She was tired and vertigo had been bothering her a lot lately, but she was scared by the possibility that Peggy Talbert might find out about that dirt—that she might climb up there to run her finger along the molding when no one was in the room, and then tell everyone about it—this would be unthinkable disgrace. Margaret had never been one to take disgrace easily, nor to lie down in the face of great difficulty. Tying a bandanna around her hair, she prepared herself for action, and unlimbered her vacuum cleaner. Four walls in twelve rooms contained many hundred feet of molding, and the stepladder was heavy for an old woman. The suction pipe of the vacuum cleaner was awkward to lift up to the ceiling; the hose was too short, and the wire kept getting twisted as Margaret tried to pull the machine along the floor. She leaned out as far as she could from the top of the stepladder to clean as much space as possible before having to climb down and move all her equipment farther along the wall. It was a desperate battle, but in her lust to get at the dirt, Margaret had superhuman energy. She might have got the molding, in the living room at least, completely clean, if the hose of the vacuum cleaner had not wound around her legs like a snake. She fell from the top of the stepladder with her arms outstretched, and she uttered one piercing shriek before her head struck the metal cylinder of the vacuum cleaner on the floor. The machine kept purring, and when Helen came in two hours later, it was keening over her as though she were dead.

But she wasn't. She was only hopelessly injured at the age of seventy-two—with a badly fractured skull and three broken ribs and a triple-broken leg. An ambulance took her to the hospital, where she lay unconscious for three days. When she came to, she insisted upon being taken home. The doctors said it was inadvisable for a person so ill to go home, but the fact that the nurses and attendants didn't pay much attention to her, except to attend to her bodily needs, infuriated her, and she raised so much hell that the doctors decided she might as well die at home as anywhere else.

Margaret was established in state in her big bedroom, with a radio and a television set and an air conditioner and a large dinner bell which she was supposed to use if she needed help quickly, and which she rang constantly. Everyone waited on Margaret because the doctors said that she would live only a few weeks at most and her last days on earth should be made as pleasant as possible, poor dear; anyone could see that.

Only she didn't die quickly; weeks went by, and she was still there, loudly clanging her dinner bell. Helen began to hope (certainly the word was not "fear") that she was eternal, that she would recover, in spite of what the doctors said, and lie there forever complaining that no one cared about a poor dying old woman, no one cared at all, not even her husband, who still spent most of his time at athletic events; oh, he was a great sportsman, Bruce was, Margaret said.

It was a great comfort to have her mother home, Helen told her friends; having her with them in her last days meant a great deal. Of course, one difficulty was that Margaret abused the nurses so much that none stayed more than a week, and Helen finally had to give her mother the sponge baths and all the rest of it, but it was a great joy to tend her mother herself, Helen said.

Molly put off her visit to Florida until spring, and John, upon hearing about it, spent Christmas with Bart to preclude the possibility of Bart's demanding that he spend the spring vacation with him. Throughout the Christmas vacation Molly was pressed into service as a nurse. She was taught how to give her grandmother sponge baths, and it was evil of her to think that the withered old body with the ribs showing through the yellowed skin and the nipples without breasts were ugly. Oh, it was proof of the evil within her that she was sickened to the point of nausea, she told herself. Margaret was her poor, kind old granny whom she should love dearly, and the old lady had never done a wicked thing, not in her whole life, and it was cruel of Molly to get to the point where the very smell of the medicines in her room caused nausea, even before she opened the door.

That was not a gay holiday season for Molly. The usual topic of conversation at the breakfast table was Margaret's weight. Because of her broken bones, she couldn't be placed on the scales, but she was obviously getting thinner at an alarming pace. By New Year's Day, her head was like a skull, but sometimes she seemed to be gaining; that was the puzzling thing. Sometimes she looked healthier, and Helen would say, "I think the poor dear has put on a few pounds," and Bruce would agree before excusing himself to watch an early morning movie before the start of the wrestling matches.

Obviously Molly couldn't be spared to return to school. Poor Margaret might go at any time, her mother said. Miss Summerfield, the headmistress of the school, said Molly was so far advanced in her studies that it wouldn't hurt her to miss a few weeks, and the child could stay home as long as she was needed. No one had any idea that Margaret could last so long. In January the doctors were mildly surprised that she was still alive, and by February they were astonished. The woman certainly has an enormous will to live, one tired young physician said as he heard the clang of her dinner bell while he was walking down the stairs from her room; she must have led a rich life.

At the end of February, Margaret was still alive; emaciated grotesquely and unable to lift the heavy bell now, but living, with her cold eyes glittering brightly. Helen thought that probably Molly shouldn't go back to school that year because she was needed so much at home, but to everyone's astonishment, old Margaret drew the line there. In a faint voice she said her granddaughter should go along; a young girl shouldn't be prevented from graduating from school by someone else's sickness.

On March second, Molly returned to Briarwood Manor, surprised to find herself almost loving the place, but only a week later Margaret died, and Molly had to go home.

It was a beautiful funeral, all Helen's friends said. The casket cost four thousand dollars and was guaranteed to last forever. The undertaker fixed Margaret up so she looked so *natural,* all her friends said; just like her old self.

The inside of the casket was lined with cream-colored satin done up in flounces which old Bruce couldn't look at because it was just like the counterpanes on the beds in an establishment he had visited every year in Buffalo when he got his Christmas bonus. Helen and Margaret had never found out about his Christmas bonus, and in good years it had lasted several nights. The combination of the satin flounces and the Christmas decorations on the streets made old Bruce extremely nervous, never mind some other details, like the rouge on poor dead Margaret's cheeks, she, who had never worn rouge in her life. It wasn't appropriate for Bruce to go to wrestling matches the week his wife died. He would have got drunk if liquor didn't upset his stomach, but as things were he simply stayed in his room and watched the wrestling on television, his small eyes blazing with pleasure as one man jumped high in the air and landed on the belly of another.

Poor Helen delayed the burial of Margaret; she hated to see her go, she said. For three days the old lady lay in state in the undertaker's parlor, while the family took turns standing watch over her. The purpose of this was to allow all her friends to pay their final respects, and counting the membership of the entire D.A.R., quite a few came. Much of the time, however, no one was in the small room where the casket lay, and Molly found it disturbing to sit there on a straight-backed chair waiting for callers.

Finally Margaret was laid to rest in the cemetery and a high marble tower representing the aspirations of humanity or something similar was placed over her. It was far taller than any of the other tombstones nearby, thus achieving for Margaret a final victory over her neighbors.

Helen went into deep mourning and so did Molly, of course. Helen had everything but their underwear dyed black. It had never really seemed possible to Helen that her mother would die, and now she was gone, abject fear came as well as relief. She looked closely at Bruce, and saw that he didn't look well. At seventy-three, there was a pallor upon him; he was still pear-shaped, but he appeared to be gradually deflating, like a balloon with a slow leak. Soon he would die, Helen thought, and someday Molly would get married, and then she would be alone. Never in her life had Helen been alone. Her mother had had sitters for her up till the time she got married because "a young girl should not be left alone in the house." The prospect of living alone in the big house Ken had bought for her parents terrified Helen, and the vast amount of crying she did that week was not only for her dead mother. Tearfully she made Molly promise that if she ever got married she would allow her to live with her. Helen considered having Molly drop out of Briarwood instead of returning, but she had only three months to go before graduating, and no one in Helen's block had ever graduated from such a place before.

On March 15, Molly returned to her school. She was so numbed that she found it difficult to think of spending her spring vacation with her father and with John. Two whole weeks with John would determine whether he really liked her or not, she thought, and with panic pictured herself trying to talk steadily the entire time. That would be the end of the relationship, she suspected, and soon there would not even be his letters to look forward to. Overcome by exhaustion, Molly felt almost constantly as though she were about to cry.

25

Helen was terrified by the thought of Molly spending two weeks with Ken. For a long while Helen had been exaggerating all of Ken's faults, real and imagined, and he came back to her in memory as an ogre, a beast. He was, after all, an admitted adulterer, and although she tried not to think about it, Helen rather imagined that he and that woman he had married lay around all day doing nothing but make love. As if it weren't bad enough to send a pure young girl into an atmosphere like that, there was the appalling fact that that woman had a son who would probably be there too, under the very same roof with Molly, and heaven knew what that woman and Ken would let the young people do, or even encourage. Helen's mind boggled at the possibilities her imagination conjured up. What she couldn't understand was why the law actually permitted Molly to visit her father, even after all the facts had been examined by the court. More than that, the judge insisted that Molly be allowed to stay with her father a month a year if she wished, and Helen's lawyer told her that if she tried to block it, Ken might stop his alimony payments. Helen felt almost as though all the policemen in the world were descending upon her with legal decrees forcing her to commit her innocent daughter to a brothel.

As the time for the visit grew close, Helen couldn't sleep. Old Bruce, her aging father, coughed a lot, and as she lay awake at night listening to him, she half hoped he would get so sick that Molly would have to come home again and be a nurse. Certainly the court couldn't object to the dear girl coming home in an emergency, with her grandfather sick, dying, perhaps, of a broken heart caused by the death of his beloved wife.

While waiting to go to Florida, Sylvia had a premonition that something would prevent the visit, or that if not, it would somehow turn out disastrously. She had a clear feeling that her punishment was not completed yet, that she would not be absolved of her sins until something terrible occurred. There was a temptation for her to go around apologizing to everyone in an attempt to ward off the blow. At midnight she once wrote Bart a long letter telling him she was sorry she had married him without loving him and that she realized now that many of the troubles they had had were her own fault. The next morning she tore it up, but she couldn't tear the recurrent apologies from her mind. One of her nightmares was of John and Molly drowning together while in Florida. They would go off in a boat, the way they had long ago as children, only this time they would never come back. From this dream Sylvia woke up crying. It took Ken a long while to soothe her, and he was shocked when she admitted that she half hoped the children wouldn't come for Easter vacation, because she feared for them so.

Early in March Ken and Sylvia left the small farm they had bought in Connecticut and opened their house in Florida. Driving past the old motel Ken had bought for her, Sylvia averted her eyes, and she was glad he had decided to sell it. The place was closed now, and looked somehow sinister. Remembering some obviously unmarried couples who had come there while she was manager, Sylvia felt as though she had been the keeper of a bawdy house, and this increased her forebodings of disaster.

Despite her premonitions, Sylvia worked hard to prepare for the coming of the children. A week before they were to arrive, Molly's room upstairs and John's downstairs were spotlessly clean, with new blankets and counterpanes on the beds, and new curtains at the windows. The visit should be a fresh start for everyone, Sylvia told herself, and it seemed suitable to renew everything: the rugs on the floor, the towels, the linen. Molly was expected to arrive on April 3, with John coming four days later when his vacation started. From the twenty-fifth of March on, Sylvia worked in the kitchen, helping the cook to prepare a feast to be stored in the deep freezer. She made eight cherry pies, which had always been John's favorite, and a dozen chocolate layer cakes, which Ken said Molly liked, and she bought ducks, great roasts of beef, thick steaks—enough food, Ken said smilingly, to last them all a year.

Sylvia also laid in stores of Coca Cola and ginger ale before reflecting that after all, John had just turned eighteen, and Molly was seventeen: perhaps they'd rather have beer, or stronger fare. This thought bothered her, and she asked Ken whether he thought they ought to serve the children liquor. "If they ask for it," he said. "I don't think I'd volunteer it. We'll just have to play this thing by ear."

On the day before Molly was expected, Sylvia made arrangements to have flowers delivered for almost every room in the house. She ordered calla lilies, roses and spring blossoms of all descriptions.

When Ken smilingly said, "Whom are you planning to bury?" she whirled on him and replied, "Don't say that! Please! Knock on wood!"

During the last days of their waiting Sylvia worried a lot about whether a real reconciliation with their children could be achieved, or whether this was going to turn out to be just a frozen courtesy visit. In the back of Sylvia's mind was the dread that Todd Hasper had talked to John; no, it was more than a dread, it was a certainty, it was logical, taking into account the kind of man Hasper was. At night when she thought of this she covered her face with her hands, the gesture now becoming habitual; she often went to sleep that way. I have to remember that even youngsters are merciful, she thought; at least I have to pray for that. How strange that she could never even imagine talking to John about the things Hasper probably had told him. Such matters could not be talked about by a mother and son; the understanding and the forgiveness, if there were to be any, could not spring from explanation, and after all, Sylvia thought, even if she could discuss such matters, what was there to be said?

She worried about Ken's meeting Molly almost as much as her own reconciliation with John. The big man was like a child looking forward to Christmas, she thought; he seemed to assume his daughter would come running immediately to his arms, that their separation had been merely geographical.

"You don't want to get your hopes up," she said to him. "You might be in for a disappointment."

"Why do you say that?"

"I don't know. I have a feeling . . ."

Her heart jumped when the telephone rang at eleven o'clock on the evening of March 30, and before she picked up the receiver she knew something had gone wrong, that the visit was imperiled. She was not surprised when the operator said there was a long-distance call from Buffalo for Mr. Kenneth Jorgenson, but the look on his face when he picked up the receiver was odd. "Hello?" Ken said, "Who is it?" That was the first time Sylvia had ever heard that deep voice sound frightened.

"It's me!" Helen said, her voice shrill with fear at her own daring, her own sudden midnight decision.

"Helen! What's the matter?"

"It's Dad! Poor Dad."

"Is he dead?"

"No, but he's so sick, and I'm afraid Molly won't be able to go South. We need her here."

"Now look!" Ken said, his deep voice suddenly rumbling louder, sounding as though it could easily carry to Buffalo without the aid of a telephone. "Don't try to pull that!"

"Why, I don't know what you mean! He's got bronchitis, and a terrible cough, and the doctor said, a man his age . . ."

"Get a nurse."

"Why, he might die when she was away, and she'd never forgive herself."

There was a pause while Ken clenched and unclenched his free hand. "What's his temperature?" he said suddenly. "The truth now, because I'm going to call his doctor."

"It's not the temperature, it's his poor lungs, at his age . . ."

"Helen, you listen here! You stop this foolishness and let Molly come down here, or I'll cause you more trouble than you've ever dreamed of. You won't get another cent out of me until this thing is straightened out. I'll get every lawyer in New York on your tail."

"It's an emergency . . ." Helen said weakly.

"You better have a doctor's sworn testimony to prove it!"

"Molly could come some other time . . ."

"I want her here now."

"She doesn't really want to come. I can't force the child."

"Is she there?"

"No. She's at school. I just talked to her."

"I'll call her myself in the morning."

Ken slept hardly at all that night. At ten the next morning he telephoned Briarwood Manor. It took a long while to get Molly to the phone.

"Hello?" Molly said suddenly, her voice sounding timid and far away.

"Molly, baby, I'm going to be terribly disappointed if you can't get down here for your vacation," Ken said, and the note of pleading in his voice shocked Sylvia. If Molly doesn't come, I bet John won't, she thought—he's really coming to see her, not us. There would be no visit after all, Sylvia thought as she listened to Ken's sad voice, and she was caught in a collision of disappointment and relief.

"Do you *want* to come?" Ken kept saying to Molly. "Do you *want* to?" There was a silence before he said, "Don't cry! Don't cry! Oh, *please* come down here! We need each other!"

There was a pause before he put the receiver down. His face was glistening with sweat when he said, "She is coming."

Sylvia said nothing. The fear was churning in her again that it would be better, far better, if everything were postponed. *You shouldn't have begged her*, she wanted to say, but that would have hurt him too much. The rest of the day Sylvia hoped for the telephone to ring again, but it didn't.

Molly's plane was due at five the next afternoon. Carla had not seemed overjoyed at the prospect of "a new big sister" arriving and went off to spend the day with friends. Ken insisted on leaving the house at four, although it was only a ten-minute drive to the airport. Sometimes the planes got in early, he said, especially with a tail wind, and anybody could see that the wind was blowing hard from the north. In the waiting room, he paced back and forth restlessly, dressed in his best linen suit, with his handkerchief neatly folded in his breast pocket, and a new necktie of the pale blue Molly liked. Sylvia sat with her hands folded in her lap, bent over like a nun in church. When the plane was announced, she had to run to keep up with Ken as he strode to the gate. Behind a rope barrier he stood in the midst of a knot of people, watching intently as the door of the plane was opened. The stairway on wheels was rolled up, and out stepped a girl, but it was the stewardess. Next there was a fat man with a briefcase, and a woman holding a child. A seemingly endless procession of people came out; one would never have thought the plane could hold so many. Last of all came Molly.

"There she is!" Ken shouted, a deep bellow that carried all the way to the plane, and bursting from the knot of people, he vaulted the rope barrier, and ran toward her. She stood on the platform high up, by the plane door, a slender girl in a blue coat with the wind whipping the skirts about her legs, holding her hat on her head with one hand, and she looked confused as that enormous man ran toward her, came bounding up the steps, and crushed her in his arms. *Oh no, he shouldn't have done that*, Sylvia thought; *these things have to go slow and easy*, but it was too late to say that. Ken came toward her, so wrapped up in his own joy at seeing his daughter that he didn't notice the strained look on Molly's face, the frightened, puzzled eyes. "Here she is!" he said jubilantly to Sylvia, "Hasn't she grown up to be *beautiful?*"

"Hello, dear," Sylvia said in a low voice, and held out her hand, because she was suddenly afraid Molly would flinch if she kissed her. My God, maybe she knows all about me too, Sylvia thought with horror, and was about to let her hand drop when Molly clasped it shyly, and said, "Hello . . ." Molly stopped suddenly, because she had almost added "Mrs. Hunter," and she couldn't say "Mrs. Jorgenson," and certainly not "Mother," and "Sylvia" sounded wrong too, as though she were trying to get chummy with her or something. The three of them walked to the car, and Ken drove them home, talking enthusiastically about all the wonderful things they were going to do, now they were all getting together again.

"John is coming Thursday," Ken said, his voice a little roguish.

"That's nice," Molly replied, attempting a casual tone of politeness, but sounding completely uninterested instead.

Ken glanced at her sharply, and for the first time noticed how pale she was, how tense. "Are you feeling all right, honey?" he asked.

"Yes," she said.

When they went into the living room, Molly stood in front of a mirror by a vase of calla lilies and slowly took off her hat. "If you'll excuse me, I think I'd like to take a little rest before dinner," she said in her gentle voice. "The plane ride was a little rough."

"Of course!" Ken and Sylvia said in unison.

After she had gone upstairs, Ken strode restlessly back and forth in the living room. "It's perfectly natural for her to be shy at first," he said. "Let's have a cocktail, Sylvia—I feel like one tonight."

Sylvia stirred up some Martinis. When Molly came down she glanced at the pitcher on the table and said, "Do you mind if I have one?"

"Sure," Ken said. He got up and poured it. As Molly took the glass he noticed that there was a barely perceptible nervous tremor in her hand. "It's good to have you home again!" he said too heartily. "You don't know how I've been looking forward to this!"

Molly took a sip of the Martini and put the glass down. "Thank you," she replied, obviously trying her best to respond. Turning to Sylvia, she smiled and mechanically said, "I also want to thank you for the beautiful flowers in my room."

"That's all right, dear," Sylvia replied, and reaching for the pitcher of Martinis, was shocked at a sudden urge she felt to get drunk. Without pouring herself a drink, she put the pitcher down. "I think it's about time for dinner to be served," she said.

At breakfast on the morning of the day John was to arrive, Molly said she was going to take a long walk on the beach, looking for shells down by the inlet. She asked Ken not to wait for her if she wasn't back in time to go to the airport.

"Try to make it," Ken said, sounding puzzled. "I think poor John would be hurt if you weren't there. You used to be such good friends."

"I'll try," Molly said, but there was that in her tone which forbade urging, a note of dignity more than shyness. As soon as she had finished her coffee, she changed into her bathing suit, and putting on a beach coat to protect herself from the sun, she set out, walking slowly, with her head bent down, but not looking for shells. It was necessary to forget the pages of poetry she had sent him, she told herself. Probably he had forgotten it himself, and anyway, it wasn't really important whether he liked her or not; she could survive. It was silly to depend so much on his letters anyway.

Houses had been built all along the row of dunes since Molly had been in Florida, but she was too preoccupied to see them. Children ran past her throwing sand. A hairy man in swimming trunks whistled at her as she walked by, but she didn't hear him. Instinctively her feet took her north, where there was privacy, for when the hurricanes came bursting through there in the fall, the seas raged high on the beach on both sides of the inlet, and the marching rows of houses stopped cautiously a quarter mile away. Climbing to the crest of the dunes nearest the inlet, she sat with a piece of salty grass between her lips, and stared out to sea.

An hour before John's plane was due, Sylvia changed into her best white dress and combed her hair. Glancing into the mirror, she saw that insomnia and the strain of the past few days had made her appear haggard. Well, she thought grimly, if Hasper has talked to him, I look the part. One little drink before going to the airport wouldn't hurt, she thought, and took two.

The important thing is not to have a lot of preconceptions of what he will be like now, she thought. He is older, he will be going to college next year, and I must not stand here expecting to meet a young boy.

John was one of the first out of the airplane. He came down the stairway of the unloading platform a strong eighteen-year-old, but when Carla went running out to meet him his smile was boyish. Sylvia stood stock-still as he came toward her, and then his arm was around her, there was the scent of shaving lotion, and she had been kissed, briefly and politely, by her son. "It's good to see you, Mother," he said. "You're looking awfully well."

"So are you," she thought she said, but her lips moved inaudibly, and she had to say it again: "So are you."

How gracefully he walked! How courteous he was as he chatted with Ken, how affectionate with Carla! How at ease! With what polish he opened the car door for her, helping her in, and shutting the door firmly but without too loud a slam. And what implacable reserve there was beneath all those good manners, Sylvia thought; how secret were the eyes above those smiling lips.

"Isn't Molly here?" he asked when they got in the car, almost succeeding in sounding casual.

"She walked down to the inlet, and I guess she misjudged the time," Ken said. "She'll probably be home when we get there."

"You've got quite a surprise in store for you," Sylvia said, trying to sound gay. "Molly has become quite something to see."

John made no reply, and for the first time Sylvia noticed that his face was pale.

Molly was not in the living room and not in her room when they got home; she was nowhere to be seen, and the hurt in John's eyes was more than he could conceal. They sat down on the terrace overlooking the sea, and his eyes kept traveling up and down the beach, but she was nowhere. Sylvia tried to make polite conversation with him while his eyes kept searching the sand. I have forgotten the silent, secret ways of youth, Sylvia thought; of course she didn't want to go to the airport, she wanted to meet him alone. Smiling, she said to John, "I think I'll take a little rest. Why don't you take a walk on the beach?"

"Can I go?" Carla asked.

"You stay with me," Sylvia replied. "Ken, you promised you'd help Carla fix her radio."

"Sure," Ken said, rather bewilderedly. "Now?"

"Please, Daddy," Carla said, and they went upstairs together.

Sylvia went inside and stood at the window watching John go walking down the beach, a tall young man in a brown gabardine suit, leaning forward to face the wind. Putting her hand up to shield her eyes from the sun, she watched him out of sight.

He saw a girl from a distance, a small person in a blue bathing suit sitting on a yellow beach coat on the sand, high on the dunes, with her back toward him, facing the inlet. Probably it was she, he thought, forcing himself not to run. Even when he was close to her he could not be sure. Then his shadow, preceding him on the sand, fell across her, and she glanced up: the heart-shaped face, the big eyes—Molly. They must have said something, but no words remained in his memory afterward, only the way she looked, her dark hair, the thin gold chain around her neck, the old-fashioned locket given her by her mother resting just at the beginning of the swell of her breasts, her incredible grace: Molly, at seventeen.

He sat down beside her, apparently without words, or at least without words which meant enough to be remembered. He glanced down at her ankles, slim and graceful, the marvelous tendons of her foot, taut beneath the skin.

For about five minutes they sat together there, staring out to sea where the breakers curled over, crashing in upon themselves. They glanced secretly at each other, but looked away quickly again. A family of picnickers, a middle-aged couple and their children, came and spread out a tablecloth on the sand a few hundred feet away, and shouted hoarsely at their children, giving orders concerning the unpacking of baskets, the opening of Thermos jugs, and the gathering of firewood. Impatiently John and Molly stood up, and started down the beach, walking in the soft sand, oddly matched, with her in her bathing suit, and him in his brown gabardine suit. Their hands, swinging as they walked, touched, and he took hers.

"It's wonderful to see you again," he said.

Part Four

SPEAK NOW

26

"JOHNNY'S GOT A GIRL FRIEND!" Carla, who was then twelve years old, said four days later.

"Yes," John said. "I have."

He was in his bathing trunks now with a towel thrown casually over his shoulders to hide a small splotch which embarrassed him unbearably.

"I can see why you're on the boxing team," Ken said. "You've got quite a set of shoulders there."

"Actually, I don't like boxing very much," John replied.

He left them as soon as he could and ran swiftly to the beach, where Molly was awaiting him. It embarrassed them less to leave the house individually, and to meet in private. Wearing her blue bathing suit, she was sitting just above the reach of the tide. "Hello!" he called exuberantly as he ran. "Sorry I'm late!"

He was all of three minutes late. She stood up, smiling, with the wind blowing her hair across her face. "I haven't been waiting long," she said.

They started walking down the beach together, their hands automatically locking, the wind at their backs. Near the inlet at the end of the beach they paused. Three shrimp boats were putting out to sea, fighting the breakers on the bar and the rush of the incoming tide. A flock of gulls hovered like a great wheel turning over them. Farther up the inlet was a hollow created in the sand by the surf during the last hurricane. Semi-surrounded by high banks which were covered with tall grass and stunted palmetto trees, it offered at least a measure of privacy. John wanted to take Molly there, but the fear mounted in him that she would refuse, that in all probability she was willing to hold his hand simply as an act of friendship, far different in its implications from accompanying him to a lonely spot. If he did ask her to go there with him, he thought, or if he simply headed in that direction, she might refuse, saying, perhaps, "Why do you want to go there, Johnny?" She might even feel indignant, shocked, angry, disgusted, jerking her hand from his forever because he had misinterpreted a comradely gesture, and then, of course, he would be left standing there on the beach stammering apologies, and the sky would fall, all dreams would shatter and come crashing down like broken glass around his feet. Torn by his desire to be alone with her, away from the eyes of the swimmers and picnickers and gatherers of shells, and by the fear of ruining what was already a kind of perfection, he stood tongue-tied. Then, with the feeling that he was taking an immense gamble, risking everything on one sentence, he said, "Let's go in there where we can sit sheltered from the wind."

"All right," she said.

They walked into an amphitheater of broken dunes. Beneath their feet the sand, shading from tan to gray to white, was still stippled by the action of the waves. When they found themselves shielded from passers-by, they sat down awkwardly, with their backs against the steep slope of the dune, their legs stretched straight out in front of them, their hands still clasped, their faces tense, almost agonized. He wanted to put his arm around her waist, to pull her toward him; he wanted to touch her shoulder, but again the fear rose within him, redoubled. Maybe, indeed probably, she had come there with him just to get out of the wind. "Johnny!" she might say if he touched her, "Johnny Hunter, you stop that! Why, the idea! Johnny, you should be ashamed of yourself!" She might slap him, she might go screaming down the beach calling for help, she might tell her father, the police; and worst of all, he might find that he inspired in her only disgust, that she didn't love him, that no woman could ever love him at all. If he tried to kiss her she might recoil in horror, as though touched by the snout of a pig, and then he would know, as he had always suspected, that there was something repugnant about him, and that he was condemned to loneliness. He would have to walk back up the beach then, knowing that she would soon abandon him for someone else; that she had been kind, but that no one could in the last analysis be kind enough to overlook the fact that he was too repellent to be loved.

After sitting frozen by these thoughts for a minute, John moved toward her a little, cautiously enough to make it look like an accident if she recoiled, ready to pull back and say with elaborate casualness, "*Sorry!*" His muscles were so tight that his arms ached. She let go of his hand suddenly, perhaps in alarm. He put his arm back in a tortuous, cramped position, not touching her, but then she leaned toward him, and he let his arm down on her shoulders. Thus the incredible came to pass, he played Russian roulette and won, or at least she allowed him to place his arm around her shoulders, and did not scream or run.

They sat in a very cramped position, their bodies rigid, he leaning forward with his arm around her warm shoulders, she half turned to rest against him, and he was afraid to speak, afraid to move a quarter of an inch for fear she would pull away from him. A strand of her hair blew across his lips; he bent his head down; the fragrance of her hair and skin seemed to grow more and more intense until he took her by both shoulders and turned her to him, thinking now she will run, now I have betrayed myself, but I cannot help it, and he kissed her on the lips, finding them soft, inquiring, maybe responding, maybe not. Terrified that she would pull away, he kissed her again, and he was not sure of her consent until he felt her place her hand on the back of his head, caressing him softly. Then a shudder went through him, and feeling that the greatest of all imaginable crises had passed, he looked up and found her smiling at him. In slow motion he reached out his hand and touched her gently on the cheek, and the old words sounded newly invented.

"I love you," they both said.

He stretched out on the sand beside her. "You are," he said, saying something he had been aching to say for the past four years, something he had been afraid to say, "you are more beautiful than I can believe."

"I'm glad," she said. "It's nice to know you like the way I look." There was a pause, and then she added, "Johnny, you aren't fooling me, are you?"

"I love you so much you make me tremble," he said. He held his hand out to her, and it was true, at that moment he was trembling, as though just rescued from the face of a cliff. She caught his hand and held it tightly against her cheek. "I was scared to death you didn't really like me," she said.

"Me too. I was afraid that if I tried to kiss you, you'd run."

She laughed and he kissed her again, burying his face in her neck, tasting the saltness of her skin. Then the laughter stopped, and there was the incredible softness and warmth, beauty beyond old dreams, so long forbidden.

"No, Johnny," she finally said, pulling away from him.

"Are you angry?" he asked in panic.

"No, but I am afraid."

"I want to marry you," he said.

"We can't. Not for years."

"We could run away together," he said.

"It would be silly, Johnny. You've got to go to college, and the army, and all the rest."

"That will be six or seven years!" he said in horror.

"We can still see each other. Often."

"But we have to go back to school in a week," he said, astonished to find that this prospect remained even on these days of wonder.

"Where are you going to be next summer?" she asked.

"Pine Island. Could you visit us there?"

"I'm afraid Mother is going to keep me in Buffalo again," she said miserably.

"Maybe we could get together in the fall," he said. "I start at Harvard in September and girls often come for weekends."

"Mother would never let me."

The thought of the lonesome months ahead sobered them. They kissed more deeply than before, and he found it difficult to stop. "I don't want to scare you," he groaned. "I'll take you home now if you want."

She said nothing.

"Oh, Molly!" he said, and she did not pull away from his kiss.

For Molly there was fear, counterbalanced by the knowledge that the word "no" struck him like a stone in the face. There was the vision of his stalking away as so many boys had after dancing with her, his need unmet, her loneliness remaining. There were the kisses, the kisses. . . . There was the moment of panic, the pain, in which a thousand hideous voices seemed to scream. There were the fears upon fears mounting and echoing against each other; there was the feeling of being imprisoned, of being unable to escape; there was the vision of her father crying. She seemed to be in a circle of mocking faces chanting *shame!* The thin, horrified scream of her mother ululated constantly in the back of her mind. There was the vision of her dead grandmother shaking a finger at her, telling her that monstrous things would happen if this were not forbidden. There was the incongruous stink of sweat, the sharp hot breaths, the animal sounds, the sudden image of a lamb being eaten by a lion—terror. At one time she tried to pull away from him, but he held her in a grip of iron. And then the bad part was over, and she found herself not with a beast of prey, but a man who worshiped her. His face was dumb with adoration, he was suddenly as gentle as a father with a child, and she knew finally that he belonged to her, that she had paid a great price, but that he was hers, and that she could not deny him when he begged forgiveness.

There was also joy. Since childhood she had thought of her body as something that had to be hidden, not only because of the unimaginable things, the wickedness, the sin, but also because she thought clothes were a necessary deception to hide some mysterious, fundamental ugliness of flesh. But on that day Molly found that in the eyes of one person at least she was, astonishingly enough, perfect; that she had nothing to hide; and that she could cause delight. It was an incredible luxury to stretch proudly there on the sand before him, bearing him gifts in the sun. There was the absence of all defenses, the easy communication between them, the fringe benefits of love.

Afterward there was the talking, the first time that either of them had ever talked to anyone, really, which is to say, the first time they had ever talked about anything which mattered. He told Molly all about Bill Norris, about how it had been to wake up at night and see that empty cot, perfectly made up, in that lonely room. He went on, the words rushing out in an orgy of truth, telling how the boys had jerked the covers off Bill, how Bill had lived for two years in the midst of cruelty and jeers, how the headmaster had covered up, how even he himself had ended by finding it impossible to tell Bill's mother what had happened to her son. He told her also about the lonely summer he had spent at camp. She in turn told him in detail about her troubles at school, about why she had had to stop meeting him in New York, and about Margaret's death. The fact that it is occasionally possible to talk about things next to the heart was an extraordinary discovery. It was as though they had always been alone in a desert world bereft of people, and for the first time met a human being; it was as though they had been deaf and dumb from birth and just found the power of speech; it was astonishing, this discovery that conversation can go beyond ordinary communication, that language when combined with love can conquer the separateness of people. He remembered the letters they had written each other, the funny mincing phrases, the sense that there was nothing to write about, except in poems or songs, and he said, "Why haven't we ever been able to talk before?"

"Because we were afraid," she said, stretching like a cat in the sun, fragile and delicate.

After about an hour they got dressed and started toward the house, walking slowly along the beach, pausing often, John still talking rapidly, gesticulating with his arms, laughing, picking her up in a torrent of words, explaining his whole life. She listened gravely. He told her about his father, about the day of his mother's departure and the night, and was understood.

As they approached their house John did not feel oppressed by the necessity to keep a secret. There was not the slightest temptation to tell anyone, neither to boast nor to confess. He walked into the living room of his mother's home without seeing the people around him. When Molly went upstairs to her room, Sylvia started asking John questions about his school, and more to avoid an irritating interruption of his thoughts than anything else, he sat down at the piano and played his mother every song he knew, saving only the one he had written himself. Sylvia was astonished to find he could play so well.

But for Molly it was different. When she left John and started climbing the stairs to her room, she experienced a sudden dizziness so strong that she almost fell. At the head of the stairs Ken, who had heard her footsteps, emerged from his bedroom smiling, and said, "Hi, baby. Did you find some good shells?"

"No," she said, her voice tight, tears almost coming, and hurried to her room as fast as she could without running. Totally confused, Ken stood mutely looking after her, wondering what he had done wrong.

That night Molly sat across from John at the middle of a long table with her father at one end and Sylvia at the other while an aged Negress served a festive dinner. Molly had a terrifying compulsion then to speak out, to tell the truth. "Dad," she would say, and her father would glance up, his big alert face looking tired, as it had lately. "Dad," she would say, "Johnny took me out in the dunes today, and I think I may be going to have a baby." She imagined her father turning on John then in a rage.

The waitress took away a dish of pea soup, one of the favorite dishes which Molly had barely touched, and replaced it with a platter of rare roast beef, the very smell of which nauseated Molly. She glanced away from it, and she had another vision then, a horrifying one, of herself saying, "Dad, do you know what I did today?" and following that question with every obscenity she had ever seen chalked on lavatory walls, the short hideous words spewing from her mouth like vomit. Then her father would arise and smite her, perhaps kill her, she imagined.

"Molly, aren't you hungry?" Sylvia asked.

"Oh yes, I'm going to eat," Molly replied. Eating was extremely difficult, but she felt it necessary to give the impression that she was feeling perfectly well. John was looking at her worriedly, and she smiled timorously at him.

After dinner she went to her room, saying she wanted to read. Her head throbbed; there was a feeling that the top of it was going to blow off. Holding both hands pressed to her ears, she threw herself down on her bed. That night she had dreams which she did not remember upon awaking, but which made her flail her arms, knocking over a lamp on the bedside table, causing her father to rush in crying, "What's the matter?"

With scared eyes she blinked at the big man in the blue bathrobe at the foot of her bed. "I guess I must have had a nightmare," she said.

In the morning Molly arose with a profound sense of disaster. After forcing down her breakfast, she put on her bathing suit, went to the beach and sat huddled on the sand, a forlorn and dejected figure in the bright morning sun.

John soon appeared in swimming trunks, buoyant and self-confident, and threw himself down beside her in the sand, a young athlete astride the world. He took her hand and touched her wrist, a gesture of infinite tenderness, and he said, "I hope you're feeling better."

"We can't hold hands here," she said. "Someone might see."

"Is there a law against it?"

"Johnny! It's not good taste!"

"All right," he said, and let her hand go.

An old man in short trousers who was walking without shoes at the water's edge looked at them curiously.

"Let's get out of here, Johnny," Molly said. "Let's take a walk."

Striding along the beach, John asked her about her school, and she described it, finding him easy to talk to, but oddly enough, their new ease of communication did not include her fear, her terror, her guilt—that was a dark island within her, unapproachable even to him.

Two old women with big straw hats were casting from the beach into the inlet. Wearing faded cotton dresses almost to their ankles, they shouted gaily to each other, and ran up and down the beach whooping with glee like children whenever one of them caught a fish. To escape their curious stares Molly led the way to the secret place in the dunes, and almost immediately John kissed her, pulling her tight against him.

"No!" she said desperately.

He stopped immediately, taken aback. "Why?"

"Because I'm still afraid." That, the understatement of the year.

"Of having a baby?"

"Yes. That and other things I can't explain."

"If you did find out you were going to have one, we could get married right away."

"No!" she said.

"Wouldn't you like to get married?"

"No. Not now. Not that way."

"I know you're right, and that we should be sensible and wait and all that," John said in a monotone.

"Yes," she said with great earnestness. "We've got to be good."

"I don't know what it means to be good," he said miserably.

"Are you bad, Johnny?" she asked, shocked. "Do you do this with other girls?"

"No," he said. "I just don't know what the word means, the word 'good.' Will it be 'good' to see each other hardly at all for the next four or five years? Is loneliness 'good'?"

"That's not what I mean," she said.

"I think your shoulders are good," he said. "I give these tendons in your foot a mark of excellent."

"No, Johnny! Please!"

"Can't I even hold your hand?"

"Of course, but you *don't* stop."

"I just want to hold your hand," he said.

The wind rustled the grass on the dunes, making the palmetto leaves whisper, and she started suddenly, believing someone was there. It would be bad to be seen in such a secluded spot, she thought, even if they were only holding hands. Behind the sandbanks anyone might be lurking—small boys, vagrants, bird watchers, Peeping Toms, her father taking a morning walk. The shadows on the sand, even the clouds in the sky, seemed full of scowling faces with eyes. She sat rigid with fear, and she said, "Johnny, we shouldn't be seen here. Let's take a walk."

"All right," he said. "If that's what you want."

"How about a swim?"

"I hate swimming," he said. "The water looks cold."

"I'm asking you to go swimming with me. Then you're coming home with me and you're going to chat with Dad and your mother. It's important that we be very normal."

"Sure," he said.

"How would you like to rent some bicycles? I haven't ridden a bike in ages."

"That would be fun," he said, brightening.

"Let's go," she said. "I'll race you into the water."

In a blur of motion she was off in front of him, her feet kicking up a spray of sand. Just at the water's edge he caught up with her, and they plunged into the sea together, emerging from the first comber breathless, but shouting like Indians in battle.

27

THROUGHOUT THE VACATION the atmosphere in Ken's house became more and more tense. Molly's shyness and reserve increased. She didn't seem capable of sitting and talking with either Sylvia or Ken, and when they addressed her, she had a habit of averting her eyes. Sylvia became convinced that Molly must have heard such terrible things about Ken and herself that it was torture for the poor child to be polite, as she was obviously trying to be. John played the piano almost every minute he wasn't off somewhere with Molly, and on the few occasions Sylvia tried to engage him in conversation, he was courteous but evasive. There was a troubled look in his eyes, and in the music he played there was a wild mixture of elation and despair. Molly was obviously the cause of the elation, Sylvia thought; of the despair, she felt herself to be the mother. Her only consolation was that some day both Molly and John would grow old enough to forgive. All children go through a stage of despising their parents, she told herself grimly; divorce just makes matters a little worse.

On the last afternoon of Molly's vacation John and she sat on the beach in the place the hurricane had made crashing through the dunes, but it was not secret enough. "Anyone could come along," Molly said.

No place to go.

"Molly," he said suddenly, "the place where I used to live, the old motel—it's closed, locked up and for sale."

"Oh, no, Johnny!" she said. "Not an empty house. The very thought gives me the creeps."

"No one could find us there."

"No," she said.

"I know that place. There's a loose window in the cellar. I could get in."

"It scares me just to think about."

"You keep worrying about people seeing us," he said. "I thought . . ."

"Please, Johnny, for the last time, I beg you. No."

"All right," he said. "I don't want to scare you. I keep telling myself that." He put his hand out and touched her ankle with such infinite longing that she was moved. "Poor Johnny," she said.

"I know I'm wrong about this," he said. "Anybody would say so."

"Don't worry."

He stroked her foot. "Did you ever look at a foot?"

"Yes," she said, laughing.

"I mean, really look at it."

"Sure."

"It's very beautiful. The way it's made. This arch, like a steel spring. The marvelous things like steel cords just under the skin. It's a miracle."

"There are lots of miracles around then," she said, smiling. "Four right here."

"Yes," he said. "I would like to understand more about miracles."

"Want to be a doctor?"

"No. I would hate to take a foot apart." He encircled her ankle with his fingers. "I like it as it is."

"Kiss me, Johnny."

"No. I would only end by making myself even more miserable, or scaring you. It's no good because it's one-sided. I've just realized that."

"It's not one-sided!" she said, shocked.

"This part is."

"Johnny, it's not that I don't love you! It's just that I'm so terribly scared!"

"I know." He stretched out on his back on the sand, deeply tanned now, and lithe, but curiously in the attitude of a corpse. His eyes were closed against the sun, and his chest seemed hardly to move for breath. He said nothing.

She sat near his head, looking down at him. "I love you, Johnny," she said.

He smiled without opening his eyes. "That will be good to think about."

"It's true."

"I know it is. I love you back."

She sat staring down at him, feeling oddly as though she had killed him, the tableau complete, the murderess sitting by her victim's side. He seemed utterly relaxed, his face serene, the voice friendly, no forced melancholy, but indefinably dead.

"We'll write often, Johnny," she said. "Every day."

"And sometimes twice."

"I'm sorry Mother won't let me visit you. Maybe I can make her change her mind."

"Maybe."

"Next summer maybe I can talk her into letting me go to Pine Island."

"That would be wonderful."

"Mother might change her mind about your visiting me at school, and you could, anyway."

He rolled over on his side, facing her, and said, "We've got to face facts, Molly. Your mother is going to make it just as tough on us as she possibly can. She wants to break us up, and maybe she'll succeed, at least for a long while."

"We can stick it out," Molly said.

"I've been lying here trying to imagine what it's going to be like. With no fooling, Molly. Sunday when I start back to school. My old room. It's a thing I'm trying to get used to."

"Me too. I don't look forward to it, either."

"I know," he said.

"We play volley ball every day at three. I hate volley ball."

He laughed.

"We also play field hockey," she said. "There is an enormous girl who keeps rushing down on me. I just get out of her way, and it makes the other girls angry."

"Don't dispute her," he said. "I want no broken bones."

"We have to carry books on our head to learn to stand straight," she said. "There's a teacher there by the name of Miss Wriggly. Honest. And she wriggles when she walks, in a kind of horrible way."

Molly got to her feet, turning, to John's astonishment, into an expert mimic. "Miss Wriggly says, 'Now, girls, you must realize how important it is to know how to enter a room. You should pause at the door, and you should imagine that all eyes are upon you. It doesn't make a bit of difference whether it's true. You should *feel* it. You should carry yourself like a queen.' Then," Molly concluded, "she comes wriggling in. Like this."

She gave a convincing demonstration of a stilted, mincing gait.

"Do queens walk like that?" John asked, laughing.

"I never saw one. I don't think Miss Wriggly has, either."

"I love the way you walk," John said. "Don't let Miss Wriggly change it."

"She wouldn't like to hear you say that," Molly said. "She says, 'Molly Carter, what am I going to do? You *won't* learn how to enter a room and you *won't* learn how to sit.' "

"To sit?" John asked in astonishment.

"Yes. We're supposed to sit like this." Folding her hands neatly in front of her, Molly sank in a highly circumspect manner to the sand.

"I love the way you sit," John said. "Don't let her change it."

"School's not going to be so bad after this, Johnny," she said softly. "Nothing's going to be so bad. You've done me good."

"Come on," he said briskly, sitting up. "We've got to go back. There's a dance at the hotel tonight. Want to go?"

"Johnny," she said, catching him by the hand. "Kiss me once."

"No!" he said brusquely. "There's no point in making this any tougher."

"Is a kiss tough?"

"Oh, Molly. Stopping after one is. I'm trying my best to do what you want."

"Right now, I want a kiss."

He gave her one. When it was over she said, "I'll go with you tonight. Wherever you want."

"Don't offer that," he said bluntly. "I don't have the strength to refuse."

"I wouldn't offer if I wanted you to refuse."

"Oh, Molly!" he said, pulling her to him and burying his face in her hair. "I don't want to do awful things to you."

"They're not awful things."

"I don't want to make you scared."

"I love you, Johnny," she said. "Don't ever forget that."

"I'm going to ask you to go into the motel first and make sure everything's all right," Molly said very reasonably while they were walking back along the beach. "I'll tell Dad we're going to the movies. That will give us plenty of time."

"All right," John said.

"Down at the Bijou they're showing *King Kong* again. I saw that ages ago at school, so if they ask me questions about it, I'll know the answers."

"Good," John said. "Molly, if you don't want to do this, for God's sake, don't."

"Hush. Have you seen *King Kong*?"

"No."

"Well, you better know about it in case they ask you how you liked the movie. It's a real old one they keep reviving. There's this big ape, a gorilla or something from a prehistoric age. He carries this girl, Fay Wray, I think it is, off in the palm of his hand."

"Oh, Molly," he said. "I'm beginning to feel awful."

"Why?"

"I'm making you do something you don't want to do."

"I never do things I don't want to do," she said. "Ask Miss Wriggly."

"You're sure about this? All these plans make it so sort of cold-blooded."

"We have to be practical," she said. "Now listen about *King Kong*, because Dad might get suspicious, and he might ask you questions, and Johnny . . ."

"Yes?"

"Johnny," she said with dreadful earnestness. "I don't want to be caught. You said there was a way not to have a baby."

"Yes."

"Can you do that?"

"Yes."

"This is horrible," she said. "Why does it have to be so horrible?"

"I don't know," he said in real confusion. "The horrible part—I don't know."

"Is it worth it, Johnny?"

"No." The word sounded false. "It's not worth it to you," he added.

"It is to me if it is to you."

"No, Molly," he said. "The hell with it. I'll take you to that dance and tomorrow I'll get on the train, and that will be that. We'll write letters."

"It's worth it to you," she said conclusively.

"Yes," he said. "I can't lie about it. I don't know why, but yes. I don't care much about consequences. I know that sounds horrible. Maybe I'm horrible. I don't know."

"All right, Johnny," she said. "If it's that important to you, it's that important to me."

They continued walking down the beach. "About *King Kong*," she said. "In case anybody asks you. In the end, this big gorilla, or whatever it is, climbs the Empire State Building, and these airplanes come and kill him. He bats at them like flies, but they kill him. It's kind of sad."

"Sounds terrible," John said.

"If anybody asks you, just talk about the end," Molly said. "That's the part that everybody remembers."

He left her at the house, got a flashlight, and went to reconnoiter the old motel. By that time it was almost dark.

The cellar window of the motel was as loose as he remembered it. He opened it easily, and lowered himself into a small storage room.

Pitch blackness. He turned on the flashlight. The room was piled high with terrace furniture covered with dust. He found his way to the stairs, holding his hand over the flashlight so that it could not be seen from outside, the beam making his fingers glow red and satanic in the dark. The old familiar kitchen, the hall. The little lobby was ghostly with sheet-shrouded furniture, and there was the smell of mothballs. Then he came to the curved staircase with the cool wrought-iron railing he had run his hand along so many times before. He hurried up it and went to his old room. There it was, with the bed on which he had cried so often. Two chairs were piled on top of it, a box of books, and a desk. The whole pyramid was covered by sheets. He took the sheets off, put the furniture in the old places, and dusted the room with one of the sheets. In the bottom drawer of the bureau he found a silk-covered comforter packed with moth flakes. He shook it out and covered the mattress on the bed.

On the way out he glanced at his mother's old room. The closed door looked ominous. He walked down the familiar hall, and opened it. In the corner was the empty armchair where his mother had often sat. Now it was covered by a sheet. Dead silence.

Still keeping his hand over the light to allow only a faint glow, he walked back to his own room. The smell of moth flakes was overpowering. The catch on the window opened easily, and he slid up the sash. Fresh air. Outside, the surf pounded with the old familiar roar, and a half moon was just climbing out of the sea. The wind bent the faded muslin curtains into the shape of wings.

He went downstairs to a side door, which was bolted from the inside, as it always had been, and went out, leaving it so it could be opened from the outside. He walked six blocks to the drugstore. A tall old man with bushy eyebrows stood behind the counter. Steeling himself, John whispered to him.

"Young man," the druggist said quite loudly, "how old are you?"

John glanced around. There was no one else in the store. "Twenty-one," he said in a low voice.

"Young man, I doubt it. I have four children of my own and eight grandchildren. I see no reason why the fact that I'm a pharmacist should place me under an obligation to contribute to the . . ."

John walked out. He was trembling. Looking at his watch, he saw it was almost eight, when he had said he would meet Molly.

The wizened colored maid let him in the front door. Ken was

sitting in the living room reading a newspaper. "Hello," he said, smiling and looking up. "I suppose you want Molly."

"Yes," John said. "We're going to the movies. *King Kong*."

"She's upstairs," Ken said. "She'll be down in a minute."

John got a copy of the *Saturday Evening Post* with a picture of a little girl with pigtails on the cover. He sank down in an easy chair and started to read a story about a cowboy and a pretty schoolteacher. Then there was a footstep. He looked up. Molly was standing before him in a dress that was yellow, almost the color of gold, quite formal. She had put a white magnolia blossom in her hair. "Come on, Johnny," she said. "Let's go."

"Kind of dressed up for the movies, aren't you?" Ken asked.

"We might stop in at the dance afterward," Molly said.

They walked out the front door and down the driveway.

"We can't go," John said. "The druggist wouldn't sell me one. Maybe I can get a taxi and try somewhere else." His voice sounded tortured.

"Poor Johnny," she said. "It must have been horrible."

"It was."

"We'll just have to be careful," she said.

"No. I'll take you to the dance."

"Do you want to?"

"No!"

"Is the motel all right?"

"Yes! Why does this have to be so terrible?"

"It doesn't," she said.

The side door opened at his touch, and they climbed the dusty stairs silently together, his hand glowing over the flashlight beam. When he opened the door to his room, he saw that moonlight was streaming through the window, and he put the flashlight out. The wind from the sea was fresh. She stood in the center of the room with the moonlight glinting on her golden dress. "Oh, Molly," he said. "I'll never forget . . ."

28

ALL THAT EVENING Ken was restless. At eleven-thirty he gave up trying to read and went to his bedroom, where Sylvia had already retired. No light was on when he opened the door, but he knew she was awake and having an asthma attack. The rasping of her breath was torturous. "Is it giving you a hard time tonight, darling?" he asked. As his eyes got used to the darkness, he saw that she was sitting up in bed.

"I'm afraid so," she replied wryly.

"Have you used the nebulizer?"

"Not yet. The darn stuff keeps me awake."

He undressed, slipped on his pajamas and got into bed. Sleep did not come. It seemed like a long while before she said, "Ken, what time is it?"

Snapping on the light on the bedside table, he glanced at his wrist watch and said, "Quarter after twelve."

"Shouldn't the children be home from the movies by now?"

"They said they might go on to the dance at the hotel afterward."

"Oh." There was a sound of a match striking and a sudden glare as Sylvia lit a cigarette.

"I wish you wouldn't smoke in bed," he said.

"I'll be careful."

"It's dangerous," he retorted, feeling ridiculously irritable. "You shouldn't do it."

"I said I'd be careful!" Her voice was sharp.

"I'm sorry." He closed his eyes and tried to concentrate on mathematical problems, a procedure which had always worked better for him than counting sheep. Through the open window came the distant music of a radio turned too loud, and the growl of a truck's gears on the state highway. It seemed to Ken that hours passed. It was hot.

"Ken," Sylvia whispered. "Are you still awake?"

"Yes."

"What time is it?"

He put the light on again. "Almost one o'clock."

"When is the dance over?"

"One, I think."

"They ought to be home pretty soon."

"Now don't lie there worrying about them!" he said impatiently.

"I can't help it."

"There's nothing to worry about!"

"I don't know, Ken. They're terribly in love. Surely you can't miss seeing that."

"Of course."

"It isn't easy at that age. They're both so intense!"

"That's natural, isn't it?"

"Yes, but I've been lying here thinking that we should talk to them. Do you think we should?"

"What about?" He kept his voice deliberately noncommittal.

"I don't know. It seems as though we ought to be able to help them. We went through so nearly the same thing ourselves."

"Don't make the mistake of ascribing our experiences to them. They're different people."

"I know, but . . ."

"What do you think we should say to them?"

"I don't know. That they should take it a little easy, I guess."

"Do you think that would help?"

"Poor Johnny's been hurt so much! I don't want anything else to happen."

"Molly wouldn't hurt anybody, for heaven's sake!"

"Not on purpose. But sometimes I wonder if she knows what she's doing. A girl that age . . . Beauty is such a terrible power."

"Molly isn't like that!"

"Oh, I know," Sylvia said in confusion. "But they're both so young!"

"They're going to be all right," Ken replied.

"What time is it?"

"Quarter after one."

"They ought to be home pretty soon."

But at two Molly and John were not home, and they were still out at three. "Darn it, I *will* have a talk with that boy," Ken said angrily. "He's got to learn to be more responsible!"

"Don't put all the blame on him. I imagine Molly has something to do with it."

"I'll have a talk with her too," Ken said grimly. Lying in the darkness with his ears straining for the sound of a door closing or of footsteps on the stairs, Ken was shocked at the series of thoughts to which his worried imagination was subjecting him. There was, grotesque in its ugliness, the image of John making love to Molly, of his hand on her breast, of . . . That is ridiculous, Ken told himself. The old are always attributing their own guilty memories to the young. They are innocent, both of them; they are little more than children; there is something especially hideous in the concept of the worried father conjuring up such fantasies about his daughter.

But damn it, he thought, there's something that I don't trust about that boy—that unnatural courtesy; he is a Hunter after all; he's more Bart than Sylvia, he's Bart all over again.

Ken remembered with strange acuteness then the sensation of seeing Bart kiss Sylvia in the old days, his own helpless longing, the mute jealousy. . . .

Jealousy, he thought, turning over violently in his bed; that's it, I'm jealous all over again, and that's really ugly, the father jealous of his daughter's suitor. Johnny's not really like Bart; I suppose I wouldn't like any boy with Molly. It's not fair to damn Johnny because of his father.

Nevertheless, Ken found his fists doubling up at the very thought of the name "Hunter." The way the boy looked at Molly, the quick response in her eyes, the manner in which she got up immediately and followed when John left the room, without any conversation being necessary, the hours during which the two of them disappeared together, walking down the beach—suddenly these fresh memories seemed sinister to Ken and infuriating.

I will not let him take advantage of her, he thought; I shall have a talk with her; I shall warn her. It is the duty of a father to teach his daughter the ways of the world.

At half past four in the morning, while these thoughts were still revolving in Ken's mind, he heard the front door shut softly and footsteps on the stairs. He got out of bed.

"Ken!" Sylvia said. "Where are you going?"

"They're here. I'm going to have a talk with them!"

"Wait! Do it in the morning when we're all calmed down!"

"I'm going to do it now!"

"No! You'll only say things you'll regret. Wait till everybody's rested."

Disregarding her, Ken opened the bedroom door and walked into the hall. In the dim light he saw Molly and John standing halfway up the stairs, Molly a step above John, leaning over and embracing him, with John almost lifting her. "*I love you,*" Ken heard her say before his heavy tread startled them and they broke apart, their faces white, staring up at him. Instinctively Ken retreated into his room and shut his door, and he had no way of knowing how distraught and how angry his face had looked to them, what a shock his sudden appearance at the head of the stairs had been. A moment later he heard the sound of hurrying footsteps as Molly ran through the hall to her room. Leaning against his closed bedroom door, Ken pressed his forehead against the cool wood. He felt dizzy.

"Ken, are you all right?" Sylvia asked.

"Yes."

"What's the matter?"

"I guess you're right. I should wait till morning."

"Of course. Come to bed now, darling. They're home and there's nothing to worry about any more."

Back in bed, Ken lay trying to formulate the talk he was going to deliver to Molly in the morning. You must wait, the gist of it was; you must not give yourself too easily. You must be practical. You must realize that passions, once aroused, are not easily controlled. You must be sure that a boy like John is honest in his affections. It is hard for you to realize, I know, but I've heard too many young men standing in washrooms boasting of their conquests, describing each whisper of love as a personal victory. "Boy, what a night!" I've heard them boast, and I've seen the evil grins upon their faces. It sounds ridiculous to you I know, he thought of himself saying, but it would be more normal for John to be like that at his age than not.

You must learn to be master of your emotions, he thought he would say. Do not let a boy like John take advantage of you. It will be years before you can be married. Meanwhile, it is better for you to be careful, to permit a good-night kiss perhaps, but only a circumspect one.

Be chaste, he thought he would say. Oh, for your own sake, be chaste! Be conventional. It is not right for a girl your age to be out with a boy till dawn. Be home by midnight after this, and no more kisses on the stairs, no more kisses like that one . . .

All this developed in his mind into such a puritanical lecture that finally his sense of irony was aroused. What a great moralist I in my middle age have become, he thought; how stern I am about the morals of others!

Remembering his old longings for Sylvia when she had been Molly's age, remembering his dreams of going to a far land where seventeen-year-old girls could be married in the fullness of their beauty instead of wasting their youth away, he smiled wryly at himself. I should not be surprised, he thought, to find that what I want for my daughter is exactly opposite to what I wanted for myself.

Outside his window the first light of dawn turned the bedroom gray. I must be realistic when I speak to Molly, he thought; God knows I'm old enough and I've been through enough to have something sensible to say.

I cannot tell my daughter to welcome passion, to be proud of her beauty, to take joy in the giving of it, he thought. That might be a nice idyl, but it is hardly the sort of advice which would be best for her now.

He had, he recalled, heard of "modern" parents who gave their children complete license and who even provided them with contraceptives, but that thought was so hideous that he could not stomach it. That could happen only in a debauched family, he thought; that would not be encouraging love at all, that would be destroying it. Such a thing could only be the final degradation for everyone concerned.

So, he asked himself, what is my advice to my daughter? Kiss a little, but not too much. Do not allow a boy to make love to you, but do not be too angry if he tries, do not freeze yourself. Do not be too chaste nor not chaste enough at seventeen. Be a half virgin, for that is the rule of your world, and such rules cannot be trespassed against. We do not live in Samoa, no; we have our own strange customs. Allow yourself to be fondled, to be half had in the back seats of cars if you must, but always draw back in time; restrain yourself; give no final fulfillment either to yourself or to the man you love. And if you cannot be half chaste, be the complete, eternal virgin like Helen and old Margaret; be shocked by sex; be sterile. Or accomplish if you can the ideal of your world: withhold yourself completely before marriage and give yourself completely afterward. Be a quick-change artist.

How ridiculous it all is, Ken thought: there simply is no honest advice on this subject which can be passed between the generations. Shall we all maintain a frightened silence?

Look, Molly, he thought of himself as saying a little desperately. People with healthy emotional lives can love without having to find physical expression right away. Your love will be greater if you can save it. The economic capacity for parenthood is a necessary preliminary to love in this country.

What solemn nonsense, he thought; how like a YMCA counselor I begin to sound; how big the words get when the truth is left behind! "The economic capacity for parenthood is a necessary preliminary to love" indeed!

Poor Molly, he thought; after all Helen and I have put her through, I expect her to be perfectly sensible. Do not be starved, I want to say to her; do not be hungry; wait patiently for love, wait until it is convenient.

My daughter, he thought; that is the trouble; she is my daughter and oh, she's seen love run hot and cold, she has. A father has no right to be horrified at seeing his child turn out to be the image of himself. I, the great moralist, did not have such a patient youth; no, in the grove of pines with Sylvia that night, I read no moral lectures, no exhortations to virtue, and I have never really been sorry.

Do not be like me: that is really what I want to tell my daughter, he thought. And do not be like Helen, and do not be as Sylvia was at your age; do not withhold and do not give; just wait; youth should be a time of suspended animation, and I have almost forgotten the loneliness and the hunger, the impatience, and the waste, and that is good, for if I remembered those too clearly I could give no fatherly advice.

"Ken," Sylvia said, "are you still awake?"

"Yes."

"What are you thinking about?"

"I'm trying to figure out what we should say to the children."

"I wish I could talk to John, but I can't," Sylvia said. "I'm afraid he would think me an utter hypocrite."

"Molly will probably think that of me too. God knows what Helen has told her about us."

Ken finally fell into a fitful sleep. Awaking at nine, he dressed quickly and went down to breakfast. Neither Molly nor John had got up yet. At eleven Ken went upstairs and with sudden timidity knocked on Molly's door.

"Who is it?" she asked sharply.

"Me," Ken said in his deep bass. "If you're awake, I'd like to talk to you a minute."

"Come in," she said, her voice tight.

He opened the door. Molly was half sitting with the bedclothes pulled modestly up to her chin. It was immediately apparent to Ken that she knew what he had come to talk about and that she was both scared and defiant. He sat down on the foot of her bed.

"What do you want?" she asked, and her stare was so direct that he found himself momentarily tongue-tied.

"I just wanted to caution you a little . . ." he began.

"About what?"

"You and Johnny . . ."

"I'm in love with him," she said, barely above a whisper.

He answered before thinking; the words blurted themselves out automatically. "You're too young!" he said. "You've got to be sensible!" He did not mean to make his voice sound angry. He saw her expression change; it was almost as though she had slipped a mask over her face, and he knew suddenly and with despair that there would be no more confidences between them.

"We will be sensible," she said, her voice flat and ironic.

"I mean . . ." he began again, but he did not really know what he meant. For a moment they stared at each other wordlessly. "I just want to help," he said finally. "I don't want to see you get yourself into a mess."

"I know," Molly said, dropping her eyes. "If you don't mind, I'd like to get dressed now."

"All right!" he said gruffly. He got up clumsily and kissed her on the forehead. Feeling completely helpless, he left the room. In the living room he met John. Not wanting to face him at that moment, Ken said "Good morning!" rather brusquely, and brushed by him to the front door. John saw him smash his fist into the palm of his hand with exasperation, and the noise seemed almost as loud as a clap of thunder.

29

"I'M GLAD TO SEE that you are entering into more of the school's activities," Mr. Caulfield said in May, six weeks after Easter vacation.

"Yes, sir," John replied.

"Of course, your record here has been an extraordinary one, but in my report to the admissions officer at Harvard I did feel obligated to say you were an oddly solitary boy. It was the only mark against you."

"Yes, sir."

"Of course you got the scholarship anyway, but I think I will send in an addendum to my report, saying that we have helped you to become more gregarious."

"Yes, sir."

"Your being chosen leader of the band—well, it will look very good on your record, as a counterbalance to your academic and athletic distinctions," Mr. Caulfield continued. "The well-rounded boy—it's what all the colleges want. I think perhaps you might apply for a bigger scholarship."

"Thank you, sir."

"They have a few which cover room and board. I'll see what I can do for you," Mr. Caulfield concluded.

The school band, a nine-piece affair, practiced in the gymnasium every Friday night. Ted Farlough was good on the trumpet, and Fred Cohn was terrific on the drums, and the others struggled along as best they could. John walked to the gymnasium now to practice with them. Ted and the others were already warming up. "Come on, Johnny," they said. "Get on the mike."

The band swung into an old one, "East of the Sun and West of the Moon." John let them run through it once before he began. "East of the sun," he sang, "and west of the moon, we'll build a dream house for two, dear, east of the sun in the day and west of the moon at night . . ."

"Man, that's wonderful!" Art Bradshaw said. "You're wasting your time with Latin, boy."

"Thanks," John said, embarrassed. "To tell you the truth, I never liked that song. What else have we got?"

It was that evening that Mr. Nealy, newly returned to the school after a long absence, knocked on the door of John's room. "Telephone call for you," he said. "Long distance."

John hurried to the booth on the bottom floor of his dormitory. "Johnny?" Molly said, her voice taut.

"Yes! Are you all right?"

"Oh, Johnny!" the words were followed by an agonized silence.

"Molly, what is it?"

At the other end of the line there was a deep intake of breath. "It's happened," she said finally.

"Are you sure?"

"Almost."

"Where are you? Where are you now?"

"Drugstore," she said. "Near school. Had to tell you."

"Have you told anyone else?"

"The doctor!" The words were a gasp of agony. "I went out of town to see one!"

"Don't cry!" he said. "Please don't! We'll figure this out."

"How? Can you come here? I need you so much, Johnny!"

"Of course I'll come."

"When?"

"Tonight. I'll start tonight."

"Oh, thank you, Johnny! I had imagined awful things." Immeasurable relief was in her voice. "I was afraid you'd say it was no business of yours," she said.

"Molly! We're man and wife."

"Yes!"

"I suppose this is terrible to say, but I'm glad."

"Oh, Johnny!"

"Except for hurting you."

"What will we do?"

"Get married!"

"How?"

"We'll figure a way."

"I feel so ashamed!" Agony again.

"*Nuts!*" he said, the word coming out like a crack of a whip. "Don't talk like that, Molly! Cut that stuff out! We're going to handle this together, and everything will be all right, but you've got to quit being ashamed."

"I'll try," she said.

"If anybody should be ashamed, I should. Let me be ashamed for both of us. It's easier on me."

"All right." Her voice was meek.

"Now listen. Dry your eyes and go back to school and wait for me. We ought to keep this secret till we figure out what we want to do. I don't know how long it will take me to get there, but I'll make it as soon as I possibly can. We need a chance to talk and figure things out. When I come, pretend I'm your brother or something."

"They know I don't have a brother."

"O.K. So I'm asking you out on a date. Does that school let you have dates?"

"Just on weekends. On weekdays you can call on us in the common room."

"Tomorrow's Thursday," he said. "I'll be in the common room as soon as I can."

"But what are we going to *do*?" she asked.

"Give me a chance to think, but I know we can figure it out. O.K.?"

"O.K.," she said.

"I'll be there as soon as I possibly can. Goodbye, darling."

"Goodbye," she said, and before the click of her hanging up, she added, "Thank God, Johnny."

He had been calm up till then, but upon leaving the telephone booth he felt suddenly confused. He had to get permission to leave the school—if he just ran away, they would look for him, and that would add another complication. He needed money immediately. How much did a train ticket cost to Virginia? He had no idea. Could he get a plane? Again no idea. Money—that was the first thing. He ought to get a hundred dollars, and he wished he hadn't torn up the checks Sylvia had sent him. In his school bank account, he had only seven dollars left from his Easter vacation.

No money.

Nobody to borrow a hundred dollars from at Colchester Academy. The masters would ask questions, and the boys wouldn't have it to give.

No money. Panic took him. Maybe it would be simply impossible for him to go immediately.

Of course not. He could hitchhike if necessary. Make it almost as fast, with luck.

Or borrow money from the headmaster. Say there was a family emergency. Father sick. Have to make some excuse like that anyway to get permission to go. No point in having Caulfield set the cops searching for him.

But if there was a real emergency like that, wouldn't the family wire money? Old Caulfield would get suspicious if John not only wanted to leave without official word from the family, but also asked to borrow money. And if he got suspicious, he might prevent John even from hitchhiking—he might keep an eye on him or something, and even lock him in his room if he were caught slipping out with a suitcase. And then he wouldn't be able to go at all.

No. This has to be done right, John at the age of eighteen thought. No mistakes. And immediately a plan formed itself, a lie based on the truth.

"Mr. Caulfield," John said to the headmaster fifteen minutes later. "I've just received some pretty bad news. Family emergency."

"I'm sorry to hear that," Mr. Caulfield replied, his voice full of concern. "What is it?"

"It's kind of embarrassing, sir."

"You can tell me, son!" Mr. Caulfield always thought himself a very understanding person. The boys could bring him all their problems, he said.

"Well, it's my father, sir. He, well, sometimes he drinks too much."

"I'm sorry to hear that," Mr. Caulfield said, although he had heard it before from other sources. He always kept a thorough record on "the home situation."

"I guess he's been drinking too much lately, especially too much, I mean, and he's sick. The woman who worked for him quit two days ago, he was so hard to get along with. This woman, old Martha Hulbert, started driving to Florida to look for work, but in Virginia she got worried about Dad. Said her conscience bothered her about leaving him alone. So she stopped to call me up. Said she thought I should take a visit home, maybe put Dad in the hospital. I just got this long-distance call from Virginia."

"I'm sorry to hear that," Mr. Caulfield said. "Don't you have any relatives you can call on?"

"Well, you know Dad and Mother are divorced."

"It's a hard job for a young boy," Mr. Caulfield said. "Putting his father in the hospital. Especially in this sort of situation. Isn't there anyone who could help?"

"Yes, sir," John said. "All kinds of friends are on the mainland. If

Dad actually has to go to the hospital, I'll get them. But first I'd like to see."

"Couldn't one of the friends go?"

"No, sir. There's no phone on the island, and the way it is, I'd feel pretty bad asking a friend to go out, especially if Dad turned out to be O.K. I mean, Dad wouldn't like it if I asked someone to come out and see if he were sick. Kind of insulting to him. That Martha Hulbert, well, she's a queer one. She might have been exaggerating."

"I see," Mr. Caulfield said. "You're an unusually responsible boy, John. Old for your age."

"Thank you, sir. I guess we all have problems, sooner or later, I mean. There's just one thing. Of course, I can't very well get written permission from my father, and I don't have any money. Could I borrow a hundred dollars from the loan fund?"

Mr. Caulfield folded his hands in front of him. "John," he said, "I want you to know that Colchester Academy will do everything it can to help you meet your family responsibilities, but this isn't right. I can't let an eighteen-year-old boy go off alone on an errand like that."

"Why not, sir?"

"These cases can be pretty tough—nothing for a youngster to handle. We'll call the police and get them to check on your father."

"There are no police on the island. And no telephone."

"Then we'll call the Coast Guard."

"Oh. No, sir."

"Why not?"

"My father would be very angry."

"He won't know. The Coast Guard will make some excuse for dropping in."

"I think I ought to go myself," John said.

"Absolutely not," Mr. Caulfield replied. "I respect your desire, but I must forbid it."

"Oh," John said.

"John, are you all right?"

"Yes."

"Try not to worry about this too much. I'll let you know what the Coast Guard reports."

"All right," John said. "Thank you, sir. Thank you very much."

He went back to his room, took his suitcase and his seven dollars, and left the school immediately, walking fast through the woods. It already was dark, a cool May evening. The leaves were wet. When he reached the state highway, he stood beside his suitcase gesticulating at passing automobiles, a tall boy waving his thumb wildly in the glare of headlights at the side of the road.

30

AN INSURANCE SALESMAN who said he had been driving thirty-six hours without stopping picked him up first. When John offered to drive for him, he refused, and sat stolidly staring ahead through red-rimmed eyes, slapping his own face to stay awake.

"Talk to me, kid," he said. "Talk to me so I won't go to sleep."

"I don't know what to talk about."

"Tell me anything. Tell me the story of your life."

"Nothing to that."

"You've got to talk," the salesman said. "What books do you read in school?"

For two hours, while the salesman continually slapped his own face and shook his head, John told him about *The Return of the Native, The Turn of the Screw* and *Brave New World.*

At a filling station John picked up a road map, and when the salesman turned off his route, he thanked him and got out. It was almost midnight, and few cars were passing, but finally a huge truck rumbled to a stop, and a fat burly man in a dirty blue shirt opened the door of the cab, and in a deep friendly voice said, "Get in, my boy. You look to me as though you need help."

John rode for a hundred miles, when the truck turned off his route. After he had waited in a cold drizzle at the side of the road for an hour, starting at three in the morning, an old Chevrolet slowed down and backed to him. A flashlight shone in his face. "You look like a nice young man," a woman's voice said in a slight Southern accent. "Get in."

"Thank you," John said, and sat on the ragged upholstery of the front seat. The driver seemed to be quite a stout woman, but the light from the dashboard was too dim to see her clearly.

"Guess you wonder why I pick up hitchhikers," the woman said, grinding the gears as she started.

"No, ma'am."

"Got bad tires," the woman said. "One liable to go any minute. Might need help."

"I'll do what I can," John said.

"Guess you wonder why I'm driving alone this time of night. A respectable lady like me."

"No, ma'am."

"Mother's dying," the woman said. "Poor old lady, haven't seen her in three years. Hope I get there in time."

"Hope so," John said.

"I've got six kids," the woman continued. "My husband is staying home taking care of them to let me off. Not much on looks or money, my husband, but he's a good guy. That's worth a lot."

"Yes, ma'am."

"I was married young," the woman went on as the old Chevrolet rattled along the highway. "Might have done better if I'd waited. I was a looker when I was young. You wouldn't believe it to see me now, would you?"

"It's easy to believe, ma'am."

"Old Tom—that's my husband—he was the one with the girls! Just a little feller too, but oh boy, as they used to say."

"I see."

"Those things mattered then. I was a great girl for a barnyard fiddle. Brought up in Georgia—they had great fiddlers down there. And my Tom, he could dance with the best of them. Just a little feller, too."

"I guess size isn't very important," John said.

"You said it, boy! You understand! It ain't. And neither is money—not in the long run. That sounds like a lot of malarky, doesn't it? Especially to a young feller like you. I know what's important at your age—the fast girl and the fast buck. Did I nail it that time, boy? Did I nail it?" She gave a high cackle.

"You nailed it," John said.

"You understand. Well, let me tell you a story—from my life, boy, the real goods, not the malarky you read in books. My old lady—the one who's dying right now, may be dead, for all I know—she married well, at least for Georgia in those years. My old man had a big outfit, over a thousand acres, with no bank paper on it. But he is a mean bastard, a real mean bastard, and my mother hasn't had a happy day since."

"I'm sorry."

"You damn well should be. That old lady's been married almost sixty years, and that's a lot of misery, boy—sixty years can be a long miserable time. My father, he's still kicking, still fighting with her. She's had cancer in the gut, or some damn thing, for a year now, and the last time she wrote me, she said she was down to ninety pounds, her a woman that used to be able to pick me up, even when I was grown. And that old man, my sister told me, he comes into her room and fights with her yet. Sits right by her bed, with her in pain, and tells her she was never no good to him, and he'll say that until she's dead."

This left John speechless.

"You hear me, boy?" the woman said.

"I hear you. I'm kind of tired. I haven't had any sleep for a long while."

"Put your head down, boy, and shut your eyes. Don't let my talking bother you. I just talk to keep myself awake, because I like to figure things out. A time of death—it makes you think, boy, you know that? Makes you think what's important. Say, where do you want to get out? I'll wake you up."

"I'm going to Briarwood," John said drowsily. "In Virginia."

"Going right through there. I'll wake you up. Don't let my talking bother you, but don't expect me to stop. You know what's important, boy, when you get right down to it?"

"No, ma'am."

"The small things—take care of them and the big ones will take care of themselves. Take my husband, he knows I want to go see my old lady before she dies. He don't begrudge me the gas money, though he ain't having it easy now. He stays home from his job to look after the kids. When he gets mad he cusses me like any man will. When he wants me in bed he wants me, and he won't take no, even now. But there's never a mean word to him, really, never a plan to hurt. This morning when I started, he gave me a road map he had all marked out with the route for me to take. It's the small things which are important, the stuff that holds us up."

"Yes, ma'am," John said, and went to sleep.

What seemed only a short time afterward, she awoke him by poking him hard with her fist. "Get up, boy!" she said. "This is your stop. Briarwood!"

He opened his eyes in confusion. The sun was shining brightly, and outside the window of the car was an unfamiliar street. For a moment he didn't know where he was, or why. "Briarwood?" he asked.

"Yes. You live here, boy?"

"No," he said. "Just visiting. Thanks for the ride very much."

Carrying his suitcase, he walked bewilderedly across the street, causing a milk truck to honk wildly at him as it veered by.

The first problem was where to leave his suitcase. In a Greyhound Bus terminal he found a locker. "Can you tell me where the Briarwood school is?" he asked a thin man behind the ticket counter.

"Public or the other?"

"The other."

"Straight down Main Street, just outside of town."

John started to walk. The spring air was warm in Virginia, and he carried his coat on his arm. The town of Briarwood was unusually quiet, and there was little traffic on the streets. Passing a bank, John glanced at a clock on a post outside and saw that it was not yet nine, much too early to call at a girls' school. He went back to the bus terminal, and feeling suddenly weak, discovered that he was hungry. At the lunch counter he ate two soggy doughnuts and drank a glass of milk, spending fifteen cents. The hamburgers smelled good, but he didn't order one, because he didn't know how long his seven dollars would have to last.

Maybe I could reach her now by telephone, he thought; she ought to know I'm here. Going to a booth, he found a tattered telephone book, and looked up the school number.

"Briarwood Manor," a crisp feminine voice answered.

"Could I speak to Miss Molly Carter, please?"

"Miss Carter will be in chapel now. All the girls are in chapel. Who is this, please?"

"A friend of the family," John said, keeping his voice carefully casual. "My father and I just happened to be driving through town on our way south, and I promised Miss Carter I'd call. I know it's awfully early, but she knew we were planning to pass by, and she wanted us to pick up some clothes or something from her to deliver to her mother. Both our families have winter places down in Palm River."

"I see," the person at the other end of the wire said.

"It's a terrible hour to call, I know, but could you tell Miss Carter I'm here, and get her to telephone me when she gets out of chapel? My name is John Hunter, and I'm calling from the bus terminal." He gave her the number.

"I'll give Miss Carter the message," the voice said, and there was a click.

John sat down on a wooden bench near the telephone booth. It was five minutes after nine. He imagined Molly sitting in chapel, her face white and serious in prayer. As she filed out with the other girls, maybe, a teacher would tap her on the arm and give her his message. She would be glad. The thought of this strengthened John, and he didn't feel so tired. Quarter after nine, but still the telephone didn't ring. How long does chapel last up there, anyway, he thought.

A fat woman carrying many bundles approached the telephone booth and wedged herself in, balancing the bundles on her lap. Leaving the door open, she placed a call and in a loud voice said, "Well, sweetie, I'm here. Ain't you going to come and get me?"

A pause. Then she said, "O.K. I'll take a cab."

Almost as soon as the fat woman left the booth, the telephone rang and John jumped to answer. "Hello," he said.

"Johnny! You're here!"

"Are you all right?"

"Now I am."

"Listen. I told the girl at the school that I'm a friend of the family, and that my father and I are driving through on the way south. I said I was supposed to pick up a package of clothes or something."

"I know," Molly said. "She told me."

"Did you give us away?"

"No."

"Good. I don't want the school to call your mother yet. When can I see you?"

"You can meet me in the common room right away. It's in the center building—the biggest one. I'll bring a box of clothes."

"Do you have any money?"

"Not much."

"We're going to need money," he said.

"I have my fur coat. Maybe we could sell it. A girl at school said it must have cost five thousand dollars."

"Bring the coat," he said.

It took him fifteen minutes to walk to the school, which proved to be a collection of imposing brick buildings a rich man had given in memory of his wife. John found the common room easily, a lounge elaborately furnished with reproductions of Early American antiques. At the near end of it was a reception desk with a telephone switchboard at which a plain girl, a scholarship student, sat studying a book on plane geometry. No one else was in the room.

"My name is John Hunter," he said. "I believe Miss Molly Carter is to meet me here."

"I'll tell her you've come," the girl replied, glancing up and revealing a painfully bad complexion. "Won't you sit down?"

John sat down in the farthest corner of the room. The girl did something with the switchboard and said, "Molly. Your caller's here." Her voice carried easily to the place where John sat, and he thought, We'll have to whisper.

Three minutes passed. A tall, elderly woman in black, probably a widow, John thought, came in and paused at the switchboard. "I'm Alice Cunningham's mother," she said in a sad voice. "Will you tell her I'm here?"

"Yes, Mrs. Cunningham," the receptionist said. "Won't you sit down?"

The woman sat down only a short distance from John. "Isn't it a lovely day out?" she said.

"Yes," John replied.

"I just got off the train from New York," the woman said. "It's such a tiring trip."

"Yes," John repeated. On the pretext of getting a magazine, he took another chair farther away, and she looked at him curiously. Another minute passed. The woman in black stared at him.

Molly suddenly came into the room, holding herself erect, but looking pale. Over her left arm she carried her fur coat and under her right arm she carried an empty dress box. She walked across the floor with quiet dignity. "Hello, John," she said in a perfectly normal voice. "It's good to see you."

The woman in black continued to stare. Molly sat as close to John as she could without appearing odd, and they leaned toward each other.

"Molly," John whispered. "This is very simple. We're going to get married."

"I'm afraid of what Dad will do," Molly said.

"He won't be able to do anything after we're married. And I think my father will help us. I'm going to see him."

"Couldn't we just run away?"

"That would be silly. We've got to be practical, Molly. I want to get married and live on the island, at least until we can figure things out. I think we can count on my father."

"I wish we could on mine," she said.

"Don't think too far ahead. Right now, I'll sell the coat, and I'll go up and see Dad. Then I'll come back here for you, and we'll figure out what to do next."

"Good," she said, and added in a low voice, as she had on the telephone, "Thank God, Johnny."

31

AT THE BUS TERMINAL in Briarwood John bought a ticket for Richmond, the nearest big city on the way north. It was only about an hour's ride, and it was not yet noon when he got there. With the fur coat over one arm and holding his suitcase with the other, he walked the busy streets looking for a pawnshop. At last he found one, with three big gold balls suspended overhead. The window had iron grillwork on it to prevent burglaries. For a moment John stood looking in. Lying in the pawnshop were a row of ugly-looking revolvers, three cameras, dozens of gold wrist watches, and a silver trumpet.

The owner of the pawnshop was a thin man with rimless spectacles and very little hair. "Good morning," he said to John in a mild Southern accent.

"I would like to sell this," John said and handed the coat across the white marble counter.

The man studied the fur closely. He looked at the label inside.

Then he spread the coat out on the counter and looked it over minutely. "I'll give you twenty dollars," he said quietly.

"Twenty dollars!" John said. "That coat cost five thousand dollars."

"I know," the man said.

"Give it back and I'll take it somewhere else," John replied indignantly.

"No," the man said quietly. "Take your twenty dollars and leave."

"What do you mean?"

"Or I'll call the police," the man said. "Would you like to explain to them where you got that coat?"

"You son-of-a-bitch!" John said.

The man shrugged wearily, and rang open his cash drawer.

If he did tell the police, I'd have to call Molly to get her to explain, John thought, and the school might find out, and would tell her mother, and that is not the way for her to be informed. The owner of the pawnshop shoved two ten-dollar bills across the counter. John picked up the money.

"Now get out of here and don't come back," the pawnbroker said.

"Give me my ticket," John replied. The man handed it to him.

Walking out of the pawnshop, John clenched his fists so tightly that his fingernails bit into the palms of his hands, and he felt suddenly weak. Slowly he walked around the corner. I'm hungry, he thought—that's why I feel like this. He went to a diner and ordered a hot dog. While it was being cooked, he took out his money and counted it: twenty-four dollars and eighty-five cents. If I can't get money from Dad, he thought, I'll need this to take Molly to Buffalo or Connecticut or wherever we go next. I'll also have to buy a bus ticket from Boston to Harvesport, because there won't be much traffic for hitchhiking this early in the year, and I'll have to pay Captain Andrews to take me out to the island. So I better hitchhike from here to Boston, and save as much as I can.

After eating his hot dog, John walked until he came to a filling station. There he got a road map, and a tall Negro with a scar across his nose pointed the way to the state highway. "You wait here a while, and maybe somebody will give you a lift there," the Negro said. "Cops might pick you up if you thumb yourself a ride here in the city."

A stocky man in a pickup truck drove up for gas. John walked up to him. "You bound north out of town?" he asked.

The man looked at him suspiciously. "Maybe," he said.

"I'd like a ride," John said quietly.

"Where are you going, boy?"

"To Boston. My father is sick."

"I'm sorry to hear that," the man said. "Toss your suitcase in back. I'll take you out to where you can get a ride."

They drove to a truck terminal. "Wait here," the stocky man said. "I know some of these guys. Let me see what I can do for you." He left. Huge trailer trucks were parked in rows all around John, some loaded with oranges and grapefruit, some with refrigerator engines whirring over their cabs. John sat staring at the many license plates each of them carried: Florida, Virginia, New York, Massachusetts.

"Hello there!" a jovial, white-haired man in a blue shirt said. "Hear you want to go to Boston."

"Yes, sir."

"See that ten-ton job over there with the grapefruit? Hop in. You'll be there in nine hours," the man said.

John slept the entire way to Boston. There he spent seven dollars and thirty-two cents for a bus ticket to Harvesport, Maine.

When the bus left Boston it was crowded with trout fishermen carrying creels and rods in canvas cases. One man had a battered felt hat covered by brightly feathered dry flies, with the tiny barbed hooks embedded in the hatband. The fishermen talked a great deal, laughing and swapping information about different rivers. John slept.

"Hey, boy!" the bus driver said hours later. "Ain't you going to Harvesport?"

"Yes," John said, coming suddenly awake.

"We're here."

It was dark. John got out of the bus and was surprised to find it was unusually cold for May. A bitter wind was blowing from the north. He turned up his coat collar and walked down to the wharf where Herb Andrews moored his vessel, the *Mary Anne*. The old Gloucester schooner was there, but no light showed on deck or below. John banged the flat of his hand three times on the hatch. Almost immediately Herb's voice answered from below. "Who's there?"

"Me, John Hunter."

"What the hell do you want?"

"I want to go out to the island."

"For God's sake, boy. Do you know what time it is?"

"No," John said in confusion. "I just got off the bus."

"It's midnight," Herb said. "I'll take you in the morning."

"I'll make it worth your while if you'll take me tonight," John said.

"Go to sleep. Don't waste your money. Want a bunk?"

"I want to go tonight," John replied.

"It's a rotten night out. Blowing a gale."

"I'm in a hurry."

"Don't stand there and shout," Herb said. "Come below."

John shoved the hatch open and descended the companionway. Herb Andrews, dressed only in long woolen underwear, climbed from his bunk and lit an oil lamp. "Now what's the matter, boy?"

"I got word that my father is ill, and I have to go out and see him," John said. "If it's blowing too hard, I guess I could get the Coast Guard to take me out."

"I'll take you. I didn't know it was an emergency."

"Thanks," John said. "I'll pay what I can."

"Just the usual rate," Herb replied gruffly. "But you'll have to help out on deck. My brother's ashore."

The big Diesel engine coughed, and then chortled quietly to itself.

"Now stand by the spring line," Herb said. "I'll take care of the stern line."

The stern line splashed as Herb let it go. He shoved the clumsy gearshift ahead, and spun the schooner's big wheel. Slowly she nudged her bow into the wharf, with her stern out. "*Now,*" Herb said, hauling the gearshift lever into reverse, "let go your spring line."

John let it go with a splash, and the big schooner backed majestically into the harbor. The wind was already whining in her rigging.

The bay was black, with only two lights showing ashore. Herb's face glowed in the light from the binnacle, and the running lights made a blur of green to starboard and red to port, reflected on the wet decks.

"How can you see?" John asked, peering into the murk ahead.

"This old tub knows the way to the island without me," Herb replied, "but you're going to have to hang on."

When they cleared the breakwater the wind hit them hard. The *Mary Anne* heeled over with her lee rail awash, as though she were under full sail. Spray arched across her decks, and she started to buck, to drop with dizzying speed, to crash into the waves, and suddenly rear up again.

"*Hi Yeeeeee!*" Herb called at the top of his lungs. "You show 'em, old girl!"

"Can she take this?" John asked, appalled as the bow slammed into a sea with the impact of a truck hitting a brick wall.

"She's built for it, boy!" Herb said. "A good vessel can take anything she has to take."

The timbers shuddered and groaned, but the *Mary Anne* held steady to her course, and when Herb tested the pumps, he found no leak.

It took almost two hours to get to the island, bucking the north wind, but finally they entered the harbor, and there was a sudden stillness which was abruptly broken by Todd Hasper's dog. The current Satan was a huge black beast which looked like a panther. As the ship approached, he came charging out on the wharf and raged back and forth, baring his teeth and barking in a frenzy. Herb Andrews trained a searchlight on him. "What do you want me to do?" he asked. "I can't put you ashore there."

"I don't know," John said, suddenly bewildered. Why would the dog be loose if Bart were on the island? The fear that his father had died, that the lie he had told Caulfield about his father was turning out to be all too true, possessed John, but there didn't seem to be any way to go ashore to investigate without being torn to ribbons.

"I've got a shotgun below," Herb said, letting the schooner circle near the wharf while the dog continued to growl out his fury. "Why don't you blow his goddamn head off?"

"Wait," John said. High up on the shore he saw a lantern weaving down the path. When it reached the wharf, Herb Andrews turned his searchlight in that direction. Todd Hasper, dressed in a tattered overcoat, stood caught in the beam, an old man with a deeply lined face, a hooked nose, and a malignant stare. He stood glaring into the searchlight without a word.

"It's me, John Hunter!" John called. "Hold your dog!"

The old man did not appear to have heard. Andrews cut off the vessel's engine to reduce the noise, and handed John a megaphone. *"It's me, John Hunter!"* he called again at the top of his lungs. *"Hold your dog!"*

Without a word, the old man turned and started back up the path, leaving the dog raging at the end of the wharf. "Listen!" John called in anger. "Hold your dog or I'll shoot him!" Hasper hesitated. To Herb, John said, "Get me that gun, will you?"

Herb ducked below and produced a double-barreled shotgun. "It's loaded," he said. "Let me do it. This is something I've wanted to do for years."

"Give him a warning shot first," John said.

Herb fired into the water. At the sound of the report Hasper ran to the end of the wharf, and above the growls of the dog, they could hear him shouting, "No! No!"

"Hold him then," John said grimly.

Hasper attached a chain leash to the brute's collar and stood with both feet braced. As the schooner came alongside, the dog appeared to go insane, and Hasper needed all his strength to restrain him. Herb Andrews handed John the shotgun. "Here," he said. "You better take this with you. The crazy bastard is liable to let go."

With the gun under his arm, John started to step ashore.

"Wait," Herb shouted. "You better take a lantern too. The wharf is full of holes."

Carrying a lantern in one hand and the gun in the other, John stepped onto the wharf. Herb left his searchlight upon Hasper and the maddened dog. "Is Dad here?" John shouted to Hasper, but either the old man didn't want to answer, or he couldn't hear anything above the protests of his beast. In disgust, John turned, and picking his way around holes and sagging timbers, walked ashore. When he got to the path he started to run. The shriek of the wind in the branches overhead was shrill.

It is not strange to find no lights showing, he told himself as he approached the garage behind the high old house on the hill. It's two-thirty in the morning, and of course the lights are out. But something else was strange. There were no footprints but the dog's in the mud anywhere around the front door of the garage apartment. Stronger than ever John had the premonition that his father was sick, if not dead.

No, he thought, that is absurd. If he were sick, Todd Hasper would take care of him and I would have been told if he were dead.

Why weren't Hasper's tracks in the mud?

Maybe no one is here, John thought. Maybe Dad got sick and moved in with Hasper.

Full of terror, John walked up the dark front steps, almost slipping on dog droppings, and banged on the door. There was no answer. The image of a dead man inside loomed clearly in his mind, a man dead, perhaps, for several weeks. He leaned the gun against the side of the house and set the lantern down. "Dad!" he called at the top of his lungs. "Dad! Dad! Let me in!" And he rained blows upon the door, slugging it with the flat of both hands, until the whole building shook.

"Yes?" Bart's thin voice answered suddenly from inside. "Yes? Yes? Who's there?"

"It's me! Your son! It's John!"

The door opened and Bart, wearing a soiled and rumpled lieutenant commander's uniform, stood there holding a candle in a shaking hand. He had not shaved for weeks, and from his chin hung a thin, almost Oriental-looking beard. "John!" he said in astonishment. "John! What are you doing here?"

"I came to talk to you about something," John said.

"Why do you have a gun?"

"I'm afraid of the dog."

"Are you all right? Is something wrong?"

"Everything's fine. Let's get some coffee and we can talk."

"All right," Bart said, and lit an oil lantern.

"What happened to the electricity?" John asked.

"That bastard Hasper—we had a fight. So he cut me off."

"A fight?"

"Crazy son-of-a-bitch," Bart said. "He won't keep the dog chained any more, even though he killed all the goddamn sheep and goats he was supposed to protect. I'm going to get rid of him." He lit another lantern.

"Does the dog attack you?"

"I never go out of the house any more anyway. Except in summer."

"How do you get your food?"

"Got whole supply in the cellar. Had Andrews bring it over. I'm completely self-sufficient here."

John went to the kitchen to brew coffee. The sight of his father with the old uniform and thin gray beard had shocked him, and his hand shook when he put the pot on the stove.

"You look cold." Bart said. "Don't you want a real drink?"

"No, thanks."

"You're wise. Stay off it as long as you can." Bart got a bottle from a cupboard, poured himself a quarter tumbler full of whisky, and took a swallow. He shuddered, and then lit a cigarette. "What did you come here for?" he asked.

John sat down across the kitchen table from him. "Father, I'm in love," he said.

Barton gave a short high laugh. "At your age, that's not surprising. Who is it, the little Jorgenson girl?"

"Yes."

"Well, congratulations," Barton said, not unkindly. "She's a pretty little thing."

"I want to get married."

"Now?"

"Now," John said.

"You're too young. It's absurd. Marriage at eighteen!"

"I still want to get married."

Bart glanced at him sharply. "Are you in trouble?"

"No. Or yes. I just want to get married and I need help."

"Oh, no!" Bart groaned. "Not so young!"

"We're going to be all right," John said evenly. "I would like to get married and come here."

"Oh, Lord!" Bart groaned.

"I want to borrow money. Some day I'll repay it."

"Jesus Christ!" Bart said in despair.

"Maybe I can still go to college," John said. "But right now we want to come here."

With a shaking hand Bart lifted his glass to his lips.

"You once said you had some money in a trust fund," John continued. "I need maybe three hundred dollars now to get married and come back here."

Bart got up and began pacing up and down the floor. "It's not a question of money," he said.

"What else?"

"You don't see it the way I do," Bart replied, continuing to pace and to drink. "My God. You sit there, a boy eighteen years old, and I stand here, forty-one years old, and we see two entirely different things."

"What do you see?"

"First let's get to what you see. You see a pretty girl. You see that it's wonderful to be in love. You don't feel any shame, John, even though you've done a terrible thing to a nice youngster. All you see is love and the pretty girl, and that's not enough."

"I think I see more than that," John said.

"You see responsibility—you're good that way, better than I. But that's not enough."

"What else is there?"

"I'll tell you what I see," Barton said, his voice rising. "I'll tell you the truth, John. It's painful, but we better have it out."

"What truth?"

"Let's start with me. It concerns you. I'm not much of a father, John—I've never been. There are all kinds of things wrong with me that you're getting old enough to think about, because they affect you, because they're part of my poor inheritance and yours. I said we see things differently, and we do. I see things straight."

He paused and took another drink, spilling a few drops on the floor.

"What?"

"I'm going to say it, John. It's tough, but sometimes the truth has to be said. I'm a little crazy, Johnny—everybody knows that. But it's like the joke, where the man says, 'I may be crazy, but I'm not stupid.' That's true of me."

"What has that got to do with us?"

"I'll tell you," Barton said. "Let's face it." He paused in his pacing and confronted John squarely, pointing his finger at his face. "You're the son of an alcoholic, Johnny. You're the grandson of a suicide, well covered up. You didn't know that, did you? You've got a real bad inheritance, and at eighteen you've made a girl pregnant. Don't you see what it is, Johnny? No romance. It's a damn sordid piece of business, and we're all trapped in it, and we can't get out."

"That has nothing to do with this."

"It doesn't? Me and Sylvia, your rotten mother! Sleeping with the tutor when she was younger than you. You're getting old enough to understand, Johnny. No more secrets. The cat's out of the bag—all the cats, the terrible, mangy, howling obscene cats of inheritance. You've got to see them. They'll kill you if you leave them in the dark!"

"I don't see how they apply to me." John spoke mechanically. He was standing now, very erect, with his back against the window.

"You're one of them, Johnny. A mangy cat, one of us. Me the alcoholic. Your mother a good deal worse, and now you, Johnny, eighteen with a pregnant girl. You see what I see, Johnny? It's enough to make me cry!"

"Molly isn't like that."

"All you see is a pretty girl!"

"My Molly—she isn't like that."

"Don't be sentimental!" Barton shot out. "You're old enough to face facts. You're not going to get married, you're going to repair yourself."

"No."

"I'll pay for a psychiatrist, not a minister!"

"I'm going to get married."

"I'll tell you what will happen if you do. You'll bring one more miserable child into the world, one more alcoholic, one more seducer of the young!"

"No!"

"I've got a good mind, John, in spite of the liquor, and I'm going to insist on an intelligent solution."

"What?"

"With my mother's trust fund, I'll give you money for an abortion." Barton's face became contorted. "Abortion isn't always a bad thing," he said. "I wish my mother had been aborted before I was born."

"Molly!" John said.

"I won't help you get married!"

"Molly!" John repeated.

"You've got to see reason! You can't help being corrupt, but you don't have to be stupid! If you marry you'll get divorced before you're twenty-one!"

"Molly!" John said. "She's . . ."

"You're as bad as your mother!"

"Molly," John said. "She's not the way you say. Maybe I am. I don't know. But my Molly, she's not an alley cat. I don't know. You say just a pretty girl, but it's more. It's more! I say this, goddamn you bastard father, goddamn your great intelligent mind, in spite of everything you say, *it's more!*"

Turning, he fled the house.

32

Outside the door of the garage apartment, John grabbed his gun and his lantern, and started to run back to the wharf. Halfway down the hill he paused in confusion. Where was he going? He had almost no money left. What was he going to do? Hitchhike back to Molly, and get her from the school—certainly he couldn't leave her alone there. But where would they go? I'll get a job, he thought; maybe I can get a job playing the piano, or at least as a laborer. But it would take time to do that, and meanwhile he needed money, enough to support them for a few days at least, until they could get married. Money—it seemed to him that everything depended upon getting that, or something to sell. Standing there in the darkness with the wind whistling in his ears, he suddenly had an idea, and ran back up the hill, not to the garage, but to the old inn itself. His mind was working fast and clearly now. All the doors and windows would be locked of course. No, there was a French door leading to the veranda. Hurrying to it, he found that it had been covered by a heavy wooden storm door, but there was a window nearby with the glass exposed. Without hesitation, he broke one pane with the stock of the shotgun, reached in and tried to open the latch. It was so rusty and covered with old paint that it would not budge. Standing back impatiently, he seized the gun by the barrel and wielded it like a club, smashing all the panes and the window frame. Climbing gingerly through, he let himself down to the floor inside, and held the lantern high. In its feeble light the living room of the old inn looked like a monstrous cavern. The piano, where he had sat playing as a boy, was covered with a torn sheet. It was cold, and the broken glass he had scattered over the floor glittered like ice. Moving quickly without any attempt to be quiet, John went to the basement. It was damp there, and there was the patter of rats' feet ahead of him. Opening the door of a storage room, he found some old suitcases, covered with the tattered remains of labels of European resorts his parents and grandparents had long ago visited. The leather was speckled with green mold, but some of the bags were still serviceable. Choosing one of medium size, John went back to the living room and started rifling through the drawers of the old cherry highboy. There he found the leather box containing the ivory chess set his grandfather had brought home from India, and the French clock, lying carefully packed in newspapers. Ripping the sheet from the piano, he swathed the clock and its glass dome in it, and packed it with the chess set in the suitcase. Next he went to the closet off the pantry where the ornate silver his grandmother had received as a wedding present was stored in a heavy teak chest. The top tray held rolls of musty velvet with pockets in which teaspoons were kept. He packed all he thought he could carry in the suitcase, closed it and shoved it through the broken window. Without a backward glance he climbed after it, scratching his wrist slightly on a jagged piece of glass. Awkwardly carrying the gun and the lantern in one hand and the heavy bag in the other, he hurried down the hill to the wharf. Todd Hasper's dog was still snarling in the distance, and the wind seemed to be blowing harder.

At the end of the wharf he paused, fearful of stumbling in the dark and falling through the rotten wood. It would not help Molly now if I broke my leg or killed myself, he thought, visualizing the inky waters swirling beneath. Heavy clouds scudded over the sky, covering the moon and stars. Nothing could be seen outside the small circle of lamplight, and the end of the wharf was invisible in the midst of the rushing tide. John put down his burdens and rested before continuing.

"Hello there!" he shouted as the dim shape of the schooner along the end of the wharf loomed ahead.

"Hello!" Herb Andrews answered. "What have you got there?"

"Some things of mine. Watch out, they're heavy!"

John helped Herb to cast off the lines and they returned to Harvesport. He slept aboard the schooner that night. In the morning he washed his face in a bucket of cold water, changed his clothes, and carrying the heavy suitcase, went ashore to catch a bus back to Boston.

In Scollay Square he toured the shops, carrying only one object at a time to reduce the suspicion that he was a thief. This time he felt no anger when low prices were quoted; in fact, he felt no emotion at all. The world had blurred, as in a dream; his senses had been deadened. The honking of traffic, the garish signs advertising tattoo parlors, bars and dance halls, the swirling crowd of sailors on the streets, the opaque faces of the men behind the counters of the secondhand stores, all these seemed to merge into a pattern of confusion too fantastic to matter. The well-remembered curlicues on the handles of his grandmother's teaspoons lost their familiarity on the shop counters. Passing a store window, he saw a dim reflection of himself, a wavering figure carrying a French clock wrapped in a sheet, like a baby in swaddling clothes, a shadow without substance, and he had the curious sensation of being unsure whether he were alive or dead.

A jeweler gave him a good price for the clock. Altogether, he was able to raise almost four hundred dollars on the contents of the suitcase. On the way to the bus station, he passed a secondhand car lot which displayed an ancient Plymouth selling for ninety-nine dollars. Thinking of all the traveling he had ahead of him, John bought the car. It was important, he thought, to start saving every penny from the beginning. Not only would the car get him to Virginia, and wherever they were going afterward almost as cheaply as a bus, but it could even be a place for them to sleep, if necessary. A man with a car could not be said to be entirely homeless.

On the way to Briarwood, John picked up every hitchhiker, until the car was full. At one time he was carrying a soldier on leave from Texas, or perhaps absent without leave, John thought; the father of a family of six out on the road in search of work; a merchant marine sailor going to see his girl in Georgia; and a small man who sat absolutely still, hour after hour, without giving any information about himself at all, but who occasionally smiled for his own mysterious reasons.

It was Sunday when John got to Briarwood, and a tea for the young girls and their callers was being held in the common room of the school. Several girls who had had permission to be away for the weekend had just returned, and were saying goodbye to their escorts. The common room was a gay and busy place.

Molly met him there at five in the afternoon, still pale, but with no sign of defeat in her face or bearing. They sat with their heads bent close over a cup of tea while youngsters laughed all around them. Briefly he told her what had happened.

"What are we going to do?" she asked.

"Go to Richmond, or some place, and get married. After that . . ."

"What?"

"I've got enough money to last a long while," he said. "We'll have plenty of time to think."

"I won't be so afraid when we're married," she said.

"Can you think of an excuse to get away from school? I don't want them to call the police."

"Miss Summerfield is awfully hard to fool."

"I guess we better just go then," John said, and stood up. Molly was afraid someone would stop her if she got her suitcase, so without delay they walked out of the common room, and looking as casual as possible, climbed into his car.

The old engine started without hesitation, and he drew away from the curb. While in the town he drove slowly to avoid drawing attention, but when they got on the open highway he bore down on the accelerator, anxious to leave Briarwood behind. For five minutes they drove without talking. He had thought he would be happy as soon as he was alone with her, but the silence between them was leaden. He wanted to ask if she was happy, but the question would have sounded ironic. On Molly's pale face there was determination and courage, but not joy.

"A small town might be better," he said abruptly.

"What?"

"It might be easier to get married in a small town than in Richmond."

"All right."

Molly, he wanted to say, oh, Molly, what's happening to us? Running away to get married ought to be romantic or something, it ought not be like this.

"I love you," he said suddenly. "I love you, Molly."

"Oh, Johnny!"

"What's the matter?"

"What are we going to do?"

"Get married, of course!"

"I mean afterward."

"I'll get a job. There are all kinds of things I can do."

There was a short silence before she said, "We've been kidding ourselves, Johnny."

"What are you talking about?"

"I don't think anyone will even marry us. We're too young."

"We can say we're older."

"They'll know."

"They can't stop us!" he said defiantly, and drove a little faster.

But Molly's prediction proved accurate. When they entered the dingy brick building which served as the town hall of Rocksford, a small city twenty miles from Briarwood, and said they wanted a marriage license, a thin, baldheaded clerk in a sweat-stained shirt looked at them expressionlessly and said, "How old are you?"

"Twenty-one," John said hastily, not knowing the legal age for marriage, but guessing it must be that. "We're both twenty-one."

"Do you have your birth certificates?" the clerk asked, and perhaps Molly imagined that there was contempt on his face. On a bench at the side of the room a newspaper rustled, and she saw a half dozen men who were loafing there staring at them.

"No," John said. "We'll have to send for them."

"Come back when you have them," the clerk said, and abruptly turned his back to them, as though the very sight of their faces embarrassed him. A tall man in faded overalls who was sitting on the end of the bench spat into a spittoon. Molly put her hand on John's arm when they walked out and had difficulty restraining an impulse to run.

"We can go to another state," John said as they got back in the car. "I'm sure there are places where we can get married."

"Yes," she said, trying to forget the faces of the men on the bench who had stared at her. The wedding guests, she thought, trying to fight off hysteria, recalling the man who had spat, with the brown teeth and stubbly beard, and the fat, dough-faced derelict beside him with the watery eyes.

John started the car. Outside of the town the road ran uphill, and the old car groaned as John shifted first into second gear, and then into third. The motor knocked alarmingly.

"Where are we going?" Molly asked.

"I thought we might try Maryland," he said, not at all sure that they were going in the direction of Maryland, but ashamed to admit that he really had no destination, no purpose in driving except to get away from the staring clerk and the faces on the bench. When they got to the top of the hill, the road dipped precipitously downward, a long, steep slope, at the end of which the highway curved under a railroad bridge. John shifted into high gear, and the old car started to pick up speed. He sat stiffly at the wheel, and as the speedometer crept above the fifty mark, he meant to apply the brake, but he didn't—there was a fascination in letting the acceleration continue. The car swayed. At the bottom of the hill the railroad bridge loomed larger, with white letters on the black iron just too far away to be read. The speedometer passed the sixty mark, and John suddenly remembered Bill Norris. The thought occurred to him that all he would have to do now was nothing, precisely nothing, and all their problems would take care of themselves, for if he just did nothing a few seconds longer, the car would be going seventy when it reached that railroad bridge and it would be impossible to turn or stop in time. John glanced at Molly, and saw that she was glancing hypnotically at the bridge. Her face showed no fear, but her fists were clenched tightly in her lap. The letters on the bridge were clear now: ATLANTIC SEABOARD ROUTE. Just a few more seconds and there would be no more decisions to be made, he thought, but then jerked his head, snapping himself out of the trance, and in panic applied the brakes, bringing the car under control just in time to make the turn. Bending over with her face in her lap, Molly started to cry, the first time he had seen her cry in years. Pulling the car to the side of the road in the shadow of the railroad bridge, he put his arms around her and found that she was trembling violently. For a minute they clung together. Then, in a strangely detached voice, she said, "This is silly, Johnny. We're going to have to tell Dad and your mother. We can't do it alone."

"How about your mother?"

"She'll die," Molly said simply.

"I don't know what my mother will do."

"We better go see them and face it out."

"Yes," he said.

"They can't really do anything but help us. Not with me the way I am." The words sounded reasonable, but there was no conviction in her voice.

"I think your father will be all right," John said, but his words too rang hollow. The image of Ken's distraught face at the head of the stairs was strong in his mind.

"We don't have to hurry, do we?" Molly said. "I'm awfully tired."

"No, we don't have to hurry." He turned the car around and headed slowly north, toward Connecticut.

With the decision made, the tension eased a little. It was companionable to go droning along the highway with Molly half asleep on his shoulder. "I wish we could go on like this forever," she said. "I wish we'd never get there."

"Don't say that," he said.

"Superstitious?"

"Yes. Knock on wood."

A big truck roared by, almost crowding the tiny Plymouth off the road. John slowed down. "Do you want to stop at a hotel tonight?" he asked.

"I'm afraid they'd ask to see our marriage license."

"They wouldn't."

"I hate the way they'd look at us," she said. "Let's sleep in the car."

"All right."

At an Army-Navy store in the next town he bought two pillows and two blankets. At dusk he turned off the highway onto a small dirt road in the woods, and parked under a large oak tree. Huddled in the back seat with Molly, he felt cramped but warm. Once he was awakened in the night by the sound of rain on the car's thin metal roof. Molly's face was a dim shape at his shoulder, and he realized that her eyes were wide open. He kissed her, pulling her to him, his shoulders twisting awkwardly in the cramped back seat of the car.

"No, Johnny!" she said. "Not now!" Suddenly she started to cry again. He held her tightly, and it was a long while before she dozed off.

The next morning they got out and ran in circles around their car to work the knots out of their muscles. A gray cow put her head over a wire fence nearby and watched them solemnly.

"If we got a Sterno stove, I could cook breakfast," Molly said. "It would be cheaper than restaurants, and Johnny . . ."

"What?"

"Let's stay here a little longer. We don't have to hurry . . ."

They bought the stove and some groceries at the next town, and returned to their secret place in the woods. The old Plymouth could be used as a home for weeks, if necessary, they told each other.

33

MOLLY WAS MISSED at Briarwood Manor Academy for Girls when she had been gone only a few hours, and Miss Summerfield, the aging headmistress, was notified. She was not particularly surprised: she remembered the rumors about Molly meeting a boy in New York and she had not run a girls' school for more than thirty years without learning a few of the signs. Since returning from Easter vacation, Molly had been even more pale and withdrawn than she usually was. The child was too pretty for her own good, Miss Summerfield thought, and reflected the tensions of a broken home. Miss Summerfield recognized a candidate for trouble when she saw one, and she had been keeping an eye on Molly.

Although it wasn't published in the brochures used to advertise Briarwood Manor, there had been quite a number of "mishaps" over the years, and Miss Summerfield had grown skilled in handling them. Now she started by having the faculty conduct a quiet search of the campus and buildings. An elderly Latin teacher was dispatched to tour the ice-cream shops and the movie theater in the town. She knew her job well, and was able to chat with the men selling tickets at the bus and railroad stations without raising suspicions. After inquiring whether a girl of Molly's description had been seen, she explained that she was trying to deliver a message from the child's parents concerning a minor change of traveling plans. She always finished by smiling graciously and saying it really wasn't important at all.

When no clue concerning Molly's whereabouts had been received by nightfall, Miss Summerfield telephoned Helen Carter. Such calls were always painful to make; the mothers often were harder to handle than the girls. Over the years Miss Summerfield had developed a number of techniques for breaking bad news, and when her secretary told her that Mrs. Helen Carter in Buffalo was on the wire, the phrases rolled to her lips with little effort.

"Mrs. Carter," she said. "How-do-you-do. This is Miss Summerfield at Briarwood. I have been a headmistress now for a good many years, and I have learned that this sort of thing is very rarely cause for great alarm, but I thought I ought to notify you that Molly apparently has left the school. Youth is a tempestuous time. Our receptionist saw her walk out with a young man this afternoon and . . ."

Miss Summerfield held the receiver away from her ear and sighed. She detested hysterics.

Ken, Sylvia and Carla were just sitting down to dinner in their house in Connecticut when the telephone rang. "I'll get it," Ken said, walked to the hall, and picked up the receiver. "Helen!" he said, sounding shocked, and Sylvia stood up slowly, letting the napkin fall from her lap.

"What's the matter?" Carla said, but no one answered her.

For what seemed a very long time, Ken listened silently with the telephone at his ear. "Now, Helen," he finally said, his deep voice sounding infinitely sad, "you've got to get hold of yourself. It doesn't do any good . . ."

"Carla," Sylvia said, "would you mind waiting in your room for a few minutes? We'll explain later."

"All right," Carla said bewilderedly, and slowly walked upstairs.

"No!" Ken said into the telephone.

There was silence again, and then Ken said loudly and firmly, "Helen, you stop this. Call a doctor and get him to give you a sedative and go to bed. I'll handle this. Yes. Yes. Yes. I'll handle it. Yes. Good night."

He hung up and turned toward Sylvia, his big face gone shockingly gray and old. "Molly has run away from school, probably with John," he said, and picking up the receiver, called Colchester Academy. Sylvia sat down, feeling weak. She heard Ken asking questions over the telephone, and then he put the receiver down again. "John's been missing for three days," he said. "The school's been in touch with Bart. He told them not to search."

"They've probably eloped," Sylvia said in a low voice.

He glanced at her, his face deathlike. "Kids, seventeen and eighteen!" he said. Doubling up his fist then, he brought it down on the telephone table with a crash. "God damn Johnny!" he said. "God damn him!" He drew in his breath sharply. The whirr of the oil burner in the cellar sounded loud.

"We are all damned," Sylvia said in a flat voice.

Shaking his head like a prizefighter who has been hit hard, he sat flexing his fingers. Then he saw that Sylvia was crying. Quickly he went to her. "I'm sorry," he said.

Her sobs erupted then, welling from deep within her, bending her head to her lap, forcing her clenched teeth apart. He picked her up like a child and carrying her over to the sofa, sat cradling her in his arms. "They're not dead," he said grimly.

"How do you know? Maybe . . ."

"They wouldn't do that."

"Anyway . . ." Her sobs interrupted her and he hugged her, rocking back and forth on the couch, repeating, "Hush, hush. They're not dead. We don't have to make this too much of a tragedy."

"Death isn't the only tragedy!"

Impatiently he jumped up, and leaving her on the couch, he began pacing up and down the living room. His heavy tread made the house tremble, and his deep voice rumbled when he said, "I've been a fool. I'm not going to despair! I won't!"

"Are you going to celebrate?"

"Somebody's got to stay sane around here! Helen's talking about suicide, for God's sake!"

"But where are they? What will they do?"

"They'll come here! I know those kids! They'll come here!"

"And even then what can be done? Are they going to set up housekeeping at seventeen and eighteen?"

"God damn it!" Ken said, and he brought his fist down in the palm of his hand with a deafening crack. "They're going to get married if they haven't already, and they're going to finish their education!"

"She may be pregnant. That's probably why they ran away."

"All right!" Ken said, and he brought his fist down in the palm of his hand with a loud crack again. "Are you worrying about what the neighbors will say?"

"No," she said, "but God knows what kind of trouble they're getting into. If they get scared . . ."

He wheeled on her. "No!" he said. "Don't you know them? My Molly isn't an idiot servant girl! And don't you know your own son?"

"It's our fault," Sylvia said, her voice toneless. "We don't even have the right to be indignant."

"Let's have no more accusations!" he retorted. "We've had too much of that." Holding out his big hands with the fingers outstretched in front of him, he said, "It's not a question of who's going to throw the first stone, it's a question of who's going to start building with it!"

"What are you going to build?" she asked bitterly.

"There's everything to build! They're going to need our help. Are you going to comfort them by offering to share their guilt? Nonsense! They're going to need our love, money and advice, in that order, not a group psychoanalysis!"

Sylvia said nothing.

"Look!" he added suddenly. "This doesn't have to be all bad. A youthful marriage isn't such an ugly thing, it's not all hideous! If you and I had fought things through and had got married when we were that age, wouldn't it have been better for us?"

"Yes."

"These aren't youngsters who don't know their own minds! They're no juvenile delinquents, for God's sake! This at least will get Molly out of Helen's house, and it will get John away from Bart! Do you think life would have been better for them the other way?"

"There was no way for them."

"They're finding their way!" he said, bringing his fist down hard into the palm of his hand again. "We gave them a problem and they're solving it! *Why are you crying?*"

"I'll tell you why I'm crying!" Sylvia said desperately. "Because we've destroyed them! You and Bart and I—all of us! We've destroyed them. After causing this, how can any of us have any self-respect?"

"Why are they destroyed?" he retorted. "If we all have courage and common sense, why can't something good be made of this? What's so goddamn terrible about two youngsters in love?"

"Can I come down now?" Carla asked, descending the stairs.

"Not yet," Sylvia replied.

"Do you mind telling me what's the matter?"

"Molly has left her school," Ken said in a low voice. "We're a little worried about her."

"She's probably marrying Johnny," Carla said. "I always knew she would."

They ate dinner slowly, and the waiting was hard. All evening Ken paced back and forth, saying, "They'll come here! I know they will!"

"How long does it take to get here from Briarwood?" Sylvia asked.

"Depends on how they're coming. Maybe twelve hours by train or bus, if they get good connections. You can't tell. Maybe they're flying." He continued to pace, impatiently smashing his fist into the palm of his hand every few minutes.

"When did they leave?"

"The girl at the reception desk saw them walk out at about three in the afternoon."

"They probably won't get here till tomorrow morning—maybe not till afternoon," Sylvia said.

"Maybe they're hitchhiking—it could take longer that way," Ken said.

At eleven o'clock the telephone rang, and he jumped to answer. "I have a long-distance call for Mr. Kenneth Jorgenson from Buffalo, New York," the operator said.

Ken grimaced. "Buffalo," he said to Sylvia, and to the operator added, "All right. I'm Jorgenson."

It was old Bruce Carter, sounding very tired and far away. "Have you heard anything new?" he asked.

"No. How's Helen?"

"All right. She tried to swallow a whole bottle of sleeping pills, but I got them away from her in time."

"Good," Ken said grimly. "Get her to a hospital."

"Anyway, she's knocked herself out for a while," old Bruce concluded. "Be sure and call me if you hear anything."

"All right," Ken said, and hung up. It seemed entirely logical to him that Helen would finally turn against herself. After telling Sylvia about it, he said, "Anything is better for Molly than living in that house. Anything!"

At three in the morning Ken said that keeping a night vigil was ridiculous; the children were bound to arrive in the morning. He and Sylvia went to bed, but could not sleep. At dawn he got up, and to occupy his mind, began to spade up the garden energetically, preparing to plant new rose bushes. Sylvia got dressed at dawn and tried to read. Later she got Carla off to school and made the beds, but after that there was nothing to do but wait.

It was one o'clock before John and Molly reached Stamford, Connecticut, and asked the way to Redding. As they approached it, Molly became more and more strained. "I think you ought to let me out at their driveway, and come back later," she said to John. "It might be better if I told them alone."

"Why?" he asked indignantly.

"I think I might be able to handle Dad better alone if he gets angry."

"I'm not going to leave you," John said flatly. "If anybody's going to get angry, I want to be there." A muscle in his cheek flickered, and he held the steering wheel so tightly that his knuckles went white.

The mailbox outside Ken's house with the name "Jorgenson" was freshly painted. Neither of them said a word as they turned into the driveway. In a small garden at the front of the house they immediately saw Ken on his knees. At the sound of the car, he stood up, holding his trowel, a big man with the black loam still clinging to his trousers, and when Molly got out of the car, he dropped the trowel. She ran to him, starting to cry as she touched him, and threw both arms around his neck, burying her face in his shoulder, and he hugged her, saying, "Molly! Molly!" but she couldn't speak. John came and stood beside them, his body bent, his fists clenched nervously at his sides, and he looked dumbly at Ken. Suddenly, to John's horror, tears started down his cheeks; he made no sound, but his shoulders shook, and Ken, holding his daughter in one arm, swept out the other and clasped the boy to him, holding the two of them tight against his barrel-like chest, his big head bent over theirs. Then through Molly's sobs he heard the sentence, almost indistinguishable at first, but repeated, the one sentence, "Daddy, Daddy, baby, baby, I'm going to have a baby, oh Daddy, I'm going to have a baby. . . ."

"All right!" Ken said, the two words exploding out of him as an affirmation, almost a prayer. Molly looked up and saw him smiling at her. "Come into the house," he said.

They followed him meekly and sat in the living room. "Sylvia!" Ken called. "The children are here!"

Sylvia came down the stairs, pale, with one hand up, smoothing her hair, but when she saw John she ran to him, and for the first time in years, his body was not rigid when she hugged him, and she felt him hug her back. He stood there, taller than she, and she pulled his head down on her shoulder. "Molly and I are going to have . . ." he said.

"I know." They sat on the couch together. "It was my fault," John began.

"No," Molly said. Breaking away from her father, she ran to him, and suddenly the four of them were all hugging each other, saying it was everybody's fault and no one's fault, and the crying got mixed up with the laughter of sudden relief.

34

THE NEXT DAY Ken conferred with his lawyer and discovered that to get a marriage license, John and Molly would have to get either the written consent of the parent in whose custody they had been put, or a waiver. "Under the circumstances," the lawyer said delicately, "the probate judge would readily grant a waiver. Such cases are far from uncommon, and the State makes legal provision for them, but it might be wiser and more dignified to keep this a family affair. Let's get consent if we can."

When Molly talked to her mother over the telephone, Helen was still so groggy from drugs that she only mumbled incoherently, but her lawyer got her to give her legal consent to the marriage. John sent Bart a short note. "Dear Dad," he wrote, "As I told you, I want to get married. Mother and Mr. Jorgenson are helping us. I can get legal waiver of the age requirement, but I would much prefer to have your permission. If you would sign the enclosed papers, I would be grateful. If you would care to come to the wedding Friday morning, we would like to have you."

Arrangements were made for this letter to be delivered to Bart by Herb Andrews. Bart's reply came three days later. It was a long one.

DEAR SON,

Your letter reached me just as I was preparing to go to the hospital in Portland. I don't know how long I'll be there—weeks or months, I guess, for the ulcers have kicked up worse than ever. My hand shakes as I write this, and I realize there is a certain irony in any advice from my pen, but I shall persist.

You say you want me to consent to your marriage, and in the same sentence you point out that you will get married anyway. All right. I give my legal consent, and I've signed the enclosed papers simply because there's no point in making things difficult for you if you have unalterably made up your mind. But I don't give my approval.

As I dimly remember the marriage ceremony, the minister at one time or another says, "If anyone here knows just cause why this man and this woman should not be joined in holy matrimony, let him now speak or forever hold his peace." I shall speak now in this letter. And I'm a sober wedding guest, Johnny, cold sober.

I feel it is my obligation to point out that at the age of eighteen you have made a serious mistake which cannot be whitewashed by a lot of foolish sentimentality. You have, if you will forgive a rather nauseous phrase, got a girl into trouble, but more than that, you have got yourself into a great deal of trouble, all the worse because you don't appear to realize it. There are of course many ways in which you can explain away your mistake; it is, undoubtedly, a logical outcome of your heredity and environment. You are suffering the sins of your fathers and also repeating them. Regardless of that, I beg to point out, your mistake exists, and your only choice is whether to minimize it or to compound it.

Now let us try to look at this thing rationally. Superficially marriage may appear to be a practical solution. I suppose that Ken Jorgenson can easily support you, and he is the cheerful type who would probably do so without complaint. When you get into college, you will also have the small trust fund which we discussed. There is, I admit, no economic barrier here, but don't imagine for a minute that this will make things easy.

Statistically, the odds against very youthful marriages are not encouraging—that's a matter of record. You don't know your own minds at your age, nor what sort of adults you and your girl will become. Being supported by others will be a corrosive experience. Beyond that, I think you're going to miss a lot of fun by accepting responsibilities so early. Youth is supposed to be a carefree time. It hasn't been for you, but that is all the more reason why you should be free to relax and enjoy life in the next three or four years. You should be going to dances and football games next year, not helping to hang out diapers. That probably sounds frivolous to you, but some of the best parts of life are frivolous.

If you persist in getting married, there are strong currents you will have to swim against. The tradition of delaying marriage until one can support a family is most respected in the richest nations, especially among those families who don't really have to worry about money. That may not make sense, but it's a fact: only poor people marry young. Your segment of the world will raise an eyebrow at you, and more than that, you will incur scorn.

I have not even touched yet upon the question of morality, a word which you may think odd to come from this shaking pen. Even so, I have observed that there is some rough moral law at work in the world, that sinners generally pay, in one way or another. As I write this, I have the most fearful pain in my belly, so I speak with authority on the theme of punishment. Anyway, the point is, Johnny, that according to any obvious ethic, you have committed a sin of fairly generous proportions. It is not right for young boys to fall into bed with young girls while they are not yet out of preparatory school, and I suspect that no matter how tolerant and sophisticated we all are, there is a punishment awaiting you somewhere along the line. Even if there really is no inflexible moral law at work in the world, we have all had morality dinned into our ears through so many generations that psychological laws have been created which operate with all the rigor of an Old Testament God. You have sinned, or at least at heart you think you have sinned, and if God does not punish you, you will punish yourself. Here is the great danger, I think, for I fear that your desire to get married, and probably your girl's desire, is simply a wish to punish yourselves, "to do the right thing," to seek absolution, and these are not mature motives for marriage.

You may think that the solution I posed to you when I last saw you would be the ultimate crowning of immorality, but in all honesty, I don't. This is a pretty hard-boiled world, Johnny, and the good or evil of any action can be judged only by the long-range effect it has on everyone concerned. If you and your girl get married for largely neurotic reasons and have a child and, perhaps only a few years later, get divorced, you will have added greatly to the sum of the world's unhappiness, and will have set the whole wheel of our misery spinning for yet another generation. I say stop this affair now, as, after all, can rather easily be done. Acknowledge your mistake, erase it. If you and your girl are actually fond of each other, you can get married at the proper time, when you're both old enough to know what you're doing.

Before you make any final decision, I think you would be wise to show this letter to your mother, and to get her opinion. Regardless of the differences which existed between us, I never accused her of being anything but practical.

And now I must change the subject and conclude not as an adviser, but as a supplicant. I'm sick and I need your help, Johnny. I have no idea how long I will have to be in the hospital, and the island should not be left untended. It has been necessary for me to give notice to poor Hasper—he's too old now to do any real work, and I really think that with senility, he has become unhinged. He's had notice for some time now, but he's given no sign of preparing to go. This is simply more than I can handle in my present condition, and I'd appreciate it if you'd take charge.

What I'm really asking, Johnny, is that you come here. The inn will be yours some day, perhaps not too far in the future. You have received many bad things in your inheritance; the island is one good thing. I hope you can devise a way to keep it.

I must go now, for Herb Andrews is waiting. I do not look forward to the hospital, but oh, God, my belly is aching, and I have not been able to hold food since you left. There! To my other sins, I have added self-pity—I did not mean to do that. Visit me if you can, and take care of the island, at least until July, when the others come. Life is a battle against great odds. I profoundly hope you do not get married, but if you do, I wish you happiness. Maybe life is only a dice game, after all. If so, our family is due for a winner.

Hastily,

DAD

Sitting on the couch beside Molly in Ken's living room, John read the letter slowly. The muscle under his cheek flickered. When he was through, he handed the letter to Molly. "I guess we better go out to the island as soon as we're married," he said.

Molly showed no sign of emotion while she read the letter, except that she kept opening and closing one hand. Giving the five sheets of paper back to John, she said, "I'm sorry he's sick. Of course we'll go."

John passed the letter to Sylvia. Her lips tightened when she read it. A reply to Bart cried out in her mind: I've learned from Ken that this is more than a question of right and wrong, she wanted to say. It's a question of meeting a problem and solving it with love, and we all have at least a fighting chance! Handing the letter back to John, she said, "Don't let it discourage you," and was about to attempt a whole counterargument to Bart when she realized that words wouldn't help. Molly and John were looking at each other with mute intensity. The letter had shocked Molly, Sylvia realized, and they could not talk about it with her there. John was trying to be matter-of-fact and calm, but with his eyes he was trying to reassure Molly. They should be alone, Sylvia thought, and glancing at her watch she said, "I've got to meet Ken," a sentence which made no sense, for Ken had gone to New York on business and was not expected back for three hours. Quickly she left the room.

Damn Bart, Sylvia thought as she got into her car and slammed the door. What a fine wedding present *he* had to give: a prophecy of doom, a glib espousal of defeat, a charming display of confidence in the probability of disaster. *Damn* him, she thought, he should not have sent such a letter now—that is not at all what the children need.

Driving without any particular destination, Sylvia found that reply after reply to Bart kept forming in her mind. How strange it is, she wanted to say. A father can buy his daughter fur coats and automobiles without much criticism, and he can allow her to spend any amount on parties, but to help her to marry is considered somehow immoral. Parents can give a son a big enough allowance to permit all kinds of hell raising; they can pay his liquor bills and directly or indirectly they can subsidize the entertainment of every harlot in town, but they cannot help him to get married young; no, there is something especially wicked about that.

The difference between this and the sordid little case history you make it, she imagined herself continuing in an impassioned speech, the difference is something Ken taught me about. It is summed up in the one small word, *love*. That one word which you, Bart, never mentioned in all your long letter, that invisible quality of which you have such small knowledge can change all this from defeat into a kind of triumph.

Yes, triumph, she thought of herself saying, a triumph against loneliness, a triumph for the children and a triumph for Ken and me, a triumph for love, both the love they have for each other and the love Ken and I have for them.

Sylvia found she was driving too fast. Deliberately she slowed down. Bart would consider her fancy rhetoric silly, she reflected ruefully, and she could imagine his reply: Why Sylvia, how cheerful you have become!

Yes, I am cheerful, she would reply, and that is a beautiful word when correctly used.

Even in her imagination this sounded hollow to Sylvia, and with a sinking sensation she realized why: she was not feeling particularly triumphant or cheerful at the moment. On the contrary, she was full of apprehension, and dreaded Friday, the day of the wedding. Since the children had returned, she had been trying to imagine how it would be. There would be few guests, for they had no friends nearby who were capable of attending such a short-notice wedding without embarrassment. Old Bruce, Molly's grandfather, had said he would come from Buffalo and Helen planned to attend "if she were well enough." Those two would certainly do little to create a joyous atmosphere, Sylvia thought grimly. Carla would be full of innocent excitement about serving as a bridesmaid again, and Ken would be hearty. Sylvia could picture him passing out glasses of champagne, trying to change an atmosphere of pathos to one of celebration. And even the children might not appear happy. Sylvia imagined them standing together before the minister looking subdued, even scared, babes in the woods, not figures of triumph. Luckily Bart would not be there, for he almost certainly would be drunk, but his sober self which had arrived by mail was even worse, Sylvia thought. Now Bart would be an invisible presence as soon as the wedding march began, even if she did get the minister to omit from the ceremony the passage inviting objectors to speak now.

It is up to Ken and me to prevent this from being a pathetic affair, Sylvia thought with determination, and on impulse turned her car toward Stamford. Perhaps it was silly, but she had a sudden desire to buy a new dress to wear at the wedding, and some clothes to add to the already elaborate trousseau she had ordered for Molly.

When she got to the dress shop, Sylvia's enthusiasm ran away with her. She bought armfuls of lingerie and dresses of many colors for Molly, and a pale yellow dress with a widely flared skirt for herself. In a curious way, anything that enhanced the beauty of women seemed an answer to her worries, a reply to Bart, a refutation of despair. This thought confused her, for it did not seem reasonable, but it persisted. As though arming Molly, she continued to buy her clothes. A flowing afternoon dress of pale blue silk might be suitable for Molly to wear at her wedding, she thought, for the child had said she didn't want a formal white gown. A black evening dress with a gold belt, a pair of red leather pumps, a chaste housecoat of cream-colored satin—all these Sylvia bought as a surprise for Molly. When the bill was presented, it was enormous, and Sylvia suffered a twinge of guilt, but then she thought, this is ridiculous; Ken is the last person who would ever resent my buying clothes for Molly. He can easily afford them, and when am I going to quit questioning good fortune?

Wealth should not be ostentatious and beauty should not be flaunted, she thought, imagining with pleasure how Molly's youthful figure would look in some of the clothes she had bought her, but they also should not be buried; yes, they are fundamentally gifts from God which should be appreciated. Feeling more lighthearted, she filled the back seat of her car with packages and drove to the station to meet Ken. When he came toward her, standing well above the crowd, she had the curious sensation of seeing him for the first time. How big he looks, she thought, how incredibly strong! That too seemed an answer to her worries: the fortunate possession of such a powerful ally. Of course the children have a fight ahead of them, she thought, but they have on their side the beauty and the strength of youth, love and a sense of humor, and those are the weapons of the angels. They go well-armed with strong friends.

She kissed Ken with unusual warmth when he climbed into the car. "Wow!" he said, smiling. "What's that for?"

"Gratitude," she said.

That night Sylvia asked Molly to her room and presented her with her new clothes. Molly seemed pleased and smilingly tried them on, but there was still a reserve about her, a sort of melancholy lurking just beneath the surface which worried Sylvia. In her new blue silk dress Molly pirouetted with a curious combination of youthful grace and dignity before Sylvia's full-length mirror. "It's beautiful," she said in a soft voice. "I can't thank you enough."

"Molly!" Sylvia said suddenly, almost without thinking. "Don't be afraid!"

"Afraid?" She made the word barely audible.

"I didn't mean to be abrupt." Sylvia brushed her hand over her forehead in confusion. "I want you to be happy," she said, feeling that the words sounded ridiculous. "You have a wonderful father and you're about to be married to a fine young man. There isn't anything for you to fear." That wasn't at all what she had meant to say. Molly's peculiarly direct way of looking at her was disquieting. Sylvia paused in confusion.

"I know," Molly said.

"It's just that I don't want you to worry about anything," Sylvia continued, making her voice sound down-to-earth, and then she added, "Does the idea of having a baby scare you?"

There was a moment of silence. "A little," Molly said. Her tone was precise, as thought she had just measured her fear with a scientific instrument.

"It's nothing to be scared of. You're lucky to be so young. Ken and I would like to have a baby, but sometimes it's not so easy to get pregnant when you're older."

"Yes," Molly said, and glanced down. "I can't thank you enough for the clothes," she added.

"It's a pleasure to give them to you, darling," Sylvia replied, and wished she had not started the conversation.

Downstairs Sylvia found John talking earnestly with Ken about arrangements which were being made to enable him and Molly to take special examinations in the summer. If they passed these, they could graduate from their schools, and it was probable that John could enter college in the fall as had been planned. "Even if I can't go to Harvard, there are plenty of other places," John said. He sounded anxious.

"I don't think marriage will prejudice any university against you," Ken replied. "I wouldn't worry about it."

But John continued to sound and to look worried. He had worked out a budget which he wanted to go over with Ken, and he had already made inquiries about apartments in Cambridge for the following fall. He should be this practical and this responsible, Sylvia thought. I should be grateful for that. What celebration do I expect of the children? Do I want them to go madly dancing about the house singing a hymn to Hymen? Do I want John to lie with Molly in the garden feeding her grapes? I have become a fool.

Yet the children did not seem happy while they prepared for the wedding, Sylvia thought, and there was nothing to joke about in that. Trying to understand this, she prepared for bed. When Ken came upstairs a few minutes later she said, "Ken, do you think there's anything troubling the children that they haven't told us?"

"No. What makes you think so?"

"I can't explain it. They seem so sort of joyless."

"They've been through an awful lot. It takes time for that sort of thing to wear off."

"I wish they weren't so solemn. It's absurd, I guess, but I want them to celebrate. I never hear them laugh . . ."

"It takes time," he repeated. "It always does."

On Friday Sylvia awoke at dawn. She went to the window and seeing that the sky was almost clear and that the few clouds on the horizon were white, she was grateful. She had dreaded a rainy day for the wedding. Going downstairs, she had a sudden idea: why not have the ceremony in the garden instead of in the living room? The piano could be moved out on the terrace. The forsythia was blooming and a few of the rose bushes were in blossom. Sylvia had had a clear conception of what the proceedings in the living room would be like, with Helen, in all probability, wringing her hands in the corner by the fireplace, and the thought of changing the whole setting appealed to her. Helen, who had arrived with Bruce at a hotel in Stamford the night before, would still be there, but it would be good to get the whole ceremony out into the sunlight.

The wedding was scheduled for eleven o'clock. At ten the big black Cadillac arrived with Bruce and Helen. As she had been since the death of old Margaret, Helen was in mourning. She had been instructed by her doctor to take a sedative in preparation for this occasion, and she appeared rather vague when Ken and Sylvia greeted her. Old Bruce was wearing a blue serge which he always referred to as his funeral suit. He was not without dignity as he stood supporting his ailing daughter on his arm, trying to help her make conversation with her former husband. Wasn't it lucky, he said, that the weather had turned out so well for the wedding, and the garden certainly was a fine place for it, wasn't it? Yes, Helen said in a weak voice at regular intervals, oh yes. She sounded like a small bird chirping.

To Sylvia's dismay, Helen asked to see Molly before the ceremony. The child should be left in peace while she dressed for her wedding, Sylvia thought, but there was no way to forbid her mother. Sylvia escorted Helen to Molly's room and knocked. "Molly, your mother's here," she said.

"Come in," Molly replied in a clear, firm voice.

When they opened the door, they found Molly in her new blue gown, sitting on the edge of her bed. At the sight of Helen, she stood up, looking almost incredibly beautiful, Sylvia thought, with her glossy dark hair brushed back from her fine forehead, and the full blue skirt billowing out all around her. "Hello, Mother," she said. "I'm glad you came."

Helen kissed her, a swift peck on the cheek, and began to cry. "I felt I should be here, dear," she said in a broken voice. Taking a handkerchief from her pocket, she began dabbing at her eyes. Molly, who was a little taller than her mother, put her arm around her and patted her shoulder, saying, "It's all right, Mother, it's all right," and they stood together there for almost a minute, curiously reversing their roles of mother and child.

"I think that perhaps we should go downstairs now, Helen," Sylvia said from the door. Obviously in deep grief, Helen turned and meekly followed her. She sat next to old Bruce, twisting her hands precisely as Sylvia had imagined her doing. Now there's a figure of joy, Sylvia thought, first with bitterness and then with sudden compassion. Oh, let the wedding bells ring out; let us burn incense and dance the whole night through to celebrate the nuptial rites. What is so gay as a wedding in the garden in the spring?

At eleven o'clock the minister, who had been talking with Ken in the house, came out and stood alone by a stone wall at the end of the garden. He was a rather stout man, only half as tall as the young lilac bushes at each side of him. A few minutes later John, wearing a white linen suit, walked from the house to the garden and stood nervously in front of the minister. On the terrace a spinster who taught music at the local high school began playing the wedding march, hitting the keys as hard as she could to make the music carry to the end of the garden. Carla came down the steps from the terrace. She was beaming. Twenty-five feet behind her walked Ken, also dressed in a linen suit, and at his side, with one hand on his arm, walked Molly. The wind ruffled her skirt and she looked precisely as all brides pray to look, Sylvia thought, except that she was too pale. The piano, beaten so hard, sounded tinny and oddly irreverent. Sylvia was glad when Ken and Molly reached the minister, and the music stopped. Ken stepped rather awkwardly to one side, leaving Molly beside John. Somewhere in the distance a crow called and was answered raucously by another. The minister cleared his throat, and in a highly cultivated tenor voice which to Sylvia sounded monstrously like Bart's, he began the marriage ceremony. The sun shone so blindingly on his white surplice and on the suits of John and Ken that it was difficult to look at them. Helen cried audibly.

It was the first such ceremony Sylvia had ever attended which seemed so long. The minister read several prayers from a book, some of which he had difficulty finding. While he riffled the pages, he coughed discreetly, and always in the background there was the sound of Helen's snuffling. John stood very straight, and when it came time to put the ring on Molly's finger, he did so without fumbling.

"You may kiss the bride," the minister finally said, and Molly tilted her face up with her eyes closed. Looking as though they were in a trance, they brushed their lips together, and the ceremony was over.

The brief reception which followed on the terrace was so much the way Sylvia had imagined that it was like reliving a dream. With a rather set smile Ken handed out glasses of champagne. Old Bruce said one glass would be enough because it disturbed his stomach, and Helen used hers to wash down a pill. John and Molly stood together, looking like proud youngsters on graduation day.

Finally it was over. John and Molly walked toward their old Plymouth, which had already been packed. Carla threw a handful of rice at them and they were off, bound for Pine Island. Sylvia, in her new yellow dress, stood at the edge of the terrace looking after them, and she was shocked at a sudden desire to swear. It shouldn't be like this, she thought with rising anger. I wish we were savages. I wish we had garlanded them with flowers. We should be singing.

But of course there was no singing. Helen and Bruce left immediately in their Cadillac, closely followed by the minister and the piano player. Carla went upstairs to change her dress, leaving Ken and Sylvia alone on the terrace. The garden with its empty chairs seemed strangely forlorn. Ken came toward her, carrying a bottle of champagne. "There's plenty left for us to celebrate," he said.

Wordlessly she turned to him and threw both arms around his neck. With his free arm he held her tight. He didn't say anything, but when the embrace was over, Sylvia felt better. Smiling, she picked up an empty glass and held it toward him. "Let the celebration begin," she said.

35

It was a strange start for a honeymoon. The first day John stopped in Portland, where he felt impelled by conscience to visit his father in the hospital. They found Bart in a ward full of the sick and the dying. In the bed on one side of him was an aged fat man with his face nearly covered by bandages, and in the bed on the other side of him was a swarthy thin man who coughed constantly. Throughout the visit the eyes of both these patients remained almost hungrily on John and Molly, and it was difficult to talk much. Bart was so weak that he could not lift his head from the pillow. He said "Thank you" in a low voice when John said they were on their way to the island, and he said "Good luck" when John told him that he and Molly had been married. Other than that he said nothing. His exhausted eyes shifted restlessly from John's face to Molly's and he seemed relieved when they said goodbye. The smell of ether and illness seemed to cling to them as they left the hospital.

The morning they got to the island there was the difficult business of getting rid of Todd Hasper, who had simply ignored the fact that Bart had fired him. As they moored the schooner, Hasper did not come down to the wharf, but they could hear his dog barking somewhere in the distance. "You stay here, Molly," John said. "I'll go see him."

"Be careful," Molly replied.

"You better take the gun," Herb Andrews said. "Here are your keys."

John walked slowly ashore with the shotgun in one hand and a large bunch of keys in the other. At the top of the hill Hasper, holding the dog on a leash, stepped suddenly from behind the old inn. The dog flattened his ears and bared his teeth, but made almost no sound. Hasper looked older and thinner than John had remembered him.

"Hello, Todd," John said.

"What are you here for?"

"I'm going to stay awhile. When are you leaving?"

"I ain't planning to leave."

"I thought Dad asked you to."

Hasper spat contemptuously. "He was drunk," he said.

"Well, I'm not drunk, and I'm telling you to leave now. The boat will wait while you get your things."

"Who the hell are you to give orders?"

The dog growled and strained at his leash. John pulled back both hammers of the shotgun, and there was a soft click. "Be careful not to let that dog go," he said.

Hasper glared at him malignantly.

"If you don't leave, I'll get the police from Harvesport," John said. "If we have to, we'll shoot the dog and carry you aboard the schooner tonight. I'll give you an hour to pack."

"All right!" Hasper said. "You can stew in your own evil—you and your whole family!" He turned and walked toward his cabin with the dog trotting obediently beside him. He disappeared inside and shut the door. John returned to the schooner. "Is everything all right?" Molly asked.

"I think so, but I won't believe he's gone till he's aboard ship. While we're waiting for him, we might as well unload our gear."

"I bet we have to tie him down to a stretcher," Herb Andrews said as he handed up the suitcases and the boxes of groceries. "I don't know why your father put up with him as long as he did."

But in the end no violence was necessary. With surprising meekness the old man came down the hill carrying a large duffel bag on his shoulder and leading the dog. Wordlessly he picked his way over the rotten wharf and dropped the bag to the deck of the schooner. He looked crestfallen and tired. Even the dog, reflecting his mood, did not seem particularly fierce any more. He followed him to the forecastle of the ship, and whined as Hasper tied him to the anchor bitts. Hasper glared balefully at Molly but said nothing. The sun was hot, and the dog started to pant.

John handed Andrews the gun. "Thanks a lot, Herb," he said.

Andrews grinned. "Good to have you back, Johnny! You and your pretty new Missus!"

"Thanks!" Molly said, and jumped nimbly to the wharf. She looked graceful balancing there, as though poised for flight, with her candy-striped skirt billowing out in the wind. John waited beside her while Herb backed the big schooner off and headed out of the harbor. Then he picked up the suitcases. "Watch out, Molly," he said. "This is an easy place to break a leg."

"I'm all right!"

At the head of the wharf he paused and put the suitcases down. Conscious now of being the only people on the island, they stood looking up the hill toward the dilapidated old inn, which suddenly appeared sinister. Without the barking of the dog, the island seemed strangely quiet. The wind sighing in the trees and the distant whisper of the surf sounded eerie.

Briskly John carried the suitcases and the boxes of groceries to the wide veranda of the inn. After fumbling with the keys for a moment, he opened the front door and they walked into the cavernous living room. Glass from the window he had broken when he came to get the silver and the other things to sell still littered the floor. "Johnny!" Molly said. "What happened here?"

He told her. "I'll fix it temporarily with a storm window," he concluded.

"It must have been awful for you," she said.

"Not so bad. Come and I'll show you where we're going to stay."

He carried the suitcases to the master bedroom, put up the shades, and opened the wide windows which overlooked the harbor and the garden where he had trimmed the lilacs and the hydrangeas. A fragrant wind swept through the musty room. While Molly began to dust and to make up the beds, he went downstairs, his footsteps echoing in the empty hall. He picked up the glass and put on a storm window from another part of the house. After taking the groceries to the kitchen, he went to the cellar to turn on the water and start the generator which made electricity for the inn. When everything was in working order, he went upstairs and lay on the bed watching Molly hang up her dresses, taking pleasure in the sinuous way she moved as she held up a pale green skirt to get the wrinkles out of it. Busily she stored in drawers some cream-colored lingerie which smelled of lavender. When she had finished, he took the empty suitcases to the cellar. Upon returning to the bedroom, he found Molly at an open window, looking pensively down into the garden. The hum of bees was in the air. At the sound of his footsteps she turned toward him. Standing there in a shaft of yellow sunbeams in her white blouse and candy-striped skirt, she looked phantasmal to John, as though she had just been created in a blaze of light. He kissed her, bending her to him. *"Oh, Molly!"* he said with agony.

She put her hand gently on his cheek. "What?"

"I can't touch you without wanting to make love to you. I can't even look at you, and I'm always afraid that you don't feel anything that I feel, that I'm taking advantage of being your husband, and . . ."

"Hush," she said.

"I know you're still afraid!"

"No, Johnny . . ."

His voice was tortured. "We've got to face the truth, Molly! You don't feel what I do. You never have. At least we don't have to lie about it! You just married me because . . ."

"Don't insult me, Johnny."

"Does it make it any worse to say it?"

"Kiss me."

"No!"

"Don't say no to me now, Johnny. I'm trying."

"It's horrible that you have to try."

"It's not horrible. I asked you to kiss me. Am I going to be refused?"

He kissed her, feeling her lips part timidly. It was a long if gentle kiss. When it was over she said, "Slowly, Johnny—we have plenty of time."

Later that day they took a long walk down the beach. As they sat watching the colors of the harbor deepen with dusk, John had an intense conviction he would never forget anything that was happening. The fine, almost feathery texture of the sun-silvered driftwood they gathered for a fire became a part of his memory, to be conserved decades after the wood was ashes, and the call of the gulls that night was lastingly recorded.

This feeling that everything he experienced was somehow permanent persisted. There was, for instance, the picture of Molly the determined housewife, a young woman with a bandanna around her head, spending the second morning of her honeymoon scrubbing on her hands and knees, cleaning the garage apartment, which Bart had left in indescribable disorder. There was the serious face of Molly the fledgling intellectual, insisting that she not be interrupted while she tried to write verse, and an hour later there was the sensual picture of Molly standing with elaborate insouciance on the wharf, like a Balinese girl, wearing nothing but a crimson beach towel pinned around her waist, and eating a banana.

At three o'clock of the second morning they spent on the island a thunderstorm struck the old inn. Half asleep, John sat up in bed suddenly with the roar of the wind in his ears. The rain was battering the windowpanes and whipping the foliage. At the instant of awaking, he was confused, half feeling that he was a boy again, alone, with Bart lying sick and drunk in the next room. The well-remembered sounds of loneliness were all around him, the bang of a loose shutter, the lashing of the tree branches, and the rising tempo of the surf. A deadly, familiar sense of desolation gripped him until suddenly there was a flash of lightning. In its glare he saw Molly lying beside him, with her hair streaming back over the pillow, and one tanned shoulder emerging from a swirl of white sheet. Then it was dark again. The clap of thunder which followed awoke her. "Johnny," she said. "Are you there?"

"Yes," he said.

She sighed, rolled closer to him, and went back to sleep. For a long while he lay awake listening to the storm. The steady beat of the rain sounded peaceful and good.

ABOUT THE AUTHOR

SLOAN WILSON *is 37 years old. He is, of course, best known as the author of* The Man in the Gray Flannel Suit, *but he is also the author of a little-known novel written ten years before called* Voyage to Somewhere, *and of dozens of pieces for* The New Yorker, Harper's *and other magazines. It took him fifteen years to attain the rank of a full-time professional novelist. He has been a third-class blacksmith in a shipyard, a sailing instructor, a Coast Guard officer in command of small supply ships to Greenland and the South Pacific, a newspaper reporter, foundation executive, an English professor, a public-relations man, a magazine editor, Education Editor for the New York* Herald Tribune *and Assistant Director of the White House Conference on Education. He, his wife and their three children live in Pound Ridge, New York.*